Centers of the Self

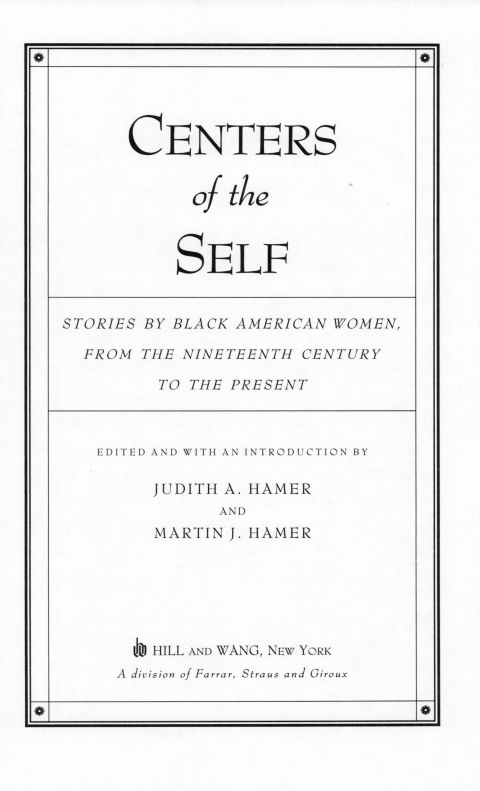

CENTERS

of the

SELF

STORIES BY BLACK AMERICAN WOMEN,

FROM THE NINETEENTH CENTURY

TO THE PRESENT

EDITED AND WITH AN INTRODUCTION BY

JUDITH A. HAMER

AND

MARTIN J. HAMER

HILL AND WANG, NEW YORK

A division of Farrar, Straus and Giroux

LIBRARY OF CONGRESS CATALOGING-IN-PUBLICATION DATA
Centers of the self : stories by black American women from the
nineteenth century to the present / edited and with an introduction
by Judith A. Hamer and Martin J. Hamer.—1st ed.
p.   cm.
1. Short stories, American—Afro-American authors.   2. Short
stories, American—Women authors.   3. Afro-American women—Fiction.
4. Afro-Americans—Fiction.   I. Hamer, Judith A.   II. Hamer, Martin
J.
PS647.A35C46   1994   813'.01099287'08996073—dc20   94-14724   CIP

We would like to thank the authors, their agents, and their publishers for permission to include
the following stories.

"Willie Bea and Jaybird," copyright © 1991 by Tina McElroy Ansa. First published in *Callaloo*,
vol. 14, no. 1. Reprinted by permission of the author.

"My Man Bovanne," from *Gorilla, My Love*, copyright © 1972 by Toni Cade Bambara.
Reprinted by permission of the author.

"Marigolds," by Eugenia Collier, copyright © 1969 Johnson Publishing Co., Inc. Reprinted by
permission of the author and *Negro Digest*.

"Damon and Vandalia," from *Fifth Sunday, Stories by Rita Dove*, copyright © 1985 by Rita
Dove. Reprinted by permission of the author.

"Requiem for Willie Lee," by Frenchy Hodges. Reprinted by permission of *Ms.* Magazine ©
1979.

"Jevata," from *White Rat*, copyright © 1977, by Gayl Jones. Reprinted by permission of the
author.

"Song of Roland," copyright © 1993 by Jamaica Kincaid. First published in *The New Yorker*,
April 12, 1993. Reprinted by permission of the author.

"To Da-Duh, in Memoriam," copyright © 1967, 1983 by Paule Marshall. From *Reena and
Other Stories*. Published by permission of the author and the Feminist Press at the City
University of New York.

"Sister Detroit," copyright © 1978 by Colleen McElroy, from *Jesus and Fat Tuesday*, Creative
Arts Books. Reprinted by permission of the author.

"Key to the City," copyright © 1965 by Diane Oliver. First printed in *Red Clay Reader II* (1965).
Reprinted by permission of the Estate of Diane Oliver.

"Miss Muriel," copyright © 1963 by Ann Petry; copyright renewed 1991 by Ann Petry. Reprinted
by permission of Russell & Volkening, New York, NY, as agents for the author.

"Hoodoo," copyright © 1988 by Connie Porter. First published in *The Southern Review*. Re-

To our daughters
and the past generations of fathers
whose surnames they proudly carry,
Jill Taylor Hamer,
Fern Smalls Hamer,
Kim Thompson Hamer

❂

Many people helped us to make this a better book in our first collaborative effort. We extend special thanks to our readers—my sister Carolyn Brown, Victoria Arana, Robert Bone, Renée Beach-Halliburton, Regina Pomeranz-Krummel, and Carla Peterson—for their honest and sometimes stinging criticism of the introduction. We thank our friends, who through their questions and comments confirmed that this was an important project and that we could do it together. We thank the staff of the General Research and Reference Division of the Schomburg Center for Research in Black Culture—including those energetic young people who pleasantly fetch books and fiche and copy pages—especially the librarians Sharon Howard, Genette McLaurin, and Betty Odabashian. Their motto ought to be "If it exists, we can find it." And we thank Marta Campbell of the Westport Public Library.

Contents

Centers of the Self

Introduction

*We are the subjects of our own narrative, witnesses to and
participants in our own experience, and, in no way coinciden-
tally, in the experiences of those with whom we have come in
contact . . . And to read imaginative literature by and about us
is to choose to examine centers of the self and to have the opportunity to compare these centers with the "raceless" one with
which we are, all of us, most familiar.*
  Toni Morrison, "Unspeakable Things Unspoken:
  The Afro-American Presence in American Literature"

*And what is wrong in woman's
  life
In man's cannot be right.*
  Frances Ellen Watkins Harper, "A Double Standard"

Anna Julia Cooper (1858–1964), whose 1892 book of essays, *A Voice from
the South*, is considered to be one of the earliest texts of the black feminist
movement, set down what can serve as the justification for this anthology
when she wrote, "It is not the intelligent woman vs. the ignorant woman;
nor the white woman vs. the black, the brown, and the red—it is not
even the cause of woman vs. man. Nay, 'tis woman's strongest vindication
for speaking that *the world needs to hear her voice.*"[1]

More than half a century later, in 1950, that "voice" was heard when
Gwendolyn Brooks became the first black American to win the Pulitzer
Prize for poetry. Twenty years later, in 1970, black women opened a
floodgate that changed African-American literature forever. Toni Cade
Bambara published the anthology *The Black Woman*, the first of its kind
to allow women to speak their minds on issues relevant to their lives.
That same year, as if on cue, Toni Morrison's *The Bluest Eye* and Alice
Walker's *The Third Life of Grange Copeland* rounded out the triumvirate
that would begin a renaissance. Now, exactly a century and two years
after Cooper's prophetic remark, Toni Morrison has become the first black
woman to be awarded the Nobel Prize. The growing success of black
women's writing in the past twenty years is awesome. In 1992 they had

3

three books on the best-seller list at the same time: Terry McMillan's *Waiting to Exhale*, Morrison's *Jazz*, and Walker's *Possessing the Secret of Joy*. Phenomenal sales figures indicate that their work has been accepted by an audience more sophisticated and integrated than has ever existed for black male writers.

Black women writers have also produced an impressive body of short stories. Some were published at the turn of the century, when their writings enjoyed modest popularity. Many were published during the Harlem Renaissance and in the years after the 1970s, as women writers gained increased access to the marketplace. Together, these short stories from the past and the present represent a unique body of literature that has not been adequately recognized. [2]

The twenty-seven short stories in this anthology document some of the thoughts and deeds of nineteenth- and twentieth-century black women. Read against the black American concerns and feminist aspirations that existed when each piece was published, these stories provide a sense of black women's attitudes that expands the views provided in novels by black women. [3] Most of the stories fall into the general category of social realism, where the writer arranges the elements in the story to give the illusion of actual experience. These stories explore various themes: among them, the results of men's mistreatment of women (S. A. Williams's "Tell Martha Not to Moan" and Colleen McElroy's "Sister Detroit"), family love (Walker's "To Hell with Dying" and Paule Marshall's "To Da-Duh, in Memoriam"), erotic love (Dove's "Damon and Vandalia" and Jamaica Kincaid's "Song of Roland"), and the complexities of relationships (Marita Bonner's "One Boy's Story," Toni Cade Bambara's "My Man Bovanne," and Gayl Jones's "Jevata"). Others, like Fannie Barrier Williams's "After Many Days" and Jessie Redmon Fauset's "Mary Elizabeth," belong to a radically different category, domestic allegories. Rather than attempting to imitate reality, they present a fictive society where blacks gain acceptance by hard work, frugality, and spirituality. With their perfect-world themes, these works resemble the white utopian novels of the post-Reconstruction years. Three other early stories are as meaningful today as when they were first published. Frances Ellen Watkins Harper's "Two Offers" asks whether marriage is preferable to social activism and spinsterhood; Angelina Weld Grimké's "Goldie" examines the futility of revenge; and Nella Larsen's "Sanctuary" questions the age-old homily that blood is thicker than water.

The significance of the short story as a literary genre cannot be overstated. If one of the functions of art is to help society look at itself, to raise levels of consciousness by exposing beliefs that have too long been taken for granted, then the short story serves this function well. It focuses intensely on specific situations. It frequently reflects current circumstances, since it can often be written in a matter of months, and it provides a many-faceted journal of everyday life, a window on society. For example, in the anthology *Short Fiction by Black Women, 1900–1920*, edited by Elizabeth Ammons, the stories deal with a host of early twentieth-century black concerns, including

> the church, schoolteaching, love, poverty, lynching, passing, sisterhood, uplift, slavery, marriage, mothering, dreaming, lying, laughing, dying . . . They voice opinions on political issues . . . [discuss] black men's sexism, color prejudice within the black community, votes for women, and the sexual exploitation of black women by white men.[4]

Finally, because the short story is generally published by black-owned magazines and journals, it more readily reflects the moods and attitudes of black people.

None of these attributes of the short story is unusual once it is realized that, although the modern story is a literary convention barely a century and a half old, its origins lie in myths and ancient folktales that go back thousands of years. The earliest form of the short story is generally thought to date back to the jataka, fables of the births of the Buddha in various animal guises, which were set down around 483 B.C.[5] From this source came such stories as "The Goose That Laid the Golden Eggs." Other traditional stories came from Greek myth and *The Arabian Nights*. Still others were first collected and written down by the Grimm brothers and philologists in Italy and France. Their tales include the stories about Bluebeard, Cinderella, and Sleeping Beauty.

Perhaps the most stunning information to emerge from the research on the ancient short story is that the substance of a number of the Grimms' tales can be found among most racial and ethnic groups, including the Native North Americans, East and West Africans, Maoris and Samoans, and even the ancient Egyptians, as attested to by papyri found in tombs.[6] The short story, then, be it myth or legend, proverb or anecdote, an ancient story or a modern one told after dinner, seems to serve a fundamental function in all societies. It is a way to celebrate our fantasies, to mark our presence in time, to pass down our loves, fears, and foibles from one generation to the next.

Edgar Allan Poe, considered the father of the modern short story, defined it in 1842 when he suggested criteria for its length and dramatic design. It should be short enough to be read at one sitting, thereby taking advantage of the "immense force derivable from totality"—a force so powerful that it can make the body tense, raise the blood pressure, so engross the reader that she may not even hear another person enter or leave the room. Poe believed that, "in the whole composition there should be no word written of which the tendency, direct or indirect, is not to the one pre-established design."[7] For like poetry, if a word is misplaced or is superfluous or if there is a loss of balance or the momentum is not right, the story will not work.

In 1842, the same year that Poe published his critical essay, the Russian writer Nicolai Gogol published "The Overcoat," which dramatically changed the short story's subject matter. Poe's stories focus on one of three subjects: the study of passive horror ("The Pit and the Pendulum," about the Spanish Inquisition), the murder mystery ("The Murders in the Rue Morgue"), and scientific puzzles and thrills ("The Gold Bug"). Gogol, however, in writing about a clerk who makes sacrifices in order to buy a new overcoat only to have it stolen the first evening he wears it, moved the short story from romanticism to realism. Many critics believe that this story was the first to present the "little man" and that it brought an end to the ancient short stories where heroes were always kings or gentlemen. Today's short story is so routinely about common people that the Russian phrase "We all spring from Gogol's 'Overcoat' " cannot be taken lightly.

Since brevity and drama are hardly enough to define the short story, over the years critics have added other criteria. Many—such as trope (e.g., metaphor, metonym), topoi (theme), motif (subtheme), characterization (the development of characters with whom the reader strongly identifies, either positively or negatively), and plot (how is this story going to turn out?)—are taken from the novel. Others, like believability, eloquent use of the vernacular, showing as opposed to telling, were added as twentieth-century critics strove to better define the form.

There has long been a movement away from the tight plot. Chekhov is credited with having struck out the beginning and the end of the story, leaving us with the so-called plotless middle action. The plotless story gives us another variation, where nothing is resolved and a particular, isolated action simply moves to a more general plane. Or it allows the author to begin as near as possible to the end of an action, compressing an event in an attempt to reach its core. In other plotless tales, the "action is small, [but] its meanings are large."[8] Yet none of these criteria has limited this increasingly sophisticated art form. For the short story, Nadine Gordimer tells us, has the power to show us exactly "that quality of human life where contact is more like the flash of fireflies . . . where the only thing one can be sure of [is] the present moment."[9] The short story can also probe the labyrinthine recesses of the tormented soul. Perhaps that is why revelation, epiphany, and the moment of illumination are so appropriate to the genre, for in life as in this art insights often occur during that one moment of focused intensity.

Thus, we have two sets of criteria: the denotative definitions laid down by Poe and elaborated upon by later critics, and the connotative standards developed by writers as they experiment with the form. These criteria, of course, are race- and gender-neutral. To claim anything else—that because the criteria were established by white writers they do not apply to blacks, or that black women should be held to different standards— marginalizes the importance of all black writers' work. While one's liking a story or not is often a matter of personal taste, a knowledge of criteria can only help in making a decision. As the black critic George Kent eloquently states, a critic is

a kind of intelligent (hopefully) reader mediating between the writer and the audience, with very strong obligations to both. Obligations to the writer in trying as hard as you can to know what he's doing, and obligations to the audience . . . to try to speak stimulatingly enough about the work so that the audience will understand [its] particular customs and conventions . . . and how [it] relates . . . to its own tradition.[10]

Hence, we offer the following critical road map.

In 1859 Frances Ellen Watkins Harper published "The Two Offers." Although African-American men had already published three tales, none qualifies as a modern short story. The first two strain a reader's willing suspension of disbelief. Lemuel Hayes's narrative, published in the then-equivalent of a modern-day paperback and entitled *Mystery Developed; or, Russell Colvin, (Supposed to Be Murdered,) in Full Life; and Stephen and Jesse Boorn, (His Convicted Murderers,) Rescued from Ignominious Death by Wonderful Discoveries* (1820), fails to explain crucial murder evidence.[11] Frederick Douglass's "The Heroic Slave" (1840), also published as a paperback, expects the reader to believe that an escaped slave and a white man who helps him could run into each other by pure chance three times in as many states over the course of more than five years. The odds of this happening are remote, and credibility is a key requirement of the modern short story. The third tale, William Wells Brown's "A True Story of Slave Life," which appeared in the *Anti-Slavery Advocate* (1852), is, based on our research, a true story. It tells of a ten-year-old fair-skinned slave girl who is abandoned by her white "master" and father. She is taken in by the family of a "coloured gentleman," Robert Purvis, and four years later is placed in the family of "his father-in-law, the late venerable James Forten." Mrs. Forten encourages the girl's father to visit her, and, smitten by her beauty and surprised that she has lost "the uncouthness of the Southern slave life," he agrees to her future support.[12]

Harper's story about marriage, however, meets the criteria for a modern short story: It is well structured, having a beginning, a middle, and an end. It credibly dramatizes the lives of three common people, such as the husband of one of the women: "And yet moments of deep contrition would sweep over him, when he would resolve to abandon the wine-cup forever, when he was ready to forswear the handling of another card . . ." And it raises important questions: Is marriage preferable to social commitment and spinsterhood? Is a woman's place only in the home? The pre–Civil War readers of Harper's day "assumed that the aim of literature was education. They expected it to . . . argue . . . or exhort, to point out the lessons in their everyday experiences . . ."[13] Harper's story appeared in the *Anglo-African American*, a magazine designed to educate and to encourage, to speak for and to black Americans. It undoubtedly reached free blacks, like herself, living and working in the North. By deliberately making the story ethnically neutral,[14] Harper provokes a discussion about class, equality, and equal opportunity rather than one specifically about racial injustice. Harper raised questions that were probably central to the lives of many women. Her story, then, is essentially about choices a woman must make.

The two largest secular outlets for black women's fiction did not appear until the turn of the century. *The Colored American Magazine*, founded in 1900, and *The Crisis*, founded in 1910 as the official organ of the National Association for the Advancement of Colored People,[15] were started during the darkest days of post-Reconstruction, when African Americans were rapidly losing faith in their newly won freedom. However, the literary critic Claudia Tate, whose *Domestic Allegories of Political Desire* examines black women's novels of this period, points out that many African Americans still believed they could realize their desire to become full citizens by simply adopting the middle-class values of the dominant society. Despite the lynching of some four thousand blacks between 1889 and 1920,[16] many African Americans saw goals such as marriage, voting, professional attainment, and intellectual and cultural refinement as more important than an individual's racial designation.[17] Thus some of the writers, in order to encourage these values, created domestic allegories in which blacks participated in the social institutions of the period. Fannie Barrier Williams's "After Many Days" (1902) tells the story of a well-bred young woman who, though she appears to be white, is unknowingly a fair-skinned "negro." Betrothed to a white man, she learns of her race by accident from a servant, and puts the matter before her intended to test his love for her. If he marries her, his decision will show that race is less important than education and class and, by inference, that the respectability of marriage is within reach of all "negroes," providing they have skills and social graces.

Jessie Redmon Fauset's "Mary Elizabeth" (1919) also stresses the value of participating in white society's social institutions through marriage. Like "After Many Days," this piece is also a domestic allegory: in both stories the black middle-class women learn something from black servants. The structure of "Mary Elizabeth," a story within a story, is an age-old technique (used most effectively in Chaucer's *Canterbury Tales*) in which the narrator introduces a storyteller, whose tale has greater credibility since it does not appear to be the voice of the author. In this case the apparent story, narrated by a solidly middle-class black woman named Sally and occurring in the present, examines the importance of marriage. The secondary story, however, has greater impact because it is told by Sally's maid, Mary Elizabeth, and for added emphasis it is told in dialect. Its theme is slavery's effect on the lives of Mary Elizabeth's parents. Though in love with one another, they were sold separately. Twenty-six years later, freed and married to newfound mates, they are miraculously reunited, and the question they must answer is whether they should leave their present spouses to resume their first love. Their decision not to leave their spouses may have been a way of pointing out to readers the importance of the Christian marriage ceremony—as far more significant than the parodic ritual of "jumpin' the broom" by which slaves had once been forced to marry.[18] The story also exploits the tradition of the wise but uneducated slave, often portrayed in the works of the black writer Charles Chestnutt (1858–1932). These domestic allegories created an instructive but fictive world, where art did not imitate reality.[19] In doing so, they ignored white racial authority. But domestic allegories were inconsistent with the thrust of the modern short story, which emphasized real life. It was not long before such social realism took hold anew. "Black women writers," Tate points out, "slowly abandoned the assumption that art was meant to represent human ideals in favor of its recording the daily struggle to live a moral and ethical life."[20]

Alice Dunbar-Nelson's "The Stones of the Village" (1910), Angelina Weld Grimké's "Goldie" (1920), Marita Bonner's "One Boy's Story" (1925), and Nella Larsen's "Sanctuary" (1930) are examples of the renewed emphasis on social realism in black women's literature that began shortly after the turn of the century and has continued to this day. These stories also derive their momentum from overt conflict in a dramatic plot. At the outset of each story, the reader is given a line of progression to follow—a clear statement of the conflict, or a hint of it—and the action moves toward a crisis and then a final resolution. Paraphrasing E. M. Forster in *Aspects of the Novel*, if we say, "The king died and then the queen died," we have only narrative, a sequential telling of events; but if we say, "The king died and then the queen died of grief," we have plot, a causal relating of events. The socially realistic stories depart from the earlier narratives by unmasking their racial protest. Dunbar-Nelson's "The Stones of the Village" turns on the events in the life of a young lawyer, Victor Grabert, who passes for white. The story, which takes place in a real as opposed to a fictive environment, protests the racist mind-set that forces an extremely bright and capable young man to hide his true identity. It pleads the black cause with white readers, who might find it easy to identify with characters who look and act as whites do but who would suffer horrible indignities if their true racial identity were known.[21] One can almost relish Dunbar-Nelson's anticipatory pleasure with her white readers' discomfort over Grabert's final statement:

Oh, what a glorious revenge he had on those little white village boys! . . . He had taken a diploma from their most exclusive college; he had broken down the barriers of their social world; he had taken the highest possible position among them and, aping their own ways, had shown them that he, too, could despise this inferior race they despised. Nay, he had taken for his wife the best woman among them all, and she had borne him a son. Ha, ha! What a joke on them all!

Grabert's comment also offers a sobering message to black readers. The lawyer exhibits the abnormal behavior pattern whereby the oppressed becomes the oppressor.[22] To the everlasting dismay of his fellow sufferers, he takes on all the oppressor's worst attitudes. As Grabert explains, he "had shown them that he, too, could despise this inferior race they despised." This is an obvious reference to a "Negro" lawyer whom Grabert refers to as his bête noire, who comes before Grabert when he is a judge and contributes to his downfall. Could Grabert's shoddy treatment of the lawyer be a veiled call by Dunbar-Nelson for racial solidarity among dark-skinned blacks and mulattoes? The story was never published in Dunbar-Nelson's lifetime, because her editor at *The Atlantic Monthly* felt it was unsuitable for the white readers of the time.[23]

While Grabert's problems are caused by his and society's refusal to accept his blackness, white readers would have been able to equivocate about their individual responsibility for his plight. Grimké's "Goldie" (1920), however, like the rest of her small body of work, places the blame for racism squarely on whites. Tate points out that the story, written during the Harlem Renaissance, marks two important aesthetic transitions, in American literary history in general and in African-American literary history in particular:

> In U.S. literary culture, [Grimké's works] designate a point where the growing social alienation that would later be identified as the modern condition intersects Victorian positivism . . . In specifically black literary culture, Grimké's writings mark a place where the domestic plots of social optimism become outmoded, and the explicit depictions of social alienation and racial protest commence to satisfy the expectations of twentieth-century black readers.[24]

"Goldie" begins with the simple dramatic statement "He had never thought of the night, before, as so sharply black and white" (a foreshadowing of the conflict to come). The reader follows the story through the eyes of a young black man who, summoned to the South by his fearful sister, walks, with a sense of foreboding, through the woods to her home and toward an inevitable series of vengeful events. The story derives its power from the perfect manipulation of the dramatic elements that govern plot. Grimké uses flashbacks to portray the young man, Victor Forrest, his love for his sister, Goldie, and their childhood and parents. Yet Victor Forrest is never described. Faceless and incorporeal, he moves daringly through the dark woods, and we know him only by his musings and his fears. Goldie is described as a sweet young child-woman, whose lifetime desires are a home and a child. Having created a potential victim and a possible savior, Grimké develops the plot by using numerous anxiety-producing images: the woods that seemed like "an ocean that had flowed down in a great rolling black wave of flood to the very lips of the road itself"; "the dank, black oppressiveness of the air"; "a very pallid, slightly crumpled moon sliding furtively down the west"; an unsettling "keening." And as we reach, with Victor, his destination, we are forced as he is to view things by the light of an inadequate matchstick, seeing only what he sees, our vision as unable as his to comprehend things. The dénouement is as chilling as the events leading up to it. The reader experiences more than is promised.

Grimké's work also seems to mark the decline of the "true woman" heroine, who was generally fair-skinned and whose beauty was equated with wisdom and goodness. In her place we have the heroine, like Goldie, in whom deeds rather than looks determine character. In Bonner's "One Boy's Story" (1925), another example of social realism, the tale is told by a young boy who describes his mother, Louise, as having a "roundish plump, brown face" and "black hair all curled up on the end like a nice autumn leaf." The story is a surprisingly fresh rendering of the Oedipus tale, but its motif, or subtheme, is racism. "One Boy's Story" provides a rare look at a black woman's painful love for a white man. Wishing to end their relationship, Louise laments: "Dear Jesus! With your help I'll free myself." Given the consistent view in nineteenth-century black literature that black women must avoid the advances of white men because of the latter's transgressions during slavery and the subsequent claims by white society that black women were unchaste, this story is remarkable just in its telling. However, such situations may have been far more common than we have been led to believe; for Louise also has a black suitor, and when he finds out about her white lover, his telling response is: "Just like nigger women." At the end of the story the boy is punished. The harshness of that punishment is perhaps due to the severity of the mother's transgressions. Since the story was published in the mid-1920s, when interracial relationships were beginning to gain acceptance among the avant-garde, Bonner may have used a mythical source to help legitimize her controversial subject matter.

In Larsen's "Sanctuary" (1930), set in the Great Depression, a black mother's choice between racial solidarity and justice brings into question the age-old homily that "blood is thicker than water." Civil rights for blacks were still routinely denied, and the mother's choice is perhaps more understandable, given the lawlessness of Southern white sheriffs. Interestingly, the stories by Dunbar-Nelson, Grimké, Bonner, and Larsen confront the racial system head-on, and all reflect the violence it embraces.

Dorothy West's "The Typewriter" (1944) and Ann Petry's "Miss Muriel" (1958) are also racial protest stories, but their messages are more oblique.

"The Typewriter," a poignant story of a black man who has not and probably will not realize his innate potential, is an apt reflection of the time when blacks were allowed only menial work. For instance, the first black telephone operator was not hired until 1945, just before the end of World War II. "Miss Muriel" (1958) differs from the other social-realism tales in that its protest elements are concealed in a love story. A very long story, it saunters through a summer, like condensation building on a glass of lemonade, as its precocious narrator, a twelve-year-old girl, watches her beautiful aunt Sophronia being courted by both an elderly white shoemaker, Mr. Bemish, and a carefree young black musician, Chink Johnson. This exquisite story takes a gentle look at interracial longing during our tumultuous civil rights period when the nation believed integration—in schools and communities—was the solution to the black/white problem. It also subtly "signifies" on countless slave stories, where the virile white slaver has his way with a black woman.[25] Petry has re-aligned "the signifier," the story's outcome, so that when Mr. Bemish is forced to compete fairly with Chink Johnson, Bemish loses. Nonetheless, even though his loss is predictable, there is a pathos about the resolution.

S. A. Williams's "Tell Martha Not to Moan" (1968) and Ntozake Shange's "comin to terms" (1979), both written during the women's liberation movement, are classic portrayals of women who protest their treatment by men. These character-driven stories are so engrossing that, as Maugham once said of Chekhov's work, "You do not seem to be reading stories at all . . ." It appears that the "author has had an emotion, and . . . is able so to put it into words . . . Yet if you try to tell one of the stories, there is nothing to tell."[26] "comin to terms" (1979), the shortest piece in the anthology, engages the reader in a young woman's painful examination of her relationship with her live-in boyfriend. By refusing to have sex on demand, she attempts to free herself from male domination. He, however, sees her gesture as heresy. Sadly, written over one hundred years after slavery, the protagonist is still fighting for control over her body. A poetic story, it is more to be felt than understood, for here, indeed, "the action is small, [but] its meanings are large."

In "Tell Martha Not to Moan" (1968), a young country girl falls in love with an out-of-work jazz musician. She becomes pregnant and he leaves her. Beyond that summary, there is really nothing more to tell, but so much more to glean, for the characters give us a privileged look into the workings of black families and the black community. Martha's tale shows a common generational pattern: the frequent failure of some black fathers to support their families (Martha's father did not support his family, and now the fathers of Martha's children are not supporting Martha and their children), and the pattern of unflagging support of black mothers for their daughters, regardless of their lifestyle. The story protests men's treatment of women. But it is not difficult to see the women's complicity. Martha's mother was apparently willing to become pregnant by a man who did not stay around, and now Martha is equally willing to bear children for the same type of man: "What I want to marry for anyway?" Martha exclaims. "Get somebody like daddy always coming and going and every time he go leave a baby behind."

Another character-driven story, Alice Walker's "To Hell with Dying" (1967), is about family and community love. Its characters are similar to those in "Tell Martha Not to Moan." In Walker's story the protagonist, Mr. Sweet, is an alcoholic who, when drunk, often pretends he is dying. The children of a neighboring family pretend to revive him with hugs, kisses, and tickles. The men in both "To Hell with Dying" and "Tell Martha" appear to be dreamers who are unable to hold ordinary jobs. The women in the stories—Martha, her mother, and Mrs. Sweet—despair of their men, to such an extent in Mrs. Sweet's case that she seems, unconsciously, to be raising her son to fail: "[She] loved her 'baby' . . . and worked hard to get him the 'li'l necessaries' of life, which turned out mostly to be women." "To Hell with Dying" broadens its focus by showing that Mr. Sweet's neighbors feel a responsibility toward him that may be part of an African community tradition that survived slavery.

Colleen McElroy's "Sister Detroit" (1978), a unique women's liberation protest story, depicts a newlywed working-class woman whose husband is missing in action in Vietnam. The heroine eventually challenges male authority—ironically with one of its most powerful symbols, the car:

> But for the women, those cars were the excuses that helped their men stay as fickle as the tornadoes that occasionally passed through the heart of town, the winds that sometimes danced through living rooms and took everything a family had managed to scrape out of a pinch-penny job, and sometimes turned corners down the centers of streets as if they were following traffic patterns. For the women those cars were merely another way to haul them from the house to a day job—"the hook between Miss Ann and the killing floor," as Autherine Franklin would say—because, for the women, the cars were to be looked at and paid for, but never driven.

●

McElroy's mastery of the short story is so deft, her prose so seamless, that there is not the faintest hint of the power of this statement until the end of the story. "Sister Detroit" perfectly reflects conditions for women during the 1960s, where nothing was resolved and a particular, isolated action simply moved to a more general plane.

Diane Oliver's "Key to the City" (1965) and Sonia Sanchez's "After Saturday Night Comes Sunday" (1971) demonstrate the strength of women in the face of adversity. Oliver's story, written around the time of the third black migration from the South, deals with a family's migration North. The mother's strength is revealed in the story's epiphany, which comes when her oldest child realizes what the mother has suspected all along, as the family waits in the empty Chicago bus station for their father. In "After Saturday Night Comes Sunday" (1971), written during the era of the emerging drug culture, a woman must face a terrible reality in a moment of panic, when confronted with a problem over which she has no control. Toni Cade Bambara's "My Man Bovanne" (1972), a reflective piece published during the Black Power movement, uses humor and sarcasm to focus on the strength of a middle-aged woman. At issue is how she should comport herself in front of her grown children, who criticize her behavior. Because the mother narrates the story in black English, which is often equated with ignorance, the reader might expect very little from her. However, she turns out to be extremely insightful and instructive, as she shows her children, to their dismay, that her generation is still capable of romantic love and knowledgeable in the ways of advancing black power. This story also signifies on "Mary Elizabeth," since in both stories the person with the knowledge is the one least expected to have it.

Written during the decade of changing sexual attitudes, Tina McElroy Ansa's "Willie Bea and Jaybird" (1991) also demonstrates a woman's strength in the face of adversity. What begins as a loving relationship between two unlikely people—Willie Bea, an unattractive young wife, "five feet tall, ninety pounds, stick legs, Coke-bottle glasses," and her handsome husband, Jaybird, who calls her "fine"—is tested when the woman finds out a terrible truth about her husband. As the story ends, she is lying in bed silently sorting the facts, knowing but preferring not to know what she has just learned.

Gayl Jones's "Jevata," Ann Allen Shockley's "The World of Rosie Polk," and Jamaica Kincaid's "Song of Roland" are love stories. But they also, perhaps inadvertently, deftly defy stereotypes of black women that have long been the staple of American literature. Most of us are familiar with the stereotypical images of the "southern Black woman sharecropper with

. . . children peering from a dark, rickety, dust-ridden shack . . .”; the
"bad-busting Mammy . . . and the Sex-kitten"; and the "Afro-Caribbean
primitive, superstitious, hip-swinging . . . mulatto women."[27] Such dis-
tortions have prevailed in literature for over a century. Now as the black
woman as artist and arbiter becomes, more and more, the source of "her-
own symbol-making,"[28] she can describe herself as the complex, multi-
faceted person she is.

Contrast the "bad-busting Mammy" with the protagonist in Jones's story
"Jevata" (1977). Written in the later years of the women's liberation movement, the story concerns a divorced, middle-aged mother with three children, a young boyfriend, Freddy, and a past suitor who has become a
friend. When Freddy is asked why he went with Jevata in the first place
he answers:

> "We was standing up close to each other [at a carnival] . . . and then
> all of a sudden Miss Jevata kind of turned her head to me, you know,
> and said kind of quiet-like, 'You know, Miss Jevata could teach you
> how to swallow lightning,' she said. That was all she said. She didn't
> say nothing else and she didn't say that no more. I don't even know
> if anybody else heard her. But I think that's why I went back with
> her."

Yet Jevata is a lonely, vulnerable woman caught in a fatalistic relationship,
as are the other characters in this highly complex story. It is as if Jones
is asking us to explore the immense scope of human tragedy on a small,
personal scale.

Or, compare the stereotype of the forsaken black sharecropper woman
with the migrant worker Rosie in Shockley's contemporary story "The
World of Rosie Polk" (1987). Rosie is thirty-four years old, with graying
hair and cheeks hollow from missing teeth. The history of her children
is a testament to her misfortune: Mary, born when Rosie was fifteen—
father unknown—died one week after birth; Lula, "gone off with a boy
three years ago"; Lonnie, killed at a crap game in Maryland. Charlie,
now eight, travels with Rosie from camp to camp as she picks crops, trying
but never discharging her debt to the crew leader. Yet despite her dismal
circumstances, Rosie's spirit is never crushed:

> "Sick of trucks," she went on, letting her longtime pent-up frustra-
> tions cascade out at [the crew boss]. "All my life, I been doin' nothin'
> but gittin' on and off trucks. Ridin' and gittin' no place."

Or, look anew at the "Afro-Caribbean primitive." In Kincaid's "Song of Roland" (1993), she is an intelligent, twenty-odd-year-old, plain-looking Caribbean woman erotically in love with an older, "unpolished" married man. The story derives its tension from a reversal of roles and signifies on the famous eleventh-century French narrative poem "The Song of Roland," which tells of the heroic death of Charlemagne's greatest knight, who is betrayed and killed in a pagan ambush. Kincaid evokes the medieval warrior when her protagonist (who remains nameless—a suggestion that she is every(wo)man?) says of her lover: "His name was Roland. He was not a hero, he did not even have a country . . . And he did not have a history . . ." Both the poem and the story are narratives of death by betrayal. But in her version, Kincaid's protagonist symbolically kills Roland by shedding *her* blood each month, when "small drops of blood spilt from inside me, evidence of my refusal to accept his silent offering . . ." "The World of Rosie Polk," "Jevata" and "Song of Roland" carry a common motif that, in many ways, is similar to one fostered in much of the current literature of black women: the fear of the real differences that may be encountered when stereotypes are eschewed in favor of life.

One of the wonders of the modern short story is its ability to capture the inconclusive and fragmentary nature of reality, to allow us to perceive anew what we already know ("Memory believes before knowing remembers"[29]) but are unable to articulate. Frenchy Hodges's "Requiem for Willie Lee," Connie Porter's "Hoodoo," and Rita Dove's "Damon and Vandalia" allow us to sense unconditional love, explore our anxieties over spiritualism, and stand at the rim of the vortex of carnal knowledge.

Hodges's "Requiem for Willie Lee" (1979) owes its power primarily to the first-person storytelling technique of the folktale and to the fatalistic drive of the legend. About the leader of a gang and a vacationing schoolteacher, it is a story of the failed relationship between teacher and student and, symbolically, mother and son. "He was my student who'd failed," the teacher says, "and I was the teacher who'd failed him." The tale is a tour de force in its use of images and language: "The day was dark and the woods were dark and the clouds were dark in the sky." Willie Lee is "country-sun-and-rain-black." A "Wonder Bread truck . . . [is] filled with guns-ready police." There is a new verb: he "came paining into my arms." The schoolteacher even shares her inner thoughts in the manner of a Greek chorus, probing, counseling, and attempting to heal: "Why couldn't you stop, Willie Lee, when it started going wrong and kept on going that way? You're not a fool . . ." The teacher's final words—"I comforted the dying man, making a requiem for him, for myself, and for all the world's people who only know life through death"—can be likened to the Greek *caritas* of I Corinthians 13, a love that "bears all things, believes all things, hopes all things, endures all things."

In Dove's highly innovative story "Damon and Vandalia" (1985), a young black woman, Vandalia, decides to have an affair with a white homosexual, Damon, who does not know that he is also bisexual. The plot revolves around the decisions they make as they court during one summer. The power of the story comes from its format, which alternates between the viewpoints of Damon and Vandalia. After they make love Vandalia reflects:

> When we had finished, he placed his palm between my legs, cupping and defining, his face as wondering as a child's, amazed that that's all there was—no magic, no straining muscular desire.

Published during the decade when diverse lifestyles moved to center stage, this story, in throwing off the yoke of female subservience, crosses sexual, racial, and social lines to probe the complexity of unusual human relations. Precisely for these reasons and because it must be, literally, mined for its treasures, "Damon and Vandalia" is a gem.

Finally, there is Porter's "Hoodoo" (1988). The narrator describes an albino girl's dream of a black boy who brings her color, and then the narrative takes a step back in time. The story's power comes from African Americans' spiritual connection to the dreaded Middle Passage. For our forebears did not come alone. They carried with them a system of meaning and belief "recreated from memory, preserved by oral narration, improvised upon in ritual . . . and willed to . . . subsequent generations . . ."[30] Hoodoo, voodoo, juju men, witch doctors, and conjure women are part of a thousand-year-old tradition[31] and remind us of the great myths of our West African ancestors' Yoruba religion.

The stories in this book deal with centers of the self. They examine, define, and distill feelings that, in some cases, have become central themes in our black literary canon. In all probability, "Goldie" and "Requiem for Willie Lee" will be read by future generations as examples of our terrible past; "Sister Detroit" and "Sanctuary," for the dilemma of protagonists who defy the state; "Damon and Vandalia," "Song of Roland," and "comin to terms," for their portrayal of women defining their own sexuality and breaking free of male sexual bonds at the end of the twentieth century.

The literary works of African Americans are currently receiving great attention. This change has been brought about by a national climate that is in many ways, despite problems, less negative for blacks than it has been in the past. It is also a result of the new and, we hope, lasting national and international recognition of African-American literary achievements, exemplified during the past twenty-odd years by the works of women. This anthology acknowledges the short-story genre in that literary tradition, whose importance to all Americans is inestimable. We hope this collection will allow readers to focus on the purpose, quality, and signal position of these works. It is our fervent desire that these stories will also simply give pleasure to readers for many years to come.

Judith A. Hamer
Martin J. Hamer
Westport, Connecticut
February 1994

The Two Offers

•

(1859)

Frances Ellen Watkins Harper

"What is the matter with you, Laura, this morning? I have been watching you this hour, and in that time you have commenced a half dozen letters and torn them all up. What matter of such grave moment is puzzling your dear little head, that you do not know how to decide?"

"Well, it is an important matter: I have two offers for marriage, and I do not know which to choose."

"I should accept neither, or to say the least, not at present."

"Why not?"

"Because I think a woman who is undecided between two offers has not love enough for either to make a choice; and in that very hesitation, indecision, she has a reason to pause and seriously reflect, lest her mar- riage, instead of being an affinity of souls or a union of hearts, should only be a mere matter of bargain and sale, or an affair of convenience and selfish interest."

"But I consider them both very good offers, just such as many a girl would gladly receive. But to tell you the truth, I do not think that I regard either as a woman should the man she chooses for her husband. But then if I refuse, there is the risk of being an old maid, and that is not to be thought of."

"Well, suppose there is, is that the most dreadful fate that can befall a woman? Is there not more intense wretchedness in an ill-assorted marriage—more utter loneliness in a loveless home—than in the lot of the old maid who accepts her earthly mission as a gift from God, and strives to walk the path of life with earnest and unfaltering steps?"

"Oh! What a little preacher you are. I really believe that you were cut out for an old maid, that when nature formed you, she put in a double portion of intellect to make up for a deficiency of love; and yet you are kind and affectionate. But I do not think that you know anything of the grand, overmastering passion, or the deep necessity of woman's heart for loving."

"Do you think so?" resumed the first speaker; and bending over her work she quietly applied herself to the knitting that had lain neglected by her side during this brief conversation; but as she did so, a shadow flitted over her pale and intellectual brow, a mist gathered in her eyes, and a slight quivering of the lips revealed a depth of feeling to which her companion was a stranger.

But before I proceed with my story, let me give you a slight history of the speakers. They were cousins, who had met life under different auspices. Laura Lagrange was the only daughter of rich and indulgent parents, who had spared no pains to make her an accomplished lady. Her cousin, Janette Alston, was the child of parents rich only in goodness and affection. Her father had been unfortunate in business and, dying before he could retrieve his fortunes, left his business in an embarrassed state. His widow was unacquainted with his business affairs; and when the estate was settled, hungry creditors had brought their claims, and the lawyers had received their fees, she found herself homeless and almost penniless, and she who had been sheltered in the warm clasp of loving arms found them too powerless to shield her from the pitiless pelting storms of adversity. Year after year she struggled with poverty and wrestled with want, till her toil-worn hands became too feeble to hold the shattered chords of existence, and her tear-dimmed eyes grew heavy with the slumber of death. Her daughter had watched over her with untiring devotion, had closed her eyes in death and gone out into the busy, restless world, missing a precious tone from the voices of earth, a beloved step from the paths of life. Too self-reliant to depend on the charity of relations, she endeavored to support herself by her own exertions, and she had succeeded. Her path for a while was marked with struggle and trial; but instead of uselessly repining, she met them bravely, and her life became not a thing of ease and indulgence, but of conquest, victory, and accomplishments.

At the time when this conversation took place, the deep trials of her life had passed away. The achievements of her genius had won her a position in the literary world, where she shone as one of its bright particular stars. And with her fame came a competence of worldly means, which gave her leisure for improvement, and the riper development of her rare talents. And she, that pale intellectual woman whose genius gave life and vivacity to the social circle, and whose presence threw a halo of beauty and grace around the charmed atmosphere in which she moved, had at one period of her life known the mystic and solemn strength of an all-absorbing love. Years faded into the misty past, had seen the kindling of her eye, the quick flushing of her cheek, and the wild throbbing of her heart, at tones of a voice long since hushed to the stillness of death. Deeply, wildly, passionately, she had loved. Her whole life seemed like the pouring out of rich, warm, and gushing affections. This love quickened her talents, inspired her genius, and threw over her life a tender and spiritual earnestness. And then came a fearful shock, a mournful waking from that "dream of beauty and delight." A shadow fell around her path; it came between her and the object of her heart's worship; first a few cold words, estrangement, and then a painful separation; the old story of woman's pride—digging the sepulchre of her happiness, and then a new-made grave, and her path over it to the spirit world; and thus faded out from that young heart her bright, brief, and saddened dream of life.

Faint and spirit-broken, she turned from the scenes associated with the memory of the loved and lost. She tried to break the chain of sad associations that bound her to the mournful past; and so, pressing back the bitter sobs from her almost breaking heart, like the dying dolphin, whose beauty is born of its death anguish, her genius gathered strength from suffering and wondrous power and brilliancy from the agony she hid within the desolate chambers of her soul. Men hailed her as one of earth's strangely gifted children, and wreathed the garlands of fame for her brow when it was throbbing with a wild and fearful unrest. They breathed her name with applause, when through the lonely halls of her stricken spirit there was an earnest cry for peace, a deep yearning for sympathy and heart-support.

But life, with its stern realities, met her; its solemn responsibilities confronted her, and turning, with an earnest and shattered spirit, to life's duties and trials, she found a calmness and strength that she had only imagined in her dreams of poetry and song. We will now pass over a period of ten years, and the cousins have met again. In that calm and lovely woman, in whose eyes is a depth of tenderness tempering the flashes of her genius, whose looks and tones are full of sympathy and love, we recognize the once smitten and stricken Janette Alston. The bloom of her girlhood has given way to a higher type of spiritual beauty, as if some unseen hand has been polishing and refining the temple in which her lovely spirit found its habitation; and this has been the fact. Her inner life has grown beautiful, and it is this that has been constantly developing the outer. Never, in the early flush of womanhood, when an absorbing love had lit up her eyes and glowed in her life, had she appeared so interesting as now when, with a countenance which seems overshadowed with a spiritual light, she bends over the death-bed of a young woman, just lingering at the shadowy gates of the unseen land.

"Has he come?" faintly but eagerly exclaimed the dying woman. "Oh! How I have longed for his coming, and even in death he forgets me."

"Oh, do not say so, dear Laura, some accident may have detained him," said Janette to her cousin; for on that bed, from whence she will never rise, lies the once beautiful and light-hearted Laura Lagrange, the brightness of whose eyes has long since been dimmed with tears, and whose voice has become like a harp whose every chord is tuned to sadness—whose faintest thrill and loudest vibrations are but the variations of agony. A heavy hand was laid upon her once warm and bounding heart, and a voice came whispering through her soul that she must die. But, to her, the tidings were a message of deliverance—a voice hushing her wild sorrows to the calmness of resignation and hope. Life had grown so weary upon her head—the future looked so hopeless—she had no wish to tread again the track where thorns had pierced her feet and clouds overcast her sky; and she hailed the coming of death's angel as the footsteps of a welcome friend.

And yet, earth had one object so very dear to her weary heart. It was her absent and recreant husband; for, since that conversation, she had accepted one of her offers, and become a wife. But, before she married, she learned that great lesson of human experience and woman's life: to love the man who bowed at her shrine, a willing worshipper. He had a pleasing address, raven hair, flashing eyes, a voice of thrilling sweetness, and lips of persuasive eloquence; and being well versed in the ways of the world, he won his way to her heart, and she became his bride, and he was proud of his prize. Vain and superficial in his character, he looked upon marriage not as a divine sacrament for the soul's development and human progression, but as the title-deed that gave him possession of the woman he thought he loved. But alas for her, the laxity of his principles had rendered him unworthy of the deep and undying devotion of a pure-hearted woman; but, for a while, he hid from her his true character, and she blindly loved him, and for a short period was happy in the consciousness of being beloved; though sometimes a vague unrest would fill her soul, when, overflowing with a sense of the good, the beautiful, and the true, she would turn to him, but find no response to the deep yearnings of her soul—no appreciation of life's highest realities—its solemn grandeur and significant importance. Their souls never met, and soon she found a void in her bosom that his earth-born love could not fill. He did not satisfy the wants of her mental and moral nature—between him and her there was no affinity of minds, no intercommunion of souls.

Talk as you will of woman's deep capacity for loving, of the strength of her affectional nature. I do not deny it; but will the mere possession of any human love fully satisfy all the demands of her whole being? You may paint her in poetry or fiction as a frail vine, clinging to her brother man for support and dying when deprived of it; and all this may sound well enough to please the imaginations of school-girls, or love-lorn maidens. But woman—the true woman—if you would render her happy, it needs more than the mere development of her affectional nature. Her conscience should be enlightened, her faith in the true and right established, and scope given to her Heaven-endowed and God-given faculties. The true aim of female education should be, not a development of one or two, but all the faculties of the human soul, because no perfect womanhood is developed by imperfect culture. Intense love is often akin to intense suffering, and to trust the whole wealth of a woman's nature on the frail bark of human love may often be like trusting a cargo of gold and precious gems to a bark that has never battled with the storm, or buffeted the waves. Is it any wonder, then, that so many life-barks go down, paving the ocean of time with precious hearts and wasted hopes? that so many float around us, shattered and dismasted wrecks? that so many are stranded on the shoals of existence, mournful beacons and solemn warnings for the thoughtless, to whom marriage is a careless and hasty rushing together of the affections? Alas that an institution so fraught with good for humanity should be so perverted, and that state of life, which should be filled with happiness, become so replete with misery.

And this was the fate of Laura Lagrange. For a brief period after her marriage her life seemed like a bright and beautiful dream, full of hope and radiant with joy. And then there came a change—he found other attractions that lay beyond the pale of home influences. The gambling saloon had power to win him from her side, he had lived in an element of unhealthy and unhallowed excitements, and the society of a loving wife, the pleasures of a well-regulated home, were enjoyments too tame for one who had vitiated his tastes by the pleasures of sin. There were charmed houses of vice, built upon dead men's loves, where, amid a flow of song, laughter, wine, and careless mirth, he would spend hour after hour, forgetting the cheek that was paling through his neglect, heedless of the tear-dimmed eyes peering anxiously into the darkness, waiting, or watching his return.

The influence of old associations was upon him. In early life, home had been to him a place of ceilings and walls, not a true home built upon goodness, love, and truth. It was a place where velvet carpets hushed his tread, where images of loveliness and beauty, invoked into being by paint- er's art and sculptor's skill, pleased the eye and gratified the taste, where magnificence surrounded his way and costly clothing adorned his person; but it was not the place for the true culture and right development of his soul. His father had been too much engrossed in making money, and his mother in spending it, in striving to maintain a fashionable position in society, and shining in the eyes of the world, to give the proper direction to the character of their wayward and impulsive son. His mother put beautiful robes upon his body, but left ugly scars upon his soul; she pampered his appetite, but starved his spirit. Every mother should be a true artist, who knows how to weave into her child's life images of grace and beauty, the true poet capable of writing on the soul of childhood the harmony of love and truth, and teaching it how to produce the grandest of all poems—the poetry of a true and noble life. But in his home, a love for the good, the true and right, had been sacrificed at the shrine of frivolity and fashion. That parental authority which should have been preserved as a string of precious pearls, unbroken and unscattered, was simply the administration of chance. At one time obedience was enforced by authority, at another time by flattery and promises, and just as often it was not enforced at all. His early associations were formed as chance directed, and from his want of home-training, his character received a bias, his life a shade, which ran through every avenue of his existence and darkened all his future hours.

Oh, if we would trace the history of all the crimes that have o'ershad- owed this sin-shrouded and sorrow-darkened world of ours, how many might be seen arising from the wrong home influences, or the weakening of the home ties. Home should always be the best school for the affections, the birthplace of high resolves, and the altar upon which lofty aspirations are kindled, from whence the soul may go forth strengthened, to act its part aright in the great drama of life, with conscience enlightened, affec- tions cultivated, and reason and judgment dominant. But alas for the young wife. Her husband had not been blessed with such a home. When he entered the arena of life, the voices from home did not linger around his path as angels of guidance about his steps; they were not like so many messages to invite him to deeds of high and holy worth. The memory of no sainted mother arose between him and deeds of darkness; the earnest prayers of no father arrested him in his downward course; and before a year of his married life had waned, his young wife had learned to wait and mourn his frequent and uncalled-for absence. More than once had she seen him come home from his midnight haunts, the bright intelligence of his eye displaced by the drunkard's stare, and his manly gait changed to the inebriate's stagger; and she was beginning to know the bitter agony that is compressed in the mournful words "a drunkard's wife."

And then there came a bright but brief episode in her experience; the angel of life gave to her existence a deeper meaning and loftier significance: she sheltered in the warm clasp of her loving arms a dear babe, a precious child, whose love filled every chamber of her heart, and felt the fount of maternal love gushing so new within her soul. That child was hers. How overshadowing was the love with which she bent over its helplessness, how much it helped to fill the void and chasms in her soul. How many lonely hours were beguiled by its winsome ways, its answering smiles and fond caresses. How exquisite and solemn was the feeling that thrilled her heart when she clasped the tiny hands together and taught her dear child to call God "Our Father."

What a blessing was that child. The father paused in his headlong career, awed by the strange beauty and precocious intellect of his child; and the mother's life had a better expression through her ministrations of love. And then there came hours of bitter anguish, shading the sunlight of her home and hushing the music of her heart. The angel of death bent over the couch of her child and beaconed it away. Closer and closer the mother strained her child to her wildly heaving breast, and struggled with the heavy hand that lay upon its heart. Love and agony contended with death, and the language of the mother's heart was

> *Oh, Death, away! That innocent is mine;*
> *I cannot spare him from my arms*
> *To lay him, Death, in thine.*
> *I am a mother, Death; I gave that darling birth*
> *I could not bear his lifeless limbs*
> *Should moulder in the earth.*

But death was stronger than love and mightier than agony and won the child for the land of crystal founts and deathless flowers, and the poor, stricken mother sat down beneath the shadow of her mighty grief, feeling as if a great light had gone out from her soul, and that the sunshine had suddenly faded around her path. She turned in her deep anguish to the father of her child, the loved and cherished dead. For a while his words were kind and tender, his heart seemed subdued, and his tenderness fell upon her worn and weary heart like rain on perishing flowers, or cooling waters to lips all parched with thirst and scorched with fever; but the change was evanescent, the influence of unhallowed associations and evil habits had vitiated and poisoned the springs of his existence. They had bound him in their meshes, and he lacked the moral strength to break his fetters and stand erect in all the strength and dignity of a true manhood, making life's highest excellence his ideal and striving to gain it.

And yet moments of deep contrition would sweep over him, when he would resolve to abandon the wine-cup forever, when he was ready to forswear the handling of another card, and he would try to break away from the associations that he felt were working his ruin; but when the hour of temptation came his strength was weakness, his earnest purposes were cobwebs, his well-meant resolutions ropes of sand, and thus passed year after year of the married life of Laura Lagrange.

She tried to hide her agony from the public gaze, to smile when her heart was almost breaking. But year after year her voice grew fainter and sadder, her once light and bounding step grew slower and faltering. Year after year she wrestled with agony and strove with despair, till the quick eyes of her brother read, in the paling of her cheek and the dimming eye, the secret anguish of her worn and weary spirit. On that wan, sad face, he saw the death-tokens, and he knew the dark wing of the mystic angel swept coldly around her path. "Laura," said her brother to her one day, "you are not well, and I think you need our mother's tender care and nursing. You are daily losing strength, and if you will go I will accompany you." At first, she hesitated, she shrank almost instinctively from pre-senting that pale, sad face to the loved ones at home. That face was such a tell-tale; it told of heart-sickness, of hope deferred, and the mournful story of unrequited love. But then a deep yearning for home sympathy woke within her a passionate longing for love's kind words, for tenderness and heart-support, and she resolved to seek the home of her childhood and lay her weary head upon her mother's bosom, to be folded again in her loving arms, to lay that poor, bruised, and aching heart where it might beat and throb closely to the loved ones at home.

A kind welcome awaited her. All that love and tenderness could devise was done to bring the bloom to her cheek and the light to her eye; but it was all in vain; hers was a disease that no medicine could cure, no earthly balm would heal. It was a slow wasting of the vital forces, the sickness of the soul. The unkindness and neglect of her husband lay like a leaden weight upon her heart and slowly oozed away its life-drops. And where was he that had won her love, and then cast it aside as a useless thing, who rifled her heart of its wealth and spread bitter ashes upon its broken altars? He was lingering away from her when the death-damps were gathering on her brow, when his name was trembling on her lips! Lingering away!—when she was watching his coming, though the death films were gathering before her eyes, and earthly things were fading from her vision. "I think I hear him now," said the dying woman, "surely that is his step"; but the sound died away in the distance. Again she started from an uneasy slumber. "That is his voice! I am so glad he has come."

Tears gathered in the eyes of the sad watchers by that dying bed, for they knew that she was deceived. He had not returned. For her sake they wished for his coming. Slowly the hours waned away, and then came the sad, soul-sickening thought that she was forgotten, forgotten in the last hour of human need, forgotten when the spirit, about to be dissolved, paused for the last time on the threshold of existence, a weary watcher at the gates of death. "He has forgotten me," again she faintly murmured, and the last tears she would ever shed on earth sprung to her mournful eyes. As she clasped her hands in silent anguish, a few broken sentences issued from her pale and quivering lips. They were prayers for strength and earnest pleading for him who had desolated her young life by turning its sunshine to shadows, its smiles to tears. "He has forgotten me," she murmured again, "but I can bear it, the bitterness of death is passed, and soon I hope to exchange the shadows of death for the brightness of eternity, the rugged paths of life for the golden streets of glory, and the care and turmoils of earth for the peace and rest of heaven." Her voice grew fainter and fainter; they saw the shadows that never deceive flit over her pale and faded face, and knew that the death angel waited to soothe their weary one to rest, to calm the throbbing of her bosom and cool the fever of her brain. And amid the silent hush of their grief the freed spirit, refined through suffering and brought into divine harmony through the spirit of the living Christ, passed over the dark waters of death as on a bridge of light, over whose radiant arches hovering angels bent.

They parted the dark locks from her marble brow, closed the waxen lids over the once bright and laughing eye, and left her to the dreamless slumber of the grave. Her cousin turned from that death-bed a sadder and wiser woman. She resolved more earnestly than ever to make the world better by her example, gladder by her presence, and to kindle the fires of her genius on the altars of universal love and truth. She had a higher and better object in all her writings than the mere acquisition of gold or acquirement of fame. She felt that she had a high and holy mission on the battlefield of existence, that life was not given her to be frittered away in nonsense or wasted away in trifling pursuits. She would willingly espouse an unpopular cause but not an unrighteous one. In her the downtrodden slave found an earnest advocate; the flying fugitive remembered her kindness as he stepped cautiously through our Republic, to gain his freedom in a monarchial land, having broken the chains on which the rust of centuries had gathered. Little children learned to name her with affection, the poor called her blessed, as she broke her bread to the pale lips of hunger. Her life was like a beautiful story, only it was clothed with the dignity of reality and invested with the sublimity of truth. True, she was an old maid, no husband brightened her life with his love, or shaded it with his neglect. No children nestling lovingly in her arms called her Mother. No one appended Mrs. to her name; she was indeed an old maid, not vainly striving to keep up an appearance of girlishness when departed was written on her youth. Not vainly pining at her loneliness and isolation: the world was full of warm, loving hearts, and her own beat in unison with them. Neither was she always sentimentally sighing for something to love; objects of affection were all around her, and the world was not so wealthy in love that it had no use for hers; in blessing others she made a life and benediction, and as old age descended peacefully and gently upon her, she had learned one of life's most precious lessons: that true happiness consists not so much in the fruition of our wishes as in the regulation of desires and the full development and right culture of our whole natures.

After Many Days

A Christmas Story

•

(1902)

Fannie Barrier Williams

Christmas on the Edwards plantation, as it was still called, was a great event to old and young, master and slave comprising the Edwards household. Although freedom had long ago been declared, many of the older slaves could not be induced to leave the plantation, chiefly because the Edwards family had been able to maintain their appearance of opulence through the vicissitudes of war and the subsequent disasters, which had impoverished so many of their neighbors. It is one of the peculiar characteristics of the American Negro, that he is never to be found in large numbers in any community where the white people are as poor as himself. It is, therefore, not surprising that the Edwards plantation had no difficulty in retaining nearly all of their former slaves as servants under the new regime.

The stately Edwards mansion, with its massive pillars and spreading porticoes, gleaming white in its setting of noble pines and cedars, is still the pride of a certain section of old Virginia.

One balmy afternoon a few days before the great Christmas festival, Doris Edwards, the youngest granddaughter of this historic Southern home, was hastening along a well-trodden path leading down to an old white-washed cabin, one of the picturesque survivals of plantation life before the war. The pathway was bordered on either side with old-fashioned flowers, some of them still lifting a belated blossom, caught in the lingering balm of autumn, while faded stalks of hollyhock and sun-flower, like silent sentinels, guarded the door of this humble cabin.

Through the open vine-latticed window, Doris sniffed with keen delight the mingled odor of pies, cakes, and various other dainties temptingly

31

spread out on the snowy kitchen table waiting to be conveyed to the "big house" to contribute to the coming Christmas cheer.

Peering into the gloomy cabin, Doris discovered old Aunt Linda, with whom she had always been a great favorite, sitting in a low chair before the old brick oven, her apron thrown over her head, swaying back and forth to the doleful measure of a familiar plantation melody, to which the words "Lambs of the Upper Fold" were being paraphrased in a most ludicrous way. As far back as Doris could remember, it had been an unwritten law on the plantation that when Aunt Linda's "blues chile" reached the "Lambs of the Upper Fold" stage, she was in a mood not to be trifled with.

Aunt Linda had lived on the plantation so long she had become quite a privileged character. It had never been known just how she had learned to read and write, but this fact had made her a kind of leader among the other servants, and had earned for herself greater respect even from the Edwards family. Since she'd been a house servant for many years, her language was also better than that of the other servants, and her spirits were very low indeed when she lapsed into the language of the "quarters." There was also a tradition in the family that Aunt Linda's coming to the plantation had from the first been shrouded in mystery. In appearance she was a tall yellow woman, straight as an Indian, with piercing black eyes, and bearing herself with a certain dignity of manner, unusual in a slave. Visitors to the Edwards place would at once single her out from among the other servants, sometimes asking some very uncomfortable questions concerning her. Doris, however, was the one member of the household who refused to take Aunt Linda's moods seriously, so, taking in the situation at a glance, she determined to put an end to this "mood" at least. Stealing softly up on the old woman, she drew the apron from her head, exclaiming, "O, Aunt Linda, just leave your 'lambs' alone for today, won't you? Why, this is Christmas time, and I have left all kinds of nice things going on up at the house to bring you the latest news, and now, but what is the matter anyway?" The old woman slowly raised her head, saying, "I might of knowed it was you, you certainly is gettin' might sassy, chile, chile, how you did fright me sure. My min' was way back in ole Carolina, jest befoh another Christmas, when de Lord done lay one hand on my pore heart, and wid de other press down de white lids over de blue eyes of my sweet Alice. O, my chile, can I evah forget dat day?" Doris, fearing another outburst, interrupted the moans of the old woman by playfully placing her hand over her mouth, saying: "Wait a minute, Auntie, I want to tell you something. There are so many delightful people up to the house, but I want to tell you about two of them especially.

Sister May has just come and has brought with her her friend, Pauline Sommers, who sings beautifully, and she is going to sing our Christmas carol for us on Christmas Eve. With them is the loveliest girl I ever saw, her name is Gladys Winne. I wish I could describe her, but I can't. I can only remember her violet eyes; think of it, Auntie, not blue, but violet, just like the pansies in your garden last summer." At the mention of the last name, Aunt Linda rose, leaning on the table for support. It seemed to her as if some cruel hand had reached out of a pitiless past and clutched her heart. Doris gazed in startled awe at the storm of anguish that seemed to sweep across the old woman's face, exclaiming, "Why, Auntie, are you sick?" In a hoarse voice, she answered: "Yes, chile, yes, I's sick." This poor old slave woman's life was rimmed by just two events, a birth and a death, and even these memories were hers and not hers; yet the mention of a single name has for a moment blotted out all the intervening years, and in another lowly cabin, the name of Gladys is whispered by dying lips to breaking hearts. Aunt Linda gave a swift glance at the startled Doris, while making a desperate effort to recall her wandering thoughts, lest unwittingly she betray her loved ones to this little chatterer. Forcing a ghastly smile, she said, as if to herself, "As if there was only one Gladys in all dis worl, yes and heaps of Winnes, too, I reckon. Go on chile, go on, ole Aunt Linda is sure getting ole and silly." Doris left the cabin bristling with curiosity, but fortunately for Aunt Linda, she would not allow it to worry her pretty head very long.

The lovely Gladys Winne, as she was generally called, was indeed the most winsome and charming of all the guests that composed the Christmas party in the Edwards mansion. Slightly above medium height, with a beautifully rounded form, delicately poised head crowned with rippling chestnut hair, curling in soft tendrils about neck and brow, a complexion of dazzling fairness with the tint of the rose in her cheeks, and the whole face lighted by deeply glowing violet eyes. Thus liberally endowed by nature, there was further added the charm of a fine education, the advantage of foreign travel, contact with brilliant minds, and a social prestige through her foster parents that fitted her for the most exclusive social life.

She had recently been betrothed to Paul Westlake, a handsome, wealthy, and gifted young lawyer of New York. He had been among the latest arrivals, and Gladys' happiness glowed in her expressive eyes, and fairly scintillated from every curve of her exquisite form. Beautifully gowned in delicate blue of soft and clinging texture draped with creamy lace, she was indeed as rare a picture of radiant youth and beauty as one could wish to see.

But, strange to say, Gladys' happiness was not without alloy. She had one real or fancied annoyance, which she could not shake off, though she tried not to think about it. But as she walked with Paul, through the rambling rooms of this historic mansion, she determined to call his attention to it. They had just passed an angle near a stairway, when Gladys nervously pressed his arm, saying, "Look, Paul, do you see that tall yellow woman; she follows me everywhere, and actually haunts me like a shadow. If I turn suddenly, I can just see her gliding out of sight. Sometimes she becomes bolder, and coming closer to me, she peers into my face as if she would look me through. Really there seems to be something uncanny about it all to me; it makes me shiver. Look, Paul, there she is now, even your presence does not daunt her." Paul, after satisfying himself that she was really serious and annoyed, ceased laughing, saying, "My darling, I cannot consistently blame anyone for looking at you. It may be due to an inborn curiosity; she probably is attracted by other lovely things in the same way, only you may not have noticed it." "Nonsense," said Gladys, blushing. "That is a very sweet explanation, but it doesn't explain in this case. It annoys me so much that I think I must speak to Mrs. Edwards about it." Here Paul quickly interrupted. "No, my dear, I would not do that; she is evidently a privileged servant, judging from the right-of-way she seems to have all over the house. Mrs. Edwards is very kind and gracious to us, yet she might resent any criticism of her servants. Try to dismiss it from your mind, my love. I have always heard that these old 'mammies' are very superstitious, and she may fancy that she has seen you in some vision or dream, but it ought not to cause you any concern at all. Just fix your mind on something pleasant; on me, for instance." Thus lovingly rebuked and comforted, Gladys did succeed in forgetting for a time her silent watcher. But the thing that annoyed her almost more than anything else was the fact that she had a sense of being irresistibly drawn toward this old servant by a chord of sympathy and interest, for which she could not in any way account.

But the fatal curiosity of her sex, despite the advice of Paul, whom she so loved and trusted, finally wrought her own undoing. The next afternoon, at a time when she was sure she would not be missed, Gladys stole down to Aunt Linda's cabin determined to probe this mystery for herself. Finding the cabin door ajar, she slipped lightly into the room.

Aunt Linda was so absorbed by what she was doing that she heard no sound. Gladys paused upon the threshold of the cabin, fascinated by the old woman's strange occupation. She was bending over the contents of an old hair chest, tenderly shaking out one little garment after another of a baby's wardrobe, filling the room with the pungent odor of camphor and lavender.

The tears were falling and she would hold the little garments to her bosom, crooning some quaint cradle song, tenderly murmuring, "O, my lam', my poor lil' lam'," and then, as if speaking to someone unseen, she would say: "No, my darlin', no, your ole mother will shorely nevah break her promise to young master, but O, if you could only see how lovely your little Gladys has growed to be! Sweet, innocent Gladys, and her pore ole granma must not speak to or tech her, mus' not tell her how her own ma loved her and dat dese ole hans was de fust to hold her, and mine de fust kiss she ever knew; but O, my darlin', I will nevah 'tray you, she shall nevah know." Then the old woman's sobs would break out afresh, as she frantically clasped the tiny garments, yellow with age but dainty enough for a princess, to her aching heart.

For a moment Gladys, fresh and sweet as a flower, felt only the tender sympathy of a casual observer, for what possible connection could there be between her and this old colored woman in her sordid surroundings. Unconsciously she drew her skirts about her in scorn of the bare suggestion, but the next moment found her transfixed with horror, a sense of approaching doom enveloping her as in a mist. Clutching at her throat, and with dilated unseeing eyes, she groped her way toward the old woman, violently shaking her, while in a terror-stricken voice she cried, "O Aunt Linda, what is it?" With a cry like the last despairing groan of a wounded animal, Aunt Linda dropped upon her knees, scattering a shower of filmy lace and dainty flannels about her. Through every fibre of her being, Gladys felt the absurdity of her fears, yet in spite of herself, the words welled up from her heart to her lips: "O Aunt Linda, what is it, what have I to do with your dead?" With an hysterical laugh she added, "Do I look like someone you have loved and lost in other days?" Then the simple-hearted old woman, deceived by the kindly note in Gladys' voice, and not seeing the unspeakable horror growing in her eyes, stretched out imploring hands as to a little child, the tears streaming from her eyes, saying, "O, Gladys," not "Miss Gladys" now, as the stricken girl quickly notes, "you is my own sweet Alice's little chile. O, honey, I's your own dear granma. You's beautiful, Gladys, but not more so den you own sweet ma, who loved you so."

The old woman was so happy to be relieved of the secret burden she had borne for so many years, that she had almost forgotten Gladys' presence, until she saw her lost darling fainting before her very eyes. Quickly she caught her in her arms, tenderly pillowing her head upon her ample bosom, where as a little babe she had so often lain.

For several minutes the gloomy cabin was wrapped in solemn silence. Finally Gladys raised her head and, turning toward Aunt Linda her face, from which every trace of youth and happiness had fled, in a hoarse and almost breathless whisper said: "If you are my own grandmother, who then was my father?" Before this searching question these two widely contrasted types of Southern conditions stood dumb and helpless. The shadow of the departed crime of slavery still remained to haunt the generations of freedom.

Though Aunt Linda had known for many years that she was free, the generous kindness of the Edwards family had made the Emancipation Proclamation almost meaningless to her.

When she now realized that the fatal admission, which had brought such gladness to her heart, had only deepened the horror in Gladys' heart, a new light broke upon her darkened mind. Carefully placing Gladys in a chair, the old woman raised herself to her full height, her right hand uplifted like some bronze goddess of liberty. For the first time and for one brief moment she felt the inspiring thrill and meaning of the term *freedom*. Ignorant of almost everything as compared with the knowledge and experience of the stricken girl before her, yet a revelation of the sacred relationships of parenthood, childhood, and home, the common heritage of all humanity swept aside all differences of complexion or position.

For one moment, despite her lowly surroundings and dusky skin, an equality of blood, nay superiority of blood, tingled in old Aunt Linda's veins, straightened her body, and flashed in her eye. But the crushing process of over two centuries could not sustain in her more than a moment of asserted womanhood. Slowly she lowered her arm, and, with bending body, she was again but an old slave woman with haunting memories and a bleeding heart. Then with tears and broken words, she poured out the whole pitiful story to the sobbing Gladys.

"It was this way, honey, it all happened jus before the wah, way down in ole Carolina. My lil' Alice, my one chile, had growed up to be so beautiful. Even when she was a tiny lil' chile, I used to look at her and wonder how de good Lord evah 'lowed her to slip over my doorsill, but nevah min' dat chile, dat is not you alls concern. When she was near 'bout seventeen years ole, she was dat prutty that the white folks was always askin' of me if she was my own chile, the ide, as if her own ma, but den that was all right for dem, it was jest case she was so white, I knowed.

"Tho' I lived wid my lil' Alice in de cabin, I was de housemaid in de 'big house,' but I'd nevah let Alice be up thar wid me when there was company, case, well I jest had to be keerful, nevah mind why. But one day, young Master Harry Winne was home from school, and they was a celebratin', an' I was in a hurry; so I set Alice to bringin' some roses fron de garden to trim de table, and there young master saw her, an' came after me to know who she was; he say he thought he knowed all his ma's company, den I guess I was too proud, an' I up an' tells him dat she was my Alice, my own lil' gel, an' I was right away scared dat I had tole him, but he had seen huh; dat was enough, O my pore lam'!" Here the old woman paused, giving herself up for a moment to unrestrained weeping. Suddenly she dried her eyes and said: "Gladys, chile, does you know what love is?" Gladys' cheeks made eloquent response, and with one swift glance, the old woman continued, "Den you knows how they loved each other. One day Master Harry went to ole Master and he say: 'Father, I know you'll be awful angered at me, but I will marry Alice or no woman'; den his father say—but nevah min' what it was, only it was enough to make young master say dat he'd nevah forgive his pa, for what he say about my lil' gurl.

"Some time after that my Alice began to droop an' pine away like; so one day I say to her: 'Alice, does you an' young master love each other?' Den she tole me as how young master had married her, and that she was afeard to tell even her ma, case they mite sen' him away from her forever. When young master came again he tole me all about it; jest lak my gurl had tole me. He say he could not lib withou' her. After dat he would steal down to see her when he could, bringing huh all dese pritty laces and things, and she would sit all day and sew an' cry lak her heart would break.

"He would bribe ole Sam not to tell ole Master, saying dat he was soon goin' to take huh away where no men or laws could tech them. Well, after you was bohn, she began to fade away from me, gettin' weaker every day. Den when you was only a few months ole, O, how she worshipped you! I saw dat my pore unhappy lil' gurl was goin' on dat long journey away from her pore heart-broke ma, to dat home not made with hans, den I sent for young master, your pa. O, how he begged her not to go, saying dat he had a home all ready for her an' you up Norf. Gently she laid you in his arms, shore de mos' beautiful chile dat evah were, wid your great big violet eyes looking up into his, tho' he could not see dem for the tears dat would fall on yo sweet face. Your ma tried to smile; reaching out her weak arms for you, she said, 'Gladys.' An' with choking sobs she made us bofe promise, she say, 'Promise that she shall never know that her ma was a slave or dat she has a drop of my blood, make it all yours, Harry, nevah let her know.' We bofe promised, and that night young master tore you from my breaking heart, case it was best. After I had laid away my poor unhappy chile, I begged ole Master to sell me, so as to sen' me way off to Virginia, where I could nevah trace you nor look fer you, an' I nevah have." Then the old woman threw herself upon her knees, wringing her hands and saying: "O my God, why did you let her fin' me?" She had quite forgotten Gladys' presence in the extremity of her distress at having broken her vow to the dead and perhaps wrought sorrow for the living.

Throughout the entire recital, told between heartbreaking sobs and moans, Gladys sat as if carved in marble, never removing her eyes from the old woman's face. Slowly she aroused herself, allowing her dull eyes to wander about the room at the patchwork-covered bed in the corner; then through the open casement, from which she could catch a glimpse of a group of young Negroes, noting their coarse features and boisterous play; then back again to the crouching, sobbing old woman. With a shiver running through her entire form, she found her voice, which seemed to come from a great distance: "And I am part of all this! O, my God, how can I live; above all, how can I tell Paul, but I must and will; I will not deceive him though it kill me."

At the sound of Gladys' voice Aunt Linda's faculties awoke, and she began to realize the awful possibilities of her divulged secrets. Aunt Linda had felt and known the horrors of slavery; but could she have known that after twenty years of freedom, nothing in the whole range of social disgraces could work such terrible disinheritance to man or woman as the presence of Negro blood, seen or unseen; she would have given almost life itself rather than to have condemned this darling of her love and prayers to so dire a fate.

The name of Paul, breathed by Gladys in accents of such tenderness and despair, aroused Aunt Linda to action. She implored her not to tell Paul or anyone else. "No one need ever know, no one ever can or shall know," she pleaded. "How could any fin' out, honey, if you did not tell them?" Then seizing one of Gladys' little hands, pink and white and delicate as a rose leaf, and placing it beside her own old and yellow one, she cried: "Look chile, look, could anyone ever fin' the same blood in dese two hans by jest looking at em? No, honey, I has done kep dis secret all dese years, and now I pass it on to you an you mus' keep it for yourself for the res' of de time, deed you mus', no one need evah know."

To her dying day Aunt Linda never forgot the despairing voice of this stricken girl, as she said: "Ah, but I know, my God, what have I done to deserve this?"

With no word of pity for the suffering old woman, she again clutched her arm, saying in a stifled whisper: "Again I ask you, who was, or is my father, and where is he?" Aunt Linda cowered before this angry goddess, though she was of her own flesh and blood, and softly said: "He is dead; died when you were about five years old. He lef you heaps of money, and in the care of a childless couple, who reared you as they own; he made 'em let you keep his name, I can't see why." With the utmost contempt Gladys cried, "Gold, gold, what is gold to such a heritage as this? An ocean of gold cannot wash away this stain."

Poor Gladys never knew how she reached her room. She turned to lock the door, resolved to fight this battle out for herself; then she thought of kind Mrs. Edwards. She would never need a mother's love so much as now. Of her own mother, she dared not even think. Then, too, why had she not thought of it before, this horrible story might not be true. Aunt Linda was probably out of her mind, and Mrs. Edwards would surely know.

By a striking coincidence Mrs. Edwards had noticed Linda's manner toward her fair guest, and knowing the old woman's connection with the Winne family, she had just resolved to send for her and question her as to her suspicions, if she had any, and at least caution her as to her manner.

Hearing a light tap upon her door, she hastily opened it. She needed but one glance at Gladys' unhappy countenance to tell her that it was too late; the mischief had already been done. With a cry of pity and dismay, Mrs. Edwards opened her arms and Gladys swooned upon her breast. Tenderly she laid her down, and when Gladys had regained consciousness, she sprang up, crying, "O Mrs. Edwards, say that it is not true, that it is some horrible dream from which I shall soon awaken?" How gladly would this good woman have sacrificed almost anything to spare this lovely girl, the innocent victim of an outrageous and blighting system, but Gladys was now a woman and must be answered. "Gladys, my dear," said Mrs. Edwards, "I wish I might save you further distress, by telling you that what I fear you have heard, perhaps from Aunt Linda herself, is not true. I am afraid it is all too true. But fortunately in your case no one need know. It will be safe with us and I will see that Aunt Linda does not mention it again, she ought not to have admitted it to you."

Very gently Mrs. Edwards confirmed Aunt Linda's story, bitterly inveighing against a system which mocked at marriage vows, even allowing a man to sell his own flesh and blood for gain. She told this chaste and delicate girl how poor slave girls, many of them most beautiful in form and feature, were not allowed to be modest, not allowed to follow the instincts of moral rectitude, that they might be held at the mercy of their masters. Poor Gladys writhed as if under the lash. She little knew what painful reasons Mrs. Edwards had for hating the entire system of debasement to both master and slave. Her kind heart, Southern born and bred as she was, yearned to give protection and home to two beautiful girls, who had been shut out from her own hearthstone, which by right of justice and honor was theirs to share also. "Tell me, Gladys," she exclaimed, "which race is the more to be despised? Forgive me, dear, for telling you these things, but my mind was stirred by very bitter memories. Though great injustice has been done, and is still being done, I say to you, my child, that from selfish interest and the peace of my household, I could not allow such a disgrace to attach to one of my most honored guests. Do you not then see, dear, the unwisdom of revealing your identity here and now? Unrevealed, we are all your friends—" The covert threat lurking in the unfinished sentence was not lost upon Gladys. She arose, making an effort to be calm, but, nervously seizing Mrs. Edwards' hand, she asked: "Have I no living white relatives?" Mrs. Edwards hesitated a moment, then said: "Yes, a few, but they are very wealthy and influential, and now living in the North; so that I am very much afraid that they are not concerned as to whether you are living or not. They knew, of course, of your birth; but since the death of your father, whom they all loved very much, I have heard, though it may be only gossip, that they do not now allow your name to be mentioned."

Gladys searched Mrs. Edwards' face with a peculiarly perplexed look; then, in a plainer tone of voice, said: "Mrs. Edwards, it must be that only Negroes possess natural affection. Only think of it, through all the years of my life, and though I have many near relatives, I have been cherished in memory and yearned for by only one of them, and that an old and despised colored woman. The almost infinitesimal drop of her blood in my veins is really the only drop that I can consistently be proud of." Then, springing up, an indescribable glow fairly transfiguring and illuminating her face, she said: "My kind hostess, and comforting friend, I feel that I must tell Paul, but for your sake we will say nothing to the others, and if he does not advise me, yes, command me, to own and cherish that lonely old woman's love, and make happy her declining years, then he is not the man to whom I can or will entrust my love and life."

With burning cheeks, and eyes hiding the stars in their violet depths, her whole countenance glowing with a sense of pride conquered and love exalted, beautiful to see, she turned to Mrs. Edwards and, tenderly kissing her, passed softly from the room.

For several moments, Mrs. Edwards stood where Gladys had left her. "Poor deluded girl," she mused. "Paul Westlake is by far one of the truest and noblest young men I have ever known, but let him beware, for there is even now coming to meet him the strongest test of his manhood principles he has ever had to face; beside it, all other perplexing problems must sink into nothingness. Will he be equal to it? We shall soon see."

Gladys, in spite of the sublime courage that had so exalted her but a moment before, felt her resolution weaken with every step. It required almost a superhuman will to resist the temptation to silence, so eloquently urged upon her by Mrs. Edwards. But her resolution was not to be thus lightly set aside; it pursued her to her room, translating itself into the persistent thought that, if fate is ever to be met and conquered, the time is now; delays are dangerous.

As she was about to leave her room on her mission, impelled by an indefinable sense of farewell, she turned, with her hand upon the door, as if she would include in this backward glance all the dainty furnishings, the taste and elegance everywhere displayed, and of which she had felt so much a part. Finally her wandering gaze fell upon a fine picture of Paul Westlake upon the mantel. Instantly there flashed into her mind the first and only public address she had ever heard Paul make. She had quite forgotten the occasion, except that it had some relation to a so-called "Negro problem." Then out from the past came the rich tones of the beloved voice as with fervid eloquence he arraigned the American people for the wrongs and injustice that had been perpetrated upon a weak and defenseless people through centuries of their enslavement and their few years of freedom.

With much feeling he recounted the pathetic story of this unhappy people when freedom found them, trying to knit together the broken ties of family kinship and their struggles through all the odds and hates of opposition, trying to make a place for themselves in the great family of races. Gladys' awakened conscience quickens the memory of his terrible condemnation of a system and of the men who would willingly demoralize a whole race of women, even at the sacrifice of their own flesh and blood.

With Mrs. Edwards' words still ringing in her ears, the memory of the last few words stings her now as then, except that now she knows why she is so sensitive as to their real import.

This message, brought to her from out of a happy past by Paul's pictured face, has given to her a light of hope and comfort beyond words. Hastily closing the door of her room, almost eagerly, and with buoyant step, she goes to seek Paul and carry out her mission.

To Paul Westlake's loving heart, Gladys Winne never appeared so full of beauty, curves, and graces, her eyes glowing with confidence and love, as when he sprang eagerly forward to greet her on that eventful afternoon. Through all the subsequent years of their lives the tenderness and beauty of that afternoon together never faded from their minds. They seemed, though surrounded by the laughter of friends and festive preparations, quite alone—set apart by the intensity of their love and happiness.

When they were about to separate for the night, Gladys turned to Paul, with ominous seriousness, yet trying to assume a lightness she was far from feeling, saying: "Paul, dear, I am going to put your love to the test tomorrow, may I?" Paul's smiling indifference was surely test enough, if that were all, but she persisted. "I am quite in earnest, dear; I have a confession to make to you. I intended to tell you this afternoon, but I could not cloud this almost our last evening together for a long time perhaps, so I decided to ask you to meet me in the library tomorrow morning at ten o'clock, will you?"

"Will I," Paul replied; "my darling, you know I will do anything you ask; but why tomorrow, and why so serious about the matter; besides, if it be anything that is to affect our future in any way, why not tell it now?" As Gladys was still silent, he added: "Dear, if you will assure me that this confession will not change your love for me in any way, I will willingly wait until tomorrow or next year; any time can you give me this assurance?" Gladys softly answered: "Yes, Paul, my love is yours now and always; that is, if you will always wish it." There was an expression upon her face he did not like, because he could not understand it, but tenderly drawing her to him, he said: "Gladys, dear, can anything matter so long as we love each other? I truly believe it cannot. But tell me this, dear, after this confession do I then hold the key to the situation?" "Yes, Paul, I believe you do; in fact, I know that you will." "Ah, that is one point gained, tomorrow; then it can have no terrors for me," he lightly replied.

Gladys passed an almost sleepless night. Confident, yet fearful, she watched the dawn of the new day. Paul, on the contrary, slept peacefully and rose to greet the morn with confidence and cheer. "If I have Gladys' love," he mused, "there is nothing in heaven or earth for me to fear."

At last the dreaded hour of ten drew near; their "Ides of March" Paul quoted, with some amusement over the situation.

The first greeting over, the silence became oppressive. Paul broke it at last, saying briskly: "Now, dear, out with this confession; I am not a success at conundrums; another hour of this suspense would have been my undoing," he laughingly said.

Gladys, pale and trembling, felt all of her courage slipping from her; she knew not how to begin. Although she had rehearsed every detail of this scene again and again, she could not recall a single word she had intended to say. Finally she began with the reminder she had intended to use as a last resort: "Paul, do you remember taking me last spring to hear your first public address; do you remember how eloquently and earnestly you pleaded the cause of the Negro?" Seeing only a growing perplexity upon his face, she cried: "O, my love, can you not see what I am trying to say? O, can you not understand? But no, no, no one could ever guess a thing so awful"; then sinking her voice almost to a whisper and with averted face, she said: "Paul, it was because you were unconsciously pleading for your own Gladys, for I am one of them."

"What nonsense is this," exclaimed Paul, springing from his chair; "it is impossible, worse than improbable, it cannot be true. It is the work of some jealous rival; surely, Gladys, you do not expect me to believe such a wild, unthinkable story as this!" Then, controlling himself, he said: "O, my darling, who could have been so cruel as to have tortured you like this? If any member of this household has done this thing let us leave them in this hour. I confess I do not love the South or a Southerner, with my whole heart, in spite of this 'united country' nonsense; yes, I will say it, and in spite of the apparently gracious hospitality of this household."

Gladys, awed by the violence of his indignation, placed a trembling hand upon his arm, saying: "Listen, Paul, do you not remember on the very evening of your arrival here, of my calling your attention to a tall turbaned servant with piercing eyes? Don't you remember I told you how she annoyed me by following me everywhere, and you laughed away my fears, and lovingly quieted my alarm? Now, O Paul, how can I say it, but I must, that woman, that Negress, who was once a slave, is my own grandmother." Without waiting for him to reply, she humbly but bravely poured into his ears the whole pitiful story, sparing neither father nor mother, but blaming her mother least of all. Ah, the pity of it!

Without a word, Paul took hold of her trembling hands, and, drawing her toward the window with shaking hand, he drew aside the heavy drapery; then, turning her face so that the full glory of that sunlit morning fell upon it, he looked long and searchingly into the beautiful beloved face, as if studying the minutest detail of some matchless piece of statuary. At last he found words, saying: "You, my flower, is it possible that there can be concealed in this flawless skin, these dear violet eyes, these finely chiseled features, a trace of lineage or blood, without a single characteristic to vindicate its presence? I will not believe it; it cannot be true." Then, baffled by Gladys' silence, he added, "And if it be true, surely the Father of us all intended to leave no hint of shame or dishonor on this, the fairest of his creations."

Gladys felt rather than heard a deepened note of tenderness in his voice and her hopes revived. Then suddenly his calm face whitened and an expression terrible to see swept over it. Instinctively Gladys read his thought. She knew that the last unspoken thought was of the future, and because she, too, realized that the problem of heredity must be settled outside the realm of sentiment, her breaking heart made quick resolve.

For some moments they sat in unbroken silence; then Gladys spoke: "Goodbye, Paul, I see that you must wrestle with this life problem alone as I have; there is no other way. But that you may be wholly untrammeled in your judgment, I want to assure you that you are free. I love you too well to be willing to degrade your name and prospects by uniting them with a taint of blood, of which I was as innocent as yourself, until two days ago.

"May I ask you to meet me once more, and for the last time, at twelve o'clock tonight? I will then abide by your judgment as to what is best for both of us. Let us try to be ourselves today, so that our own heartaches may not cloud the happiness of others. I said twelve o'clock because I thought we would be less apt to be missed at that hour of general rejoicings than at any other time. Goodbye, dear, till then." Absently Paul replied: "All right, Gladys, just as you say; I will be here."

At the approach of the midnight hour Paul and Gladys slipped away to the library, which had become to them a solemn and sacred trysting place.

Gladys looked luminously beautiful on this Christmas Eve. She wore a black gauze dress flecked with silver, through which her skin gleamed with dazzling fairness. Her only ornaments were sprigs of holly, their brilliant berries adding the necessary touch of color to her unusual pallor. She greeted Paul with gentle sweetness and added dignity and courage shining in her eyes.

Eagerly she scanned his countenance and sought his eyes, and then she shrank back in dismay at his set face and stern demeanor.

Suddenly the strength of her love for him and the glory and tragedy which his love had brought to her life surged through her, breaking down all reserve. "Look at me, Paul," she cried in a tense whisper. "Have I changed since yesterday; am I not the same Gladys you have loved so long?" In a moment their positions had changed and she had become the forceful advocate at the bar of love and justice; the love of her heart overwhelmed her voice with a torrent of words; she implored him by the sweet and sacred memories that had enkindled from the first their mutual love, by the remembered kisses, their afterglow flooding her cheeks as she spoke, and "O, my love, the happy days together." She paused, as if the very sweetness of the memory oppressed her voice to silence, and, helpless and imploring, she held out her hands to him.

Paul was gazing at her as if entranced, a growing tenderness filling and thrilling his soul. Gradually he became conscious of a tightening of the heart at the thought of losing her out of his life. There could be no such thing as life without Gladys, and when would she need his love, his protection, his tenderest sympathy so much as now?

The light upon Paul's transfigured countenance is reflected on Gladys' own, and as he moves toward her with outstretched arms, in the adjoining room the magnificent voice of the beautiful singer rises in the Christmas carol, mingling in singular harmony with the plaintive melody as sung by a group of dusky singers beneath the windows.

The Stones of the Village

(1910)

Alice Dunbar-Nelson

Victor Grabert strode down the one wide, tree-shaded street of the village, his heart throbbing with a bitterness and anger that seemed too great to bear. So often had he gone home in the same spirit, however, that it had grown nearly second nature to him—this dull, sullen resentment, flaming out now and then into almost murderous vindictiveness. Behind him there floated derisive laughs and shouts, the taunts of little brutes, boys of his own age.

He reached the tumbledown cottage at the farther end of the street and flung himself on the battered step. Grandmère Grabert sat rocking herself to and fro, crooning a bit of song brought over from the West Indies years ago; but when the boy sat silent, his head bowed in his hands, she paused in the midst of a line and regarded him with keen, piercing eyes.

"Eh, Victor?" she asked. That was all, but he understood. He raised his head and waved a hand angrily down the street towards the lighted square that marked the village center.

"Dose boy," he gulped.

Grandmère Grabert laid a sympathetic hand on his black curls, but withdrew it the next instant.

"*Bien,*" she said angrily. "Fo' what you go by dem, eh? W'y not keep to yo'self? Dey don' want you, dey don' care fo' you. H'ain' you got no sense?"

"Oh, but Grandmère," he wailed piteously, "I wan' fo' to play."

The old woman stood up in the doorway, her tall, spare form towering menacingly over him.

"You wan' fo' to play, eh? Fo' w'y? You don' need no play. Dose boy"—she swept a magnificent gesture down the street—"dey fools!"

"Eef I could play wid—" began Victor, but his grandmother caught him by the wrist, and held him as in a vise.

"Hush," she cried. "You mus' be goin' crazy," and still holding him by the wrist, she pulled him indoors.

It was a two-room house, bare and poor and miserable, but never had it seemed so meagre before to Victor as it did this night. The supper was frugal almost to the starvation point. They ate in silence, and afterwards Victor threw himself on his cot in the corner of the kitchen and closed his eyes. Grandmère Grabert thought him asleep, and closed the door noiselessly as she went into her own room. But he was awake, and his mind was like a shifting kaleidoscope of miserable incidents and heartaches. He had lived fourteen years, and he could remember most of them as years of misery. He had never known a mother's love, for his mother had died, so he was told, when he was but a few months old. No one ever spoke to him of a father, and Grandmère Grabert had been all to him. She was kind, after a stern, unloving fashion, and she provided for him as best she could. He had picked up some sort of an education at the parish school. It was a good one after its way, but his life there had been such a succession of miseries, that he rebelled one day and refused to go any more.

His earliest memories were clustered about this poor little cottage. He could see himself toddling about its broken steps, playing alone with a few broken pieces of china which his fancy magnified into glorious toys. He remembered his first whipping too. Tired one day of the loneliness which even the broken china could not mitigate, he had toddled out the side gate after a merry group of little black and yellow boys of his own age. When Grandmère Grabert, missing him from his accustomed garden corner, came to look for him, she found him sitting contentedly in the center of the group in the dusty street, all of them gravely scooping up handsful of the gravelly dirt and trickling it down their chubby bare legs. Grandmère snatched at him fiercely, and he whimpered, for he was learning for the first time what fear was.

"What you mean?" she hissed at him. "What you mean playin' in de strit wid dose niggers?" And she struck at him wildly with her open hand.

He looked up into her brown face surmounted by a wealth of curly black hair faintly streaked with gray, but he was too frightened to question.

It had been loneliness ever since. For the parents of the little black and yellow boys, resenting the insult Grandmère had offered their offspring,

sternly bade them have nothing more to do with Victor. Then when he
toddled after some other little boys, whose faces were white like his own,
they ran him away with derisive hoots of "Nigger! Nigger!" And again,
he could not understand.

Hardest of all, though, was when Grandmère sternly bade him cease
speaking the soft, Creole patois that they chattered together, and forced
him to learn English. The result was a confused jumble which was no
language at all; that when he spoke it in the streets or in the school, all
the boys, white and black and yellow, hooted at him and called him
"White nigger! White nigger!"

He writhed on his cot that night and lived over all the anguish of his
years until hot tears scalded their way down a burning face, and he fell
into a troubled sleep wherein he sobbed over some dreamland miseries.

The next morning, Grandmère eyed his heavy, swollen eyes sharply,
and a momentary thrill of compassion passed over her and found expression in a new tenderness of manner towards him as she served his breakfast.
She too, had thought over the matter in the night, and it bore fruit in an
unexpected way.

Some few weeks after, Victor found himself timidly ringing the doorbell
of a house on Hospital Street in New Orleans. His heart throbbed in
painful unison to the jangle of the bell. How was he to know that old
Madame Guichard, Grandmère's one friend in the city, to whom she
had confided him, would be kind? He had walked from the river landing
to the house, timidly inquiring the way of busy pedestrians. He was hungry
and frightened. Never in all his life had he seen so many people before,
and in all the busy streets there was not one eye which would light up
with recognition when it met his own. Moreover, it had been a weary
journey down the Red River, thence into the Mississippi, and finally here.
Perhaps it had not been devoid of interest, after its fashion, but Victor
did not know. He was too heartsick at leaving home.

However, Mme. Guichard was kind. She welcomed him with a vol-
ubility and overflow of tenderness that acted like balm to the boy's sore
spirit. Thence they were firm friends, even confidants.

Victor must find work to do. Grandmère Grabert's idea in sending him
to New Orleans was that he might "mek one man of himse'f" as she
phrased it. And Victor, grown suddenly old in the sense that he had a
responsibility to bear, set about his search valiantly.

It chanced one day that he saw a sign in an old bookstore on Royal
Street that stated in both French and English the need of a boy. Almost
before he knew it, he had entered the shop and was gasping out some
choked words to the little old man who sat behind the counter.

The old man looked keenly over his glasses at the boy and rubbed his bald head reflectively. In order to do this, he had to take off an old black silk cap which he looked at with apparent regret.

"Eh, what you say?" he asked sharply, when Victor had finished.

"I—I—want a place to work," stammered the boy again.

"Eh, you do? Well, can you read?"

"Yes, sir," replied Victor.

The old man got down from his stool, came from behind the counter, and, putting his finger under the boy's chin, stared hard into his eyes. They met his own unflinchingly, though there was the suspicion of pathos and timidity in their brown depths.

"Do you know where you live, eh?"

"On Hospital Street," said Victor. It did not occur to him to give the number, and the old man did not ask.

"*Trés bien,*" grunted the bookseller, and his interest relaxed. He gave a few curt directions about the manner of work Victor was to do, and settled himself again upon his stool, poring into his dingy book with renewed ardor.

Thus began Victor's commercial life. It was an easy one. At seven, he opened the shutters of the little shop and swept and dusted. At eight, the bookseller came downstairs, and passed out to get his coffee at the restaurant across the street. At eight in the evening, the shop was closed again. That was all.

Occasionally, there came a customer, but not often, for there were only odd books and rare ones in the shop, and those who came were usually old, yellow, querulous bookworms, who nosed about for hours, and went away leaving many bank notes behind them. Sometimes there was an errand to do, and sometimes there came a customer when the proprietor was out. It was an easy matter to wait on them. He had but to point to the shelves and say, "Monsieur will be in directly," and all was settled, for those who came here to buy had plenty of leisure and did not mind waiting.

So a year went by, then two and three, and the stream of Victor's life flowed smoothly on its uneventful way. He had grown tall and thin, and often Mme. Guichard would look at him and chuckle to herself, "Ha, he is lak one beanpole, yaas, *mais*—" and there would be a world of unfinished reflection in that last word.

Victor had grown pale from much reading. Like a shadow of the old bookseller, he sat day after day poring into some dusty yellow-paged book, and his mind was a queer jumble of ideas. History and philosophy and old-fashioned social economy were tangled with French romance and classic mythology and astrology and mysticism. He had made few friends, for his experience in the village had made him chary of strangers. Every week, he wrote to Grandmère Grabert and sent her part of his earnings. In his way he was happy, and if he was lonely, he had ceased to care about it, for his world was peopled with images of his own fancying.

Then all at once, the world he had built about him tumbled down, and he was left staring helplessly at its ruins. The little bookseller died one day, and his shop and its books were sold by an unscrupulous nephew who cared not for bindings or precious yellowed pages, but only for the grossly material things that money can buy. Victor ground his teeth as the auctioneer's strident voice sounded through the shop where all once had been hushed quiet, and wept as he saw some of his favorite books carried away by men and women, whom he was sure could not appreciate their value.

He dried his tears, however, the next day when a grave-faced lawyer came to the little house on Hospital Street, and informed him that he had been left a sum of money by the bookseller.

Victor sat staring at him helplessly. Money meant little to him. He never needed it, never used it. After he had sent Grandmère her sum each week, Mme. Guichard kept the rest and doled it out to him as he needed it for carfare and clothes.

"The interest of the money," continued the lawyer, clearing his throat, "is sufficient to keep you very handsomely, without touching the principal. It was my client's wish that you should enter Tulane College, and there fit yourself for your profession. He had great confidence in your ability."

"Tulane College!" cried Victor. "Why—why—why—" Then he stopped suddenly, and the hot blood mounted to his face. He glanced furtively about the room. Mme. Guichard was not near; the lawyer had seen no one but him. Then why tell him? His heart leaped wildly at the thought. Well, Grandmère would have willed it so.

The lawyer was waiting politely for him to finish his sentence.

"Why—why—I should have to study in order to enter there," finished Victor lamely.

"Exactly so," said Mr. Buckley, "and as I have, in a way, been appointed your guardian, I will see to that."

Victor found himself murmuring confused thanks and good-byes to Mr. Buckley. After he had gone, the boy sat down and gazed blankly at the wall. Then he wrote a long letter to Grandmère.

A week later, he changed boarding places at Mr. Buckley's advice, and entered a preparatory school for Tulane. And still, Mme. Guichard and Mr. Buckley had not met.

It was a handsomely furnished office on Carondelet Street in which Lawyer Grabert sat some years later. His day's work done, he was leaning back in his chair and smiling pleasantly out of the window. Within was warmth and light and cheer; without, the wind howled and gusty rains beat against the windowpane. Lawyer Grabert smiled again as he looked about at the comfort, and found himself half pitying those without who were forced to buffet the storm afoot. He rose finally and, donning his overcoat, called a cab and was driven to his rooms in the most fashionable part of the city. There he found his old-time college friend, awaiting him with some impatience.

"Thought you never were coming, old man" was his greeting.

Grabert smiled pleasantly. "Well, I was a bit tired, you know," he answered, "and I have been sitting idle for an hour or more, just relaxing, as it were."

Vannier laid his hand affectionately on the other's shoulder. "That was a mighty effort you made today," he said earnestly. "I, for one, am proud of you."

"Thank you," replied Grabert simply, and the two sat silent for a minute.

"Going to the Charles' dance tonight?" asked Vannier finally.

"I don't believe I am. I am tired and lazy."

"It will do you good. Come on."

"No, I want to read and ruminate."

"Ruminate over your good fortune of today?"

"If you will have it so, yes."

But it was not simply his good fortune of that day over which Grabert pondered. It was over the good fortune of the past fifteen years. From school to college and from college to law school he had gone, and thence into practice, and he was now accredited a successful young lawyer. His small fortune, which Mr. Buckley, with generous kindness, had invested wisely, had almost doubled, and his school career, while not of the brilliant, meteoric kind, had been pleasant and profitable. He had made friends, at first, with the boys he met, and they in turn had taken him into their homes. Now and then, the Buckleys asked him to dinner, and he was seen occasionally in their box at the opera. He was rapidly becoming a social favorite, and girls vied with each other to dance with him. No one had asked any questions, and he had volunteered no information concerning himself. Vannier, who had known him in preparatory school days, had said that he was a young country fellow with some money, no connections, and a ward of Mr. Buckley's, and somehow, contrary to the usual social custom of the South, this meagre account had passed muster. But Vannier's family had been a social arbiter for many years, and Grabert's personality was pleasing, without being aggressive, so he had passed through the portals of the social world and was in the inner circle.

One year, when he and Vannier were in Switzerland, pretending to climb impossible mountains and in reality smoking many cigars a day on hotel porches, a letter came to Grabert from the priest of his old-time town, telling him that Grandmère Grabert had been laid away in the parish churchyard. There was no more to tell. The little old hut had been sold to pay funeral expenses.

"Poor Grandmère," sighed Victor. "She did care for me after her fashion. I'll go take a look at her grave when I go back."

But he did not go, for when he returned to Louisiana, he was too busy, then he decided that it would be useless, sentimental folly. Moreover, he had no love for the old village. Its very name suggested things that made him turn and look about him nervously. He had long since eliminated Mme. Guichard from his list of acquaintances.

And yet, as he sat there in his cosy study that night, and smiled as he went over in his mind triumph after triumph which he had made since the old bookstore days in Royal Street, he was conscious of a subtle undercurrent of annoyance; a sort of mental reservation that placed itself on every pleasant memory.

"I wonder what's the matter with me?" he asked himself as he rose and paced the floor impatiently. Then he tried to recall his other triumph, the one of the day. The case of Tate vs. Tate, a famous will contest, had been dragging through the courts for seven years and his speech had decided it that day. He could hear the applause of the courtroom as he sat down, but it rang hollow in his ears, for he remembered another scene. The day before he had been in another court, and found himself interested in the prisoner before the bar. The offense was a slight one, a mere technicality. Grabert was conscious of something pleasant in the man's face; a scrupulous neatness in his dress, an unostentatious conforming to the prevailing style. The Recorder, however, was short and brusque.

"Wilson—Wilson—" he growled. "Oh, yes, I know you, always kicking up some sort of a row about theatre seats and cars. Hum-um. What do you mean by coming before me with a flower in your buttonhole?"

The prisoner looked down indifferently at the bud on his coat, and made no reply.

"Hey?" growled the Recorder. "You niggers are putting yourselves up too much for me."

At the forbidden word, the blood rushed to Grabert's face, and he started from his seat angrily. The next instant, he had recovered himself and buried his face in a paper. After Wilson had paid his fine, Grabert looked at him furtively as he passed out. His face was perfectly impassive, but his eyes flashed defiantly. The lawyer was tingling with rage and indignation, although the affront had not been given him.

"If Recorder Grant had any reason to think that I was in any way like Wilson, I would stand no better show," he mused bitterly.

However, as he thought it over tonight, he decided that he was a sentimental fool. "What have I to do with them?" he asked himself. "I must be careful."

The next week, he discharged the man who cared for his office. He was a Negro, and Grabert had no fault to find with him generally, but he found himself with a growing sympathy toward the man, and since the episode in the courtroom, he was morbidly nervous lest something in his manner betray him. Thereafter, a round-eyed Irish boy cared for his rooms.

The Vanniers were wont to smile indulgently at his every move. Elise Vannier, particularly, was more than interested in his work. He had a way of dropping in of evenings and talking over his cases and speeches with her in a cosy corner of the library. She had a gracious sympathetic manner that was soothing and a cheery fund of repartee to whet her conversation. Victor found himself drifting into sentimental bits of talk now and then. He found himself carrying around in his pocketbook a faded rose which she had once worn, and when he laughed at it one day and started to throw it in the wastebasket, he suddenly kissed it instead, and replaced it in the pocketbook. That Elise was not indifferent to him he could easily see. She had not learned yet how to veil her eyes and mask her face under a cool assumption of superiority. She would give him her hand when they met with a girlish impulsiveness, and her color came and went under his gaze. Sometimes, when he held her hand a bit longer than necessary, he could feel it flutter in his own, and she would sigh a quick little gasp that made his heart leap and choked his utterance.

They were tucked away in their usual cosy corner one evening, and the conversation had drifted to the problem of where they would spend the summer.

"Papa wants to go to the country house," pouted Elise, "and Mama and I don't want to go. It isn't fair, of course, because when we go so far away, Papa can be with us only for a few weeks when he can get away from his office, while if we go to the country place, he can run up every few days. But it is so dull there, don't you think so?"

Victor recalled some pleasant vacation days at the plantation home and laughed. "Not if you are there."

"Yes, but you see, I can't take myself for a companion. Now if you'll promise to come up sometimes, it will be better."

"If I may, I shall be delighted to come."

Elise laughed intimately. "If you 'may' " she replied, "as if such a word had to enter into our plans. Oh, but Victor, haven't you some sort of plantation somewhere? It seems to me that I heard Steven years ago speak of your home in the country, and I wondered sometimes that you never spoke of it, or ever mentioned having visited it."

The girl's artless words were bringing cold sweat to Victor's brow, his tongue felt heavy and useless, but he managed to answer quietly, "I have no home in the country."

"Well, didn't you ever own one, or your family?"

"It was old quite a good many years ago," he replied, and a vision of the little old hut with its tumbledown steps and weed-grown garden came into his mind.

"Where was it?" pursued Elise innocently.

"Oh, away up in St. Landry parish, too far away from civilization to mention." He tried to laugh, but it was a hollow, forced attempt that rang false. But Elise was too absorbed in her own thoughts of the summer to notice.

"And you haven't a relative living?" she continued.

"Not one."

"How strange. Why it seems to me if I did not have half a hundred cousins and uncles and aunts that I should feel somehow out of touch with the world."

He did not reply, and she chattered away on another topic.

When he was alone in his room that night, he paced the floor again, chewing wildly at a cigar that he had forgotten to light.

"What did she mean? What did she mean?" he asked himself over and over. Could she have heard or suspected anything that she was trying to find out about? Could any action, any unguarded expression of his have set the family thinking? But he soon dismissed the thought as unworthy of him. Elise was too frank and transparent a girl to stoop to subterfuge. If she wished to know anything, she was wont to ask out at once, and if she had once thought anyone was sailing under false colors, she would say so frankly, and dismiss them from her presence.

Well, he must be prepared to answer questions if he were going to marry her. The family would want to know all about him, and Elise herself would be curious for more than her brother, Steven Vannier's meagre account. But was he going to marry Elise? That was the question.

He sat down and buried his head in his hands. Would it be right for him to take a wife, especially such a woman as Elise, and from such a family as the Vanniers? Would it be fair? Would it be just? If they knew and were willing, it would be different. But they did not know, and they would not consent if they did. In fancy, he saw the dainty girl, whom he loved, shrinking from him as he told her of Grandmère Grabert and the village boys. This last thought made him set his teeth hard, and the hot blood rushed to his face.

Well, why not, after all, why not? What was the difference between him and the hosts of other suitors who hovered about Elise? They had money; so had he. They had education, polite training, culture, social position; so had he. But they had family traditions, and he had none. Most of them could point to a long line of family portraits with justifiable pride; while if he had had a picture of Grandmère Grabert, he would have destroyed it fearfully, lest it fall into the hands of some too curious person. This was the subtle barrier that separated them. He recalled with a sting how often he had had to sit silent and constrained when the conversation turned to ancestors and family traditions. He might be one with his companions and friends in everything but this. He must ever be on the outside, hovering at the gates, as it were. Into the inner life of his social world, he might never enter. The charming impoliteness of an intercourse begun by their fathers and grandfathers was not for him. There must always be a certain formality with him, even though they were his most intimate friends. He had not fifty cousins; therefore, as Elise phrased it, he was "out of touch with the world."

"If ever I have a son or a daughter," he found himself saying unconsciously, "I would try to save him from this."

Then he laughed bitterly as he realized the irony of the thought. Well, anyway, Elise loved him. There was a sweet consolation in that. He had but to look into her frank eyes and read her soul. Perhaps she wondered why he had not spoken. Should he speak? There he was back at the old question again.

"According to the standard of the world," he mused reflectively, "my blood is tainted in two ways. Who knows it? No one but myself, and I shall not tell. Otherwise, I am quite as good as the rest, and Elise loves me."

But even this thought failed of its sweetness in a moment. Elise loved him because she did not know. He found a sickening anger and disgust rising in himself at a people whose prejudices made him live a life of deception. He would cater to their traditions no longer; he would be honest. Then he found himself shrinking from the alternative with a dread that made him wonder. It was the old problem of his life in the village; and the boys, both white and black and yellow, stood as before, with stones in their hands to hurl at him.

He went to bed worn out with the struggle, but still with no definite idea what to do. Sleep was impossible. He rolled and tossed miserably, and cursed the fate that had thrown him in such a position. He had never thought very seriously over the subject before. He had rather drifted with the tide and accepted what came to him as a sort of recompense the world owed him for his unhappy childhood. He had known fear, yes, and qualms now and then, and a hot resentment occasionally when the outsideness of his situation was inborn to him; but that was all. Elise had awakened a disagreeable conscientiousness within him, which he decided was as unpleasant as it was unnecessary.

He could not sleep, so he arose and, dressing, walked out and stood on the banquette. The low hum of the city came to him like the droning of some sleepy insect, and ever and anon the quick flash and fire of the gashouses, like a huge winking fiery eye, lit up the south of the city. It was inexpressibly soothing to Victor—the great unknowing city, teeming with life and with lives whose sadness mocked his own teacup tempest. He smiled and shook himself as a dog shakes off the water from his coat.

"I think a walk will help me out," he said absently, and presently he was striding down St. Charles Avenue, around Lee Circle and down to Canal Street, where the lights and glare absorbed him for a while. He walked out the wide boulevard towards Claiborne Street, hardly thinking, hardly realizing that he was walking. When he was thoroughly worn out, he retraced his steps and dropped wearily into a restaurant near Bourbon Street.

"Hullo!" said a familiar voice from a table as he entered. Victor turned and recognized Frank Ward, a little oculist, whose office was in the same building as his own.

"Another night owl besides myself," laughed Ward, making room for him at his table. "Can't you sleep too, old fellow?"

"Not very well," said Victor, taking the proffered seat. "I believe I'm getting nerves. Think I need toning up."

"Well, you'd have been toned up if you had been in here a few minutes ago. Why—why—" And Ward went off into peals of laughter at the memory of the scene.

"What was it?" asked Victor.

"Why—a fellow came in here, nice sort of fellow, apparently, and wanted to have supper. Well, would you believe it, when they wouldn't serve him, he wanted to fight everything in sight. It was positively exciting for a time."

"Why wouldn't the waiter serve him?" Victor tried to make his tone indifferent, but he felt the quaver in his voice.

"Why? Why, he was a darky, you know."

"Well, what of it?" demanded Grabert fiercely. "Wasn't he quiet, well-dressed, polite? Didn't he have money?"

"My dear fellow," began Ward mockingly. "Upon my word, I believe you are losing your mind. You do need toning up or something. Would you—could you—?"

"Oh, pshaw," broke in Grabert. "I—I—believe I am losing my mind. Really, Ward, I need something to make me sleep. My head aches."

Ward was at once all sympathy and advice, and chiding to the waiter for his slowness in filling their order. Victor toyed with his food, and made an excuse to leave the restaurant as soon as he could decently.

"Good heavens," he said when he was alone. "What will I do next?" His outburst of indignation at Ward's narrative had come from his lips almost before he knew it, and he was frightened, frightened at his own unguardedness. He did not know what had come over him.

"I must be careful, I must be careful," he muttered to himself. "I must go to the other extreme, if necessary." He was pacing his rooms again, and, suddenly, he faced the mirror.

"You wouldn't fare any better than the rest, if they knew," he told the reflection. "You poor wretch, what are you?"

When he thought of Elise, he smiled. He loved her, but he hated the traditions which she represented. He was conscious of a blind fury which bade him wreak vengeance on those traditions, and of a cowardly fear which cried out to him to retain his position in the world's and Elise's eyes at any cost.

Mrs. Grabert was delighted to have visiting her her old school friend from Virginia, and the two spent hours laughing over their girlish escapades, and comparing notes about their little ones. Each was confident that her darling had said the cutest things, and their polite deference to each other's opinions on the matter was a sham through which each saw without resentment.

"But, Elise," remonstrated Mrs. Allen, "I think it so strange you don't have a mammy for Baby Vannier. He would be so much better cared for than by that harum-scarum young white girl you have."

"I think so too, Adelaide," sighed Mrs. Grabert. "It seems strange for me not to have a darky maid about, but Victor can't bear them. I cried and cried for my old mammy, but he was stern. He doesn't like darkies, you know, and he says old mammies just frighten children, and ruin their childhood. I don't see how he could say that, do you?" She looked wistfully to Mrs. Allen for sympathy.

"I don't know," mused that lady. "We were all looked after by our mammies, and I think they are the best kind of nurses."

"And Victor won't have any kind of darky servant either here or at the office. He says they're shiftless and worthless and generally no-account. Of course, he knows, he's had lots of experience with them in his business."

Mrs. Allen folded her hands behind her head and stared hard at the ceiling. "Oh, well, men don't know everything," she said, "and Victor may come around to our way of thinking after all."

It was late that evening when the lawyer came in for dinner. His eyes had acquired a habit of veiling themselves under their lashes, as if they were constantly concealing something which they feared might be wrenched from them by a stare. He was nervous and restless, with a habit of glancing about him furtively, and a twitching compressing of his lips when he had finished a sentence, which somehow reminded you of a kindhearted judge, who is forced to give a death sentence.

Elise met him at the door as was her wont, and she knew from the first glance into his eyes that something had disturbed him more than usual that day, but she forbore asking questions, for she knew he would tell her when the time had come.

They were in their room that night when the rest of the household lay in slumber. He sat for a long while gazing at the open fire, then he passed his hand over his forehead wearily.

"I have had a rather unpleasant experience today," he began.

"Yes."

"Pavageau, again."

His wife was brushing her hair before the mirror. At the name she turned hastily with the brush in her uplifted hand.

"I can't understand, Victor, why you must have dealings with that man.

He is constantly irritating you. I simply wouldn't associate with him."

"I don't," and he laughed at her feminine argument. "It isn't a question of association, cherie, it's a purely business and unsocial relation, if relation it may be called, that throws us together."

She threw down the brush petulantly, and came to his side. "Victor," she began hesitatingly, her arms about his neck, her face close to his, "won't you—won't you give up politics for me? It was ever so much nicer when you were just a lawyer and wanted only to be the best lawyer in the state, without all this worry about corruption and votes and such things. You've changed, oh, Victor, you've changed so. Baby and I won't know you after a while."

He put her gently on his knee. "You mustn't blame the poor politics, darling. Don't you think, perhaps, it's the inevitable hardening and embittering that must come to us all as we grow older?"

"No, I don't," she replied emphatically. "Why do you go into this struggle, anyhow? You have nothing to gain but an empty honor. It won't bring you more money, or make you more loved or respected. Why must you be mixed up with such—such—awful people?"

"I don't know," he said wearily.

And in truth, he did not know. He had gone on after his marriage with Elise making one success after another. It seemed that a beneficent Providence had singled him out as the one man in the state upon whom to heap the most lavish attentions. He was popular after the fashion of those who are high in the esteem of the world; and this very fact made him tremble the more, for he feared that should some disclosure come, he could not stand the shock of public opinion that must overwhelm him.

"What disclosure?" he would say impatiently when such a thought would come to him. "Where could it come from, and then, what is there to disclose?"

Thus he would deceive himself for as much as a month at a time.

He was surprised to find awaiting him in his office one day the man Wilson, whom he remembered in the courtroom before Recorder Grant. He was surprised and annoyed. Why had the man come to his office? Had he seen the telltale flush on his face that day?

But it was soon evident that Wilson did not even remember having seen him before.

"I came to see if I could retain you in a case of mine," he began, after the usual formalities of greeting were over.

"I am afraid, my good man," said Grabert brusquely, "that you have mistaken the office."

Wilson's face flushed at the appellation, but he went on bravely. "I have not mistaken the office. I know you are the best civil lawyer in the city, and I want your services."

"An impossible thing."

"Why? Are you too busy? My case is a simple thing, a mere point in law, but I want the best authority and the best opinion brought to bear on it."

"I could not give you any help—and—I fear, we do not understand each other—I do not wish to." He turned to his desk abruptly.

"What could he have meant by coming to me?" he questioned himself fearfully, as Wilson left the office. "Do I look like a man likely to take up his impossible contentions?"

He did not look like it, nor was he. When it came to a question involving the Negro, Victor Grabert was noted for his stern, unrelenting attitude; it was simply impossible to convince him that there was anything but sheerest incapacity in that race. For him, no good could come out of this Nazareth. He was liked and respected by men of his political belief, because, even when he was a candidate for a judgeship, neither money nor the possible chance of a deluge of votes from the First and Fourth Wards could cause him to swerve one hair's breadth from his opinion of the black inhabitants of those wards.

Pavageau, however, was his *bête noire*. Pavageau was a lawyer, a cool-headed, calculating man with steely eyes set in a grim brown face. They had first met in the courtroom in a case which involved the question whether a man may set aside the will of his father, who, disregarding the legal offspring of another race than himself, chooses to leave his property to educational institutions which would not have granted admission to that son. Pavageau represented the son. He lost, of course. The judge, the jury, the people and Grabert were against him; but he fought his fight with a grim determination which commanded Victor's admiration and respect.

"Fools," he said between his teeth to himself, when they were crowding about him with congratulations. "Fools, can't they see who is the abler man of the two?"

He wanted to go up to Pavageau and give him his hand; to tell him that he was proud of him and that he had really won the case, but public opinion was against him; but he dared not. Another one of his colleagues might; but he was afraid. Pavageau and the world might misunderstand, or would it be understanding?

Thereafter they met often. Either by some freak of nature, or because there was a shrewd sense of the possibilities in his position, Pavageau was of the same political side of the fence as Grabert. Secretly, Grabert admired the man; he respected him; he liked him; and because of this Grabert was always ready with sneer and invective for him. He fought him bitterly when there was no occasion for fighting, and Pavageau became his enemy, and his name a very synonym of horror to Elise, who learned to trace her husband's fits of moodiness and depression to the one source.

Meanwhile, Vannier Grabert was growing up, a handsome lad, with his father's and mother's physical beauty, and a strength and force of character that belonged to neither. In him, Grabert saw the reparation of all his childhood's wrongs and sufferings. The boy realized all his own longings. He had family traditions, and a social position which was his from birth and an inalienable right to hold up his head without an unknown fear gripping at his heart. Grabert felt that he could forgive all—the village boys of long ago, and the imaginary village boys of today—when he looked at his son. He had bought and paid for Vannier's freedom and happiness. The coins may have been each a drop of his heart's blood, but he had reckoned the cost before he had given it.

It was a source of great pride for Grabert, now that he was a judge, to take the boy to court with him, and one Saturday morning when he was starting out, Vannier asked if he might go.

"There is nothing that would interest you today, *mon fils,*" he said tenderly, "but you may go."

In fact, there was nothing interesting that day; merely a troublesome old woman, who instead of taking her fair-skinned grandchild out of the school where it had been found it did not belong, had preferred to bring the matter to court. She was represented by Pavageau. Of course, there was not the ghost of a show for her. Pavageau had told her that. The law was very explicit about the matter. The only question lay in proving the child's affinity to the Negro race, which was not such a difficult matter to do, so the case was quickly settled, since the child's grandmother accompanied him. The judge, however, was irritated. It was a hot day and he was provoked that such a trivial matter should have taken up his time. He lost his temper as he looked at his watch.

"I don't see why these people want to force their children into the white schools," he declared. "There should be a rigid inspection to prevent it, and all the suspected children put out and made to go where they belong."

Pavageau, too, was irritated that day. He looked up from some papers which he was folding, and his gaze met Grabert's with a keen, cold, penetrating flash.

"Perhaps Your Honor would like to set the example by taking your son from the schools."

There was an instant silence in the courtroom, a hush intense and eager. Every eye turned upon the judge, who sat still, a figure carven in stone with livid face and fear-stricken eyes. After the first flash of his eyes, Pavageau had gone on cooly sorting the papers.

The courtroom waited, waited, for the judge to rise and thunder forth a fine against the daring Negro lawyer for contempt. A minute passed, which seemed like an hour. Why did not Grabert speak? Pavageau's implied accusation was too absurd for denial; but he should be punished. Was His Honor ill, or did he merely hold the man in too much contempt to notice him or his remark?

Finally Grabert spoke; he moistened his lips, for they were dry and parched, and his voice was weak and sounded far away in his own ears. "My son—does—not—attend the public schools."

Someone in the rear of the room laughed, and the atmosphere lightened at once. Plainly Pavageau was an idiot, and His Honor too far above him; too much of a gentleman to notice him. Grabert continued calmly: "The gentleman"—there was an unmistakable sneer in this word, habit if nothing else, and not even fear could restrain him—"the gentleman doubtless intended a little pleasantry, but I shall have to fine him for contempt of court."

"As you will," replied Pavageau, and he flashed another look at Grabert. It was a look of insolent triumph and derision. His Honor's eyes dropped beneath it.

"What did that man mean, Father, by saying you should take me out of school?" asked Vannier on his way home.

"He was provoked, my son, because he had lost his case, and when a man is provoked he is likely to say silly things. By the way, Vannier, I hope you won't say anything to your mother about the incident. It would only annoy her."

For the public, the incident was forgotten as soon as it had closed, but for Grabert, it was indelibly stamped on his memory; a scene that shrieked in his mind and stood out before him at every footstep he took. Again and again as he tossed on a sleepless bed did he see the cold flash of Pavageau's eyes, and hear his quiet accusation. How did he know? Where had he gotten his information? For he spoke, not as one who makes a random shot in anger, but as one who knows, who has known a long while, and who is betrayed by irritation into playing his trump card too early in the game.

He passed a wretched week, wherein it seemed that his every footstep was dogged, his every gesture watched and recorded. He fancied that Elise, even, was suspecting him. When he took his judicial seat each morning, it seemed that every eye in the courtroom was fastened upon him in derision; everyone who spoke, it seemed, was but biding his time to shout the old village street refrain which had haunted him all his life, "Nigger!—Nigger!—White nigger!"

Finally, he could stand it no longer; and with leaden feet and furtive glances to the right and left for fear he might be seen, he went up a flight of dusty stairs in an Exchange Alley building, which led to Pavageau's office.

The latter was frankly surprised to see him. He made a polite attempt to conceal it, however. It was the first time in his legal life that Grabert had ever sought out a Negro; the first time that he had ever voluntarily opened conversation with one.

He mopped his forehead nervously as he took the chair Pavageau offered him; he stared about the room for an instant; then with a sudden, almost brutal directness, he turned on the lawyer.

"See here, what did you mean by that remark you made in court the other day?"

"I meant just what I said" was the cool reply.

Grabert paused. "Why did you say it?" he asked slowly.

"Because I was a fool. I should have kept my mouth shut until another time, should I not?"

"Pavageau," said Grabert softly, "let's not fence. Where did you get your information?"

Pavageau paused for an instant. He put his fingertips together and closed his eyes as one who meditates. Then he said with provoking calmness, "You seem anxious—well, I don't mind letting you know. It doesn't really matter."

"Yes, yes," broke in Grabert impatiently.

"Did you ever hear of a Mme. Guichard of Hospital Street?"

The sweat broke out on the judge's brow as he replied weakly, "Yes."

"Well, I am her nephew."

"And she?"

"Is dead. She told me about you once—with pride, let me say. No one else knows."

Grabert sat dazed. He had forgotten about Mme. Guichard. She had never entered into his calculations at all. Pavageau turned to his desk with a sigh, as if he wished the interview were ended. Grabert rose.

"If—if—this were known—to—to—my—my wife," he said thickly, "it would hurt her very much."

His head was swimming. He had had to appeal to this man, and to appeal to his wife's name. His wife, whose name he scarcely spoke to men whom he considered his social equals.

Pavageau looked up quickly. "It happens that I often have cases in your court," he spoke deliberately. "I am willing, if I lose fairly, to give up; but I do not like to have a decision made against me because my opponent is of a different complexion from mine, or because the decision against me would please a certain class of people. I only ask what I have never had from you—fair play."

"I understand," said Grabert.

He admired Pavageau more than ever as he went out of his office, yet this admiration was tempered by the knowledge that this man was the only person in the whole world who possessed positive knowledge of his secret. He groveled in a self-abasement at his position; and yet he could not but feel a certain relief that the vague, formless fear which had hitherto dogged his life and haunted it had taken on a definite shape. He knew where it was now; he could lay his hands on it, and fight it.

But with what weapons? There were none offered him save a substantial backing down from his position on certain questions; the position that had been his for so long that he was almost known by it. For in the quiet deliberate sentence of Pavageau's, he read that he must cease all the oppression, all the little injustices which he had offered Pavageau's clientele. He must act now as his convictions and secret sympathies and affiliations had bidden him act, not as prudence and fear and cowardice had made him act.

Then what would be the result? he asked himself. Would not the suspicions of the people be aroused by this sudden change in his manner? Would not they begin to question and to wonder? Would not someone remember Pavageau's remark that morning and, putting two and two together, start some rumor flying? His heart sickened again at the thought.

There was a banquet that night. It was in his honor, and he was to speak, and the thought was distasteful to him beyond measure. He knew how it all would be. He would be hailed with shouts and acclamations, as the finest flower of civilization. He would be listened to deferentially, and younger men would go away holding him in their hearts as a truly worthy model. When all the while—

He threw back his head and laughed. Oh, what a glorious revenge he had on those little white village boys! How he had made a race atone for

Wilson's insult in the courtroom; for the man in the restaurant at whom Ward had laughed so uproariously; for all the affronts seen and unseen given these people of his own whom he had denied. He had taken a diploma from their most exclusive college; he had broken down the barriers of their social world; he had taken the highest possible position among them and, aping their own ways, had shown them that he, too, could despise this inferior race they despised. Nay, he had taken for his wife the best woman among them all, and she had borne him a son. Ha, ha! What a joke on them all!

And he had not forgotten the black and yellow boys either. They had stoned him too, and he had lived to spurn them; to look down upon them, and to crush them at every possible turn from his seat on the bench. Truly, his life had not been wasted.

He had lived forty-nine years now, and the zenith of his power was not yet reached. There was much more to do, much more, and he was going to do it. He owed it to Elise and the boy. For their sake he must go on and on and keep his tongue still, and truckle to Pavageau and suffer alone. Someday, perhaps, he would have a grandson, who would point with pride to "My grandfather, the famous Judge Grabert!" Ah, that in itself, was a reward. To have founded a dynasty; to bequeath to others that which he had never possessed himself, and the lack of which had made his life a misery.

It was a banquet with a political significance; one that meant a virtual triumph for Judge Grabert in the next contest for the District Judge. He smiled around at the eager faces which were turned up to his as he arose to speak. The tumult of applause which had greeted his rising had died away, and an expectant hush fell on the room.

"What a sensation I could make now," he thought. He had but to open his mouth and cry out, "Fools! Fools! I whom you are honoring, I am one of the despised ones. Yes, I'm a nigger—do you hear, a nigger!" What a temptation it was to end the whole miserable farce. If he were alone in the world, if it were not for Elise and the boy, he would, just to see their horror and wonder. How they would shrink from him! But what could they do? They could take away his office; but his wealth, and his former successes, and his learning, they could not touch. Well, he must speak, and he must remember Elise and the boy.

Every eye was fastened on him in eager expectancy. Judge Grabert's speech was expected to outline the policy of their faction in the coming campaign. He turned to the chairman at the head of the table.

"Mr. Chairman," he began, and paused again. How peculiar it was that in the place of the chairman there sat Grandmère Grabert, as she had been wont to sit on the steps of the tumbledown cottage in the village. She was looking at him sternly and bidding him give an account of his life since she had kissed him good-bye ere he had sailed down the river to New Orleans. He was surprised, and not a little annoyed. He had expected to address the chairman, not Grandmère Grabert. He cleared his throat and frowned.

"Mr. Chairman," he said again. Well, what was the use of addressing her that way? She would not understand him. He would call her Grandmère, of course. Were they not alone again on the cottage steps at twilight with the cries of the little brutish boys ringing derisively from the distant village square?

"Grandmère," he said softly, "you don't understand—" And then he was sitting down in his seat pointing one finger angrily at her because the other words would not come. They stuck in his throat, and he choked and beat the air with his hands. When the men crowded around him with water and hastily improvised fans, he fought them away wildly and desperately with furious curses that came from his blackened lips. For were they not all boys with stones to pelt him because he wanted to play with them? He would run away to Grandmère who would soothe him and comfort him. So he arose and, stumbling, shrieking and beating them back from him, ran the length of the hall, and fell across the threshold of the door.

The secret died with him, for Pavageau's lips were ever sealed.

Mary Elizabeth

•

(1919)

Jessie Redmon Fauset

Mary Elizabeth was late that morning. As a direct result, Roger left for work without telling me goodbye, and I spent most of the day fighting the headache which always comes if I cry.

For I cannot get a breakfast. I can manage a dinner, one just puts the roast in the oven and takes it out again. And I really excel in getting lunch. There is a good delicatessen near us, and with dainty service and flowers. I get along very nicely. But breakfast! In the first place, it's a meal I neither like nor need. And I never, if I live a thousand years, shall learn to like coffee. I suppose that is why I cannot make it.

"Roger," I faltered, when the awful truth burst upon me and I began to realize that Mary Elizabeth wasn't coming. "Roger, couldn't you get breakfast downtown this morning? You know last time you weren't so satisfied with my coffee."

Roger was hostile. I think he had just cut himself shaving. Anyway, he was horrid.

"No, I can't get my breakfast downtown!" He actually snapped at me. "Really, Sally, I don't believe there's another woman in the world who would send her husband out on a morning like this on an empty stomach. I don't see how you can be so unfeeling."

Well, it wasn't "a morning like this," for it was just the beginning of November. And I had only proposed his doing what I knew he would have to do eventually.

I didn't say anything more, but started on that breakfast. I don't know why I thought I had to have hotcakes! The breakfast really was awful! The cakes were tough and gummy and got cold one second, exactly, after I took them off the stove. And the coffee boiled, or stewed, or scorched, or did whatever the particular thing is that coffee shouldn't do. Roger sawed at one cake, took one mouthful of the dreadful brew, and pushed away his cup.

"It seems to me you might learn to make a decent cup of coffee," he said icily. Then he picked up his hat and flung out of the house.

I think it is stupid of me, too, not to learn how to make coffee. But really, I'm no worse than Roger is about lots of things. Take Five Hundred. Roger knows I love cards, and with the Cheltons right around the corner from us and as fond of it as I am, we could spend many a pleasant evening. But Roger will not learn. Only the night before, after I had gone through a whole hand with him, with hearts as trumps, I dealt the cards around again to imaginary opponents and we started playing. Clubs were trumps, and spades led. Roger, having no spades, played triumphantly a Jack of Hearts and proceeded to take the trick.

"But Roger," I protested, "you threw off."

"Well," he said, deeply injured, "didn't you say hearts were trumps when you were playing before?"

And when I tried to explain, he threw down the cards and wanted to know what difference it made; he'd rather play casino, anyway! I didn't go out and slam the door.

But I couldn't help from crying this particular morning. I not only value Roger's good opinion, but I hate to be considered stupid.

Mary Elizabeth came in about eleven o'clock. She is a small, weazened woman, very dark, somewhat wrinkled, and a model of self-possession. I wish I could make you see her, or that I could reproduce her accent, not that it is especially colored—Roger's and mine are much more so—but her pronunciation, her way of drawing out her vowels, is so distinctively Mary Elizabethan!

I was ashamed of my red eyes and tried to cover up my embarrassment with sternness.

"Mary Elizabeth," said I, "you are late!" Just as though she didn't know it.

"Yas'm, Mis' Pierson," she said, composedly, taking off her coat. She didn't remove her hat—she never does until she has been in the house some two or three hours. I can't imagine why. It is a small, black, dusty affair, trimmed with black ribbon, some dingy white roses, and a sheaf of wheat. I give Mary Elizabeth a dress and hat now and then but, although I recognize the dress from time to time, I never see any change in the hat. I don't know what she does with my ex-millinery.

"Yas'm," she said again, and looked comprehensively at the untouched breakfast dishes and the awful viands, which were still where Roger had left them.

"Looks as though you'd had to git breakfast yourself," she observed brightly. And went out in the kitchen and ate all those cakes and drank that unspeakable coffee. Really she did and she didn't warm them up either.

I watched her miserably, unable to decide whether Roger was too finicky or Mary Elizabeth a natural-born diplomat.

"Mr. Gales led me an awful chase last night," she explained. "When I got home yestiddy evenin', my cousin whut keeps house for me (!) tole me Mr. Gales went out in the mornin' en hadn't come back."

Mr. Gales, let me explain, is Mary Elizabeth's second husband, an octogenarian, and the most original person, I am convinced, in existence.

"Yas'm," she went on, eating a final cold hotcake, "en I went to look fer 'im, en had the whole perlice station out all night huntin' 'im. Look like they wusn't never goin' to find 'im. But I ses, 'Jes' let me look fer enough en long enough en I'll find 'im,' I ses, en I did. Way out Georgy Avenue, with the hat on ole Mis' give 'im. Sent it to 'im all the way fum Chicago. He's had it fifteen years, high silk beaver. I knowed he wusn't goin' too fer with that hat on.

"I went up to 'im, settin' by a fence all muddy, holdin' his hat on with both hands. En I ses, 'Look here, man, you come erlong home with me, en let me put you to bed.' En he come jest as meek! No-o-me, I knowed he wasn't goin' fer with ole Mis' hat on."

"Who was old 'Mis,' Mary Elizabeth?" I asked her.

"Lady I used to work fer in Noo York," she informed me. "Me en Rosy, the cook, lived with her fer years. Ole Mis' was turrible fond of me, though her en Rosy used to querrel all the time. Jes' seemed like they couldn't git erlong. 'Member once Rosy run after her one Sunday with a knife, en I kep 'em apart. Reckon Rosy musta bin right put out with ole Mis' that day. By en by her en Rosy move to Chicaga, en when I married Mr. Gales, she sent 'im that hat. That old white woman shore did like me. It's so late, reckon I'd better put off sweepin' tel termorrer, ma'am."

I acquiesced, following her about from room to room. This was partly to get away from my own doleful thoughts—Roger really had hurt my feelings—but just as much to hear her talk. At first I used not to believe all she said, but after I investigated once and found her truthful in one amazing statement, I capitulated.

She had been telling me some remarkable tale of her first husband and I was listening with the stupefied attention to which she always reduces me. Remember she was speaking of her first husband.

"En I ses to 'im, I ses, 'Mr. Gale—' "

"Wait a moment, Mary Elizabeth," I interrupted, meanly delighted to have caught her for once. "You mean your first husband, don't you?"

"Yas'm," she replied. "En I ses to 'im, 'Mr. Gale,' I ses—"

"But Mary Elizabeth," I persisted, "that's your second husband, isn't it—Mr. Gale?"

She gave me her long drawn "No-o-me! My first husband was Mr. Gale and my second husband is Mr. *Gales*. He spells his name with a Z, I reckon. I ain't never see it writ. Ez I wus sayin' I ses to Mr. Gale—"

And it was true! Since then I have never doubted Mary Elizabeth.

She was loquacious that afternoon. She told me about her sister, "where's got a home in the country and where's got eight children." I used to read Lucy Pratt's stories about little Ephraim or Ezekiel, I forget his name, who always said "where's" instead of "who's," but I never believed it really till I heard Mary Elizabeth use it. For some reason or other she never mentions her sister without mentioning the home too. "My sister where's got a home in the country" is her unvarying phrase.

"Mary Elizabeth," I asked her once, "does your sister live in the country, or does she simply own a house there?"

"Yas'm," she told me.

She is fond of her sister. "If Mr. Gales wus to die," she told me complacently, "I'd go to live with her."

"If he should die," I asked her idly, "would you marry again?"

"Oh, no-o-me!" She was emphatic. "Though I don't know why I shouldn't, I'd come by it hones'. My father wus married four times."

That shocked me out of my headache. "Four times, Mary Elizabeth, and you had all those stepmothers!" My mind refused to take it in.

"Oh, no-o-me! I always lived with Mamma. She was his first wife."

I hadn't thought of people in the state in which I had instinctively placed Mary Elizabeth's father and mother as indulging in divorce, but as Roger says slangily, "I wouldn't know."

Mary Elizabeth took off the dingy hat. "You see, Papa and Mamma—" the ineffable pathos of hearing this woman of sixty-four, with a husband of eighty, use the old childish terms!

"Papa and Mamma wus slaves, you know, Mis' Pierson, and so of course they wusn't exackly married. White folks wouldn't let 'em. But

they wus awf'ly in love with each other. Heard Mamma tell erbout it lots
of times, and how Papa wus the han'somest man! Reckon she wus long
erbout sixteen or seventeen then. So they jumped over a broomstick, en
they wus jes as happy! But not long after I come erlong, they sold Papa
down South, and Mamma never see him no mo' fer years and years.
Thought he was dead. So she married again."

"And he came back to her, Mary Elizabeth?" I was overwhelmed with
the woefulness of it.

"Yas'm. After twenty-six years. Me and my sister where's got a home
in the country—she's really my half-sister, see Mis' Pierson—her en
Mamma en my stepfather en me wus all down in Bumpus, Virginia,
workin' fer some white folks, and we used to live in a little cabin, had a
front stoop to it. En one day an ole cullud man come by, had a lot o'
whiskers. I'd saw him lots of times there in Bumpus, lookin' and peerin'
into every cullud woman's face. En jes' then my sister she call out, 'Come
here, you Ma'y Elizabeth,' en that old man stopped, en he looked at me
en he looked at me, en he ses to me, 'Chile, is yo name Ma'y Elizabeth?'

"You know, Mis' Pierson, I thought he wus jes' bein' fresh, en I ain't
paid no 'tention to 'im. I ain't sed nuthin' ontel he spoke to me three or
four times, en then I ses to 'im, 'Go 'way fum here, man, you ain't got
no call to be fresh with me. I'm a decent woman. You'd oughta be ashamed
of yorself, an ole man like you!' "

Mary Elizabeth stopped and looked hard at the back of her poor wrinkled
hands.

"En he says to me, 'Daughter,' he ses jes' like that, 'daughter,' he ses,
'hones' I ain't bein' fresh. Is yo' name shore enough Ma'y Elizabeth?'

"En I tole him, 'Yas'r.'

" 'Chile,' he ses, 'whar is yo' daddy?'

" 'Ain't got no daddy,' I tole him peart-like. 'They done tuk 'im away
fum me twenty-six years ago, I wusn't but a mite of a baby. Sol' 'im down
the river. My mother often talks about it.' And oh, Mis' Pierson, you
shoulda see the glory come into his face!

" 'Yore mother!' he ses, kinda out of breath, 'yore mother! Ma'y Elizabeth, whar is your mother?'

" 'Back thar on the stoop,' I tole 'im. 'Why, did you know my daddy?'

"But he didn't pay no 'tention to me, jes' turned and walked up the
stoop whar Mamma wus settin'! She wus feelin' sorta porely that day. En
you oughta see me steppin' erlong after 'im.

"He walked right up to her and giv' her one look. 'Oh, Maggie,' he
shout out, 'oh, Maggie! Ain't you know me? Maggie, ain't you know me?'

"Mamma look at 'im and riz up outa her cheer. 'Who're you?' she ses kinda trimbly, 'callin' me Maggie thata way? Who're you?'

"He went up real close to her, then. 'Maggie,' he ses jes' like that, kinda sad 'n tender, 'Maggie!' and hel' out his arms.

"She walked right into them. 'Oh!' she ses, 'it's Cassius! It's Cassius! It's my husban' come back to me! It's Cassius!' They wus like two mad people.

"My sister Minnie and me, we jes' stood and gawped at 'em. There they wus, holding on to each other like two pitiful childrun, en he tuk her hands and kissed 'em.

" 'Maggie,' he ses, 'you'll come away with me, won't you? You gona take me back, Maggie? We'll go away, you en Ma'y Elizabeth en me. Won't we Maggie?'

"Reckon my mother clean forgot about my stepfather. 'Yes, Cassius,' she ses, 'we'll go away.' And then she sees Minnie, en it all comes back to her. 'Oh, Cassius,' she ses, 'I cain't go with you, I'm married again, en this time fer real. This here gal's mine and three boys, too, another chile comin' in November!' "

"But she went with him, Mary Elizabeth," I pleaded. "Surely she went with him after all those years. He really was her husband."

I don't know whether Mary Elizabeth meant to be sarcastic or not. "Oh, no-o-me, Mamma couldn't a done that. She wus a good woman. Her ole master, whut done sol' my father down river, brung her up too religious fer that, en anyways, Papa was married again, too. Had his fourth wife there in Bumpus with 'im."

The unspeakable tragedy of it!

I left her and went up to my room, and hunted out my dark blue serge dress which I had meant to wear again that winter. But I had to give Mary Elizabeth something, so I took the dress down to her.

She was delighted with it. I could tell she was, because she used her rare and untranslatable expletive.

"Haytian!" she said. "My sister where's got a home in the country, got a dress look somethin' like this but it ain't as good. No-o-me. She got hers to wear at a friend's weddin'—gal she wus riz up with. Thet gal married well, too, lemme tell you; her husband's a Sunday School sup'rintender."

I told her she needn't wait for Mr. Pierson, I would put dinner on the table. So off she went in the gathering dusk, trudging bravely back to her Mr. Gales and his high silk hat.

I watched her from the window till she was out of sight. It had been such a long time since I had thought of slavery. I was born in Pennsylvania, and neither my parents nor grandparents had been slaves; otherwise I might have had the same tale to tell as Mary Elizabeth, or worse yet, Roger and I might have lived in those black days and loved and lost each other and futilely, damnably, met again like Cassius and Maggie.

Whereas it was now, and I had Roger and Roger had me.

How I loved him as I sat there in the hazy dark. I thought of his dear, bronze perfection, his habit of swearing softly in excitement, his blessed stupidity. Just the same I didn't meet him at the door as usual, but pretended to be busy. He came rushing to me with the *Saturday Evening Post*, which is more to me than rubies. I thanked him warmly, but aloofly, if you can get that combination.

We ate dinner almost in silence for my part. But he praised everything—the cooking, the table, my appearance.

After dinner we went up to the little sitting room. He hoped I wasn't tired—couldn't he fix the pillows for me? So!

I opened the magazine and the first thing I saw was a picture of a woman gazing in stony despair at the figure of a man disappearing around the bend of the road. It was too much. Suppose that were Roger and I! I'm afraid I sniffled. He was at my side in a moment.

"Dear loveliest! Don't cry. It was all my fault. You aren't any worse about coffee than I am about cards! And anyway, I needn't have slammed the door! Forgive me, Sally. I always told you I was hard to get along with. I've had a horrible day—don't stay cross with me, dearest."

I held him to me and sobbed outright on his shoulder. "It isn't you, Roger," I told him. "I'm crying about Mary Elizabeth."

I regret to say he let me go then, so great was his dismay. Roger will never be half the diplomat that Mary Elizabeth is.

"Holy smokes!" he groaned. "She isn't going to leave us for good, is she?"

So then I told him about Maggie and Cassius. "And oh, Roger," I ended futilely, "to think that they had to separate after all those years, when he had come back, old and with whiskers!" I didn't mean to be so banal, but I was crying too hard to be coherent.

Roger had got up and was walking the floor, but he stopped then aghast.

"Whiskers!" he moaned. "My hat! Isn't that just like a woman?" He had to clear his throat once or twice before he could go on, and I think he wiped his eyes.

"Wasn't it the—" I really can't say what Roger said here—"wasn't it the darndest hard luck that when he did find her again, she should be married? She might have waited."

I stared at him astounded. "But, Roger," I reminded him, "he had married three other times, he didn't wait."

"Oh—!" said Roger, unquotable, "married three fiddlesticks! He only did that to try to forget her."

Then he came over and knelt beside me again. "Darling, I do think it is a sensible thing for a poor woman to learn how to cook, but I don't care as long as you love me and we are together. Dear loveliest, if I had been Cassius"—he caught my hands so tight he hurt them—"and I had married fifty times and had come back and found you married to someone else, I'd have killed you, killed you."

Well, he wasn't logical, but he was certainly convincing.

So thus, and not otherwise, Mary Elizabeth healed the breach.

Goldie

●

(1920)

Angelina Weld Grimké

He had never thought of the night, before, as so sharply black and white; but then, he had never walked before, three long miles, after midnight, over a country road. A short distance only, after leaving the railroad station, the road plunged into the woods and stayed there most of the way. Even in the day, he remembered, although he had not traveled over it for five years, it had not been the easiest to journey over. Now, in the almost palpable darkness, the going was hard, indeed; and he was compelled to proceed, it almost seemed to him, one careful step after another careful step.

Singular fancies may come to one, at such times: and, as he plodded forward, one came, quite unceremoniously, quite unsolicited, to him and fastened its tentacles upon him. Perhaps it was born of the darkness and the utter windlessness with the resulting great stillness; perhaps—but who knows from what fancies spring? At any rate, it seemed to him, the woods, on either side of him, were really not woods at all but an ocean that had flowed down in a great rolling black wave of flood to the very lips of the road itself and paused there as though suddenly arrested and held poised in some strange and sinister spell. Of course, all of this came, he told himself over and over, from having such a cursed imagination; but whether he would or not, the fancy persisted and the growing feeling with it, that he, Victor Forrest, went in actual danger, for at any second the spell might snap and with that snapping, this boundless, deep upon deep of horrible, waiting sea, would move, rush, hurl itself heavily and swiftly together from the two sides, thus engulfing, grinding, crushing, blotting out all in its path, not excluding what he now knew to be that most insignificant of insignificant pigmies, Victor Forrest.

But there were bright spots, here and there in the going—he found himself calling them white islands of safety. These occurred where the woods receded at some little distance from the road.

"It's as though," he thought aloud, "they drew back here in order to get a good deep breath before plunging forward again. Well, all I hope is, the spell holds O.K. beyond."

He always paused, a moment or so, on one of these islands to drive out expulsively the dank, black oppressiveness of the air he had been breathing and to fill his lungs anew with God's night air, that here, at least, was sweet and untroubled. Here, too, his eyes were free again and he could see the dimmed white blur of road for a space each way; and, above, the stars, millions upon millions of them, each one hardly brilliant, stabbing its way whitely through the black heavens. And if the island were large enough there was a glimpse, scarcely more, of a very pallid, slightly crumpled moon sliding furtively down the west.—Yes, sharply black and sharply white, that was it, but mostly it was black.

And as he went, his mind busy enough with many thoughts, many memories, subconsciously always the aforementioned fancy persisted, clung to him; and he was never entirely able to throw off the feeling of his very probable and imminent danger in the midst of this arrested wood-ocean.

—Of course, he thought, it was downright foolishness, his expecting Goldie, or rather Cy, to meet him. He hadn't written or telegraphed.— Instinct he guessed, must have warned him that wouldn't be safe; but, confound it all! This was the devil of a road.—Gosh! What a lot of noise a man's feet could make—couldn't they?—All alone like this.—Well, Goldie and Cy would feel a lot worse over the whole business than he did.—After all it was only once in a lifetime, wasn't it?—Hoofing it was good for him, anyway.—No doubt about his having grown soft.—He'd be as lame as the dickens tomorrow.—Well, Goldie would enjoy that— liked nothing better than fussing over a fellow.—If (But he very resolutely turned away from that if.)

—In one way, it didn't seem like five years and yet, in another, it seemed longer—since he'd been over this road last. It had been the sunshiniest and the saddest May morning he ever remembered.—He'd been going in the opposite direction, then; and that little sister of his, Goldie, had been sitting very straight beside him, the two lines held rigidly in her two little gold paws and her little gold face stiff with repressed emotion. He felt a twinge, yet, as he remembered her face and the way the great tears would well up and run over down her cheeks at intervals.—Proud little thing!—She had disdained even to notice them and treated them as a matter with which she had no concern.—No, she hadn't wanted him to go.—Good, little Goldie!—Well, she never knew, how close, how very close he had been to putting his hand out and telling her to turn back—he'd changed his mind and wasn't going after all.—

He drew a sharp breath.—He hadn't put out his hand.

—And at the station, her face there below him, as he looked down at her through the open window of the train.—The unwavering way her eyes had held his—and the look in them, he hadn't understood them, or didn't now, for that matter.

"Don't," he had said. "Don't, Goldie!"

"I must. Vic, I must.—I don't know.—Don't you understand I may never see you again?"

"Rot!" he had said. "Am I not going to send for you?"

—And then she had tried to smile and that had been worse than her eyes.

"You think so, now, Vic—but will you?"

"Of course."

"Vic!"

"Yes."

"Remember, whatever it is—it's all right. *It's all right.*—I mean it.—See! I couldn't smile—could I?—if I didn't?"

And then, when it had seemed as if he couldn't stand any more—he had leaned over, even to pick up his bag to get off, give it all up—the train had started and it was too late. The last he had seen of her, she had been standing there, very straight, her arms at her sides and her little gold paws two little tight fists.—And her eyes!—And her twisted smile!—God! that was about enough of that.—He was going to her, now, wasn't he?

—Had he been wrong to go?—Had he?—Somehow, now, it seemed that way.—And yet, at the time, he had felt he was right.—He still did for that matter.—His chance, that's what it had meant.—Oughtn't he to have had it?—Certainly a colored man couldn't do the things that counted in the South.—To live here, just to *live* here, he had to swallow his self-respect.—Well, he had tried, honestly, too, for Goldie's sake, to swallow his.—The trouble was he couldn't keep it swallowed—it nauseated him.—The thing for him to have done, he saw that now, was to have risked everything and taken Goldie with him.—He shouldn't have waited, as he had from year to year, to send for her.—It would have meant hard sledding, but they could have managed somehow.—Of course, it wouldn't have been the home she had had with her Uncle Ray and her Aunt Millie, still.—Well, there wasn't any use in crying over spilt milk. One thing was certain, never mind how much you might wish to, you couldn't recall the past.—

—Two years ago—(gosh!) but time flew!—when her letter had come telling him she had married Cy Harper.—Queer thing, this life!—Darned queer thing!—Why he had been in the very midst of debating whether or not he could afford to send for her—had almost decided he could.— Well, sisters, even the very best of them, it turned out, weren't above marrying and going off and leaving you high and dry—just like this.— Oh! of course, Cy was a good enough fellow, clean, steady going, true, and all the rest of it—no one could deny that—still, confound it all! how could Goldie prefer a fathead like Cy to him.—Hm!— peeved yet, it seemed!—Well, he'd acknowledge it—he was peeved all right.

Involuntarily he began to slow up.

—Good! Since he was acknowledging things—why not get along and acknowledge the rest.—Might just as well have this out with himself here and now.—Peeved first, then, what?

He came to an abrupt stop in the midst of the black silence of the arrested wood-ocean.

—There was one thing, it appeared, a dark road could do for you—it could make it possible for you to see yourself quite plainly—almost too plainly.—Peeved first, then what?—No blinking now, the truth.—He'd evaded himself very cleverly—hadn't he?—up until tonight?—No use any more.—Well, what was he waiting for?—Out with it.—Peeved first; go ahead, now.—Louder!—*Relief!*—Honest, at last.—Relief! Think of it, he had felt relief when he had learned he wasn't to be bothered, after all, with little, loyal, big-hearted Goldie.—*Bothered!*—And he had prided himself upon being rather a decent, upright, respectable fellow.—Why, if he had heard this about anybody else, he wouldn't have been able to find language strong enough to describe him—a rotter, that's what he was, and a cad.

"And Goldie would have sacrificed herself for you any time, and gladly, and you know it."

To his surprise he found himself speaking aloud.

—Why once, when the kid had been only eight years old and he had been taken with a cramp while in swimming, she had jumped in too!— Goldie, who couldn't swim a single stroke!—Her screams had done it and they were saved. He could see his mother's face yet, quizzical, a little puzzled, a little worried.

"But what on earth, Goldie, possessed you to jump in too?" she had asked. "Didn't you *know* you couldn't save him?"

"Yes, I know it."

"Then, why?"

"I don't know. It just seemed that if Vic had to drown, why I had to drown with him.—Just couldn't live *afterwards*, Momsey. If I lived *then* and he drowned."

"Goldie! Goldie!—If Vic fell out of a tree, would you have to fall out too?"

"Proberbly." Goldie had never been able to master "probably," but it fascinated her.

"Well, for Heaven's sake. Vic, do be careful of yourself hereafter. You see how it is," his mother had said.

And Goldie had answered—how serious, how quaint, how true her little face had been.—

"Yes, that's how it is, isn't it?" Another trick of hers, ending so often what she had to say with a question.—And he hadn't wished to be bothered with her!—

He groaned and started again.

—Well, he'd try to even up things a little, now.—He'd show her (there was a lump in his throat) if he could.—

For the first time Victor Forrest began to understand the possibilities of tragedy that may lie in those three little words, "If I can."

—Perhaps Goldie had understood and married Cy so that he needn't bother any more about having to have her with him. He hoped, as he had never hoped for anything before, that this hadn't been her reason. She was quite equal to marrying, he knew, for such a motive—and so game, too, you'd never dream it was a sacrifice she was making. He'd rather believe, even, that it had been just to get the little home all her own.—When Goldie was only a little thing and you asked her what she wanted most in all the world when she grew up, she had always answered:

"Why, a little home—all my own—a cunning one—and young things in it and about it."

And if you asked her to explain, she had said:

"Don't you *know*?—not *really*?"

And, then, if you had suggested children, she had answered:

"Of course, all my own; and kittens and puppies and little fluffy chickens and ducks and little birds in my trees, who will make little nests and little songs there because they will know that the trees near the little home all my own are the very nicest ever and ever."—

—Once, she must have been around fifteen, then—how well he re-membered that once—he had said:

"Look here, Goldie, isn't this an awful lot you're asking God to put over for you?"

Only teasing, he had been—but Goldie's face!

"Oh! Vic, am I?—Do you *really* think that?"

And then, before he could reply, in little, eager, humble rushes:

"I hadn't thought of it—*that* way—before.—Maybe you're right.—If —if—I gave up something, perhaps—the ducks—or the chickens—or the—birds—or the kittens—or the puppies?"

Then very slowly:

"Or-the-children?—Oh!—But I couldn't!—Not any of them.—Don't you think, perhaps—just perhaps, Vic—if—if—I'm—good—always— from now on—that—that—maybe—maybe—sometime, Vic, some-time—I—I—might?—Oh! Don't you?"—

He shut his mouth hard.

—Well, she had had the little home all her own. Cy had made a little clearing, she had written, just beyond the great live oak. Did he remember it? And did he remember, too, how much Cy loved the trees?—

—No, he hadn't forgotten that live oak—not the way he had played in it—and carved his initials all over it; and he hadn't forgotten Cy and the trees, either.—Silly way, Cy had had, even after he grew up, of mooning among them.

"Talk to me—they do—sometimes.—Tell me big, quiet things, nice things."

—Gosh! After *his* experience, *this* night among them. *Love* 'em!— Hm!—Damned, waiting, greedy things!—Cy could have them and welcome.—

—It had been last year Goldie had written about the clearing with the little home all her own in the very "prezact" middle of it.—They had had to wait a whole year after they were married before they could move in—not finished or something—he'd forgotten the reason.—How had the rest of that letter gone?—Goldie's letters were easy to remember— had, somehow, a sort of burrlike quality about them. He had it, now, something like this:

She wished she could tell him how cunning the little home all her own was, but there was really no cunning word cunning enough to describe it.—Why even the very trees came right down to the very edges of the clearing on all four sides just to look at it.—If he could only *see* how proudly they stood there and nodded their entire approval one to the other!—

Four rooms the little home, all her own, had.—Four!—And a little porch in the front and a "littler" one in the back, and a hall that had really the most absurd way of trying to get out both the front and rear doors at the same time. Would he believe it, they had to keep both the doors shut tight in order to hold that ridiculous hall in? Had he ever, in all his life, heard of such a thing? And just off of this little hall, at the right of the front door, was their bedroom, and back of this, at the end of this same very silly hall, was their dining room, and opposite, across the hall again—she hoped he saw how this hall simply refused to be ignored—again—opposite was the kitchen.—He was, then, to step back into the hall once more, but *this* time he was to pretend very hard not to see it. There was no telling, its vanity was so great, if you paid too much attention to it, what it might do. Why, the unbearable little thing might rise up, break down the front and back doors and escape; and then where'd they be, she'd like to know, without any little hall at all?—He was to step, then, quite nonchalantly—if he knew what that was—back into the hall and come forward, but this time he was to look at the room at the left of the front door; and *there*, if he pleased, he would see something really to repay him for his trouble, for here he would behold her sitting room and parlor both in one. And if he couldn't believe how perfectly adorable this little room could be and was, why she was right there to tell him all about it.—Every single bit of the little home all her own was built just as she had wished and furnished just as she had hoped. And, well, to sum it all up, it wasn't safe, if you had any kind of heart trouble at all, to stand in the road in front of the little home all her own, because it had such a way of calling you that before you knew it, you were running to it and running fast. She could vouch for the absolute truth of this statement.

And she had a puppy, yellow all over, all but his little heart—she dared him even to suggest such a thing!—with a funny wrinkled forehead and a most impudent grin. And he insisted upon eating up all the uneatable things they possessed, including Cy's best straw hat and her own Sunday go-to-meeting slippers. And she had a kitten, a grey one; and the busiest things he did were to eat and sleep. Sometimes he condescended to play with his tail and to keep the puppy in his place. He had a way of looking at you out of blue, very young, very innocent eyes that you knew perfectly well were not a bit young nor yet a bit innocent. And she had the darlingest, downiest little chickens and ducks and a canary bird, which Emma Elizabeth lent her sometimes when she went away to work, and the canary had been made of two golden songs. And outside of the little home all her own—in the closest trees—the birds were, lots of them, and they had nested there.—If, of a morning, he could only hear them singing!—As if they knew—and did it on purpose—just as she had wished.—How happy it had all sounded—and yet—and yet—once or twice—he had had the feeling that something wasn't quite right.

—He hoped it didn't mean she wasn't caring for Cy.—He would rather believe it was because there hadn't been children.—The latter could be remedied—from little hints he had been gathering lately, he rather thought it was already being remedied; but if she didn't *care* for Cy, there wasn't much to be done about that.—Well, he was going to her, at last.—She couldn't fool him—couldn't Goldie; and if that fathead, Cy, couldn't take care of her, now. Just let somebody start something.—

—That break ahead there, in the darkness, ought to be just about where the settlement was.—No one need ever tell *him* again it was only three miles from the station—he guessed he knew better.—More like ten or twenty.—The settlement, all right.—Thought he hadn't been mistaken.—So far, then, so good.

The road, here, became the main street of the little colored settlement. Three or four smaller ones cut it at right angles and then ran off into the darkness. The houses, for the most part, sat back, not very far apart; and, as the shamed moon had entirely disappeared, all he could make out of them was their silent, black little masses. His quick eyes and his ears were busy. No sound broke the stillness. He drew a deep breath of relief. As nearly as he could make out, everything was as it should be.

He did not pause until he was about midway of the settlement. Here he set his bag down, sat on it and looked at the illuminated hands of his watch. It was half past two. In the woods he had found it almost cold, but in this spot the air was warm and close. He pulled out his handkerchief, took off his hat, mopped his face, head and neck, finally the sweatband of his hat.

—Queer!—But he wouldn't have believed that the mere sight of all this, after five years, could make him feel this way. There was something to this home idea, after all.—Didn't feel, hardly, as though he had ever been away.—

Suddenly he wondered if old man Tom Jackson had fixed that gate of his yet. Curiosity got the better of him. He arose, went over and looked. Sure enough the gate swung outward on a broken hinge. Forrest grinned.

"Don't believe over much here, in change, do they?—That gate was that way ever since I can remember.—Bet every window is shut tight too. Turrible, the night air always used to be.—Wonder if my people will ever get over these things."

He came back and sat down again. He was facing a house that his eyes had returned to more than any other.

"Looks just the same.—Wonder who lives there now.—Suppose someone does.—Looks like it.—Mother sure had courage—more than I would have had—to give up a good job in the North, teaching school, to come down here and marry a poor doctor in a colored settlement. I give it to her.—Game!—Goldie's just like her—she'd have done it too."

—How long had it been since his father had died?—Nine—ten—why, it was ten years and eight since his mother—. They'd both been born there—he and Goldie.—What was that story his mother had used to tell about him when he had first been brought in to see her?—He had been six at the time.

"Mother," he had asked, "is her gold?"

"What, son?"

"I say, is her gold?"

"Oh! I see," his mother had said and smiled, he was sure, that very nice understanding smile of hers. "Why, she *is* gold, isn't she?"

"Yes, all of her. What's her name?"

"She hasn't any, yet, son."

"He ain't got no name?—Too bad!—I give her one. Hers name's Goldie, 'cause."

"All right, son, Goldie it shall be." And Goldie it had always been.—

—No, you couldn't call Goldie pretty exactly.—Something about her, though, mighty attractive.—Different looking!—That was it.—Like herself.—She had never lost that beautiful even gold color of hers.—Even her hair was "goldeny" and her long eyelashes. Nice eyes Goldie had, big and brown with flecks of gold in them—set in a little wistful, pointed face.—

He came to his feet suddenly and picked up his bag. He moved swiftly now, but not so swiftly as not to notice things still as he went.

"Why, hello!" he exclaimed and paused a second or so before going on again. "What's happened to Uncle Ray's house?—Something's not the same.—Seems larger, somehow.—Wonder what it is?—Maybe a porch.—So they do change here a little.—That there ought to be Aunt Phoebe's house.—But she must be dead—though I don't remember Goldie's saying so.—Why, she'd be way over ninety.—Used to be afraid of the dark or something and never slept without a dim light.—Gosh! If there isn't the light—just the same as ever.—And way over ninety.— Whew!—Wonder how it feels to be that old.—Bet I wouldn't like it.— Gee! What's that?"

Victor Forrest stopped short and listened. The sound was muffled but continuous, it seemed to come from the closed, faintly lighted pane of Aunt Phoebe's room. It was a sound, it struck him, remarkably like the keening he had heard in an Irish play. It died out slowly and, though he waited, it did not begin again.

"Probably dreaming or something and woke herself up," and he started on once more.

He soon left the settlement behind and, continuing along the same road, found himself (he hoped for the last time) in the midst of the arrested wood-ocean.

But the sound of that keening, although he had explained it quite satisfactorily to himself, had left him disturbed. Thoughts, conjectures, fears that he had refused, until now, quite resolutely to entertain no longer would be denied. They were rooted in Goldie's last two letters, the cause of his hurried trip South.

"Of course, there's no *real* danger.—I'm foolish, even, to entertain such a thought.—Women get like that sometimes—nervous and overwrought.—And if it is with her as I suspect and hope—why the whole matter's explained.—Why it had really sounded *frightened*!—And parts of it were—hm!—almost incoherent.—The whole thing's too ridiculous, however, to believe.—Well, when she sees me we'll have a good big laugh over it all.—Just the same, I'm glad I came.—Rather funny— somehow—thinking of Goldie—with a kid—in her arms.—Nice, though."

—Lafe Coleman!—Lafe Coleman!—He seemed to remember dimly a stringy, long white man with stringy colorless hair, quite disagreeably underclean; eyes a pale grey and fishlike.—He associated a sort of toothless grin with that face.—No, that wasn't it, either.—Ah! That was it!—He had it clearly, now.—The grin was all right but it displayed the dark and rotting remains of tooth stumps.—

He made a grimace of strong disgust and loathing.

—And—this—this—*thing* had been annoying Goldie, had been in fact, for years.—She hadn't told anybody, it seems, because she had been able to take care of herself.—But since she had married and been living away from the settlement—it had been easier for him, and much more difficult for her. He wasn't to worry, though, for the man was stupid and so far she'd always been able to outwit— What she feared was Cy. It was true Cy was amiability itself—but—well—she had seen him angry once.—Ought she to tell him?—She didn't believe Cy would kill the creature—not outright—but it would be pretty close to it.—The feeling

between the races was running higher than it used to.—There had been
a very terrible lynching in the next county only last year.—She hadn't
spoken of it before—for there didn't seem any use going into it.—As he
had never mentioned it, she supposed it had never gotten into the papers.
Nothing, of course, had been done about it, nothing ever was. Everybody
knew who was in the mob.—Even he would be surprised at some of the
names.—The brother of the lynched man, quite naturally, had tried to
bring some of the leaders to justice; and he, too, had paid with his life.
Then the mob, not satisfied, had threatened, terrorized, cowed all the
colored people in the locality.—He was to remember that when you were
under the heel it wasn't the most difficult of matters to be terrorized and
cowed. There was absolutely no law, as he knew, to protect a colored
man.—That was one of the reasons she had hesitated to tell Cy, for not
only Cy and she might be made to pay for what Cy might do, but the
little settlement as well. Now, keeping all this in mind, ought she to tell
Cy?

And the letter had ended:

"I'm a little nervous, Vic, and frightened and not quite sure of my
judgment. Whatever you advise me to do, I am sure will be right."

—On the very heels of this had come the "special" mailed by Goldie
in another town.—She hadn't dared, it seemed, to post it in Hope-
wood.—It had contained just twelve words, but they had brought him
South on the next train.

"Cy knows," it had said, "and O! Vic, if you love me, come, come,
come!"

Way down inside of him, in the very depths, a dull, cold rage began
to glow, but he banked it down again, carefully, very carefully, as he had
been able to do, so far, each time before that the thoughts of Lafe Coleman
and little Goldie's helplessness had threatened anew to stir it.

—That there ought to be the great live oak—and beyond should be
the clearing, in the very "prezact" middle of which should be the little
home all Goldie's own.—

For some inexplicable reason his feet suddenly began to show a strange
reluctance to go forward.

"Damned silly ass!" he said to himself. "There wasn't a thing wrong
with the settlement. That ought to be a good enough sign for anybody
with a grain of sense."

And then, quite suddenly, he remembered the keening.

He did not turn back to pause, still his feet showed no tendency to
hasten. Of necessity, however, it was only a matter of time before he

reached the live oak. He came to a halt beside it, ears and every sense keenly on the alert. Save for the stabbing, white stars above the clearing, there was nothing else in all the world, it seemed, but himself and the heavy black silence.

Once more he advanced but, this time, by an act of sheer will. He paused, set his jaw and faced the clearing. In the very center was a small dark mass; it must be the little home. The breath he had drawn in sharply, while turning, he emitted in a deep sigh. His knees felt strangely weak. —What he had expected to see exactly, he hardly knew. He was almost afraid of the reaction going on inside of him. The relief, the blessed relief at merely finding it there, the little house all her own!

It made him feel suddenly very young and joyous and the world, bad as it was, a pretty decent old place after all. Danger!—Of course, there was no danger.—How could he have been so absurd?—Just wait until he had teased Goldie aplenty about this. He started to laugh aloud but caught himself in time.

—No use awaking them.—He'd steal up and sit on the porch—there'd probably be a chair there or something—and wait until dawn.—They shouldn't be allowed to sleep one single second after that.—And then he'd bang on their window, and call out quite casually:

"O, Goldie Harper, this is a nice way—isn't it?—to treat a fellow; not even to leave the latch string out for him?"

He could hear Goldie's little squeal now.

And then he'd say to Cy:

"Hello, you big fathead, you!—What do you mean, anyhow, by making a perfectly good brother-in-law hoof it the whole way here, like this?"

He had reached the steps by this time and he began softly to mount them. It was very dark on the little porch and he wished he dared to light a match, but he mustn't risk anything that might spoil the little surprise he was planning. He transferred his bag from his right to his left hand, the better to feel his way. With his fingers outstretched in front of him he took a cautious step forward and stumbled over something.

"Clumsy chump!" he exclaimed below his breath. "That will about finish your little surprise I am thinking." He stood stockstill for several seconds, but there was no sound.

"Some sleepers," he commented.

He leaned over to find out what it was he had stumbled against and discovered that it was a broken chair lying on its side. Slowly he came to a standing posture. He was not as happy for some reason. He stood there, very quiet, for several moments. Then his hand stretched out before he started forward again. This time, after only a couple of steps, his hand came in contact with the housefront. He was feeling his way along, cautiously still, when all of a sudden his fingers encountered nothing but air. Surprised, he paused. He thought, at first, he had come to the end of the porch. He put out a carefully exploring foot only to find firm boards beneath. A second time he experimented, with the same result. And then, as suddenly, he felt the housefront once more beneath his fingers. Gradually it came to him where he must be. He was standing before the door and it was open, wide open!

He could not have moved if he had wished. He made no sound and none broke the blackness all about.

It was sometime afterwards when he put his bag down upon the porch, took a box of matches out of his pocket, lit one and held it up. His hand was trembling, but he managed, before it burned his fingers and he blew it out automatically, to see four things—two open doors to right and left, a lamp in a bracket just beyond the door at the left and a dirty mudtrodden floor.

The minutes went by and then, it seemed to him, somebody else called out:

"Goldie! Cy!" This was followed by silence only.

Again the voice tried, a little louder this time:

"Goldie! Cy!" —There was no response.

This other person, who seemed, somehow, to have entered into his body, moved forward, struck another match, lit the lamp and took it down out of the bracket. Nothing seemed to make very much difference to this stranger. He moved his body stiffly; his eyes felt large and dry. He passed through the open door at the left and what he saw there did not surprise him in the least. In some dim way, only he knew that it affected him.

There was not, in this room, one single whole piece of furniture. Chairs, tables, a sofa, a whatnot, all had been smashed, broken, torn apart; the stuffing of the upholstery, completely ripped out; and the entirety thrown, scattered, here, there and everywhere. The piano lay on one side, its other staved in.—Something, it reminded him of—something to do with a grin—the black notes like the rotting stumps of teeth. Oh, yes! Lafe Coleman!—That was it. The thought aroused no particular emotion in him. Only, again he knew it affected him in some far off way.

Every picture on the walls had been wrenched down and the moulding with it, the pictures themselves defaced and torn, and the glass splintered and crushed under foot. Knickknacks, vases, a china clock, all lay smashed and broken. Even the rug upon the floor had not escaped, but had been ripped up, torn into shreds and fouled by many dirty feet. The frail white curtains and window shades had gone down too in this human whirlwind; not a pane of glass was whole. The white woodwork and the white walls were soiled and smeared. Over and over the splay-fingered imprint of one dirty hand repeated itself on the walls. A wanton boot had kicked through the plastering in places.

This someone else went out of the door, down the hall, into the little kitchen and dining room. In each room he found precisely the same conditions prevailing.

There was one left, he remembered, so he turned back into the hall, went along it to the open door and entered in.—What was the matter, here, with the air?—He raised the lamp higher above his head. He saw the same confusion as elsewhere. A brass bed was overturned and all things else shattered and topsy-turvy. There was something dark at the foot of the bed. He moved nearer, and understood why the air was not pleasant. The dark object was a little dead dog, a yellow one, with a wrinkled forehead. His teeth were bared in a snarl. A kick in the belly had done for him. He leaned over; the little leg was quite stiff. Less dimly, this time, he knew that this affected him.

He straightened up. When he had entered the room there had been something he had noticed for him to do. But what was it? This stranger's memory was not all that it should be.—Oh, yes! He knew, now. The bed. He was to right the bed. With some difficulty he cleared a space for the lamp and set it down carefully. He raised the bed. Nothing but the mattress and the rumpled and twisted bed clothing. He didn't know exactly just what this person was expecting to find.

He was sitting on the steps, the extinguished lamp at his side. It was dawn. Everything was veiled over with grey. As the day came on, a breeze followed softly after, and with the breeze there came to him there on the steps a creaking, two creakings!—Somewhere there to the right, they were, among the trees. The grey world became a shining green one. Why were the birds singing like that, he wondered.—It didn't take the day long to get here—did it?—once it started. A second time his eyes went to the woods at the right. He was able to see now. Nothing there, as far as he could make out. His eyes dropped from the trees to the ground and he beheld what looked to him like a trampled path. It began there at the trees: it approached the house: it passed over a circular bed of little pansies. It ended at the steps. Again his eyes traversed the path, but this time from the steps to the trees.

Quite automatically he arose and followed the path. Quite automatically he drew the branches aside and saw what he saw. Underneath those two terribly mutilated swinging bodies, lay a tiny unborn child, its head crushed in by a deliberate heel.

Something went very wrong in his head. He dropped the branches, turned and sat down. A spider, in the sunshine, was reweaving the web someone had just destroyed while passing through the grass. He sat slouched far forward, watching the spider for hours. He wished the birds wouldn't sing so.—Somebody had said something once about them. He wished, too, he could remember who it was.

About midday, the children of the colored settlement, playing in the road, looked up and saw a man approaching. There was something about him that frightened them, the little ones in particular, for they ran screaming to their mothers. The larger ones drew back as unobtrusively as possible into their own yards. The man came on with a high head and an unhurried gait. His should have been a young face, but it was not. Out of its set sternness looked his eyes, and they were very terrible eyes indeed. Mothers with children, hanging to them from behind and peering around, came to their doors. The man was passing through the settlement now. A woman, startled, recognized him and called the news out shrilly to her man eating his dinner within. He came out, went down to the road rather reluctantly. The news spread. Other men from other houses followed the first man's example. They stood about him, quite a crowd of them. The stranger, of necessity, came to a pause. There were no greetings on either side. He eyed them over, this crowd, coolly, appraisingly, contemptuously. They eyed him, in turn, but surreptitiously. They were plainly very uncomfortable. Wiping their hands on aprons, women joined the crowd. A larger child or two dared the outskirts. No one would meet his eye.

Suddenly a man was speaking. His voice came sharply, jerkily. He was telling a story. Another took it up and another.

One added a detail here; one a detail there. Heated arguments arose over insignificant particulars; angry words were passed. Then came too noisy explanations, excuses, speeches in extenuation of their own actions, pleas, attempted exoneration of themselves. The strange man said never a word. He listened to each and to all. His contemptuous eyes made each writhe in turn. They had finished. There was nothing more that they could see to be said. They waited, eyes on the ground, for him to speak.

But what he said was:

"Where is Uncle Ray?"

Uncle Ray, it seemed was away—had been for two weeks. His Aunt Millie with him. No one had written to him, for his address was not known.

The strange man made no comment.

"Where is Lafe Coleman?" he asked.

No one there knew where he was to be found—not one. They regretted the fact, they were sorry, but they couldn't say. They spoke with lowered eyes, shifting their bodies uneasily from foot to foot.

Watching their faces he saw their eyes suddenly lift, as if with one accord, and focus upon something behind him and to his right. He turned his head. In the brilliant sunshine, a very old, very bent form leaning heavily on a cane was coming down the path from the house in whose window he had seen the dimmed light. It was Aunt Phoebe.

He left the crowd abruptly and went to meet her. When she was quite sure he was coming she paused where she was, bent over double, her two hands, one over the other, on the knob of her cane, and waited for him. No words, either, between these two. He looked down at her and she bent back her head, tremulous from age, and looked up at him.

The wrinkles were many and deep-bitten in Aunt Phoebe's dark skin. A border of white wool fringed the bright bandana tied tightly around her head. There were grey hairs in her chin; two blue rings encircled the irises of her dim eyes. But all her ugliness could not hide the big heart of her, kind yet, and brave, after ninety years on earth.

And as he stood gazing down at her, quite suddenly he remembered what Goldie had once said about those circled eyes.

"Kings and Queens may have *their* crowns and welcome. What's there to *them*?—But the kind Aunt Phoebe wears—that's different. She earned hers, Vic, earned them through many years and long of sorrow, and heartbreak and bitter, bitter tears. She bears with her the unforgetting heart.—And though they could take husband and children and sell them South, though she lost them in the body—never a word of them, since —she keeps them always in her heart.—I knew, Vic, I know—and God who is good and God who is just touched her eyes, both of them and gave her blue crowns, beautiful ones, a crown for each. Don't you *see she is of God's Elect?*"

For a long time Victor Forrest stood looking down into those crowned eyes. No one disturbed these two in the sun-drenched little yard. They, in the road, drew closer together and watched silently.

And then he spoke:

"You are to tell me, Aunt Phoebe—aren't you?—where I am to find Lafe Coleman?"

Aunt Phoebe did not hesitate a second. "Yes," she said, and told him.

The crowd in the road moved uneasily, but no one spoke.

And then Victor Forrest did a thing he had never done before: he leaned over swiftly and kissed the wrinkled parchment cheek of Aunt Phoebe.

"Goldie loved you," he said and straightened up, turned on his heel without another word and went down the path to the road. Those there made no attempt to speak. They drew closer together and made way for him. He looked neither to the right nor to the left. He passed them without a glance. He went with a steady, purposeful gait and a high head. All watched him for they knew they were never to see him alive again. The woods swallowed Victor Forrest. A low keening was to be heard. Aunt Phoebe had turned and was going more feebly, more slowly than ever toward her house.

Those that know whereof they speak say that when Lafe Coleman was found he was not a pleasant object to see. There was no bullet in him— nothing like that. It was the marks upon his neck and the horror of his blackened face.

And Victor Forrest died, as the other two had died, upon another tree.

There is a country road upon either side of which grow trees even to its very edges. Each tree has been chosen and transplanted here for a reason and the reason is that at some time each has borne upon its boughs a creaking victim. Hundreds of these trees there are, thousands of them. They form a forest—"Creaking Forest" it is called. And over this road many pass, very, very many. And they go jauntily, joyously here—even at night. They do not go as Victor Forrest went, they do not sense the things that Victor Forrest sensed. If their souls were not deaf, there would be many things for them to hear in Creaking Forest. At night the trees become an ocean dark and sinister, for it is made up of all the evil in all the hearts of all the mobs that have done to death their creaking victims. It is an ocean arrested at the very edges of the road by a strange spell. But this spell may snap at any second and with that snapping this sea of evil will move, rush, hurl itself heavily and swiftly together from the two sides of the road, engulfing, grinding, crushing, blotting out all in its way.

One Boy's Story

(1925)

Marita Bonner

I'm glad they got me shut up in here. Gee, I'm glad! I used to be afraid
to walk in the dark and to stay by myself.

That was when I was ten years old. Now I am eleven.

My mother and I used to live up in the hills right outside of Somerset.
Somerset, you know, is way up state and there aren't many people there.
Just a few rich people in big houses and that's all.

Our house had a nice big yard behind it, beside it and in front of it. I
used to play it was my fortress and that the hills beside us were full of
Indians. Some days I'd go on scouting parties up and down the hills and
fight.

That was in the summer and fall. In the winter and when the spring
was rainy, I used to stay in the house and read.

I love to read. I love to lie on the floor and put my elbows down and
read and read myself right out of Somerset and of America—out of the
world, if I want to.

There was just my mother and I. No brothers—no sisters—no father.
My mother was awful pretty. She had a roundish plump, brown face and
was all plump and round herself. She had black hair all curled up on the
end like a nice autumn leaf.

She used to stay in the house all the time and sew a lot for different
ladies who came up from the big houses in Somerset. She used to sew
and I would pull the bastings out for her. I did not mind it much. I liked
to look at the dresses and talk about the people who were to wear them.

Most people, you see, wear the same kind of dress all the time. Mrs.
Ragland always wore stiff silk that sounded like icicles on the window.

Her husband kept the tea and coffee store in Somerset and everybody said he was a coming man.

I used to wonder where he was coming to.

Mrs. Gregg always had the kind of silk that you had to work carefully for it would ravel into threads. She kept the boardinghouse down on Forsythe Street. I used to like to go to that house. When you looked at it on the outside and saw all the windows and borders running up against it you thought you were going in a palace. But when you got inside, you saw all the little holes in the carpet and the mended spots in the curtains and the faded streaks in the places where the draperies were folded.

The pale soft silk that always made me feel like burying my face in it belonged to Mrs. Swyburne. She was rich—awful rich. Her husband used to be some kind of doctor and he found out something that nobody else had found out, so people used to give him plenty of money just to let him tell them about it. They called him a specialist.

He was a great big man. Nice and tall and he looked like he must have lived on milk and beef-juice and oranges and tomato juice and all the stuff Ma makes me eat to grow. His teeth were white and strong, so I guess he chewed his crusts, too.

Anyhow, he was big but his wife was all skinny and pale. Even her eyes were almost skinny and pale. They were sad-like and she never talked much. My mother used to say that those who did not have any children did not have to talk much anyhow.

She said that to Mrs. Swyburne one time. Mrs. Swyburne had been sitting quiet like she used to, looking at me. She always looked at me anyhow, but that day she looked harder than ever.

Every time I raised up my head and breathed the bastings out of my face, I would see her looking at me.

I always hated to have her look at me. Her eyes were so sad they made me feel as if she wanted something I had.

Not that I had anything to give her, because she had all the money and cars and everything and I only had my mother and Cato, my dog, and some toys and books.

But she always looked that way at me, and that day she kept looking so long that pretty soon I sat up and looked at her hard.

She sort of smiled then and said, "Do you know, Donald. I was wishing I had a little boy just like you to pull out bastings for me, too."

"You couldn't have one just like me," I said right off quick. Then I quit talking because Ma commenced to frown even though she did not look up at me.

I quit because I was going to say, " 'Cause I'm colored and you aren't," when Ma frowned.

Mrs. Swyburne still sort of smiled; then she turned her lips away from her teeth the way I do when Ma gives me senna and manna tea.

"No," she said, "I couldn't have a little boy like you, I guess."

Ma spoke right up. "I guess you do not want one like him! You have to talk to him so much."

I knew she meant I talked so much and acted so bad sometimes.

Mrs. Swyburne looked at Ma then. She looked at her hair and face and right down to her feet. Pretty soon she said: "You cannot mind that surely. You seem to have all the things I haven't anyway." Her lips were still held in that lifted, twisted way.

Ma turned around to the machine then and turned the wheel and caught the thread and it broke and the scissors fell and stuck up in the floor. I heard her say "Jesus" to herself like she was praying.

I didn't say anything. I ripped out the bastings. Ma stitched. Mrs. Swyburne sat there. I sort of peeped up at her and I saw a big fat tear sliding down her cheek.

I kind of wiggled over near her and laid my hand on her arm. Then Ma yelled: "Donald, go and get a pound of rice! Go now, I said."

I got scared. She had not said it before and she had a lot of rice in a jar in the closet. But I didn't dare say so. I went out.

I couldn't help but think of Mrs. Swyburne. She ought not to cry so easy. She might not have had a little boy and Ma might have—but she should have been happy. She had a great big house on the swellest street in Somerset and a car all her own and someone to drive it for her. Ma only had me and our house, which wasn't so swell but it was all right.

Then Mrs. Swyburne had her husband and he had such a nice voice. You didn't mind leaning on his knee and talking to him as soon as you saw him. He had eyes that looked so smiling and happy, and when you touched his hands they were soft and gentle as Ma's, even if they were bigger.

I knew him real well. He and I were friends. He used to come to our house a lot of time and bring me books and talk to Ma while I read.

He knew us real well. He called Ma Louise and me Don. Sometimes he'd stay and eat supper with us and then sit down and talk. I never could see why he'd come way out there to talk to us when he had a whole lot of rich friends down in Somerset and a wife that looked like the only doll I ever had.

A lady gave me that doll once and I thought she was really pretty—all pale and blond and rosy. I thought she was real pretty at first, but by and by she seemed so dumb. She never did anything but look pink and pale and rosy and pretty. She never went out and ran with me like Cato did. So I just took a rock and gave her a rap up beside her head and threw her in the bushes.

Maybe Mrs. Swyburne was pale and pink and dumb like the doll and her husband couldn't rap her with a rock and throw her away.

I don't know.

Anyhow, he used to come and talk to us and he'd talk to Ma a long time after I was in bed. Sometimes I'd wake up and hear them talking. He used to bring me toys until he found out that I could make my own toys and that I liked books.

After that he brought me books. All kinds of books about fairies and Indians and folks in other countries.

Sometimes he and I would talk about the books—especially those I liked. The one I liked most was called "Ten Tales to Inspire Youth."

That sounds kind of funny but the book was great. It had stories in it all about men. All men. I read all of the stories, but I liked the one about the fellow named Orestes who went home from the Trojan War and found his mother had married his father's brother so he killed them. I was always sorry for the women with the whips of flame like forked tongues who used to worry him afterwards. I don't see why the Furies pursued him. They knew he did it because he loved his father so much.

Another story I liked was about Oedipus—a Greek, too—who put out his eyes to hurt himself because he killed his father and married his mother by mistake.

But after I read "David and Goliath," I just had to pretend that I was David.

I swiped half a yard of elastic from Ma and hunted a long time until I found a good forked piece of wood. Then I made a swell slingshot.

The story said that David asked Jehovah (which was God) to let his slingshot shoot good. "Do Thou lend Thy strength to my arm, Jehovah," he prayed.

I used to say that, too, just to be like him.

I told Dr. Swyburne I liked these stories.

"Why do you like them?" he asked me.

"Because they are about men," I said.

"Because they are about men! Is that the only reason?"

Then I told him no; that I liked them because the men in the stories were brave and had courage and stuck until they got what they wanted, even if they hurt themselves getting it.

And he laughed and said to Ma: "Louise, he has the blood, all right!"

And Ma said: "Yes! He is a true Gage. They're brave enough and put their eyes out, too. That takes courage all right!"

Ma and I are named Gage, so I stuck out my chest and said: "Ma, which one of us Gages put his eyes out?"

"Me," she said—and she was standing there looking right at me!

I thought she was making fun. So I felt funny.

Dr. Swyburne turned red and said: "I meant the other blood of course. All the Swyburnes are heroes."

I didn't know what he meant. My name is Gage and so is Ma's, so he didn't mean me.

Ma threw her head up and looked at him and says: "Oh, are they heroes?" Then she says real quick: "Donald, go to bed right now!"

I didn't want to go but I went. I took a long time to take off my clothes and I heard Ma and Dr. Swyburne talking fast like they were fussing.

I couldn't hear exactly what they said, but I kept hearing Ma say: "I'm through!"

And I heard Dr. Swyburne say: "You can't be!"

I kind of dozed to sleep. By and by I heard Ma say again: "Well, I'm through!"

And Dr. Swyburne said: "I won't let you be!"

Then I rolled over to think a minute and then go downstairs maybe.

But when I rolled over again, the sun was shining and I had to get up.

Ma never said anything about what happened, so I didn't either. She just walked around doing her work fast, holding her head up high like she always does when I make her mad.

So I never said a thing that day.

One day I came home from school. I came in the back way, and when I was in the kitchen I could hear a man in the front of the room talking to Ma. I stood still a minute to see if it was Dr. Swyburne, though I knew he never comes in the afternoon.

The voice didn't sound like his, so I walked in the hall and passed the door. The man had his back to me, so I just looked at him a minute and didn't say anything. He had on leather leggins and a sort of uniform like soldiers wear. He was stooping over the machine talking to Ma, and I couldn't see his face.

Just then I stumbled over the little rug in the hall and he stood up and looked at me.

He was a colored man! Colored just like Ma and me. You see, there aren't any other people in Somerset colored like we are, so I was sort of surprised to see him.

"This is my son, Mr. Frazier," Ma said.

I said, "Pleased to meet you," and stepped on Ma's feet. But not on purpose. You know, I kind of thought he was going to be named Gage and be some relation to us and stay at our house awhile.

I never saw many colored people—no colored men—and I wanted to see some. When Ma called him Frazier it made my feet slippery, so I stubbed my toe.

"Hello, son!" he said nice and quiet.

He didn't talk like Ma and me. He talked slower and softer. I liked him straight off, so I grinned and said: "Hello, yourself."

"How's the books?" he said then.

I didn't know what he meant at first but I guessed he meant school. So I said: "Books aren't good as the fishin'."

He laughed out loud and said I was all right and said he and I were going to be friends and that while he was in Somerset he was going to come to our house often and see us.

Then he went out. Ma told me he was driving some lady's car. She was visiting Somerset from New York and he would be there a little while.

Gee, I was so glad! I made a fishing rod for him that very afternoon out of a piece of willow I had been saving for a long time.

And one day, he and I went down to the lake and fished. We sat still on top a log that went across a little bay-like. I felt kind of excited and couldn't say a word. I just kept looking at him every once in a while and smiled. I did not grin. Ma said I grinned too much.

Pretty soon he said: "What are you going to be when you grow up, son?"

"A colored man," I said. I meant to say some more, but he hollered and laughed so loud that Cato had to run up to see what was doing.

"Sure you'll be a colored man! No way to get out of that! But I mean this: What kind of work are you going to do?"

I had to think a minute. I had to think of all the kinds of work men did. Some of the men in Somerset were farmers. Some kept stores. Some swept the streets. Some were rich and did not do anything at home but they went to the city and had their cars driven to the shop and to meet them at the train.

All the conductors and porters make a lot of scramble to get those men on and off the train, even if they looked as if they could take care of themselves.

So I said to Mr. Frazier: "I want to have an office."

"An office?"

"Yes. In the city so's I can go in to it and have my car meet me when I come to Somerset."

"Fat chance a colored man has!" he said.

"I can too have an office!" I said. He made me sore. "I can have one if I want to! I want to have an office and be a specialist like Dr. Swyburne."

Mr. Frazier dropped his pole and had to swear something awful when he reached for it, though it wasn't very far from him.

"Why'd you pick him?" he said and looked at me kind of mad-like, and before I could think of what to say he said: "Say son, does that guy come up to see your mother?"

"Sure, he comes to see us both!" I said.

Mr. Frazier laughed again but not out loud. It made me sore all over. I started to hit him with my pole, but I thought about something I'd read once that said even a savage will treat you right in his house—so I didn't hit him. Of course, he wasn't in my house exactly, but he was sitting on my own log over my fishing places and that's like being in your own house.

Mr. Frazier laughed to himself again, and then all of a sudden he took the pole I had made him out of the piece of willow I had been saving for myself and laid it across his knees and broke it in two. Then he said out loud: "Nigger women," and then threw the pole in the water.

I grabbed my pole right out of the water and slammed it across his face. I never thought of the hook until I hit him, but it did not stick in him. It caught in a tree and I broke the string yanking it out.

He looked at me like he was going to knock me in the water, and, even though I was scared, I was thinking how I'd let myself fall if he did knock me off—so that I could swim out without getting tangled in the roots under the bank.

But he didn't do it. He looked at me a minute and said: "Sorry, son! Sorry! Not your fault."

Then he put his hand on my hair and brushed it back and sort of lifted it up and said: "Like the rest."

I got up and said I was going home, and he came too. I was afraid he would come in, but when he got to my gate he said: "So long," and walked right on.

I went on in. Ma was sewing. She jumped up when I came in. "Where is Mr. Frazier?" she asked me. She didn't even say hello to me!

"I hit him," I said.

"You hit him!" she hollered. "You *hit* him! What did you do that for? Are you crazy?"

I told her no. "He said 'nigger women' when I told him that Dr. Swyburne was a friend of ours and came to see us."

Oh, Ma looked terrible then. I can't tell you how she did look. Her face sort of slipped around and twisted like the geography says the earth does when the fire inside of it gets too hot.

She never said a word at first. She just sat there. Then she asked me to tell her all about every bit that happened.

I told her. She kept wriggling from side to side like the fire was getting hotter. When I finished, she said: "Poor baby! My baby boy! Not your fault! Not your fault!"

That made me think of Mr. Frazier, so I pushed out of her arms and said: "Ma, your breast pin hurts my face when you do that!"

She leaned over on the arms of her chair and cried and cried until I cried too.

All that week I'd think of the fire inside of the earth when I looked at Ma. She looked so funny and she kept talking to herself.

On Saturday night we were sitting at the table when I heard a car drive up the road.

"Here's Dr. Swyburne!" I said, and I felt so glad I stopped eating.

"He isn't coming here!" Ma said, and then she jumped up.

"Sure he's coming," I said. "I know his motor." And I started to get up too.

"You stay where you are!" Ma hollered, and she went out and closed the door behind her.

I took another piece of cake and began eating the frosting. I heard Dr. Swyburne come up on the porch.

"Hello, Louise," he said. I could tell he was smiling by his voice.

I couldn't hear what Ma said at first, but pretty soon I heard her say: "You can't come here any more!"

That hurt my feelings. I liked Dr. Swyburne. I liked him better than anybody I knew besides Ma.

Ma stayed out a long time, and by and by she came in alone and I heard Dr. Swyburne drive away.

She didn't look at me at all. She just leaned back against the door and said: "Dear Jesus! With your help I'll free myself."

I wanted to ask her from what did she want to free herself. It sounded like she was in jail or an animal in a trap in the woods.

I thought about it all during supper, but I didn't dare say much. I thought about it and pretended that she was shut up in a prison and I was a time fighter who beat all the keepers and got her out.

Then it came to me that I better get ready to fight to get her out of whatever she was in. I never said anything to her. I carried my air rifle on my back and my slingshot in my pocket. I wanted to ask her where her enemy was, but she never talked to me about it; so I had to keep quiet too. You know, Ma always got mad if I talked about things first. She likes to talk, then I can talk afterwards.

One Sunday she told me she was going for a walk.

"Can I go?" I asked her.

"No," she said. "You play around the yard."

Then she put her hat on and stood looking in the mirror at herself for a minute. All of a sudden I heard her say to herself: "All I need is strength to fight out of it."

"Ma'am?" I thought she was talking to me at first.

She stopped and hugged my head—like I wish she wouldn't sometimes—and then went out.

I stayed still until she got out of the yard. Then I ran and got my rifle and slingshot and followed her.

I crept behind her in the bushes beside the road. I cut across the fields and came out behind the willow patch the way I always do when I am tracking Indians and wild animals.

By and by she came out in the clearing that is behind Dr. Somerset's. They call it Somerset's Grove and it's named for his folks who used to live there—just as the town was.

She sat down, so I lay down in the bushes. A sharp rock was sticking in my knee, but I was afraid to move for fear she'd hear me and send me home.

By and by I heard someone walking on the grass and I saw Dr. Swyburne coming up. He started talking before he got to her.

"Louise," he said. "Louise! I am not going to give anything up to a nigger."

"Not even a nigger woman whom you took from a nigger?" She lifted her mouth in the senna and manna way.

"Don't say that!" he said. "Don't say that! I wanted a son. I couldn't have taken a woman in my own world—that would have ruined my practice. Elaine couldn't have a child!"

"Yes," Ma said. "It would have ruined you and your profession. What did it do for me? What did it do for Donald?"

"I have told you I will give him the best the world can offer. He is a Swyburne!"

"He is *my* child," Ma hollered. "It isn't his fault he is yours!"

"But I give him everything a father could give his son!"

"He has no name!" Ma said.

"I have too!" I hollered inside of me. "Donald Gage!"

"He has no name," Ma said again, "and neither have I!" And she began to cry.

"He has blood!" said Dr. Swyburne.

"But how did he get it? Oh, I'm through. Stay away from my house, and I'll marry one of my men so Donald can be somebody."

"A nigger's son?"

"Don't say that again," Ma hollered and jumped up.

"Do you think I'll give up a woman of mine to a nigger?"

Ma hollered again and hit him right in his face.

He grabbed her wrists and turned the right one, I guess, because she fell away from him on that side.

I couldn't stand any more. I snatched out my slingshot and pulled the stone up that was sticking in my knee.

I started to shoot. Then I remembered what David said first, so I shut my eyes and said it: "Do Thou, Jehovah (which is God today), lend strength to my arm."

When I opened my eyes Ma had broken away and was running toward the road. Dr. Swyburne was standing still by the tree looking after her like he was going to catch her. His face was turned sideways to me. I looked at his head where his hair was brushed back from the side of his face.

I took aim and let the stone go. I heard him say: "Oh, my God!" I saw blood on his face and I saw him stagger and fall against the tree.

Then I ran too.

When I got home Ma was sitting in her chair with her hat thrown on the floor beside her and her head was lying back.

I walked up to her. "Ma," I said real loud.

She reached out and grabbed me and hugged my head down to her neck like she always does.

The big breast pin scratched my mouth. I opened my mouth to speak, and something hot and sharp ran into my tongue.

"Ma! Ma!" I tried to holler. "The pin is sticking in my tongue!"

I don't know what I said though. When I tried to talk again, Ma and Dr. Somerset were looking down at me and I was lying in bed. I tried to say something but I could not say anything. My mouth felt like it was full of hot bread and I could not talk around it.

Dr. Somerset poured something in my mouth, and it felt like it was on fire.

"They found Shev Swyburne in my thistle grove this afternoon," he said to Ma.

Ma look up quick. "*Found* him! What do you mean?"

"I mean he was lying on the ground—either fell or was struck and fell. He was dead from a blow on the temple."

I tried to holler but my tongue was too thick.

Ma took hold of each side of her face and held to it, then she just stared at Dr. Somerset. He put a lot of things back in his bag.

Then he sat up and looked at Ma. "Louise," he said, "why is all that thistle down on your skirt?"

Ma looked down. So did I. There was thistle down all over the hem of her dress.

"You don't think I killed him, do you?" she cried, "you don't think I did it?" Then she cried something awful.

I tried to get up but I was too dizzy. I crawled across the bed on my stomach and reached out to the chair that had my pants on it. It was hard to do—but I dragged my slingshot out of my pocket, crawled back across the bed and laid it on Dr. Somerset's knees. He looked at me for a minute.

"Are you trying to tell me that you did it, son?" he asked me.

I said yes with my head.

"My God! My God!! His own child!!!"

Dr. Somerset said to Ma: "God isn't dead yet."

Then he patted her on the arm and told her not to tell anybody nothing, and they sat down and picked all the thistle down out of the skirt. He took the slingshot and broke it all up and put it all in a paper and carried it downstairs and put it in the stove.

I tried to talk. I wanted to tell him to leave it so I could show my grandchildren what I had used to free Ma, like the men do in the books.

I couldn't talk though. My tongue was too thick for my mouth. The next day it burnt worse and things began to float around my eyes and head like pieces of wood in the water.

Sometimes I could see clearly though, and once I saw Dr. Somerset talking to another man. Dr. Somerset was saying: "We'll have to operate to save his life. His tongue is poisoned. I am afraid it will take his speech from him."

Ma hollered then: "Thank God! He will not talk! Never! He can't talk! Thank God! Oh God! I thank Thee!" And then she cried like she always does, and that time it sounded like she was laughing too.

The other man looked funny and said: "Some of them have no natural feeling of parent for child!"

Dr. Somerset looked at him and said: "You may be fine as a doctor but otherwise you are an awful fool."

Then he told the other man to go out, and he began talking to Ma.

"I understand! I understand," he said. "I know all about it. He took you away from somebody, and some of these days he might have taken Donald from you. He took Elaine from me once and I told him then God would strip him for it. Now it is all over. Never tell anyone and I will not. The boy knows how to read and write and will be able to live."

So I got a black stump in my mouth. It's shaped like a forked whip.

Some days I pretend I am Orestes with the Furies' whips in my mouth for killing a man.

Some days I pretend I am Oedipus and that I cut it out for killing my own father.

That's what makes me sick all over sometimes.

I killed my own father. But I didn't know it was my father. I was freeing Ma.

Still—I shall never write that on my paper to Ma and Dr. Somerset the way I have to talk to them and tell them when things hurt me.

My father said I was a Swyburne and that was why I liked people to be brave and courageous.

Ma says I am a Gage and that is why I am brave and courageous.

But I am both, so I am a whole lot brave, a whole lot courageous. And I am bearing my Furies and my clipped tongue like a Swyburne and a Gage—'cause I am both of them.

Sanctuary

(1930)

Nella Larsen

I

On the southern coast, between Merton and Shawboro, there is a strip
of desolation some half a mile wide and nearly ten miles long between
the sea and old fields of ruined plantations. Skirting the edge of this narrow
jungle is a partly grown-over road, which still shows traces of furrows
made by the wheels of wagons that have long since rotted away or been
cut into firewood. This road is little used, now that the state has built its
new highway a bit to the west and wagons are less numerous than
automobiles.

In the forsaken road a man was walking swiftly. But in spite of his
hurry, at every step he set down his feet with infinite care, for the night
was windless and the heavy silence intensified each sound; even the breaking of a twig could be plainly heard. And the man had need of caution
as well as haste.

Before a lonely cottage that shrank timidly back from the road the man
hesitated a moment, then struck out across the patch of green in front of
it. Stepping behind a clump of bushes close to the house, he looked in
through the lighted window at Annie Poole, standing at her kitchen table
mixing the supper biscuits.

He was a big black man with pale brown eyes in which there was
an odd mixture of fear and amazement. The light showed streaks of
gray soil on his heavy, sweating face and great hands, and on his
torn clothes. In his woolly hair clung bits of dried leaves and dead
grass.

He made a gesture as if to tap on the window, but turned away to the door instead. Without knocking he opened it and went in.

II

The woman's brown gaze was immediately on him, though she did not move. She said, "You ain't in no hurry, is you, Jim Hammer?" It wasn't, however, entirely a question.

"Ah's in trubble, Mis' Poole," the man explained, his voice shaking, his fingers twitching.

"W'at you done done now?"

"Shot a man, Mis' Poole."

"Trufe?" The woman seemed calm. But the word was spat out.

"Yas'm. Shot 'im." In the man's tone was something of wonder, as if he himself could not quite believe that he had really done this thing which he affirmed.

"Daid?"

"Dunno, Mis' Poole. Dunno."

"White man o' niggah?"

"Cain't say, Mis' Poole. White man, Ah reckons."

Annie Poole looked at him with cold contempt. She was a tiny, withered woman—fifty, perhaps—with a wrinkled face the color of old copper, framed by a crinkly mass of white hair. But about her small figure was some quality of hardness that belied her appearance of frailty. At last she spoke, boring her sharp little eyes into those of the anxious creature before her.

"An' w'at am you lookin' foh me to do 'bout et?"

"Jes' lemme stop till dey's gone by. Hide me till dey passes. Reckon dey ain't fur off now." His begging voice changed to a frightened whimper. "Foh de Lawd's sake, Mis' Poole, lemme stop."

And why, the woman inquired caustically, should she run the dangerous risk of hiding him?

"Obadiah, he'd lemme stop ef he was to home," the man whined.

Annie Poole sighed. "Yas," she admitted slowly, reluctantly, "Ah spec' he would. Obadiah, he's too good to youall no 'count trash." Her slight shoulders lifted in a hopeless shrug. "Yas, Ah reckon he'd do et. Emspecial' seein' how he allus set such a heap o' store by you. Cain't see w'at foh, mahse'f. Ah shuah don' see nuffin' in you but a heap o' dirt."

But a look of irony, of cunning, of complicity passed over her face.

She went on, "Still, 'siderin' all an' all, how Obadiah's right fon' o' you, an' how white folks is white folks, Ah'm a-gwine hide you dis one time."

Crossing the kitchen, she opened a door leading into a small bedroom, saying, "Git yo'se'f in dat dere feather baid an' Ah'm a-gwine put de clo's on de top. Don' reckon dey'll fin' you ef dey does look foh you in mah house. An Ah don' spec' dey'll go foh to do dat. Not lessen you been keerless an' let 'em smell you out gittin' hyah." She turned on him a withering look. "But you allus been triflin'. Cain't do nuffin' propah. An' Ah'm a-tellin' you ef dey warn't white folks an' you a po' niggah, Ah shuah wouldn't be lettin' you mess up mah feather baid dis ebenin', 'cose Ah jes' plain don' want you hyah. Ah done kep' mahse'f outen trubble all mah life. So's Obadiah."

"Ah's powahful 'bliged to you, Mis' Poole. You shuah am one good 'oman. De Lawd'll mos' suttinly—"

Annie Poole cut him off. "Dis ain't no time foh all dat kin' o' fiddle-de-roll. Ah does mah duty as Ah sees et 'thout no thanks from you. Ef de Lawd had gib you a white face 'stead o' dat dere black one, Ah shuah would turn you out. Now hush yo' mouf an' git yo'se'f in. An' don' git movin' and scrunchin' undah dose covahs and git yo'se'f kotched in mah house."

Without further comment the man did as he was told. After he had laid his soiled body and grimy garments between her snowy sheets, Annie Poole carefully rearranged the covering and placed piles of freshly laundered linen on top. Then she gave a pat here and there, eyed the result, and, finding it satisfactory, went back to her cooking.

III

Jim Hammer settled down to the racking business of waiting until the approaching danger should have passed him by. Soon savory odors seeped in to him and he realized that he was hungry. He wished that Annie Poole would bring him something to eat. Just one biscuit. But she wouldn't, he knew. Not she. She was a hard one, Obadiah's mother.

By and by he fell into a sleep from which he was dragged back by the rumbling sound of wheels in the road outside. For a second, fear clutched so tightly at him that he almost leaped from the suffocating shelter of the bed in order to make some active attempt to escape the horror that his capture meant. There was a spasm at his heart, a pain so sharp, so slashing that he had to suppress an impulse to cry out. He felt himself falling.

Down, down, down . . . Everything grew dim and very distant in his memory . . . Vanished . . . Came rushing back.

Outside there was silence. He strained his ears. Nothing. No footsteps. No voices. They had gone on then. Gone without even stopping to ask Annie Poole if she had seen him pass that way. A sigh of relief slipped from him. His thick lips curled in an ugly, cunning smile. It had been smart of him to think of coming to Obadiah's mother's to hide. She was an old demon, but he was safe in her house.

He lay a short while longer, listening intently, and, hearing nothing, started to get up. But immediately he stopped, his yellow eyes glowing like pale flames. He had heard the unmistakable sound of men coming toward the house. Swiftly he slid back into the heavy, hot stuffiness of the bed and lay listening fearfully.

The terrifying sounds drew nearer. Slowly. Heavily. Just for a moment he thought they were not coming in—they took so long. But there was a light knock and the noise of a door being opened. His whole body went taut. His feet felt frozen, his hands clammy, his tongue like a weighted, dying thing. His pounding heart made it hard for his straining ears to hear what they were saying out there.

"Ebenin', Mistah Lowndes." Annie Poole's voice sounded as it always did, sharp and dry.

There was no answer. Or had he missed it? With slow care he shifted his position, bringing his head nearer the edge of the bed. Still he heard nothing. What were they waiting for? Why didn't they ask about him?

Annie Poole, it seemed, was of the same mind. "Ah don' reckon youall done traipsed 'way out hyah jes' foh yo' healf," she hinted.

"There's bad news for you, Annie, I'm 'fraid." The sheriff's voice was low and queer.

Jim Hammer visualized him standing out there—a tall, stooped man, his white tobacco-stained mustache drooping limply at the ends, his nose hooked and sharp, his eyes blue and cold. Bill Lowndes was a hard one too. And white.

"W'atall bad news, Mistah Lowndes?" The woman put the question quietly, directly.

"Obadiah—" the sheriff began—hesitated—began again. "Obadiah—ah—er, he's outside, Annie. I'm 'fraid—"

"Shucks! You done missed. Obadiah, he ain't done nuffin', Mistah Lowndes. Obadiah!" she called stridently. "Obadiah! git hyah an' splain yo'se'f."

But Obadiah didn't answer, didn't come in. Other men came in. Came in with steps that dragged and halted. No one spoke. Not even Annie Poole. Something was laid carefully upon the floor.

"Obadiah, chile," his mother said softly, "Obadiah, chile." Then, with sudden alarm, "He ain't daid, is he? Mistah Lowndes! Obadiah, he ain't daid?"

Jim Hammer didn't catch the answer to that pleading question. A new fear was stealing over him.

"There was a to-do, Annie," Bill Lowndes explained gently, "at the garage back o' the factory. Fellow tryin' to steal tires. Obadiah heerd a noise an' run out with two or three others. Scared the rascal, all right. Fired off his gun an' run. We allow et to be Jim Hammer. Picked up his cap back there. Never was no 'count. Thievin' an' sly. But we'll git 'im, Annie. We'll git 'im."

The man huddled in the featherbed prayed silently. "Oh, Lawd! Ah didn't go to do et. Not Obadiah, Lawd. You knows dat. You knows et." And into his frenzied brain came the thought that it would be better for him to get up and go out to them before Annie Poole gave him away. For he was lost now. With all his great strength he tried to get himself out of the bed. But he couldn't.

"Oh, Lawd!" he moaned. "Oh, Lawd!" His thoughts were bitter and they ran through his mind like panic. He knew that it had come to pass as it said somewhere in the Bible about the wicked. The Lord had stretched out his hand and smitten him. He was paralyzed. He couldn't move hand or foot. He moaned again. It was all there was left for him to do. For in the terror of this new calamity that had come upon him, he had forgotten the waiting danger which was so near out there in the kitchen.

His hunters, however, didn't hear him. Bill Lowndes was saying, "We been a-lookin' for Jim out along the old road. Figured he'd make tracks for Shawboro. You ain't noticed anybody pass this evenin', Annie?"

The reply came promptly, unwaveringly. "No, Ah ain't sees nobody pass. Not yet."

IV

Jim Hammer caught his breath.

"Well," the sheriff concluded, "we'll be gittin' along. Obadiah was a mighty fine boy. Ef they was all like him—I'm sorry, Annie. Anything I c'n do, let me know."

"Thank you, Mistah Lowndes."

With the sound of the door closing on the departing men, power to move came back to the man in the bedroom. He pushed his dirt-caked feet out from the covers and rose up, but crouched down again. He wasn't cold now, but hot all over and burning. Almost he wished that Bill Lowndes and his men had taken him with them.

Annie Poole had come into the room.

It seemed a long time before Obadiah's mother spoke. When she did there were no tears, no reproaches; but there was a raging fury in her voice as she lashed out. "Git outen mah feather baid, Jim Hammer, an' outen mah house, an' don' nevah stop thankin' you' Jesus he done gib you dat black face."

The Gilded Six-Bits

•

(1933)

Zora Neale Hurston

It was a Negro yard around a Negro house in a Negro settlement that looked to the payroll of the G. and G. Fertilizer Works for its support.

But there was something happy about the place. The front yard was parted in the middle by a sidewalk from gate to doorstep, a sidewalk edged on either side by quart bottles driven neck down into the ground on a slant. A mess of homey flowers planted without a plan but blooming cheerily from their helter-skelter places. The fence and house were whitewashed. The porch and steps scrubbed white.

The front door stood open to the sunshine so that the floor of the front room could finish drying after its weekly scouring. It was Saturday. Everything clean from the front gate to the privy house. Yard raked so that the strokes of the rake would make a pattern. Fresh newspaper cut in fancy edge on the kitchen shelves.

Missie May was bathing herself in the galvanized washtub in the bedroom. Her dark-brown skin glistened under the soapsuds that skittered down from her washrag. Her stiff young breasts thrust forward aggressively like broad-based cones with the tips lacquered in black.

She heard men's voices in the distance and glanced at the dollar clock on the dresser.

"Humph! Ah'm way behind time t'day! Joe gointer be heah 'fore Ah git mah clothes on if Ah don't make haste."

She grabbed the clean meal sack at hand and dried herself hurriedly and began to dress. But before she could tie her slippers, there came the ring of singing metal on wood. Nine times.

Missie May grinned with delight. She had not seen the big, tall man come stealing in the gate and creep up the walk, grinning happily at the joyful mischief he was about to commit. But she knew that it was her husband throwing silver dollars in the door for her to pick up and pile beside her plate at dinner. It was this way every Saturday afternoon. The nine dollars hurled into the open door, he scurried to a hiding place behind the cape jasmine bush and waited.

Missie May promptly appeared at the door in mock alarm.

"Who dat chunkin' money in mah do'way?" she demanded. No answer from the yard. She leaped off the porch and began to search the shrubbery. She peeped under the porch and hung over the gate to look up and down the road. While she did this, the man behind the jasmine darted to the chinaberry tree. She spied him and gave chase.

"Nobody ain't gointer be chunkin' money at me and Ah not do 'em nothin'," she shouted in mock anger. He ran around the house with Missie May at his heels. She overtook him at the kitchen door. He ran inside but could not close it after him before she crowded in and locked with him in a rough and tumble. For several minutes the two were a furious mass of male and female energy. Shouting, laughing, twisting, turning, tussling, tickling each other in the ribs; Missie May clutching onto Joe and Joe trying, but not too hard, to get away.

"Missie May, take yo' hand out mah pocket!" Joe shouted out between laughs.

"Ah ain't, Joe, not lessen you gwine gimme whateve' it is good you got in yo' pocket. Turn it go, Joe, do Ah'll tear yo' clothes."

"Go on tear 'em. You de one dat pushes de needles round heah. Move yo' hand, Missie May."

"Lemme git dat paper sack out yo' pocket. Ah bet it's candy kisses."

"Tain't. Move yo' hand. Woman ain't got no business in a man's clothes nohow. Go way."

Missie May gouged way down and gave an upward jerk and triumphed.

"Unhhunh! Ah got it. It 'tis so candy kisses. Ah knowed you had somethin' for me in yo' clothes. Now Ah got to see whut's in every pocket you got."

Joe smiled indulgently and let his wife go through all of his pockets and take out the things that he had hidden there for her to find. She bore off the chewing gum, the cake of sweet soap, the pocket handkerchief as if she had wrested them from him, as if they had not been bought for the sake of this friendly battle.

"Whew! Dat play-fight done got me all warmed up," Joe exclaimed. "Got me some water in de kittle?"

"Yo' water is on de fire and yo' clean things is cross de bed. Hurry up and wash yo'self and git changed so we kin eat. Ah'm hongry." As Missie said this, she bore the steaming kettle into the bedroom.

"You ain't hongry, sugar," Joe contradicted her. "Youse jes' a little empty. Ah'm de one whut's hongry. Ah could eat up camp meetin', back off 'ssociation, and drink Jurdan dry. Have it on de table when Ah git out de tub."

"Don't you mess wid mah business, man. You git in yo' clothes. Ah'm a real wife, not no dress and breath. Ah might not look lak one, but if you burn me, you won't git a thing but wife ashes."

Joe splashed in the bedroom and Missie May fanned around in the kitchen. A fresh red and white checked cloth on the table. Big pitcher of buttermilk beaded with pale drops of butter from the churn. Hot fried mullet, crackling bread, ham hock atop a mound of string beans and new potatoes, and perched on the windowsill, a pone of spicy potato pudding.

Very little talk during the meal, but that little consisted of banter that pretended to deny affection but in reality flaunted it. Like when Missie May reached for a second helping of the tater pone. Joe snatched it out of her reach.

After Missie May had made two or three unsuccessful grabs at the pan, she begged, "Aw, Joe, gimme some mo' dat tater pone."

"Nope, sweetenin' is for us men-folks. Y'all pritty lil frail eels don't need nothin' lak dis. You too sweet already."

"Please, Joe."

"Naw, naw. Ah don't want you to git no sweeter than whut you is already. We goin' down de road a lil piece t'night, so you go put on yo' Sunday-go-to-meetin' things."

Missie May looked at her husband to see if he was playing some prank. "Sho nuff, Joe?"

"Yeah. We goin' to de ice-cream parlor."

"Where de ice-cream parlor at, Joe?"

"A new man done come heah from Chicago and he done got a place and took and opened it up for a ice-cream parlor, and bein' as it's real swell, Ah wants you to be one de first ladies to walk in dere and have some set down."

"Do Jesus. Ah ain't knowed nothin' 'bout it. Who de man done it?"

"Mister Otis D. Slemmons, of spots and places—Memphis, Chicago, Jacksonville, Philadelphia, and so on."

"Dat heavy-set man wid his mouth full of gold teethes?"

"Yeah. Where did you see 'im at?"

"Ah went down to de sto' tuh git a box of lye and Ah seen 'im standin' on de corner talkin' to some of de mens, and Ah come on back and went to scrubbin' de floor, and he passed and tipped his hat whilst Ah was scourin' de steps. Ah thought Ah never seen *him* befo'."

Joe smiled pleasantly. "Yeah, he's up to date. He got de finest clothes Ah ever seen on a colored man's back."

"Aw, he don't look no better in his clothes than you do in yourn. He got a puzzlegut on 'im and he so chuckle-headed, he got a pone behind his neck."

Joe looked down at his own abdomen and said wistfully: "Wisht Ah had a build on me lak he got. He ain't puzzlegutted, honey. He jes' got a corperation. Dat make 'm look lak a rich white man. All rich mens is got some belly on 'em."

"Ah seen de pitchers of Henry Ford and he's a spare-built man, and Rockefeller look lak he ain't got but one gut. But Ford and Rockefeller and dis Slemmons and all de rest kin be as many-gutted as dey please, Ah's satisfied wid you jes' lak you is, baby. God took pattern after a pine tree and built you noble. Youse a pretty man, and if Ah knowed any way to make you mo' pritty still, Ah'd take and do it."

Joe reached over gently and toyed with Missie May's ear. "You jes' say dat cause you love me, but Ah know Ah can't hold no light to Otis D. Slemmons. Ah ain't never been nowhere and Ah ain't got nothin' but you."

Missie May got on his lap and kissed him and he kissed back in kind. Then he went on. "All de womens is crazy 'bout 'im everywhere he go."

"How you know dat, Joe?"

"He told us so hisself."

"Dat don't make it so. His mouf is cut crossways, ain't it? Well, he kin lie jes' lak anybody else."

"Good Lawd, Missie! You womens sho is hard to sense into things. He's got a five-dollar gold piece for a stickpin and he got a ten-dollar gold piece on his watch chain and his mouf is jes' crammed full of gold teethes. Sho wisht it wuz mine. And whut make it so cool, he got money 'cumulated. And womens give it all to 'im."

"Ah don't see whut de womens see on 'im. Ah wouldn't give 'im a wink if de sheriff wuz after 'im."

"Well, he told us how de white womens in Chicago give 'im all dat gold money. So he don't 'low nobody to touch it at all. Not even put dey finger on it. Dey tole 'im not to. You kin make 'miration at it, but don't tetch it."

"Whyn't he stay up dere where dey so crazy 'bout 'im?"

"Ah reckon dey done made 'im vast-rich and he wants to travel some. He says dey wouldn't leave 'im hit a lick of work. He got mo' lady people crazy 'bout him than he kin shake a stick at."

"Joe, Ah hates to see you so dumb. Dat stray nigger jes' tell y'all anything and y'all b'lieve it."

"Go 'head on now, honey, and put on yo' clothes. He talkin' 'bout his pritty womens—Ah want 'im to see *mine*."

Missie May went off to dress and Joe spent the time trying to make his stomach punch out like Slemmons' middle. He tried the rolling swagger of the stranger, but found that his tall bone-and-muscle stride fitted ill with it. He just had time to drop back into his seat before Missie May came in, dressed to go.

On the way home that night Joe was exultant. "Didn't Ah say ole Otis was swell? Cain't he talk Chicago talk? Wuzn't dat funny whut he said when great big fat ole Ida Armstrong come in? He asted me, 'Who is dat broad wid de forte shake?' Dat's a new word. Us always thought forty was a set of figgers but he showed us where it means a whole heap of things. Sometimes he don't say forty, he jes' say thirty-eight and two, and dat mean de same thing. Know whut he tole me when Ah wuz payin' for our ice cream? He say, 'Ah have to hand it to you, Joe. Dat wife of yours is jes' thirty-eight and two. Yessuh, she's forte!' Ain't he killin'?"

"He'll do in case of a rush. But he sho is got uh heap uh gold on 'im. Dat's de first time Ah ever seed gold money. It lookted good on him sho nuff, but it'd look a whole heap better on you."

"Who, me? Missie May, youse crazy! Where would a po'man lak me git gold money from?"

Missie May was silent for a minute, then she said, "Us might find some goin' long de road some time. Us could."

"Who would be losin' gold money round heah? We ain't even seen none dese white folks wearin' no gold money on dey watch chain. You must be figgerin' Mister Packard or Mister Cadillac goin' pass through heah."

"You don't know whut been lost 'round heah. Maybe somebody way back in memorial times lost they gold money and went on off and it ain't never been found. And then if we wuz to find it, you could wear some 'thout havin' no gang of womens lak dat Slemmons say he got."

Joe laughed and hugged her. "Don't be so wishful 'bout me. Ah'm satisfied de way Ah is. So long as Ah be yo' husband, Ah don't keer 'bout nothin' else. Ah'd ruther all de other womens in de world to be dead than for you to have de toothache. Less we go to bed and git our night rest."

It was Saturday night once more before Joe could parade his wife in Slemmons' ice-cream parlor again. He worked the night shift, and Saturday was his only night off. Every other evening around six o'clock he left home, and dying dawn saw him hustling home around the lake, where the challenging sun flung a flaming sword from east to west across the trembling water.

That was the best part of life—going home to Missie May. Their whitewashed house, the mock battle on Saturday, the dinner and ice-cream parlor afterwards, church on Sunday nights, when Missie outdressed any woman in town—all, everything, was right.

One night around eleven the acid ran out at the G. and G. The foreman knocked off the crew and let the steam die down. As Joe rounded the lake on his way home, a lean moon rode the lake in a silver boat. If anybody had asked Joe about the moon on the lake, he would have said he hadn't paid it any attention. But he saw it with his feelings. It made him yearn painfully for Missie. Creation obsessed him. He thought about children. They had been married more than a year now. They had money put away. They ought to be making little feet for shoes. A little boy-child would be about right.

He saw a dim light in the bedroom and decided to come in through the kitchen door. He could wash the fertilizer dust off himself before presenting himself to Missie May. It would be nice for her not to know that he was there until he slipped into his place in bed and hugged her back. She always liked that.

He eased the kitchen door open slowly and silently, but when he went to set his dinner bucket on the table he bumped into a pile of dishes, and something crashed to the floor. He heard his wife gasp in fright and hurried to reassure her.

"Iss me, honey. Don't git skeered."

There was a quick, large movement in the bedroom. A rustle, a thud, and a stealthy silence. The light went out.

What? Robbers? Murderers? Some varmint attacking his helpless wife, perhaps. He struck a match, threw himself on guard, and stepped over the doorsill into the bedroom.

The great belt on the wheel of Time slipped and eternity stood still. By the match light he could see the man's legs fighting with his breeches in his frantic desire to get them on. He had both chance and time to kill the intruder in his helpless condition—half in and half out of his pants—but he was too weak to take action. The shapeless enemies of humanity that live in the hours of Time had waylaid Joe. He was assaulted in his weakness. Like Samson awakening after his haircut. So he just opened his mouth and laughed.

The match went out, and he struck another and lit the lamp. A howling wind raced across his heart, but underneath its fury he heard his wife sobbing and Slemmons pleading for his life. Offering to buy it with all that he had. "Please, suh, don't kill me. Sixty-two dollars at de sto'. Gold money."

Joe just stood. Slemmons looked at the window, but it was screened. Joe stood out like a rough-backed mountain between him and the door. Barring him from escape, from sunrise, from life.

He considered a surprise attack upon the big clown that stood there, laughing like a chessy cat. But before his fist could travel an inch, Joe's own rushed out to crush him like a battering ram. Then Joe stood over him.

"Git into yo' damn rags, Slemmons, and dat quick."

Slemmons scrambled to his feet and into his vest and coat. As he grabbed his hat, Joe in his fury overrode his intentions and grabbed at Slemmons with his left hand and struck at him with his right. The right landed. The left grazed the front of his vest. Slemmons was knocked a somersault into the kitchen and fled through the open door. Joe found himself alone with Missie May, with the golden watch charm clutched in his left fist. A short bit of broken chain dangled between his fingers.

Missie May was sobbing. Wails of weeping without words. Joe stood, and after a while he found out that he had something in his hand. And then he stood and felt without thinking and without seeing with his natural eyes. Missie May kept on crying and Joe kept on feeling so much; and not knowing what to do with all his feelings, he put Slemmons' watch charm in his pants pocket and took a good laugh and went to bed.

"Missie May, whut you cryin' for?"

"Cause Ah love you so hard and Ah know you don't love *me* no mo'."

Joe sank his face into the pillow for a spell, then he said huskily, "You don't know de feelings of dat yet, Missie May."

"Oh Joe, honey, he said he wuz gointer give me dat gold money and he jes' kept on after me—"

Joe was very still and silent for a long time. Then he said, "Well, don't cry no mo', Missie May. Ah got yo' gold piece for you."

The hours went past on their rusty ankles. Joe still and quiet on one bed-rail and Missie May wrung dry of sobs on the other. Finally the sun's tide crept up on the shore of night and drowned all its hours. Missie May, with her face, stiff and streaked, towards the window saw the dawn come into her yard. It was day. Nothing more. Joe wouldn't be coming home as usual. No need to fling open the front door and sweep off the porch, making it nice for Joe. Never no more breakfasts to cook; no more washing and starching of Joe's jumper-jackets and pants. No more nothing. So why get up?

With this strange man in her bed, she felt embarrassed to get up and dress. She decided to wait till he had dressed and gone. Then she would get up, dress quickly, and be gone forever beyond reach of Joe's looks and laughs. But he never moved. Red light turned to yellow, then white.

From beyond the no-man's-land between them came a voice. A strange voice that yesterday had been Joe's.

"Missie May, ain't you gonna fix me no breakfus'?"

She sprang out of bed. "Yeah, Joe. Ah didn't reckon you wuz hongry."

No need to die today. Joe needed her for a few more minutes anyhow.

Soon there was a roaring fire in the cookstove. Water bucket full and two chickens killed. Joe loved fried chicken and rice. She didn't deserve a thing and good Joe was letting her cook him some breakfast. She rushed hot biscuits to the table as Joe took his seat.

He ate with his eyes in his plate. No laughter, no banter.

"Missie May, you ain't eatin' yo breakfus'."

"Ah don't choose none. Ah thank yuh."

His coffee cup was empty. She sprang to refill it. When she turned from the stove and bent to set the cup beside Joe's plate, she saw the yellow coin on the table between them.

She slumped into her seat and wept into her arms.

Presently Joe said calmly, "Missie May, you cry too much. Don't look back lak Lot's wife and turn to salt."

The sun, the hero of every day, the impersonal old man that beams as brightly on death as on birth, came up every morning and raced across the blue dome and dipped into the sea of fire every evening. Water ran down hill and birds nested.

Missie knew why she didn't leave Joe. She couldn't. She loved him too much, but she could not understand why Joe didn't leave her. He was polite, even kind at times, but aloof.

There were no more Saturday romps. No ringing silver dollars to stack beside her plate. No pockets to rifle. In fact, the yellow coin in his trousers was like a monster hiding in the cave of his pockets to destroy her.

She often wondered if he still had it, but nothing could have induced her to ask nor yet to explore his pockets to see for herself. Its shadow was in the house whether or no.

One night Joe came home around midnight and complained of pains ·

in the back. He asked Missie to rub him down with liniment. It had been three months since Missie had touched his body and it all seemed strange. But she rubbed him. Grateful for the chance. Before morning, youth triumphed and Missie exulted. But the next day, as she joyfully made up their bed, beneath her pillow she found the piece of money with the bit of chain attached.

Alone to herself, she looked at the thing with loathing, but look she must. She took it into her hands with trembling and saw first thing that it was no gold piece. It was a gilded half dollar. Then she knew why Slemmons had forbidden anyone to touch his gold. He trusted village eyes at a distance not to recognize his stickpin as a gilded quarter and his watch charm as a four-bit piece.

She was glad at first that Joe had left it there. Perhaps he was through with her punishment. They were man and wife again. Then another thought came clawing at her. He had come home to buy from her as if she were any woman in the long house. Fifty cents for her love. As if to say that he could pay as well as Slemmons. She slid the coin into his Sunday pants pocket and dressed herself and left his house.

Halfway between her house and the quarters she met her husband's mother, and after a short talk she turned and went back home. Never would she admit defeat to that woman, who prayed for it nightly. If she had not the substance of marriage, she had the outside show. Joe must leave *her*. She let him see she didn't want his old gold four-bits too.

She saw no more of the coin for some time, though she knew that Joe could not help finding it in his pocket. But his health kept poor, and he came home at least every ten days to be rubbed.

The sun swept around the horizon, trailing its robes of weeks and days. One morning as Joe came in from work, he found Missie May chopping wood. Without a word he took the ax and chopped a huge pile before he stopped.

"You ain't got no business choppin' wood, and you know it."

"How come? Ah been choppin' it for de last longest."

"Ah ain't blind. You makin' feet for shoes."

"Won't you be glad to have a li'l baby chile, Joe?"

"You know dat 'thout astin' me."

"Iss gointer be a boy chile and de very spit of you."

"You reckon, Missie May?"

"Who else could it look lak?"

Joe said nothing, but he thrust his hand deep into his pocket and fingered something there.

It was almost six months later Missie May took to bed, and Joe went and got his mother to come wait on the house.

Missie May was delivered of a fine boy. Her travail was over when Joe came in from work one morning. His mother and the old women were drinking great bowls of coffee around the fire in the kitchen.

The minute Joe came into the room his mother called him aside.

"How did Missie May make out?" he asked quickly.

"Who, dat gal? She strong as a ox. She gointer have plenty mo'. We done fixed her wid de sugar and lard to sweeten her for de nex' one."

Joe stood silent awhile.

"You ain't ast 'bout de baby, Joe. You oughter be mighty proud cause he sho is de spittin' image of yuh, son. Dat's yourn all right, if you never git another one, dat un is yourn. And you know Ah'm mighty proud too, son, cause Ah never thought well of you marryin' Missie May cause her ma used tuh fan her foot round right smart and Ah been mighty skeered dat Missie May wuz gointer git misput on her road."

Joe said nothing. He fooled around the house till late in the day, then, just before he went to work, he went and stood at the foot of the bed and asked his wife how she felt. He did this every day during the week.

On Saturday he went to Orlando to make his market. It had been a long time since he had done that.

Meat and lard, meal and flour, soap and starch. Cans of corn and tomatoes. All the staples. He fooled around town for a while and bought bananas and apples. Way after a while he went around to the candy store.

"Hello, Joe," the clerk greeted him. "Ain't seen you in a long time."

"Nope, Ah ain't been heah. Been round in spots and places."

"Want some of them molasses kisses you always buy?"

"Yessuh." He threw the gilded half dollar on the counter. "Will dat spend?"

"Whut is it, Joe? Well, I'll be doggone! A gold-plated four-bit piece. Where'd you git it, Joe?"

"Offen a stray nigger dat come through Eatonville. He had it on his watch chain for a charm—goin' round making out iss gold money. Ha ha! He had a quarter on his tie pin and it wuz all golded up too. Tryin' to fool people. Makin' out he so rich and everything. Ha! Ha! Tryin' to tole off folkses wives from home."

"How did you git it, Joe? Did he fool you, too?"

"Who, me? Naw suh! He ain't fooled me none. Know whut Ah done? He come round me wid his smart talk. Ah hauled off and knocked 'im down and took his old four-bits way from 'im. Gointer buy my wife some good ole lasses kisses wid it. Gimme fifty cents worth of dem candy kisses."

"Fifty cents buys a mighty lot of candy kisses, Joe. Why don't you split it up and take some chocolate bars, too. They eat good, too."

"Yessuh, dey do, but Ah wants all dat in kisses. Ah got a li'l boy chile home now. Tain't a week old yet, but he kin suck a sugar tit and maybe eat one them kisses hisself."

Joe got his candy and left the store. The clerk turned to the next customer. "Wisht I could be like these darkies. Laughin' all the time. Nothin' worries 'em."

Back in Eatonville, Joe reached his own front door. There was the ring of singing metal on wood. Fifteen times. Missie May couldn't run to the door, but she crept there as quickly as she could.

"Joe Banks, Ah hear you chunkin' money in mah do'way. You wait till Ah got mah strength back and Ah'm gointer fix you for dat."

The Typewriter

·

(1944)

Dorothy West

It occurred to him, as he eased past the bulging knees of an Irish wash lady and forced an apologetic passage down the aisle of the crowded car, that more than anything in all the world he wanted not to go home. He began to wish passionately that he had never been born, that he had never been married, that he had never been the means of life's coming into the world. He knew quite suddenly that he hated his flat and his family and his friends. And most of all the incessant thing that would "clatter clatter" until every nerve screamed aloud, and the words of the evening paper danced crazily before him, and the insane desire to crush and kill set his fingers twitching.

He shuffled down the street, an abject little man of fifty-odd years, in an ageless overcoat that flapped in the wind. He was cold, and he hated the North, and particularly Boston, and saw suddenly a barefoot pickaninny sitting on a fence in the hot, Southern sun with a piece of steaming corn bread and a piece of fried salt pork in either grimy hand.

He was tired, and he wanted his supper, but he didn't want the beans, and frankfurters, and light bread that Net would undoubtedly have. That Net had had every Monday night since that regrettable moment fifteen years before when he had told her—innocently—that such a supper tasted "right nice. Kinda change from what we always has."

He mounted the four brick steps leading to his door and pulled at the bell, but there was no answering ring. It was broken again, and in a mental flash he saw himself with a multitude of tools and a box of matches shivering in the vestibule after supper. He began to pound lustily on the door and wondered vaguely if his hand would bleed if he smashed the glass. He hated the sight of blood. It sickened him.

Someone was running down the stairs. Daisy probably. Millie would be at that infernal thing, pounding, pounding . . . He entered. The chill of the house swept him. His child was wrapped in a coat. She whispered solemnly, "Poppa, Miz Hicks an' Miz Berry's orful mad. They gointa move if they can't get more heat. The furnace's birnt out all day. Mama couldn't fix it." He said hurriedly, "I'll go right down. I'll go right down." He hoped Mrs. Hicks wouldn't pull open her door and glare at him. She was large and domineering, and her husband was a bully. If her husband ever struck him it would kill him. He hated life, but he didn't want to die. He was afraid of God, and in his wildest flights of fancy couldn't imagine himself an angel. He went softly down the stairs.

He began to shake the furnace fiercely. And he shook into it every wrong, mumbling softly under his breath. He began to think back over his uneventful years, and it came to him as rather a shock that he had never sworn in all his life. He wondered uneasily if he dared say "damn." It was taken for granted that a man swore when he tended a stubborn furnace. And his strongest interjection was "Great balls of fire!"

The cellar began to warm, and he took off his inadequate overcoat that was streaked with dirt. Well, Net would have to clean that. He'd be damned—! It frightened him and thrilled him. He wanted suddenly to rush upstairs and tell Mrs. Hicks if she didn't like the way he was running things, she could get out. But he heaped another shovelful of coal on the fire and sighed. He would never be able to get away from himself and the routine of years.

He thought of that eager Negro lad of seventeen who had come North to seek his fortune. He had walked jauntily down Boylston Street, and even his own kind had laughed at the incongruity of him. But he had thrown up his head and promised himself: "You'll have an office here some day. With plate-glass windows and a real mahogany desk." But, though he didn't know it then, he was not the progressive type. And he became successively, in the years, bellboy, porter, waiter, cook, and, finally, janitor in a downtown office building.

He had married Net when he was thirty-three and a waiter. He had married her partly because—though he might not have admitted it— there was no one to eat the expensive delicacies the generous cook gave him every night to bring home. And partly because he dared hope there might be a son to fulfill his dreams. But Millie had come, and, after her, twin girls who had died within two weeks, then Daisy, and it was tacitly understood that Net was done with childbearing.

Life, though flowing monotonously, had flowed peacefully enough until that sucker of sanity became a sitting-room fixture. Intuitively at the very first he had felt its undesirability. He had suggested hesitatingly that they couldn't afford it. Three dollars: food and fuel. Times were hard, and the twenty dollars apiece the respective husbands of Miz Hicks and Miz Berry irregularly paid was only five dollars more than the thirty-five a month he paid his own Hebraic landlord. And the Lord knew his salary was little enough. At which point Net spoke her piece, her voice rising shrill. "God knows I never complain 'bout nothin'. Ain't no other woman got less than me. I bin wearin' this same dress here five years an' I'll wear it another five. But I don't want nothin'. I ain't never wanted nothin'. An' when I does as', it's only for my children. You're a poor sort of father if you can't give that child jes' three dollars a month to rent that typewriter. Ain't 'nother girl in school ain't got one. An' mos' of 'ems bought an' paid for. You know yourself how Millie is. She wouldn't as' me for it till she had to. An' I ain't going to disappoint her. She's goin' to get that typewriter Saturday, mark my words."

On a Monday, then, it had been installed. And in the months that followed, night after night he listened to the murderous "tack, tack, tack" that was like a vampire slowly drinking his blood. If only he could escape. Bar a door against the sound of it. But tied hand and foot by the economic fact that "Lord knows we can't afford to have fires burnin' an' lights lit all over the flat. You'all gotta set in one room. An' when y'get tired settin' y' c'n go to bed. Gas bill was somep'n scandalous last month."

He heaped a final shovelful of coal on the fire and watched the first blue flames. Then, his overcoat under his arm, he mounted the cellar stairs. Mrs. Hicks was standing in her kitchen door, arms akimbo. "It's warmin'," she volunteered.

"Yeh." He was conscious of his grime-streaked face and hands. "It's warmin'. I'm sorry 'bout all day."

She folded her arms across her ample bosom. "Tending a furnace ain't a woman's work. I don't blame your wife none 'tall."

Unsuspecting, he was grateful. "Yeh, it's pretty hard for a woman. I always look after it 'fore I goes to work, but some days it jes' ac's up."

"Y'oughta have a janitor, that's what y'ought," she flung at him. "The same cullud man that tends them apartments would be willin'. Mr. Taylor has him. It takes a man to run a furnace, and when the man's away all day—"

"I know," he interrupted, embarrassed and hurt, "I know. Tha's right, Miz Hicks, tha's right. But I ain't in a position to make no improvements. Times is hard."

She surveyed him critically. "Your wife called down 'bout three times while you was in the cellar. I reckon she wants you for supper."

"Thanks," he mumbled and escaped up the back stairs.

He hung up his overcoat in the closet, telling himself, a little lamely, that it wouldn't take him more'n a minute to clean it up himself after supper. After all, Net was tired and prob'bly worried what with Miz Hicks and all. And he hated men who made slaves of their womenfolk. Good old Net.

He tidied up in the bathroom, washing his face and hands carefully and cleanly so as to leave no—or very little—stain on the roller towel. It was hard enough for Net, God knew.

He entered the kitchen. The last spirals of steam were rising from his supper. One thing about Net: she served a full plate. He smiled appreciatively at her unresponsive back, bent over the kitchen sink. There was no one could bake beans just like Net's. And no one who could find a market with frankfurters quite so fat.

He sank down at his place. "Evenin', hon."

He saw her back stiffen. "If your supper's cold, 'tain't my fault. I called and called."

He said hastily, "It's fine, Net, fine. Piping."

She was the usual tired housewife. "Y'oughta et your supper 'fore you fooled with that furnace. I ain't bothered 'bout them niggers. I got all my dishes washed 'cept yours. An' I hate to mess up my kitchen after I once get it straightened up."

He was humble. "I'll give that old furnace an extra lookin' after in the mornin'. It'll las' all day tomorrow, hon."

"An' on top of that," she continued, unheeding him and giving a final wrench to her dish towel, "that confounded bell don't ring. An'—"

"I'll fix it after supper," he interposed hastily.

She hung up her dish towel and came to stand before him looming large and yellow. "An' that old Miz Berry, she claim she was expectin' comp'ny. An' she knows they must 'a' come an' gone while she was in her kitchen an' couldn't be at her winder to watch for 'em. Old liar." She brushed back a lock of naturally straight hair. "She wasn't expectin' nobody."

"Well, you know how some folks are—"

"Fools! Half the world" was her vehement answer. "I'm goin' in the front room an' set down a spell. I bin on my feet all day. Leave them dishes on the table. God knows I'm tired, but I'll come back an' wash 'em." But they both knew, of course, that he, very clumsily, would.

At precisely quarter past nine when he, strained at last to the breaking point, uttering an inhuman, strangled cry, flung down his paper, clutched at his throat, and sprang to his feet, Millie's surprised young voice, shocking him to normalcy, heralded the first of that series of great moments that every humble little middle-class man eventually experiences.

"What's the matter, Poppa? You sick? I wanted you to help me."

He drew out his handkerchief and wiped his hot hands. "I declare I must 'a' fallen asleep an' had a nightmare. No, I ain't sick. What you want, hon?"

"Dictate me a letter, Poppa. I c'n do sixty words a minute.—You know, like a business letter. You know, like those men in your building dictate to their stenographers. Don't you hear 'em sometimes?"

"Oh, sure, I know, hon. Poppa'll help you. Sure. I hear that Mr. Browning—sure."

Net rose. "Guess I'll put this child to bed. Come on now, Daisy, without no fuss.—Then I'll run up to Pa's. He ain't bin well all week."

When the door closed behind them, he crossed to his daughter, conjured the image of Mr. Browning in the process of dictating, so arranged himself, and coughed importantly.

"Well, Millie—"

"Oh, Poppa, is that what you'd call your stenographer?" she teased. "And anyway pretend I'm really one—and you're really my boss, and this letter's real important."

A light crept into his dull eyes. Vigor through his thin blood. In a brief moment the weight of years fell from him like a cloak. Tired, bent, little old man that he was, he smiled, straightened, tapped impressively against his teeth with a toil-stained finger, and became that enviable emblem of American life: a businessman.

"You be Miz Hicks, huh, honey? Course we can't both use the same name. I'll be J. Lucius Jones. J. Lucius. All them real big doin' men use their middle names. Jus' kinda looks big doin', doncha think, hon? Looks like money, huh? J. Lucius." He uttered a sound that was like the proud cluck of a strutting hen. "J. Lucius." It rolled like oil from his tongue.

His daughter twisted impatiently. "Now, Poppa—I mean, Mr. Jones, sir—please begin. I am ready for dictation, sir."

He was in that office on Boylston Street, looking with visioning eyes through its plate-glass windows, tapping with impatient fingers on its real mahogany desk.

"Ah—Beaker Brothers, Park Square Building, Boston, Mass. Ah—Gentlemen: In reply to yours at the seventh instant I would state—"

Every night thereafter in the weeks that followed, with Daisy packed off to bed, and Net "gone up to Pa's" or nodding unobtrusively in her corner, there was the chameleon change of a Court Street janitor to J. Lucius Jones, dealer in stocks and bonds. He would stand, posturing importantly, flicking imaginary dust from his coat lapel, or, his hands locked behind his back, he would stride up and down, earnestly and seriously debating the advisability of buying copper with the market in such a fluctuating state. Once a week, too, he stopped in at Jerry's, and after a preliminary purchase of cheap cigars, bought the latest trade papers, mumbling an embarrassed explanation: "I got a little money. Think I'll invest it in reliable stock."

The letters Millie typed and subsequently discarded, he rummaged for later and, under cover of writing to his brother in the South, laboriously with a great many fancy flourishes, signed each neatly typed sheet with the exalted J. Lucius Jones.

Later, when he mustered the courage, he suggested tentatively to Millie that it might be fun—just fun, of course!—to answer his letters. One night—he laughed a good deal louder and longer than necessary—he'd be J. Lucius Jones, and the next night—here he swallowed hard and looked a little frightened—Rockefeller or Vanderbilt or Morgan—just for fun, y'understand! To which Millie gave consent. It mattered little to her one way or the other. It was practice, and that was what she needed. Very soon now she'd be in the hundred class. Then maybe she could get a job!

He was growing very careful of his English. Occasionally—and it must be admitted, ashamedly—he made surreptitious ventures into the dictionary. He had to, of course. J. Lucius Jones would never say "Y'got to" when he meant "It is expedient." And, old brain though he was, he learned quickly and easily, juggling words with amazing facility.

Eventually he bought stamps and envelopes—long, important-looking envelopes—and stammered apologetically to Millie, "Honey, Poppa thought it'd help you if you learned to type envelopes, too. Reckon you'll have to do that, too, when y'get a job. Poor old man," he swallowed painfully, "came round selling these envelopes. You know how 'tis. So I had to buy 'em." Which was satisfactory to Millie. If she saw through her father, she gave no sign. After all, it was practice, and Mr. Hennessey had said that—though not in just those words.

He had got in the habit of carrying those self-addressed envelopes in his inner pocket where they bulged impressively. And occasionally he would take them out—on the car usually—and smile upon them. This one might be from J. P. Morgan. This one from Henry Ford. And a million-dollar deal involved in each. That narrow little spinster, who, upon his sitting down, had drawn herself away from his contact, was shunning J. Lucius Jones!

Once, led by some sudden, strange impulse, as an outgoing car rumbled up out of the subway, he got out a letter, darted a quick, shamed glance about him, dropped it in an adjacent box, and swung aboard the car, feeling, dazedly, as if he had committed a crime. And the next night he sat in the sitting room quite on edge until Net said suddenly, "Look here, a real important letter come today for you, Pa. Here 'tis. What you s'pose it says," and he reached out a hand that trembled. He made brief explanation. "Advertisement, hon. Thassal."

They came quite frequently after that, and despite the fact that he knew them by heart, he read them slowly and carefully, rustling the sheet, and making inaudible, intelligent comments. He was, in these moments, pathetically earnest.

Monday, as he went about his janitor's duties, he composed in his mind the final letter from J. P. Morgan that would consummate a big business deal. For days now letters had passed between them. J. P. had been at first quite frankly uninterested. He had written tersely and briefly. He wrote glowingly of the advantages of a pact between them. Daringly he argued in terms of billions. And at last J. P. had written his next letter would be decisive. Which next letter, this Monday, as he trailed about the office building, was writing itself on his brain.

That night Millie opened the door for him. Her plain face was transformed. "Poppa—Poppa, I got a job! Twelve dollars a week to start with! Isn't that *swell*!"

He was genuinely pleased. "Honey, I'm glad. Right glad," and went up the stairs, unsuspecting.

He ate his supper hastily, went down into the cellar to see about his fire, returned, and carefully tidied up, informing his reflection in the bathroom mirror, "Well, J. Lucius, you c'n expect that final letter any day now."

He entered the sitting room. The phonograph was playing. Daisy was singing lustily. Strange. Net was talking animatedly to—Millie, busy with needle and thread over a neat, little frock. His wild glance darted to the table. The pretty little centerpiece, the bowl and wax flowers all neatly arranged: the typewriter gone from its accustomed place. It seemed an hour before he could speak. He felt himself trembling. Went hot and cold.

"Millie—your typewriter's—gone!"

She made a deft little in-and-out movement with her needle. "It's the eighth, you know. When the man came today for the money, I sent it back. I won't need it no more—now!—The money's on the mantelpiece, Poppa."

"Yeh," he muttered. "All right."

He sank down in his chair, fumbled for the paper, found it.

Net said, "Your poppa wants to read. Stop your noise, Daisy."

She obediently stopped both her noise and the phonograph, took up her book, and became absorbed. Millie went on with her sewing in placid anticipation of the morrow. Net immediately began to nod, gave a curious snort, slept.

Silence. That crowded in on him, engulfed him. That blurred his vision, dulled his brain. Vast, white, impenetrable . . . His ears strained for the old familiar sound. And silence beat upon them . . . The words of the evening paper jumbled together. He read: J. P. Morgan goes—

It burst upon him. Blinded him. His hands groped for the bulge beneath his coat. Why this—this was the end! The end of those great moments —the end of everything! Bewildering pain tore through him. He clutched at his heart and felt, almost, the jagged edges drive into his hand. A lethargy swept down upon him. He could not move, nor utter sound. He could not pray, or curse.

Against the wall of that silence J. Lucius Jones crashed and died.

See How They Run

●

(1951)

Mary Elizabeth Vroman

A bell rang. Jane Richards squared the sheaf of records decisively in the large Manila folder, placed it in the right-hand corner of her desk, and stood up. The chatter of young voices subsided, and forty-three small faces looked solemnly and curiously at the slight young figure before them. The bell stopped ringing.

I wonder if they're as scared of me as I am of them. She smiled brightly.

"Good morning, children, I am Miss Richards." *As if they don't know*—the door of the third-grade room had a neat new sign pasted above it with her name in bold black capitals; and anyway, a new teacher's name is the first thing that children find out about on the first day of school. Nevertheless, she wrote it for their benefit in large white letters on the blackboard.

"I hope we will all be happy working and playing together this year." *Now why does that sound so trite?* "As I call the roll will you please stand, so that I may get to know you as soon as possible, and if you like you may tell me something about yourselves, how old you are, where you live, what your parents do, and perhaps something about what you did during the summer."

Seated, she checked the names carefully. "Booker T. Adams."

Booker stood, gangling and stoop-shouldered; he began to recite tiredly, "My name is Booker T. Adams, I'se ten years old." *Shades of Uncle Tom!* "I live on Painter's Path." He paused, the look he gave her was tinged with something very akin to contempt. "I didn't do nothing in the summer," he said deliberately.

"Thank you, Booker." Her voice was even. "George Allen." *Must*

129

remember to correct that stoop . . . Where is Painter's Path? . . . How to go about correcting those speech defects? . . . Go easy, Jane, don't antagonize them . . . They're clean enough, but this is the first day . . . How can one teacher do any kind of job with a load of forty-three? . . . Thank heaven the building is modern and well built even though it is overcrowded, not like some I've seen—no potbellied stove.

"Sarahlene Clover Babcock." *Where do these names come from? . . . Up from slavery . . . How high is up?* Jane smothered a sudden desire to giggle. Outside she was calm and poised and smiling. Clearly she called the names, listening with interest, making a note here and there, making no corrections—not yet.

She experienced a moment of brief inward satisfaction: *I'm doing very well, this is what is expected of me . . .* Orientation to Teaching . . . Miss Murray's voice beat a distant tattoo in her memory. Miss Murray with the Junoesque figure and the moon face . . . "The ideal teacher personality is one which, combining in itself all the most desirable qualities, expresses itself with quiet assurance in its endeavor to mold the personalities of the students in the most desirable patterns" . . . Dear, dull Miss Murray.

She made mental estimates of the class. *What a cross section of my people they represent,* she thought. *Here and there signs of evident poverty, here and there children of obviously well-to-do parents.*

"My name is Rachel Veronica Smith. I am nine years old. I live at Six-oh-seven Fairview Avenue. My father is a Methodist minister. My mother is a housewife. I have two sisters and one brother. Last summer Mother and Daddy took us all to New York to visit my Aunt Jen. We saw lots of wonderful things. There are millions and millions of people in New York. One day we went on a ferryboat all the way up the Hudson River—that's a great big river as wide as this town, and—"

The children listened wide-eyed. Jane listened carefully. *She speaks good English. Healthy, erect, and even perhaps a little smug. Immaculately well dressed from the smoothly braided hair, with two perky bows, to the shiny brown oxford . . . Bless you, Rachel, I'm so glad to have you.*

"—and the buildings are all very tall, some of them nearly reach the sky."

"Haw-haw"—this from Booker, cynically.

"Well, they are, too." Rachel swung around, fire in her eyes and insistence in every line of her round, compact body.

"Ain't no buildings as tall as the sky, is dere, Miz Richards?"

Crisis No. 1. Jane chose her answer carefully. *As high as the sky . . . mustn't turn this into a lesson in science . . . all in due time.* "The sky is a long way out, Booker, but the buildings in New York are very tall indeed. Rachel was only trying to show you how very tall they are. In fact, the tallest building in the whole world is in New York City."

"They call it the Empire State Building," interrupted Rachel, heady with her new knowledge and Jane's corroboration.

Booker wasn't through. "You been dere, Miz Richards?"

"Yes, Booker, many times. Someday I shall tell you more about it. Maybe Rachel will help me. Is there anything you'd like to add, Rachel?"

"I would like to say that we are glad you are our new teacher, Miss Richards." Carefully she sat down, spreading her skirt with her plump hands, her smile angelic.

Now I'll bet me a quarter her reverend father told her to say that. "Thank you, Rachel."

The roll call continued . . . Tanya, slight and pinched, with the toes showing through the very white sneakers, the darned and faded but clean blue dress, the gentle voice like a tinkling bell, and the beautiful sensitive face . . . Boyd and Lloyd, identical in their starched overalls, and the slightly vacant look . . . Marjorie Lee, all of twelve years old, the well-developed body moving restlessly in the childish dress, the eyes too wise, the voice too high . . . Joe Louis, the intelligence in the brilliant black eyes gleaming above the threadbare clothes. *Lives of great men all remind us—Well, I have them all . . . Frederick Douglass, Franklin Delano, Abraham Lincoln, Booker T., Joe Louis, George Washington . . . What a great burden you bear, little people, heirs to all your parents' stillborn dreams of greatness. I must not fail you.* The last name on the list . . . C. T. Young. Jane paused, small lines creasing her forehead. She checked the list again.

"C. T., what is your name? I only have your initials on my list."

"Dat's all my name, C. T. Young."

"No, dear, I mean what does C. T. stand for? Is it Charles or Clarence?"

"No'm, jest C. T."

"But I can't put that in my register, dear."

Abruptly Jane rose and went to the next room. Rather timidly she waited to speak to Miss Nelson, the second-grade teacher, who had the formidable record of having taught all of sixteen years. Miss Nelson was large and smiling.

"May I help you, dear?"

"Yes, please. It's about C. T. Young. I believe you had him last year."

"Yes, and the year before that. You'll have him two years, too."

"Oh? Well, I was wondering what name you registered him under. All the information I have is C. T. Young."

"That's all there is, honey. Lots of these children only have initials."

"You mean . . . Can't something be done about it?"

"What?" Miss Nelson was still smiling, but clearly impatient.

"I . . . Well . . . Thank you." Jane left quickly.

Back in Room 3 the children were growing restless. Deftly Jane passed out the rating tests and gave instructions. Then she called C. T. to her. He was as small as an eight-year-old, and hungry-looking, with enormous, guileless eyes and a beautifully shaped head.

"How many years did you stay in the second grade, C. T.?"

"Two."

"And in the first?"

"Two."

"How old are you?"

" 'Leven."

"When will you be twelve?"

"Nex' month."

And they didn't care . . . Nobody ever cared enough about one small boy to give him a name.

"You are a very lucky little boy, C. T. Most people have to take the name somebody gave them whether they like it or not, but you can choose your very own."

"Yeah?" The dark eyes were belligerent. "My father named me C. T. after hisself, Miz Richards, an dat's my name."

Jane felt unreasonably irritated. "How many children are there in your family, C. T.?"

" 'Leven."

"How many are there younger than you?" she asked.

"Seven."

Very gently, "Did you have your breakfast this morning, dear?"

The small figure in the too-large trousers and the too-small shirt drew itself up to full height. "Yes'm, I had fried chicken, and rice, and coffee, and rolls, and oranges, too."

Oh, you poor darling. You poor proud lying darling. Is that what you'd like for breakfast?

She asked, "Do you like school, C. T.?"

"Yes'm," he told her suspiciously.

She leafed through the pile of records. "Your record says you haven't been coming to school very regularly. Why?"

"I dunno."

"Did you eat last year in the lunchroom?"

"No'm."

"Did you ever bring a lunch?"

"No'm, I eats such a big breakfast, I doan git hungry at lunchtime."

"Children need to eat lunch to help them grow tall and strong, C. T. So from now on you'll eat lunch in the lunchroom"—an afterthought: *Perhaps it's important to make him think I believe him*—"and from now on maybe you'd better not eat such a big breakfast."

Decisively she wrote his name at the top of what she knew to be an already too-large list. "Only those in absolute necessity," she had been told by Mr. Johnson, the kindly, harassed principal. "We'd like to feed them all, so many are underfed, but we just don't have the money." Well, this was absolute necessity if she ever saw it.

"What does your father do, C. T.?"

"He work at dat big factory 'cross town, he make plenty money, Miz Richards." The record said "unemployed."

"Would you like to be named Charles Thomas?"

The expressive eyes darkened, but the voice was quiet. "No'm."

"Very well." Thoughtfully Jane opened the register; she wrote firmly: C. T. Young.

October is a witching month in the Southern United States. The richness of the golds and reds and browns of the trees forms an enchanted filigree through which the lilting voices of children at play seem to float, embodied like so many nymphs of Pan.

Jane had played a fast-and-furious game of tag with her class and now she sat quietly under the gnarled old oak, watching the tireless play, feeling the magic of the sun through the leaves warmly dappling her skin, the soft breeze on the nape of her neck like a lover's hands, and her own drowsy lethargy. *Paul, Paul my darling . . . how long for us now?* She had worshiped Paul Carlyle since they were freshmen together. On graduation day he had slipped the small circlet of diamonds on her finger . . . "A teacher's salary is small, Jane. Maybe we'll be lucky enough to get work together, then in a year or so we can be married. Wait for me, darling, wait for me!"

But in a year or so Paul had gone to war, and Jane went out alone to teach . . . Lansing Creek—one year . . . the leaky roof, the potbellied stove, the water from the well . . . Maryweather Point—two years . . . the tight-lipped spinster principal with the small, vicious face and the small, vicious soul . . . Three hard, lonely years and then she had been lucky.

The superintendent had praised her. "You have done good work, Miss—ah—Jane. This year you are to be placed at Centertown High— that is, of course, if you care to accept the position."

Jane had caught her breath. Centertown was the largest and best equipped of all the schools in the county, only ten miles from home and Paul—for Paul had come home, older, quieter, but still Paul. He was teaching now more than a hundred miles away, but they went home every other weekend to their families and each other . . . "Next summer you'll be Mrs. Paul Carlyle, darling. It's hard for us to be apart so much. I guess we'll have to be for a long time till I can afford to support you. But, sweet, these little tykes need us so badly." He had held her close, rubbing the nape of the neck under the soft curls. "We have a big job, those of us who teach," he had told her, "a never-ending and often thankless job, Jane, to supply the needs of these kids who lack so much."

They wrote each other long letters, sharing plans and problems. She wrote him about C. T. "I've adopted him, darling. He's so pathetic and so determined to prove that he's not. He learns nothing at all, but I can't let myself believe that he's stupid, so I keep trying."

"Miz Richards, please, ma'am." Tanya's beautiful amber eyes sought hers timidly. Her brown curls were tangled from playing, her cheeks a bright red under the tightly-stretched olive skin. The elbows jutted awkwardly out of the sleeves of the limp cotton dress, which could not conceal the finely chiseled bones in their pitiable fleshlessness. As always when she looked at her, Jane thought, *What a beautiful child!* So unlike the dark, gaunt, morose mother, and the dumpy, pasty-faced father who had visited her that first week. A fairy's changeling. *You'll make a lovely angel to grace the throne of God, Tanya! Now what made me think of that?*

"Please, ma'am, I'se sick."

Gently Jane drew her down beside her. She felt the parchment skin, noted the unnaturally bright eyes. *Oh, dear God, she's burning up!* "Do you hurt anywhere, Tanya?"

"My head, ma'am, and I'se so tired." Without warning she began to cry.

"How far do you live, Tanya?"

"Two miles."

"You walk to school?"

"Yes'm."

"Do any of your brothers have a bicycle?"

"No'm."

"Rachel!" *Bless you for always being there when I need you.* "Hurry, dear, to the office and ask Mr. Johnson please to send a big boy with a bicycle to take Tanya home. She's sick."

Rachel ran.

"Hush now, dear, we'll get some cool water, and then you'll be home in a little while. Did you feel sick this morning?"

"Yes'm, but Mot Dear sent me to school anyway. She said I just wanted to play hooky." *Keep smiling, Jane. Poor, ambitious, well-meaning parents, made bitter at the seeming futility of dreaming dreams for this lovely child . . . willing her to rise above the drabness of your own meager existence . . . too angry with life to see that what she needs most is your love and care and right now medical attention.*

Jane bathed the child's forehead with cool water at the fountain. *Do the white schools have a clinic? I must ask Paul. Do they have a lounge or a couch where they can lay one wee sick head? Is there anywhere in this town free medical service for one small child . . . born black?*

The boy with the bicycle came. "Take care of her now, ride slowly and carefully, and take her straight home . . . Keep the newspaper over your head, Tanya, to keep out the sun, and tell your parents to call the doctor." But she knew they wouldn't—because they couldn't!

The next day Jane went to see Tanya.

"She's sho' nuff sick, Miz Richards," the mother said. "She's always been a puny child, but this time she's took real bad, throat's all raw, talk all out of her haid las' night. I been using a poultice and some herb brew but she ain't got no better."

"Have you called a doctor, Mrs. Fulton?"

"No'm, we cain't afford it, an' Jake, he doan believe in doctors nohow."

Jane waited till the tide of high bright anger welling in her heart and beating in her brain had subsided. When she spoke, her voice was deceptively gentle. "Mrs. Fulton, Tanya is a very sick little girl. She is your only little girl. If you love her, I advise you to have a doctor to her, for if you don't . . . Tanya may die."

The wail that issued from the thin figure seemed to have no part in reality.

Jane spoke hurriedly. "Look, I'm going into town, I'll send a doctor out. Don't worry about paying him. We can see about that later." Impulsively she put her arms around the taut, motionless shoulders. "Don't you worry, honey, it's going to be all right."

●

There was a kindliness in the doctor's weather-beaten face that warmed Jane's heart, but his voice was brusque. "You sick, girl? Well?"

"No, sir. I'm not sick." *What long sequence of events has caused even the best of you to look on even the best of us as menials?* "I'm a teacher at Centertown High. There's a little girl in my class who is very ill. Her parents are very poor. I came to see if you would please go to see her."

He looked at her, amused.

"Of course I'll pay the bill, doctor," she added hastily.

"In that case . . . well . . . where does she live?"

Jane told him. "I think it's diphtheria, doctor."

He raised his eyebrows. "Why?"

Jane sat erect. *Don't be afraid, Jane! You're as good a teacher as he is a doctor, and you made an A in that course in childhood diseases.* "High fever, restlessness, sore throat, headache, croupy cough, delirium. It could, of course, be tonsillitis or scarlet fever, but that cough—well, I'm only guessing, of course," she finished lamely.

"Hmph." The doctor's face was expressionless. "Well, we'll see. Have your other children been inoculated?"

"Yes, sir. Doctor, if the parents ask, please tell them that the school is paying for your services."

This time he was wide-eyed.

The lie haunted her. She spoke to the other teachers about it the next day at recess. "She's really very sick, maybe you'd like to help?"

Mary Winters, the sixth-grade teacher, was the first to speak. "Richards, I'd like to help, but I've got three kids of my own, and so you see how it is?"

Jane saw.

"Trouble with you, Richards, is you're too emotional." This from Nelson. "When you've taught as many years as I have, my dear, you'll learn not to bang your head against a stone wall. It may sound hard-hearted to you, but one just can't worry about one child more or less when one has nearly fifty."

The pain in the back of her eyes grew more insistent. "I can," she said.

"I'll help, Jane," said Marilyn Andrews, breathless, bouncy newlywed Marilyn. "Here's two bucks. It's all I've got, but nothing's plenty for me." Her laughter pealed echoing down the hall.

"I've got a dollar, Richards"—this from mousy, severe little Miss Mitchell—"though I'm not sure I agree with you."

"Why don't you ask the high-school faculty?" said Marilyn. "Better still, take it up in teachers' meeting."

"Mr. Johnson has enough to worry about now," snapped Nelson. *Why, she's mad*, thought Jane, *mad because I'm trying to give a helpless little tyke a chance to live, and because Marilyn and Mitchell helped.*

The bell rang. Wordlessly Jane turned away. She watched the children troop in noisily, an ancient nursery rhyme running through her head:

> *Three blind mice, three blind mice,*
> *See how they run, see how they run,*
> *They all ran after the farmer's wife,*
> *She cut off their tails with a carving knife.*
> *Did you ever see such a sight in your life*
> *As three blind mice?*

Only this time, it was forty-three mice. Jane giggled. *Why, I'm hysterical*, she thought in surprise. *The mice thought the sweet-smelling farmer's wife might have bread and a wee bit of cheese to offer poor blind mice, but the farmer's wife didn't like poor, hungry, dirty blind mice. So she cut off their tails. Then they couldn't run anymore, only wobble. What happened then? Maybe they starved, those that didn't bleed to death. Running round in circles. Running where, little mice?*

She talked to the high-school faculty, and Mr. Johnson. Altogether she got eight dollars.

The following week she received a letter from the doctor:

Dear Miss Richards:

I am happy to inform you that Tanya is greatly improved, and with careful nursing will be well enough in about eight weeks to return to school. She is very frail, however, and will require special care. I have made three visits to her home. In view of the peculiar circumstances, I am donating my services. The cost of the medicines, however, amounts to the sum of $15. I am referring this to you as you requested. What a beautiful child!

Yours sincerely,
JONATHAN H. SINCLAIR, M.D.

P.S. She had diphtheria.

Bless you forever and ever, Jonathan H. Sinclair, M.D. For all your long Southern heritage, "a man's a man for a' that . . . and a' that!"

Her heart was light that night when she wrote to Paul. Later she made plans in the darkness. *You'll be well and fat by Christmas, Tanya, and you'll be a lovely angel in my pageant . . . I must get the children to save pennies . . . We'll send you milk and oranges and eggs, and we'll make funny little get-well cards to keep you happy.*

But by Christmas Tanya was dead!

The voice from the dark figure was quiet, even monotonous. "Jake an' me, we always work so hard, Miz Richards. We didn't neither one have no schooling much when we was married—folks never had much money, but we was happy. Jake, he tenant farm. I tuk in washing—we plan to save and buy a little house and farm of our own someday. Den the children come. Six boys, Miz Richards—all in a hurry. We both want the boys to finish school, mebbe go to college. We try not to keep them out to work the farm, but sometimes we have to. Then come Tanya. Just like a little yellow rose she was, Miz Richards, all pink and gold . . . and her voice like a silver bell. We think when she grow up an' finish school she take voice lessons—be like Marian Anderson. We think mebbe by then the boys would be old enough to help. I was kinda feared for her when she get sick, but then she start to get better. She was doing so well, Miz Richards. Den it get cold, an' the fire so hard to keep all night long, an' eben the newspapers in the cracks doan keep the win' out, an' I give her all my kivver; but one night she jest tuk to shivering an' talking all out her haid—sat right up in bed, she did. She call your name onc't or twice, Miz Richards, then she say, 'Mot Dear, does Jesus love me like Miz Richards say in Sunday school?' I say, 'Yes, honey.' She say, 'Effen I die will I see Jesus?' I say, 'Yes, honey, but you ain't gwine die.' But she did, Miz Richards . . . jest smiled an' laid down—jest smiled an' laid down."

It is terrible to see such hopeless resignation in such tearless eyes . . . One little mouse stopped running . . . *You'll make a lovely angel to grace the throne of God, Tanya!*

Jane did not go to the funeral. Nelson and Andrews sat in the first pew. Everyone on the faculty contributed to a beautiful wreath. Jane preferred not to think about that.

C. T. brought a lovely potted rose to her the next day. "Miz Richards, ma'am, do you think this is pretty enough to go on Tanya's grave?"

"Where did you get it, C. T.?"

"I stole it out Miz Adams' front yard, right out of that li'l' glass house she got there. The door was open, Miz Richards, she got plenty, she won't miss this li'l' one."

You queer little bundle of truth and lies. What do I do now? Seeing the tears blinking back in the anxious eyes, she said gently, "Yes, C. T., the rose is nearly as beautiful as Tanya is now. She will like it."

"You mean she will know I put it there, Miz Richards? She ain't daid at all?"

"Maybe she'll know, C. T. You see, nothing that is beautiful ever dies as long as we remember it."

So you loved Tanya, little mouse? The memory of her beauty is yours to keep now forever and always, my darling. Those things money can't buy. They've all been trying, but your tail isn't off yet, is it, brat? Not by a long shot. Suddenly she laughed aloud.

He looked at her wonderingly. "What you laughing at, Miz Richards?"

"I'm laughing because I'm happy, C. T.," and she hugged him.

Christmas with its pageantry and splendor came and went. Back from the holidays, Jane had an oral English lesson.

"We'll take this period to let you tell about your holidays, children."

On the weekends that Jane stayed in Centertown she visited different churches, and taught in the Sunday schools when she was asked. She had tried to impress on the children the reasons for giving at Christmastime. In class they had talked about things they could make for gifts, and ways they could save money to buy them. Now she stood by the window, listening attentively, reaping the fruits of her labors.

"I got a doll and a doll carriage for Christmas. Her name is Gladys, and the carriage has red wheels, and I got a tea set and—"

"I got a bicycle and a catcher's mitt."

"We all went to a party and had ice cream and cake."

"I got—"

"I got—"

"I got—"

Score one goose egg for Jane. She was suddenly very tired. "It's your turn, C. T." *Dear God, please don't let him lie too much. He tears my heart. The children never laugh. It's funny how polite they are to C. T. even when they know he's lying. Even that day when Boyd and Lloyd told how they had seen him take food out of the garbage cans in front of the restaurant, and he said he was taking it to some poor hungry children, they didn't laugh. Sometimes children have a great deal more insight than grownups.*

C. T. was talking. "I didn't get nothin' for Christmas, because Mamma was sick, but I worked all that week before for Mr. Bondel what owns the store on Main Street. I ran errands an' swep' up an' he give me three dollars, and so I bought Mamma a real pretty handkerchief an' a comb, an' I bought my father a tie pin, paid a big ole fifty cents for it too . . . an' I bought my sisters an' brothers some candy an' gum an' I bought me this whistle. Course I got what you give us, Miz Richards" (she had given each a small gift) "an' Mamma's white lady give us a whole crate of oranges, an' Miz Smith what live nex' door give me a pair of socks. Mamma she was so happy she made a cake with eggs an' butter an' everything; an' then we ate it an' had a good time."

Rachel spoke wonderingly. "Didn't Santa Claus bring you anything at all?"

C. T. was the epitome of scorn. "Ain't no Santa Claus," he said and sat down.

Jane quelled the age-old third-grade controversy absently, for her heart was singing. *C. T. . . . C. T., son of my own heart, you are the bright new hope of a doubtful world, and the gay new song of a race unconquered. Of them all—Sarahlene, sole heir to the charming stucco home on the hill, all fitted for gracious living; George, whose father is a contractor; Rachel, the minister's daughter; Angela, who has just inherited ten thousand dollars—of all of them who got, you, my dirty little vagabond, who have never owned a coat in your life, because you say you don't get cold; you, out of your nothing, found something to give, and in the dignity of giving found that it was not so important to receive. . . . Christ Child, look down in blessing on one small child made in Your image and born black!*

Jane had problems. Sometimes it was difficult to maintain discipline with forty-two children. Busy as she kept them, there were always some not busy enough. There was the conference with Mr. Johnson.

"Miss Richards, you are doing fine work here, but sometimes your room is a little . . . well—ah—well, to say the least, noisy. You are new here, but we have always maintained a record of having fine discipline here at this school. People have said that it used to be hard to tell whether or not there were children in the building. We have always been proud of that. Now take Miss Nelson. She is an excellent disciplinarian." He smiled. "Maybe if you ask her, she will give you her secret. Do not be too proud to accept help from anyone who can give it, Miss Richards."

"No, sir, thank you, sir, I'll do my best to improve, sir." *Ah, you dear, well-meaning, shortsighted, round, busy little man. Why are you not more concerned about how much the children have grown and learned in these past four months than you are about how much noise they make? I know Miss Nelson's secret. Spare not the rod and spoil not the child. Is that what you want me to do? Paralyze these kids with fear so that they will be afraid to move? afraid to question? afraid to grow? Why is it so fine for people not to know there are children in the building? Wasn't the building built for children?* In her room Jane locked the door against the sound of the playing children, put her head on the desk, and cried.

Jane acceded to tradition and administered one whipping. Booker had slapped Sarahlene's face because she had refused to give up a shiny little music box that played a gay little tune. He had taken the whipping docilely enough, as though used to it; but the sneer in his eyes that had almost gone returned to haunt them. Jane's heart misgave her. *From now on I positively refuse to impose my will on any of these poor children by reason of my greater strength.* So she had abandoned the rod in favor of any other means she could find. They did not always work.

There was a never-ending drive for funds. Jane had a passion for perfection. Plays, dances, concerts, bazaars, suppers, parties followed one on another in staggering succession.

"Look here, Richards," Nelson told her one day, "it's true that we need a new piano, and that science equipment, but, honey, these drives in a colored school are like the poor: with us always. It doesn't make too much difference if Suzy forgets her lines, or if the ice cream is a little lumpy. Cooperation is fine, but the way you tear into things you won't last long."

"For once in her life Nelson's right, Jane," Mary told her later. "I can understand how intense you are because I used to be like that; but, pet, Negro teachers have always had to work harder than any others and till recently have always got paid less, so for our own health's sake we have to let up wherever possible. Believe me, honey, if you don't learn to take it easy, you're going to get sick."

Jane did. Measles!

"Oh, no," she wailed, "not in my old age!" But she was glad of the rest. Lying in her own bed at home, she realized how very tired she was.

Paul came to see her that weekend, and sat by her bed and read aloud to her the old classic poems they both loved so well. They listened to their favorite radio programs. Paul's presence was warm and comforting. Jane was reluctant to go back to work.

What to do about C. T. was a question that daily loomed larger in Jane's consciousness. Watching Joe Louis's brilliant development was a thing of joy, and Jane was hard-pressed to find enough outlets for his amazing abilities. Jeanette Allen was running a close second, and even Booker, so long a problem, was beginning to grasp fundamentals, but C. T. remained static.

"I always stays two years in a grade, Miz Richards," he told her blandly. "I does better the second year."

"Do you *want* to stay in the third grade two years, C. T.?"

"I don't keer." His voice had been cheerful.

Maybe he really is slow, Jane thought. But one day something happened to make her change her mind.

C. T. was possessed of an unusually strong tendency to protect those he considered to be poor or weak. He took little Johnny Armstrong, who sat beside him in class, under his wing. Johnny was nearsighted and nondescript, his one outstanding feature being his hero worship of C. T. Johnny was a plodder. Hard as he tried, he made slow progress at best.

The struggle with multiplication tables was a difficult one, in spite of all the little games Jane devised to make them easier for the children. On this particular day there was the uneven hum of little voices trying to memorize. Johnny and C. T. were having a whispered conversation about snakes.

Clearly Jane heard C. T.'s elaboration. "Man, my father caught a moccasin long as that blackboard, I guess, an' I held him while he was live right back of his ugly head—so."

Swiftly Jane crossed the room. "C. T. and Johnny, you are supposed to be learning your tables. The period is nearly up and you haven't even begun to study. Furthermore, in more than five months you haven't even learned the two-times table. Now you will both stay in at the first recess to learn it, and every day after this until you do."

Maybe I should make up some problems about snakes, Jane mused, *but they'd be too ridiculous . . . Two nests of four snakes—Oh, well, I'll see how they do at recess.* Her heart smote her at the sight of the two little figures at their desks, listening wistfully to the sound of the children at play, but she busied herself and pretended not to notice them. Then she heard C. T.'s voice:

"Lissen, man, these tables is easy if you really want to learn them. Now see here. Two times one is two. Two times two is four. Two times three is six. If you forgit, all you got to do is add two like she said."

"Sho' nuff, man?"

"Sho'. Say them with me . . . two times one—" Obediently Johnny began to recite. Five minutes later they came to her. "We's ready, Miz Richards."

"Very well. Johnny, you may begin."

"Two times one is two. Two times two is four. Two times three is . . . Two times three is—"

"Six," prompted C. T.

In sweat and pain, Johnny managed to stumble through the two-times table with C. T.'s help.

"That's very poor, Johnny, but you may go for today. Tomorrow I shall expect you to have it letter perfect. Now it's your turn, C. T."

C. T.'s performance was a fair rival to Joe Louis's. Suspiciously she took him through in random order.

"Two times nine?"

"Eighteen."

"Two times four?"

"Eight."

"Two times seven?"

"Fourteen."

"C. T., you could have done this long ago. Why didn't you?"

"I dunno . . . May I go to play now, Miz Richards?"

"Yes, C. T. Now learn your three-times table for me tomorrow."

But he didn't, not that day, or the day after that, or the day after that . . . *Why doesn't he? Is it that he doesn't want to? Maybe if I were as ragged and deprived as he I wouldn't want to learn either.*

Jane took C. T. to town and bought him a shirt, a sweater, a pair of dungarees, some underwear, a pair of shoes, and a pair of socks. Then she sent him to the barber to get his hair cut. She gave him the money so he could pay for the articles himself and figure up the change. She instructed him to take a bath before putting on his new clothes, and told him not to tell anyone but his parents that she had bought them.

The next morning the class was in a dither.

"You seen C. T.?"

"Oh, boy, ain't he sharp!"

"C. T., where'd you get them new clothes?"

"Oh, man, I can wear new clothes any time I feel like it, but I can't be bothered with being a fancypants all the time like you guys."

C. T. strutted in new confidence, but his work didn't improve.

Spring came in its virginal green gladness and the children chafed for the out-of-doors. Jane took them out as much as possible on nature studies and excursions.

C. T. was growing more and more mischievous, and his influence began to spread throughout the class. Daily his droll wit became more and more edged with impudence. Jane was at her wit's end.

"You let that child get away with too much, Richards," Nelson told her. "What he needs is a good hiding."

One day Jane kept certain of the class in at the first recess to do neglected homework, C. T. among them. She left the room briefly. When she returned, C. T. was gone.

"Where is C. T.?" she asked.

"He went out to play, Miz Richards. He said couldn't no ole teacher keep him in when he didn't want to stay."

Out on the playground C. T. was standing in a swing, gently swaying to and fro, surrounded by a group of admiring youngsters. He was holding forth.

"I gets tired of stayin' in all the time. She doan pick on nobody but me, an' today I put my foot down. 'From now on,' I say, 'I ain't never goin' to stay in, Miz Richards.' Then I walks out." He was enjoying himself immensely. Then he saw her.

"You will come with me, C. T." She was quite calm except for the telltale veins throbbing in her forehead.

"I ain't comin'." The sudden fright in his eyes was veiled quickly by a nonchalant belligerence. He rocked the swing gently.

She repeated, "Come with me, C. T."

The children watched breathlessly.

"I done told you I ain't comin', Miz Richards." His voice was patient, as though explaining to a child. "I ain't . . . comin' . . . a . . . damn . . . tall!"

Jane moved quickly, wrenching the small but surprisingly strong figure from the swing. Then she bore him bodily, kicking and screaming, to the building.

The children relaxed and began to giggle. "Oh, boy! Is he goin' to catch it!" they told one another.

Panting, she held him, still struggling, by the scruff of his collar before the group of teachers gathered in Marilyn's room. "All right, now *you* tell me what to do with him!" she demanded. "I've tried everything." The tears were close behind her eyes.

"What'd he do?" Nelson asked.

Briefly she told them.

"Have you talked to his parents?"

"Three times I've had conferences with them. They say to beat him."

"That, my friend, is what you ought to do. Now he never acted like that with me. If you'll let me handle him, I'll show you how to put a brat like that in his place."

"Go ahead," Jane said wearily.

Nelson left the room, and returned with a narrow but sturdy leather thong. "Now, C. T."—she was smiling, tapping the strap in her open left palm—"go to your room and do what Miss Richards told you to."

"I ain't gonna, an' you can't make me." He sat down with absurd dignity at a desk.

Still smiling, Miss Nelson stood over him. The strap descended without warning across the bony shoulders in the thin shirt. The whip became a dancing demon, a thing possessed, bearing no relation to the hand that held it. The shrieks grew louder. Jane closed her eyes against the blurred fury of a singing lash, a small boy's terror, and a smiling face.

Miss Nelson was not tired. "Well, C. T.?"

"I won't. Yer can kill me but I *won't!*"

The sounds began again. Red welts began to show across the small arms and through the clinging sweat-drenched shirt.

"Now will you go to your room?"

Sobbing and conquered, C. T. went. The seated children stared curiously at the little procession. Jane dismissed them.

In his seat C. T. found pencil and paper.

"What's he supposed to do, Richards?"

Jane told her.

"All right, now write!"

C. T. stared at Nelson through swollen lids, a curious smile curving his lips. Jane knew suddenly that come hell or high water, C. T. would not write. *I mustn't interfere. Please, God, don't let her hurt him too badly. Where have I failed so miserably? . . . Forgive us our trespasses.* The singing whip and the shrieks became a symphony from hell. Suddenly Jane hated the smiling face with an almost unbearable hatred. She spoke, her voice like cold steel.

"That's enough, Nelson."

The noise stopped.

"He's in no condition to write now anyway."

C. T. stood up. "I hate you. I hate you all. You're mean and I hate you." Then he ran. No one followed him. *Run, little mouse!* They avoided each other's eyes.

"Well, there you are," Nelson said as she walked away. Jane never found out what she meant by that.

•

The next day C. T. did not come to school. The day after that he brought Jane the fatal homework, neatly and painstakingly done, and a bunch of wild flowers. Before the bell rang, the children surrounded him. He was beaming.

"Did you tell yer folks you got a whipping, C. T.?"

"Naw! I'd 'a' only got another."

"Where were you yesterday?"

"Went fishin'. Caught me six cats long as your haid, Sambo."

Jane buried her face in the sweet-smelling flowers. *Oh, my brat, my wonderful resilient brat. They'll never get your tail, will they?*

It was seven weeks till the end of term when C. T. brought Jane a model wooden boat.

Jane stared at it. "Did you make this? It's beautiful, C. T."

"Oh, I make them all the time . . . an' airplanes an' houses, too. I do 'em in my spare time," he finished airily.

"Where do you get the models, C. T.?" she asked.

"I copies them from pictures in the magazines."

Right under my nose . . . right there all the time, she thought wonderingly. "C. T., would you like to build things when you grow up? Real houses and ships and planes?"

"Reckon I could, Miz Richards," he said confidently.

The excitement was growing in her. "Look, C. T. You aren't going to do any lessons at all for the rest of the year. You're going to build ships and houses and airplanes and anything else you want to."

"I am, huh?" He grinned. "Well, I guess I wasn't goin' to get promoted nohow."

"Of course, if you want to build them the way they really are, you might have to do a little measuring, and maybe learn to spell the names of the parts you want to order. All the best contractors have to know things like that, you know."

"Say, I'm gonna have real fun, huh? I always said lessons wussent no good nohow. Pop say too much study eats out yer brains anyway."

The days went by. Jane ran a race with time. The instructions from the model companies arrived. Jane burned the midnight oil planning each day's work:

Learn to spell the following words: ship, sail, steamer—boat, anchor, airplane wing, fly.

Write a letter to the lumber company, ordering some lumber.

The floor of our model house is ten inches wide and fourteen inches long. Multiply the length by the width and you'll find the area of the floor in square inches.

Read the story of Columbus and his voyages.

Our plane arrives in Paris in twenty-eight hours. Paris is the capital city of a country named France across the Atlantic Ocean.

Long ago sailors told time by the sun and the stars. Now, the earth goes around the sun—

Work and pray, work and pray!

C. T. learned. Some things vicariously, some things directly. When he found that he needed multiplication to plan his models to scale, he learned to multiply. In three weeks he had mastered simple division.

Jane bought beautifully illustrated stories about ships and planes. He learned to read.

He wrote for and received his own materials.

Jane exulted.

The last day! Forty-two faces waiting anxiously for report cards. Jane spoke to them briefly, praising them collectively, and admonishing them to obey the safety rules during the holidays. Then she passed out the report cards.

As she smiled at each childish face, she thought, *I've been wrong. The long arm of circumstance, environment, and heredity is the farmer's wife that seeks to mow you down, and all of us who touch your lives are in some way responsible for how successful she is. But you aren't mice, my darlings. Mice are hated, hunted pests. You are normal, lovable children. The knife of the farmer's wife is double-edged for you because you are Negro children, born mostly in poverty. But you are wonderful children, nevertheless, for you wear the bright protective cloak of laughter, the strong shield of courage, and the intelligence of children everywhere. Some few of you may indeed become as the mice—but most of you shall find your way to stand fine and tall in the annals of men. There's a bright new tomorrow ahead. For every one of us whose job it is to help you grow that is insensitive and unworthy there are hundreds who daily work that you may grow straight and whole. If it were not so, our world could not long endure.*

She handed C. T. his card.

"Thank you, ma'am."

"Aren't you going to open it?"

He opened it dutifully. When he looked up, his eyes were wide with disbelief. "You didn't make no mistake?"

"No mistake, C. T. You're promoted. You've caught up enough to go to the fourth grade next year."

She dismissed the children. They were a swarm of bees released from a hive. " 'By, Miss Richards" . . . "Happy holidays, Miss Richards."

C. T. was the last to go.

"Well, C. T.?"

"Miz Richards, you remember what you said about a name being important?"

"Yes, C. T."

"Well, I talked to Mamma, and she said if I wanted a name it would be all right, and she'd go to the courthouse about it."

"What name have you chosen, C. T.?" she asked.

"Christopher Turner Young."

"That's a nice name, Christopher," she said gravely.

"Sho' nuff, Miz Richards?"

"Sure enough, C. T."

"Miz Richards, you know what?"

"What, dear?"

"I love you."

She kissed him swiftly before he ran to catch his classmates.

She stood at the window and watched the running, skipping figures, followed by the bold mimic shadows. *I'm coming home, Paul. I'm leaving my forty-two children, and Tanya there on the hill. My work with them is finished now.* The laughter bubbled up in her throat. *But Paul, oh Paul. See how straight they run!*

Miss Muriel

●

(1958)

Ann Petry

Almost every day, Ruth Davis and I walk home from school together. We walk very slowly because we like to talk to each other and we don't get much chance in school or after school either. We are very much alike. We are both twelve years old and we are freshmen in high school and we never study—well, not very much, because we learn faster than the rest of the class. We laugh about the same things and we are curious about the same things. We even wear our hair in the same style—thick braids halfway down our backs. We are not alike in one respect. She is white and I am colored.

Yesterday when we reached the building that houses my father's drugstore, we sat down on the front steps—long wooden steps that go all the way across the front of the building. Ruth said, "I wish I lived here," and patted the steps though they are very splintery.

Aunt Sophronia must have heard our voices, because she came to the door and said, "I left my shoes at the shoemaker's this morning. Please go and get them for me," and she handed me a little cardboard ticket with a number on it.

"You want to come with me, Ruth?"

"I've got to go home. I'm sure my aunt will have things for me to do. Just like your aunt." She smiled at Aunt Sophronia.

I walked part way home with Ruth and then turned back and went up Petticoat Lane toward the shoemaker's shop. Mr. Bemish, the shoemaker, is a little man with gray hair. He has a glass eye. This eye is not the same color as his own eye. It is a deeper gray. If I stand too close to him I get a squeamish feeling because one eye moves in its socket and the other eye does not.

Mr. Bemish and I are friends. I am always taking shoes to his shop to be repaired. We do not own a horse and buggy and so we walk a great deal. In fact, there is a family rule that we must walk any distance under three miles. As a result, our shoes are in constant need of repair, the soles and heels have to be replaced, and we always seem to be in need of shoelaces. Quite often I snag the uppers on the bull briars in the woods and then the tears have to be stitched.

When I went to get Aunt Sophronia's shoes, Mr. Bemish was sitting near the window. It is a big window and he has a very nice view of the street. He had on his leather apron and his eyeglasses. His glasses are small and they have steel rims. He was sewing a shoe and he had a long length of waxed linen thread in his needle. He waxes the thread himself.

I handed him the ticket and he got up from his workbench to get the shoes. I saw that he had separated them from the other shoes. These are Aunt Sophronia's store shoes. They had been polished so that they shone like patent leather. They lay alone, near the front of the table where he keeps the shoes he has repaired. He leaned toward me and I moved away from him. I did not like being so close to his glass eye.

"The lady who brought these shoes in. Who is she?"

I looked at him and raised one eyebrow. It has taken me two months of constant practice in front of a mirror to master the art of lifting one eyebrow.

Mr. Bemish said, "What's the matter with you? Didn't you hear what I said? Who was that lady who brought these shoes in?"

I moved further away from him. He didn't know it but I was imitating Dottle Smith, my favorite person in all the world. Dottle tells the most wonderful stories and he can act and recite poetry. He visits our family every summer. Anyway, I bowed to Mr. Bemish and I bowed to an imaginary group of people seated somewhere on my right and I said, "Gentlemen, be seated. Mr. Bones, who was that lady I saw you with last night?" I lowered the pitch of my voice and said, "That wasn't no lady. That was my *wife*."

"Girlie—"

"Why do you keep calling me 'girlie'? I have a name."

"I cannot remember people's names. I'm too old. I've told you that before."

"How old are you, Mr. Bemish?"

"None of your business," he said pettishly. "Who—"

"Well, I only asked in order to decide whether to agree with you that you're old enough to be forgetful. Does the past seem more real to you than the present?"

Mr. Bemish scowled his annoyance. "The town is full of children," he said. "It's the children who bring the shoes in and come and get them after I've fixed them. They run the errands. All those children look just alike to me. I can't remember their names. I don't even try. I don't plan to clutter up my mind with a lot of children's names. I don't see the same children that often. So I call the boys 'boy,' and I call the girls 'girlie.' I've told you this before. What's the matter with you today?"

"It's spring and the church green is filled with robins looking for worms. Don't you sometimes wish you were a robin looking for a worm?"

He sighed. "Now tell me, who was that lady that brought these shoes in?"

"My aunt Sophronia."

"Sophronia?" he said. "What a funny name. And she's your aunt?"

"Yes."

"Does she live with you?"

Mr. Bemish's cat mewed at the door and I let her in. She is a very handsome creature, gray, with white feet, and really lovely fur. "May-a-ling, May-a-ling," I said, patting her, "where have you been?" I always have the feeling that if I wait, if I persist, she will answer me. She is a very intelligent cat and very responsive.

"Does your aunt live with you?"

"Yes."

"Has she been living with you very long?"

"About six months, I guess. She's a druggist."

"You mean she knows about medicine?"

"Yes, just like my father. They run the store together."

Mr. Bemish thrust his hands in Aunt Sophronia's shoes and held them up, studying them. Then he made the shoes walk along the edge of the table, in a mincing kind of walk, a caricature of the way a woman walks.

"She has small feet, hasn't she?"

"No." I tried to sound like my mother when she disapproves of something.

He flushed and wrapped the shoes in newspaper, making a very neat bundle.

"Is she married?"

"Who? Aunt Sophronia? No. She's not married."

Mr. Bemish took his cookie crock off the shelf. He lives in the shop. Against one wall he has a kitchen stove, a big black iron stove with nickel fenders and a tea kettle on it, and there is a black iron sink with a pump right near the stove. He cooks his meals himself, he bakes bread, and usually there is a stew bubbling in a pot on the stove. In winter the windows of his little shop frost over, so that I cannot see in and he cannot see out. He draws his red curtains just after dusk and lights his lamps, and the windows look pink because of the frost and the red curtains and the light shining from behind them.

Sometimes he forgets to draw the curtains that separate his sleeping quarters from the rest of the shop and I can see his bed. It is a brass bed. He evidently polishes it, because it shines like gold. It has a very intricate design on the headboard and the footboard. He has a little piece of flowered carpet in front of his bed. I can see his white china pot under the bed. A dark suit and some shirts hang on hooks on the wall. There is a chest of drawers with a small mirror in a gold frame over it, and a washbowl and pitcher on a washstand. The washbowl and pitcher are white with pink rosebuds painted on them.

Mr. Bemish offered me a cookie from the big stoneware crock.

"Have a cookie, girlie."

He makes big thick molasses cookies. I ate three of them without stopping. I was hungry and did not know it. I ate the fourth cookie very slowly and I talked to Mr. Bemish as I ate it.

"I don't think my aunt Sophronia will ever get married."

"Why not?"

"Well, I never heard of a lady druggist before and I don't know who a lady druggist would marry. Would she marry another druggist? There aren't any around here anywhere except my father and certainly she couldn't marry him. He's already married to my mother."

"She looks like a gypsy," Mr. Bemish said dreamily.

"You mean my aunt Sophronia?"

Mr. Bemish nodded.

"She does not. She looks like my mother and my aunt Ellen. And my father and Uncle Johno say they look like Egyptian queens."

They are not very tall and they move quickly and their skins are brown and very smooth and their eyes are big and black and they stand up very straight. They are not alike though. My mother is business-minded. She likes to buy and sell things. She is a chiropodist and a hairdresser. Life sometimes seems full of other people's hair and their toenails. She makes a hair tonic and sells it to her customers. She designs luncheon sets and banquet cloths and guest towels and sells them. Aunt Ellen and Uncle Johno provide culture. Aunt Ellen lectures at schools and colleges. She plays Bach and Beethoven on the piano and organ. She writes articles for newspapers and magazines.

I do not know very much about Aunt Sophronia. She works in the store. She fills prescriptions. She does embroidery. She reads a lot. She doesn't play the piano. She is very neat. The men who come in the store look at her out of the corner of their eyes. Even though she wears her hair skinned-tight back from her forehead, and wears very plain clothes, dresses with long, tight sleeves and high necks, she still looks like—well, like an Egyptian queen. She is young but she seems very quiet and sober.

Mr. Bemish offered me another cookie. "I'll eat it on my way home to keep my strength up. Thank you very much," I said primly.

When I gave the shoes to Aunt Sophronia, I said, "Mr. Bemish thinks you look like a gypsy."

My mother frowned. "Did he tell you to repeat that?"

"No, he didn't. But I thought it was an interesting statement."

"I wish you wouldn't repeat the things you hear. It just causes trouble. Now every time I look at Mr. Bemish I'll wonder about him—"

"What will you wonder—I mean—"

She said I must go and practice my music lesson and ignored my question. I wonder how old I will be before I can ask questions of an adult and receive honest answers to the questions. My family always finds something for me to do. Are they not using their power as adults to give orders in order to evade the questions?

That evening, about five o'clock, Mr. Bemish came in the store. I was sitting on the bench in the front. It is a very old bench. The customers sit there while they wait for their prescriptions to be filled. The wood is a beautiful color. It is a deep, reddish brown.

Mr. Bemish sat down beside me on the bench. His presence irritated me. He kept moving his hand up and down the arms of the bench, up and down, in a quick, nervous movement. It is as though he thought he had an awl in his hand, and he is going in and out making holes in leather and then sewing, slipping a needle in and out, as he mends a saddle or a pair of boots.

My father looked at him over the top of his glasses and said, "Well, Bemish, what can I do for you?"

"Nothing. Nothing at all. I just stopped in to pass the time of day, to see how you all were—" His voice trailed away, softly.

He comes every evening. I find this very annoying. Quite often I have to squeeze myself onto the bench. Pritchett, the sexton of the Congregational church—stout, red-faced, smelling of whiskey—rings the bell for a service at seven o'clock and then he, too, sits in the front of the store, watching the customers as they come and go until closing time. He eyed Mr. Bemish rather doubtfully at first, but then ignored him.

When the sexton and Mr. Bemish were on the bench, there was just room enough for me to squeeze in between them. I didn't especially mind the sexton, because he usually went to sleep, nodding and dozing until it was time to close the store. But Mr. Bemish doesn't sit still—and the movement of his hands is distracting.

My mother finally spoke to my father about Mr. Bemish. They were standing in the back room. "Why does Mr. Bemish sit out there in the store so much?" she asked.

"Nothin' else to do."

She shook her head. "I think he's interested in Sophronia. He keeps looking around for someone."

My father laughed out loud. "That dried-up old white man?"

The laughter of my father is a wonderful sound—if you know anything about music you know he sings tenor and you know he sings in the Italian fashion with an open throat and you begin to smile, and if he laughs long enough, you laugh too, because you can't help it.

"Bemish?" he said. And he laughed so hard that he had to lean against the doorjamb in order to keep his balance.

Every night right after supper, Mr. Bemish sits in the store rubbing the arm of the bench with that quick, jerking motion of his hand, nodding to people who come in, sometimes talking to them, but mostly just sitting.

Two weeks later I walked past his shop. He came to the door and called me. "Girlie," he said, beckoning.

"Yes, Mr. Bemish?"

"Is your aunt with the peculiar name still here—that is, in town, living with you?"

"Yes, she is, Mr. Bemish."

"Don't she ever go in the drugstore?"

"Not after five o'clock, Mr. Bemish. My father doesn't approve of ladies working at night. At night we act just like other people's families. We sit around the table in the dining room and talk, and we play checkers, and we read and we—"

"Yes, yes," he said impatiently. "But don't your aunt ever go anywhere at night?"

"I don't think so. I go to bed early."

"Do you think—" And he shook his head. "Never mind, girlie, never mind," and he sighed. "Here—I just made up a fresh batch of those big cookies you like so well."

I walked down Petticoat Lane toward the drugstore eating one of Mr. Bemish's thick molasses cookies. I wished I had taken time to tell him how cozy our downstairs parlor is in the winter. We have turkey-red curtains at the windows too, and we pull the window shades and draw the curtains, and there is a very thick rug on the floor and it is a small room, so the rug completely covers the floor. The piano is in there and an old-fashioned sofa with a carved mahogany frame and a very handsome round stove and it is warm in winter; and in the summer when the windows are open, you can look right out into the back yard and smell the flowers and feel the cool air that comes from the garden.

The next afternoon, Mr. Bemish came in the drugstore about quarter past three. It was a cold, windy afternoon. I had just come from school and there was a big mug of hot cocoa for me. Aunt Sophronia had it ready and waiting for me in the back room. I had just tasted the first spoonful; it was much too hot to gulp down, and I leaned way over and blew on it gently, and inhaled the rich, chocolatey smell of it. I heard my aunt say, "Why, Mr. Bemish, what are you doing out at this hour?"

"I thought I'd like an ice-cream soda." Mr. Bemish's voice sounded breathless, lighter in weight, and the pitch was lower than normal.

I peeked out at him. He was sitting near the fountain in one of the ice-cream-parlor chairs. He looked very stiff and prim and neater than usual. He seems to have flattened his hair closer to his skull. This makes his head appear smaller. He was holding his head a little to one side. He looked like a bird but I cannot decide what bird—perhaps a chickadee. He drank the soda neatly and daintily. He kept looking at Aunt Sophronia.

He comes every day now, in the middle of the afternoon. He should have been in his shop busily repairing shoes or making boots, or making stews and cookies. Instead, he is in our store, and his light-gray eye, the one good eye, travels busily over Aunt Sophronia. His ears seem to waggle when he hears her voice, and he has taken to giggling in a very silly fashion.

He always arrives about the same time. Sometimes I sit in one of the ice-cream-parlor chairs and talk to him. He smells faintly of leather, and of shoe polish, and of wax, and of dead flowers. It was quite a while before I could place that other smell—dead flowers. Each day he stays a little longer than he stayed the day before.

I have noticed that my father narrows his eyes a little when he looks at Mr. Bemish. I heard him say to my mother, "I don't like it. I don't want to tell him not to come in here. But I don't like it—an old white man in here every afternoon looking at Sophronia and licking his chops—well, I just don't like it."

Aunt Sophronia took a sudden interest in the garden. In the afternoon, after school, I help her set out plants and sow seed. Our yard is filled with flowers in the summer; and we have a vegetable garden that in some ways is as beautiful as the flowers—it is so neat and precise-looking. We keep chickens so that we can have fresh eggs. And we raise a pig and have him butchered in the fall.

When the weather is bad and we cannot work in the garden, Aunt Sophronia and I clean house. I do not like to clean house but I do like to sort out the contents of other people's bureau drawers. We started setting Aunt Sophronia's bureau in order. She showed me a picture of her graduating class from Pharmacy College. She was the only girl in a class of boys. She was colored and the boys were white. I did not say anything about this difference in color and neither did she. But I did try to find out what it was like to be the only member of the female sex in a class filled with males.

"Didn't you feel funny with all those boys?"

"They were very nice boys."

"Oh, I'm sure they were. But didn't you feel funny being the only girl with so many young men?"

"No. I never let them get overly friendly and we got along very well."

I looked at the picture and then I looked at her and said, "You are beautiful."

She put the picture back in her top drawer. She keeps her treasures in there. She has a collar made of real lace, and a pair of very long white kid gloves, and a necklace made of gold nuggets from Colorado that a friend of my mother's left to Aunt Sophronia in her will. The gloves and the collar smell like our garden in August when the flowers are in full bloom and the sun is shining on them.

Sometimes I forget that Aunt Sophronia is an adult and that she belongs in the enemy camp, and I make the mistake of saying what I have been thinking.

I leaned against the bureau and looked down into the drawer, at the picture, and said, "You know, this picture reminds me of the night last summer when there was a female moth, one of those huge night moths, on the inside of the screen door, and all the male moths for miles around came and clung on the outside of the screen, making their wings flutter, and you know, they didn't make any sound but it was kind of scary. Weren't you—"

Aunt Sophronia closed the drawer with a hard push. "You get a broom and a dustpan and begin to sweep in the hall," she said.

On Saturday morning, after I finished washing the breakfast dishes and scrubbing the kitchen floor, I paid a call on Mr. Bemish. He is cleaning his house, too. He has taken down the red curtains that hung at the windows all winter, and the red curtains that hung in front of his bed, separating his sleeping quarters from the rest of his shop, and he was washing these curtains in a big tub at the side of his house. He was making a terrific splashing and the soapsuds were pale pink. He had his sleeves rolled up. His arms are very white and stringy-looking.

"Too much red for summer, girlie. I've got to get out the green summer ones."

He hung them on the line and poured the wash water out on the ground. It was pink.

"Your curtains ran, didn't they?" I looked at a little pink puddle left on top of a stone. "If you keep washing them, they'll be pink instead of red."

His own eye, the real eye, moved away from me, and there was something secret, and rather sly, about his expression. He said, "I haven't seen your aunt in the store lately. Where is she?"

"She's been busy fixing the garden and cleaning the house. Everybody seems to be cleaning house."

"As soon as I get my green curtains put up, I'm going to ask your aunt to come have tea."

"Where would she have tea with you?"

"In my shop."

I shook my head. "Aunt Sophronia does not drink tea in people's bedrooms and you have only that one room for your shop and there's a bed in it and it would be just like—"

"I would like to have her look at some old jewelry that I have and I thought she might have tea."

"Mr. Bemish," I said, "do you like my aunt Sophronia?"

"Now, girlie," he said, and he tittered. "Well, now, do you think your aunt likes me?"

"Not especially. Not any more than anybody else. I think you're too old for her and besides, well, you're white and I don't think she would be very much interested in an old white man, do you?"

He frowned and said, "You go home. You're a very rude girl."

"You asked me what I thought, Mr. Bemish. I don't see why you get mad when I tell you what I think. You did ask me, Mr. Bemish."

I followed him inside his shop. He settled himself near the window and started to work on a man's boot. It needed a new sole and he cut the sole out of leather. I looked out the front window. There is always enough breeze to make his sign move back and forth; it makes a sighing noise. In the winter, if there's a wind, the sign seems to groan because it moves back and forth quickly. There is a high-laced shoe painted on the sign. The shoe must once have been a deep, dark red, but it has weathered to a soft rose color.

Mr. Bemish is my friend and I wanted to indicate that I am still fond of him though I disapprove of his interest in Aunt Sophronia. I searched for some topic that would indicate that I enjoy talking to him.

I said, "Why don't you have a picture of a man's boot on your sign?"

"I prefer ladies' shoes. More delicate, more graceful—" He made an airy gesture with his awl and simpered.

I went home and I told Aunt Sophronia that Mr. Bemish is going to ask her to have tea with him.

"Will you go?"

"Of course not," she said impatiently.

Aunt Sophronia did not have tea with Mr. Bemish. He sees her so rarely in the store that he finally came in search of her.

It is summer now and the Wheeling Inn is open for the season. The great houses along the waterfront are occupied by their rich owners. We are all very busy. At night after the store is closed, we sit in the back yard. On those warm June nights, the fireflies come out, and there is a kind of soft summer light, composed of moonlight and starlight. The grass is thick underfoot and the air is sweet. Almost every night my mother and my father and Aunt Sophronia and I, and sometimes Aunt Ellen and Uncle Johno, sit there in the quiet and in the sweetness and in that curious soft light.

Last night when we were sitting there, Mr. Bemish came around the side of the house. There was something tentative in the way he came towards us. I had been lying on the grass and I sat up straight, wondering what they would do and what they would say.

He sidled across the lawn. He didn't speak until he was practically upon us. My mother was sitting in the hammock under the cherry tree, rocking gently back and forth, and she didn't see him until he spoke. He said, "Good evening." He sounded as though he was asking a question.

We all looked at him. I hoped that someone would say: What are you doing in our back yard, our private place, our especially private place? You are an intruder, go back to your waxed thread and your awl, go back to your horse and your cat. Nobody said anything.

He stood there for a while, waiting, hesitant, and then he bowed and sat down, cross-legged, on the grass, near Aunt Sophronia. She was sitting on one of the benches. And he sat so close to her that her skirt was resting on one of his trouser legs. I kept watching him. One of his hands reached towards her skirt and he gently fingered the fabric. Either she felt this or the motion attracted her attention, because she moved away from him, and gathered her skirt about her, and then stood up and said, "The air is making me sleepy. Good night."

The next afternoon I took a pair of my father's shoes to Mr. Bemish to have the heels fixed. My father wears high-laced black shoes. I left them on Mr. Bemish's worktable.

"You can get them tomorrow."

I did not look right at him. I leaned over and patted May-a-ling. "She has such a lovely name, Mr. Bemish. It seems to me a name especially suited for a cat."

Mr. Bemish looked at me over the top of his little steel-rimmed glasses. "You've got a nice back yard," he said.

"I don't think you should have been in it."

"Why not?" he asked sharply. "Did anybody say that I shouldn't have been in it?"

"No. But the front part of the building, the part where the drugstore is, belongs to everybody. The back part of the building, and upstairs in the building, and the yard are ours. The yard is a private part of our lives. You don't belong in it. You're not a part of our family."

"But I'd like to be a part of your family."

"You can't get to be a part of other people's families. You have to be born into a family. The family part of our lives is just for us. Besides, you don't seem to understand that you're the wrong color, Mr. Bemish."

He didn't answer this. He got up and got his cookie crock and silently offered me a cookie.

After I returned from the shoe shop, I sat on the wooden steps that run across the front of the drugstore. I was trying to decide how I really feel about Mr. Bemish. I always sit at the far end of the steps with my back against the tight-board fence. It is a very good place from which to observe the street, the front of the store, the church green. People walk past me not noticing that I am there. Sometimes their conversations are very unusual. I can see a long way down the path that bisects the green. It is a dirt path and not too straight. The only straight paths in town are those in front of the homes of people who have gardeners.

From where I sat I could see a man approaching. He was strolling down the path that crosses the church green. This is a most unusual way for a man to walk in Wheeling in the summer. It is during the summer that the year-round residents earn their living. They mow lawns, and cut hedges, and weed gardens, and generally look after the summer people. Able-bodied men in Wheeling walked fast in summer.

This tall, broad-shouldered man was strolling down the path. He was wearing a white suit, the pants quite tight in the leg, and he had his hands in his hip pockets, and a stiff straw hat, a boater, on the back of his head.

I sat up very straight when I discovered that this was a very dark colored man. I could not imagine where he came from. He could not possibly be a butler or a waiter even if he wanted to and spent a whole lifetime in trying. He would never be able to walk properly—he would always swagger, and who ever heard of a swaggering butler or a waiter who strolled around a table?

As he came nearer, I saw that he had a beard, an untidy shaggy beard like the beard of a goat. His hair was long and shaggy and rough-looking too. Though he was tall, with wide shoulders, the thick, rough hair on his head and the goat's beard made his head and face look too big, out of proportion to his body.

When he saw me, he came straight toward me. He bent over me, smiling, and I moved back away from him, pressing against the fence. His eyes alarmed me. Whenever I think about his eyes, I close mine, trying to shut his out. They are reddish brown and they look hot, and having looked into them, I cannot seem to look away. I have never seen anyone with eyes that color or with that strange quality, whatever it is. I described them as looking "hot," but that's not possible. It must be that they are the color of something that I associate with fire or heat. I do not know what it is.

"You lost?" he said.

"No. Are you?"

"Yup. All us colored folks is lost." He said this in a husky, unmusical voice, and turned away and went in the store.

I went in the store, too. If this unusual-looking man with the goat's beard got into a discussion of "all us colored folks is lost" with my father, I wanted to hear it.

My father said, "How-de-do?" and he made it a question.

The bearded man nodded and said, "The druggist in?"

"I'm the druggist."

"This your store?"

"That's right."

"Nice place you got here. You been here long?"

My father grunted. I waited for him to make the next move in the game we called Stanley and Livingstone. All colored strangers who came into our store were Livingstones—and it was up to the members of our family to find out which lost Mr. Livingstone or which lost Mrs. Livingstone we had encountered in the wilds of the all-white town of Wheeling. When you live in a town where there aren't any other colored people, naturally you're curious when another colored person shows up.

I sat down in the front of the store and waited for my father to find out which Mr. David Livingstone he was talking to and what he was doing in our town. But my father looked at him with no expression on his face and said, "And what did you want?"

The man with the goat's beard fished in the pocket of his tight white pants. In order to do this, he thrust his leg forward a little to ease the strain on the fabric, and thus he gave the impression that he was pawing the ground. He handed my father a piece of paper.

"I got a prescription for a lotion—"

"It'll take a few minutes," my father said, and went in the back room.

The bearded man came and sat beside me.

"Do you live here in Wheeling?" I asked.

"I work at the Inn. I'm the piano player."

"You play the piano?"

"And sing. I'm the whole orchestra. I play for the dinner hour. I play for all those nice rich white folks to dance at night. I'll be here all summer."

"You will?"

"That's right. And I've never seen a deader town."

"What's your name?"

"Chink."

"Mr. Chink—"

"No," he said, and stood up. "Chink is my first name. Chink Johnson."

Mr. Johnson is a restless kind of man. He keeps moving around even when he is sitting still, moving his feet, his hands, his head. He crosses his legs, uncrosses them, clasps his hands together, unclasps them.

"Why are you having a prescription filled?"

"Hand lotion. I use it for my hands."

My father came out of the back room, wrapped up a bottle, said, "Here you are."

Chink Johnson paid him, said good-by to me, and I said, "Good-by, Chink."

"What's his name?"

"Chink Johnson. He plays the piano at the Inn."

Chink Johnson seems to me a very interesting and unusual man. To my surprise, my father did not mention our newest Mr. Livingstone to the family. He said nothing about him at all. Neither did I.

Yet he comes in the drugstore fairly often. He buys cigarettes and throat lozenges. Sometimes he drives over from the Inn in a borrowed horse and carriage. Sometimes he walks over. My father has very little to say to him.

He doesn't linger in the store, because my father's manner is designed to discourage him from lingering or hanging around. But he does seem to be looking for something. He looks past the door of the prescription room, and on hot afternoons, the door in the very back is open and you can see our yard, with its beautiful little flower gardens, and he looks out into the yard, seems to search it. When he leaves he looks at the house, examining it. It is as though he is trying to see around a corner, see through the walls, because some sixth sense has told him that there exists on the premises something that will interest him, and if he looks hard enough, he will find it.

My mother finally caught a glimpse of him as he went out the front door. She saw what I saw—the goat's beard in silhouette, the forward thrust of his head, the thick shaggy hair—because we were standing in the prescription room looking toward the door.

"Who was that?" she asked, her voice sharp.

"That's the piano player at the Inn," my father said.

"You've never mentioned him. What is his name?"

"Jones," my father said.

I started to correct him but I was afraid to interrupt him because he started talking fast and in a very loud voice. "Lightfoot Jones," he said. "Shake Jones. Barrelhouse Jones." He started tapping on the glass case in front of him. I have never heard him do this before. He sings in the Congregational church choir. He has a pure, lyric tenor voice, and he sings all the tenor solos, the "Sanctus," "The Heavens Are Telling." You can tell from his speaking voice that he sings. He is always humming or singing or whistling. There he was with a pencil in his hand, tapping out a most peculiar rhythm on the glass of a showcase.

"Shake Jones," he repeated. "Rhythm in his feet. Rhythm in his blood. Rhythm in his feet. Rhythm in his blood. Beats out his life, beats out his lungs, beats out his liver, on a piano," and he began a different and louder rhythm with his foot. "On a pi-an-o. On a pi-an-o. On a pi—"

"Samuel, what is the matter with you? What are you talking about?"

"I'm talkin' about Tremblin' Shakefoot Jones. The piano player. The piano player who can't sit still, and comes in here lookin' around and lookin' around, prancin' and stampin' his hoofs, and sniffin' the air. Just like a stallion who smells a mare—a stallion who—"

"Samuel! How can you talk that way in front of this child?"

My father was silent.

I said, "His name is Chink Johnson."

My father roared, terrible in his anger, "His name is Duke. His name is Bubber. His name is Count, is Maharajah, is King of Lions. I don't give a good goddamn what he calls himself. I don't want him and his restless feet hangin' around. He can let his long feet slap somebody else's floor. But not mine. Not here—"

He glared at me and glared at my mother. His fury silenced us. At that moment his eyes were red-brown just like Chink Jones's, no, Johnson's. He is shorter, he has no beard, but he had at that moment a strong resemblance to Chink.

I added to his fury. I said, "You look just like Chink Johnson."

He said, "Ah!!! . . ." He was so angry I could not understand one word he said. I went out the front door, and across the street, and sat on the church steps and watched the world go by and listened to the faint hum it made as it went around and around.

I saw Mr. Bemish go in the drugstore. He stayed a long time. That gave me a certain pleasure because I knew he had come to eat his ice-cream soda, mouthful by mouthful, from one of our long-handled ice-cream-soda spoons, and to look at Aunt Sophronia as he nibbled at the ice cream. He looks at her out of the corners of his eyes, stealing sly little glances at her. I knew that Aunt Sophronia would not be in the store until much later and that he was wasting his time. It was my father's birthday and Aunt Sophronia was in the kitchen baking a great big cake for him.

If Mr. Bemish had known this, he might have dropped in on the birthday celebration, even though he hadn't been invited. After all, he had sidled into our back yard without being invited and our yard is completely enclosed by a tight-board fence, and there is a gate that you have to open to get in the yard, so that entering our yard is like walking into our living room. It is a very private place. Mr. Bemish is the only person that I know of who has come into our yard without being invited, and he keeps coming, too.

After Mr. Bemish left the store, I crossed the street and sat outside on the store steps. It was hot. It was very quiet. Old Lady Chimble crossed the church green carrying a black silk umbrella, and she opened it and used it as a sunshade. A boy went by on a bicycle. Frances Jackins (we called her Aunt Frank), the colored cook in the boardinghouse across the street, hurried across the street carrying something in a basket. She is always cross and usually drunk. She drinks gin. Mother says this is what has made Aunt Frank's lips look as though they were turned inside out and she says this is called a "gin lip." They are bright red, almost like a red gash across the dark skin of her face. I want very much to ask Aunt Frank about this—how it feels, when it happened, etc.—and someday I will, but I have not as yet had a suitable opportunity. When she is drunk, she cannot give a sensible answer to a sensible question, and when she is sober, or partially sober, she is very irritable and constantly finds fault with me. She is absolutely no relation to us; it is just that my mother got in the habit of calling her "Aunt" Frank many years ago and so we all call her that. Because I am young, she tries to boss me and to order me around, and she calls me "Miss" in a very unpleasant, sarcastic way.

She is a very good cook when she is sober. But when she is drunk, she burns everything, and she is always staggering across the street and stumbling up our back steps, with bread pans filled with dough which would not rise because she has forgotten the yeast, and with burned cakes and pies and burned hams and roasts of beef. When she burns things, they are not just scorched; they are blackened and hardened until they are like charcoal.

Almost every night she scratches at our back door. I have sharper hearing than everybody else; I can hear people walking around the side of the house and no one else has heard them—anyway, I always hear her first. I open the door suddenly and very fast, and she almost falls into the kitchen and stands there swaying, and fouling our kitchen with the sweetish smell of gin and the dank and musty odor of her clothes.

She always has a dip of snuff under her upper lip and she talks around this obstruction, so that her voice is peculiar. She speaks quickly to keep the snuff in place, and sometimes she pauses and works her upper lip, obviously getting the snuff in some special spot. When she comes to the back door at night, she puts the basket of ruined food just inside the door, on the floor, and says to my mother, "Here, Mar-tha, throw this away. Throw it a-way for me. Give it to the hens. Feed it to the pig—"

She turns all two-syllable words into two separate one-syllable words. She doesn't say "Martha" all in one piece. She separates it, so that it becomes "Mar-tha"; she doesn't say "away," but "a-way." It is a very jerky kind of speech.

I am always given the job of burying the stuff in the back yard, way down in the back. I dig a hole and throw the blackened mess into it and then cover it with lime to hasten decomposition and discourage skunks and dogs.

Sometimes I hide behind the fence and yell at her on her way back across the street:

> *Ole Aunt Frankie*
> *Black as tar*
> *Tried to get to heaven*
> *In a 'lectric car.*
> *Car got stalled in an underpass,*
> *Threw Aunt Frankie right on her ass.*

Whenever I singsong this rhyme at her, she invariably tries to climb over the fence, a furious, drunken old woman, threatening me with the man's umbrella that she carries. I should think she would remember from past performances that she cannot possibly reach me. But she always tries. After several futile efforts, she gives up and goes back to the boardinghouse across the street. A lot of old maids and widows live there. No gentlemen. Just ladies. They spend their spare time rocking on the front porch, and playing whist, and looking over at the drugstore. Aunt Frank spends her spare time in the kitchen of the boardinghouse, rocking and emptying bottle after bottle of gin.

But on the day of my father's birthday, she was sober; at least, she walked as though she were. She had a basket on her arm with a white napkin covering its contents. I decided she must have made something special for my father's supper. She went in the drugstore, and when she came out, she didn't have the basket. She saw me sitting on the steps but she ignored me.

Aunt Sophronia came and stood in the window. She had washed the glass globes that we keep filled with blue, red, and yellow liquid. She was wearing a dark skirt and a white blouse. Her hair was no longer skinned tight back from her forehead; it was curling around her forehead, perhaps because she had been working in the garden, bending over, and the hairpins that usually hold it so tightly in place had worked themselves loose. She didn't look real. The sun was shining in the window and it reflected the lights from the jars of colored water back on her face and her figure, and she looked golden and rose-colored and lavender and it was as though there was a rainbow moving in the window.

Chink Johnson drove up in his borrowed horse and carriage. He stood and talked to me and then started to go in the store, saw Aunt Sophronia, and stood still. He took a deep breath. I could hear him. He took off the stiff straw hat that he wore way back on his head and bowed to her. She nodded, as though she really didn't want to, and turned away and acted as though she were very busy.

He grabbed my arm and actually pinched it.

"What are you doin'?" I said angrily. "What is the matter with you? Let go my arm."

"Shut up," he said impatiently, pinching harder. His fingers felt as though they were made of iron. "Who is that?"

I pried his fingers loose and rubbed my arm. "Where?"

"In the window. Who is that girl in the window?"

"That's my aunt Sophronia."

"Your aunt? Your aunt?"

"Yes."

He went in the store. One moment he was standing beside me and the next moment he had practically leaped inside the store.

I went in, too. He was leaning in the window, saying, "Wouldn't you like to go for a walk with me this Sunday?" She shook her head. "Well, couldn't you go for a ride with me? I'll call for you—"

Aunt Sophronia said, "I work every day."

"Every day?" he said. "But that's not possible. Nobody works every day. I'll be back tomorrow—"

And he was gone. Aunt Sophronia looked startled. She didn't look angry, just sort of surprised.

I said, "Tomorrow and tomorrow and tomorrow—" And I thought, well, she's got two suitors now. There's this Shake Jones Livingstone, otherwise known as Chink Johnson, and there's Mr. Bemish. I do not think I would pick either one. Mr. Bemish is too old even though he is my friend. I think of Chink Johnson as my friend, too, but I do not think he would make a good husband. I tried to decide why I do not approve of him as a husband for Aunt Sophronia. I think it is because Aunt Sophronia is a lady and Chink Johnson is—well—he is not a gentleman.

That night at supper we celebrated my father's birthday. At that hour nobody much came in the store. Pickett, the sexton, sat on the bench in the front and if anybody came in and wanted my father, he'd come to the back door and holler for him.

There was a white tablecloth on the big oak dining-room table, and we used my mother's best Haviland china and the sterling-silver knives and forks with the rose pattern, and there was a pile of packages by my father's plate, and there were candles on the cake and we had ice cream for dessert. My old enemy, Aunt Frank, had delivered Parker House rolls for his birthday and had made him a milk-panful of rice pudding, because my father has always said that when he dies he hopes it will be because he drowns in a sea composed of rice pudding, that he could eat his weight in rice pudding, that he could eat rice pudding morning, noon, and night. Aunt Frank must have been sober when she made the pudding, for it was creamy and delicious and I ate two helpings of it right along with my ice cream.

I kept waiting for Aunt Sophronia to say something about Chink Johnson. He is a very unusual-looking man and we've never had a customer, colored or white, with that kind of beard. She did not mention him. Neither did I. My father has never mentioned him—at least not at the table. I wonder if my father hopes he will vanish. Perhaps they are afraid he will become a part of the family circle if they mention him.

Chink Johnson has become a part of the family circle and he used the same method that Mr. Bemish used. He just walked into the yard and into the house. I was upstairs, and I happened to look out of the window, and there was Chink Johnson walking up the street. He opened our gate, walked around the side of the house and into our back yard. I hurried to the back of the house and looked out the window and saw him open the screen door and go into the kitchen. He didn't knock on the door either, he just walked in.

For the longest time I didn't hear a sound. I listened and listened. I must have stood still for fifteen minutes. Then I heard someone playing our piano. I knew it must be Chink Johnson because this was not the kind of music anyone in our house would have been playing. I ran downstairs. My mother had been in the cellar, and she came running up out of the cellar, and my father came hurrying over from the drugstore. We all stood and looked and looked.

Chink was sitting at our piano. He had a cigarette dangling from his lower lip, and the smoke from the cigarette was like a cloud—a blue-gray, hazy kind of cloud around his face, his eyes, his beard, so that you could only catch glimpses of them through the smoke. He was playing some kind of fast, discordant-sounding music and he was slapping the floor with one of his long feet and he was slapping the keys with his long fingers.

Aunt Sophronia was leaning against the piano looking down at him. He did not use music when he played, and he never once looked at the keyboard, he just kept looking right into Aunt Sophronia's eyes. I thought my father would tell Chink to go slap somebody else's floor with his long feet, but my mother gave him one of those now-don't-say-a-word looks and he glared at Chink and went back to the drugstore.

Chink stayed a long time, he played the piano, he sang, or rather I guess you would say he talked to the music. It is a very peculiar kind of musical performance. He plays some chords, a whole series of them, and he makes peculiar changes in the chords as he plays, and then he says the words of a song—he doesn't really sing, but his voice does change in pitch to, in a sense, match the chords he is playing, and he does talk to a kind of rhythm which also matches the chords. I sat down beside him and watched what he was doing, and listened to the words he said, and though it is not exactly music as I am accustomed to hearing it, I found it very interesting. He told me that what he does with those songs is known as the "talkin' blues." Only he said "*talk*in' " and he made "blues" sound like it was two separate words, not just a two-syllable word, but two distinct words.

I have been trying to play the piano the way he does but I get nothing but terrible sounds. I pretend that I am blind and keep my eyes closed all the time while I feel for chords. He must have a special gift for this because it is an extremely difficult thing that he is doing and I don't know whether I will ever be able to do it. He has a much better ear for music than I have.

Chink Johnson comes to see Aunt Sophronia almost every day. Sometimes when I look out in the back yard, Mr. Bemish is out there too. He always sits on the ground, and at his age, I should think it might give him rheumatism. He must be a very brave little man or else his love for Aunt Sophronia has given him great courage. I say this because Chink Johnson is very rude to Mr. Bemish and he stares at him with a dreadfully cruel look on his face. If I were small and slender and old like Mr. Bemish, I would not sit in the same yard with a much bigger, much younger man who obviously did not want me there.

I have thought a great deal about Mr. Bemish. I like him. He is truly a friend. But I do not think he should be interested in Aunt Sophronia —at least not in a loving kind of way. The thing that bothers me is that I honestly cannot decide whether I object to him as a suitor for her because he is white or because he is old. Sometimes I think it is for both reasons. I am fairly certain it isn't just because he's old. This bothers me. If my objections to him are because he's white (and that's what I told him, but I often say things that I know people do not want to hear and that they particularly do not want to hear from someone very much younger than they are), then I have been trained on the subject of race just as I have been "trained" to be a Christian. I know how I was trained to be a Christian—Sunday school, prayers, etc. I do not know exactly how I've been "trained" on the subject of race. Then why do I feel like this about Mr. Bemish?

Shortly after I wrote that, I stopped puzzling about Mr. Bemish because summer officially started—at least for me. It is true that school had been out for a long time, and we are wearing our summer clothes, and the yard is filled with flowers—but summer never really gets under way for me until Dottle Smith comes for his yearly visit.

Dottle and Uncle Johno went to school together. They look sort of alike. They are big men and they are so light in color they look like white men. But something in them (Dottle says that it is a "cultivated and developed and carefully nourished hatred of white men") will not permit them to pass for white. Dottle teaches English and elocution and dramatics at a school for colored people in Georgia, and he gives lectures and readings during the summer to augment his income. Uncle Johno is the chief fund-raising agent for a colored school in Louisiana.

I believe that my attitude towards Mr. Bemish stems from Dottle Smith. And Johno. They are both what my father calls race-conscious. When they travel on trains in the South, they ride in Jim Crow coaches until the conductor threatens to have them arrested unless they sit in the sections of the train reserved for whites. They are always being put out of the colored sections of waiting rooms, and warned out of the colored sections of towns, and being refused lodgings in colored rooming houses on the grounds that they would be a source of embarrassment—nobody would be able to figure out why a white man wanted to live with colored people, and they would be suspected of being spies, but of what kind or to what purpose, they have never been able to determine.

I have just reread what I have written here, and I find that I've left out the reason why I am writing so much about Dottle. Yesterday afternoon when I came back from an errand, there was a large, heavy-looking bag —leather, but it was shaped like a carpetbag—near the bench where the customers sit when they wait for prescriptions. I recognized it immediately. I have seen that bag every summer for as far back as I can remember. I wondered if Dottle had come alone this time or if he had a friend with him. Sometimes he brings a young man with him. These young men look very much alike—they are always slender, rather shy, have big dark eyes and very smooth skin just about the color of bamboo.

I looked at Dottle's big battered old bag sitting on the floor near the bench, and I could almost see him, with his long curly hair, and I could hear him reciting poetry in his rich, buttery voice. He can quote all the great speeches from *Hamlet*, *Macbeth*, *Richard II*, and he can recite the sonnets.

I loved him. He was lively and funny and unexpected. Sometimes he would grab my braid and shout in his best Shakespearean voice, "Seize on her Furies, take her to your torments!"

I looked at Dottle's battered bag and I said to my father, "Is he alone? Or has he got one of those pretty boys with him?"

My father looked at me over the top of his glasses. "Alone."

"How come he had to leave his bag here?"

"Well, the Ecckles aren't home. Ellen's gone on vacation—"

"Why does Aunt Ellen always go on vacation when Dottle comes?"

My father ignored this and went on talking. "Johno's gone to Albany collecting money for the school."

"Where is Dottle now?"

"I'm right here, sugar," and Dottle Smith opened the screen door and came in. He looked bigger than he had the summer before. He hugged me. He smelled faintly of lavender.

"You went and grew, honey," he said, and took off his hat and bowed. It was a wide-brimmed panama, and he had on a starched white shirt, and a flowing Byronic kind of black tie, and I looked at him with absolute delight. He was being a Southern "cunnel" and he was such an actor— I thought I could see lace at his wrists, hear mockingbirds sing, see a white-columned mansion, hear hoofbeats in the distance, and hear a long line of slaves, suitably clad as footmen and coachmen and butlers and housemen, murmur, Yess, massah, Yes, massah. It was all there in his voice.

"Why, in another couple years I'll be recitin' poetry to you. How's your momma? This summer I'll have to teach you how to talk. These Yankah teachers you've got all talk through their noses. They got you doin' the same thing—"

For two whole days I forgot about Chink Johnson and Mr. Bemish and Aunt Sophronia. Dottle liked to go fishing and crabbing; he liked to play whist; and he could tell the most marvelous stories and act them out.

The very next day Dottle and Uncle Johno and I went crabbing. We set out early in the morning with our nets and our fishing lines and the rotten meat we used for bait, and our lunch and thermos bottles with lemonade in them. It was a two-mile walk from where we lived to the creek where we caught crabs.

There was a bridge across the creek, an old wooden bridge. Some of the planks were missing. We stood on this bridge or sat on it and threw our lines in the water. Once in a great while a horse and wagon would drive across and set the planks to vibrating. Johno and Dottle would hop off the bridge. But I stayed on and held to the railing. The bridge trembled under my feet, and the horse and wagon would thunder across, and the driver usually waved and hollered, "I gotta go fast or we'll all fall in."

The water in the creek was so clear I could see big crabs lurking way down on the bottom; I could see little pieces of white shells and beautiful stones. We didn't talk much while we were crabbing. Sometimes I lay flat on my stomach on the bridge and looked down into the water, watching the little eddies and whirlpools that formed after I threw my line in.

Before we ate our lunch, we went wading in the creek. Johno and Dottle rolled up the legs of their pants, and their legs were so white I wondered if they were that white all over, and if they were, how they could be colored. We sat on the bank of the creek and ate our lunch. Afterwards Dottle and Johno told stories, wonderful stories in which animals talk, and there are haunted houses and ghosts and demons, and old colored preachers who believe in heaven and hell.

They always started off the same way. Dottle said to Johno, "Mr. Bones, be seated."

Though I have heard some of these stories many, many times, Dottle and Johno never tell them exactly the same. They change their gestures, they vary their facial expressions and the pitch of their voices.

Dottle almost always tells the story about the colored man who goes in a store in a small town in the South and asks for Muriel cigars. The white man who owns the store says (and here Johno becomes an outraged Southern white man), "Nigger, what's the matter with you? Don't you see that picture of that beautiful white woman on the front of this box? When you ask for them cigars, you say *Miss* Muriel cigars!"

Though Uncle Johno is a good storyteller, he is not as good, not as funny or as dramatic as Dottle. When I listen to Dottle I can see the old colored preacher who spent the night in a haunted house. I see him approaching the house, the wind blowing his coattails, and finally he takes refuge inside because of the violence of the storm. He lights a fire in the fireplace and sits down by it and rubs his hands together, warming them. As he sits there, he hears heavy footsteps coming down the stairs (and Dottle makes his hand go thump, thump, thump on the bank of the creek) and the biggest cat the old man has ever seen comes in and sits down, looks at the old preacher, looks around, and says, "Has Martin got here yet?" The old man is too startled and too nervous to answer. He hears heavy footsteps again—thump, thump, thump. And a second cat, much bigger than the first one, comes in, and sits down right next to the old preacher. Both cats stare at him, and then the second cat says to the first cat, "Has Martin got here yet?" and the first cat shakes his head. There is something so speculative in their glance that the old man gets more and more uneasy. He wonders if they are deciding to eat him. The wind howls in the chimney, puffs of smoke blow back into the room. Then another and bigger cat thumps down the stairs. Finally there are six enormous cats, three on each side of him. Each one of these cats has asked the same question of the others—"Martin got here yet?" A stair-shaking tread begins at the top of the stairs, the cats all look at each other, and the old man grabs his hat, and says to the assembled cats, "You tell Martin ah been here but ah've gone."

I clapped when Dottle finished this story. I looked around, thinking how glad I am he is here and what a wonderful place this is to listen to stories. The sun is warm but there is a breeze and it blows through the long marsh grass which borders the creek. The grass moves, seems to wave. Gulls fly high overhead. The only sound is the occasional cry of a gull and the lapping of water against the piling of the bridge.

Johno tells the next story. It is about an old colored preacher and a rabbit. The old man tries to outrun an overfriendly and very talkative rabbit. The rabbit keeps increasing in size. The old man runs away from him and the rabbit catches up with him. Each time the rabbit says, "That was some run we had, wasn't it, brother?" Finally the old man runs until he feels as though his lungs are going to burst and his legs will turn to rubber, and he looks back and doesn't see the rabbit anywhere in sight. He sits down on a stone to rest and catch his breath. He has just seated himself when he discovers the rabbit sitting right beside him, smiling. The rabbit is now the same size as the preacher. The rabbit rolls his eyes and lisps, "That wath thome run we had, wathn't it?" The old man stood up, got ready to run again, and said, "Yes, that was some run we had, brother, but"—he took a deep breath—"you ain't *seen* no runnin' yet."

After they finished telling stories, we all took naps. Dottle and Johno were wearing old straw hats, wide-brimmed panamas with crooked, floppy brims. Dottle had attached a piece of mosquito netting to his, and it hung down across his shoulders. From the back he looked like a woman who was wearing a veil.

When we woke up it was late in the afternoon and time to start for home. I ran part of the way. Then I sat down by the side of the road, in the shade, and waited until they caught up with me.

Dottle said, "Sugar, what are you in such a hurry for?"

I said, laughing, "Miss Muriel, you tell Martin I been here but I've gone and that he ain't *seen* no runnin' yet."

I got home first. Chink Johnson was in the store. When Dottle and Johno arrived, I introduced Chink to my uncles, Johno and Dottle. They didn't seem much impressed with each other. Johno nodded and Dottle smiled and left. Chink watched Dottle as he went toward the back room. Dottle has a very fat bottom and he sort of sways from side to side as he walks.

Chink said, "He seems kind of ladylike. He related on your mother's side?"

"He's not related at all. He's an old friend of Uncle Johno's. They went to school together. In Atlanta, Georgia." I sounded very condescending. "Do you know where that is?"

"Yeah. Nigger, read this. Nigger, don't let sundown catch you here. Nigger, if you can't read this, run anyway. If you can't run—then vanish. Just vanish out. I know the place. I came from there."

My father was standing outside on the walk talking to Aunt Frank, so I felt at liberty to speak freely and I said, "Nigger, what are you talkin' about you want Muriel cigars. You see this picture of this beautiful red-headed white woman, nigger, you say *Miss* Muriel."

Chink stood up and he was frowning and his voice was harsh. "Little girl, don't you talk that way. I talk that way if I feel like it but don't you ever talk that way."

I felt as though I had been betrayed. One moment he was my friend and we were speaking as equals and the next moment, without warning, he is an adult who is scolding me in a loud, harsh voice. I was furious and I could feel tears welling up in my eyes. This made me angrier. I couldn't seem to control my weeping. Recently, and I do not know how it happened, whenever I am furiously angry, I begin to cry.

Chink leaned over and put his hand under my chin, lifted my face, saw the tears, and he kissed my cheek. His beard was rough and scratchy. He smelled like the pine woods, and I could see pine needles in his hair and in his beard, and I wondered if he and Aunt Sophronia had been in the woods.

"Sugar," he said gently, "I don't like that Miss Muriel story. It ought to be told the other way around. A colored man should be tellin' a white man, 'White man, you see this picture of this beautiful colored woman? *White* man, you say *Miss* Muriel!' "

He went out of the store through the back room into the yard just as though he were a member of the family. It hadn't taken him very long to reach this position. Almost every afternoon he goes for a walk with Aunt Sophronia. I watch them when they leave the store. He walks so close to her that he seems to surround her, and he has his head bent so that his face is close to hers. Once I met them strolling up Petticoat Lane, his dark face so close to hers that his goat's beard was touching her smooth brown cheek.

My mother used to watch them too, as they walked side by side on the dirt path that led to the woods—miles and miles of woods. Sometimes he must have said things that Aunt Sophronia didn't like, because she would turn her head sharply away from him.

I decided that once you got used to his beard and the peculiar color and slant of his eyes, why you could say he had an interesting face. I do not know what it is about his eyes that makes me think of heat. But I know what color they are. They are the color of petrified wood after it's been polished, it's a red brown, and that's what his eyes are like.

I like the way he plays the piano, though I do not like his voice. I cannot get my mother to talk about him. My father grunts when I mention Chink's name and scowls so ferociously that it is obvious he does not like him.

I tried to find out what Aunt Sophronia thought of him. Later in the day I found her in the store alone and I said, "Do you like Chink Johnson?"

She said, "Run along and do the supper dishes."

"But do you?"

"Don't ask personal questions," she said, and her face and neck flushed.

She must have liked him though. She not only went walking with him in the afternoon, but on Sunday mornings he went to church with her. He wore a white linen suit and that same stiff straw hat way back on his head. He brought her presents—a tall bottle of violet eau de cologne, a bunch of Parma violets made of silk, but they looked real. On Sundays, Aunt Sophronia wore the violets pinned at her waist and they made her look elegant, like a picture in a book.

I said, "Oh, you look beautiful."

My mother said dryly, "Very stylish."

We all crossed the street together on Sunday mornings. They went to

church. I went to Sunday school. Sunday school was out first and I waited
for them to come down the church steps. Aunt Sophronia came down
the church steps and he would be so close behind her that he might have
been dancing with her and matching his leg movements to hers. Suddenly
he was in front of her and down on the path before she was and he turned
and held out his hand. Even there on the sidewalk he wasn't standing
still. It is as though his feet and his hands are more closely connected to
his heart, to his central nervous system, than is true of other people, so
that during every waking moment he moves, tapping his foot on the floor,
tapping his fingers on a railing, on somebody's arm, on a table top. I
wondered if he kept moving like that when he was asleep, tapping quarter
notes with his foot, playing eighth notes with his right hand, half notes
with his left hand. He attacked a piano when he played, violated it—
violate a piano? I thought, violate Aunt Sophronia?

He stood on the dirt path and held out his hand to Aunt Sophronia,
smiling, helping her down the church steps.

"Get your prayers said, sugar?" he said to me.

"Yes. I said one for you and one for the family. Aunt Sophronia, you
smell delicious. Like violets—"

"She does, doesn't she?"

We walked across the street to the drugstore, hand in hand. Chink was
in the middle and he held one of my hands and one of Aunt Sophronia's.
He stays for dinner on Sundays. And on Sunday nights we close the store
early and we all sit in the back yard, where it is cool. Mr. Bemish joined
us in the yard. At dusk the fireflies come out, and then as the darkness
deepens, bats swoop around us. Aunt Sophronia says, "Oooooh!" and
holds on to her head, afraid one might get entangled in her hair.

Dottle took out one of his big white handkerchiefs and tied it around
his head, and said in his richest, most buttery voice, " 'One of the nocturnal or crepuscular flying mammals constituting the order Chiroptera.' "

Dottle sprawled in a chair and recited poetry or told long stories about
the South—stories that sometimes had so much of fear and terror and
horror in them that we shivered even though the air was warm. Chink
didn't spend the evening. He sat in one of the lawn chairs, tapping on
the arm with his long, flexible fingers, and then left. Mr. Bemish always
stays until we go in for the night. He takes no part in the conversation,
but sits on the ground, huddled near Aunt Sophronia's skirts. Once when
a bat swooped quite close, Aunt Sophronia clutched his arm.

Sometimes Dottle recites whole acts from *Macbeth* or *Hamlet* or all of
the Song of Solomon, or sometimes he recited the loveliest of Shake-

speare's sonnets. We forget the bats swooping over our heads, ignore the mosquitoes that sting our ankles and our legs, and sit mesmerized while he declaims, "Shall I compare thee to a summer's day?"

The summer is going faster and faster—perhaps because of the presence of Aunt Sophronia's suitors. I don't suppose Dottle is really a suitor, but he goes through the motions. He picks little bouquets for her—bachelor buttons and candytuft—and leaves them on the kitchen table. He always calls her "Miss Sophronia." If we are outdoors and she comes out to sit in the yard, he leaps to his feet, and bows and says, "Wait, wait. Befo' you sit on that bench, let me wipe it off," and he pulls out an enormous linen handkerchief and wipes off the bench. He is always bowing and kissing her hand.

By the middle of August it was very hot. My father had the store painted, and when the blinds were taken down, the painter found whole families of bats clinging together in back of the blinds. Evidently they lived there. I couldn't get hold of one, although I tried. They were the most peculiar-looking creatures. They looked almost like a person who wears glasses all the time and then suddenly goes without them, and they have a kind of peering look.

Chink Johnson is always in our house or in the store or in the yard or going for walks with Aunt Sophronia. Whenever he is not violating the piano at the Inn, he is with Aunt Sophronia—

He taught her how to dance—in the back yard, without any music, just his counting and clapping his hands. His feet made no sound on our thick grass. On two different sunny afternoons, he gave her dancing lessons, and on the third afternoon, he had her dancing. She was laughing and she was lively-looking and she looked young. He persuaded her to take off her shoes and she danced in her bare feet. Fortunately, nobody knows this but me.

He took her fishing. When they came back, she was quite sunburned but her eyes were shining as though they held the reflected light from the sun shining on water.

Just in that one short summer he seemed to take on all kinds of guises—fisherman, dancer, singer, churchgoer, even delivery boy.

One morning someone knocked at the back door and there was Chink Johnson with our grocery order, saying to my Aunt Sophronia, "Here's your meat, ma'am, and your vegetables," touching his hat, bowing, un-loading the crate of groceries, and then sitting down at the kitchen table as though he owned it, drinking a cup of coffee that no one had offered him, just pouring it out of the enamel pot that stays on the stove, finding cream and sugar himself, and sitting there with his legs thrust way out in front of him, and those terribly tight pants he wears looking as though they were painted on his thighs.

Sometimes when he sits in our kitchen, he laughs. His laughter is not merry. When my father laughs, the sound makes you laugh, even when you don't know what he is laughing about.

When Chink Johnson laughs, I look away from him. The sound hurts my ears. It is like the ugly squawk of some big bird that you have disturbed in the woods and it flies right into your face, pecking at your eyes.

It has been a very interesting summer. I have begun to refer to it in the past tense because there isn't much left of a summer by the middle of August. On Thursday afternoon, Aunt Sophronia and I saw that other ladies liked Chink Johnson too.

Thursday afternoon is traditionally maids' day off and Chink Johnson drove the maids from the Inn into town, in a wagon, late in the day. He stopped in front of the store with a wagon full of girls in long skirts, giggling, leaning against him, a kind of panting excitement in that wagon, their arms around him; they whispered to him, they were seized by fits of laughter, shrieks of laughter.

They came in the store and bought hairnets and hairpins and shampoo and Vaseline and hair tonics and cough medicines and court plaster and a great many items that they did not need, because it was a pleasure to be spending money, and to be free of the tyranny of the housekeepers' demands—or so my mother said—some young and attractive, some not so young, about ten of them.

Aunt Sophronia was in the store and she waited on them, studying them. Every once in a while one would go to the door, and yell, "We'll be out in a minute, Chink. Just a little while!" and wave at him and throw kisses at him.

Then they were gone, all at once, piling into the wagon, long full skirts in disarray. One of them sat in Chink's lap, laughing, looking up into his face, and saying, "Let's go in the woods. Chink take us in the woods. I'll help drive."

Aunt Sophronia and I stood in the doorway and watched them as they drove off, going towards the pine woods. The wagon seemed to be filled with wide skirts, and ruffled petticoats, all suddenly upended because Chink said, "Giddup, there!" and hit the horse with the whip, cracked it over the horse's ears, and the horse started off as though he were a race horse.

It was late when they went past the store, going home. Sitting in the back yard, we could hear the horse racing, and the girls squealing and laughing, and Chink singing a ribald song, about "Strollin', and Strollin'."

Dottle stopped right in the middle of a poem and Mr. Bemish straightened up so that he was not quite so close to Aunt Sophronia's skirts. It was like having Chink Johnson right there in the back yard with us, the rough, atonal voice, the red-brown eyes that looked hot, literally hot, as though if you touched them you would have to withdraw your fingers immediately because they would be scorched or singed or burned, the jutting beard, the restless feet and hands.

We sat absolutely still. We could hear the rattling of the wagon, the clop-clop of the horse's hoofs and above it the laughter of the girls, and, dominating that sound, Chink Johnson's voice lifted in song. Even after they were so far away we could not possibly hear them, these sounds seemed to linger in the air, faint, far-off.

It was a warm night, brilliant with light from the moon. I pictured the girls as sitting on top of Chink, all around him, on his arms, in his lap, on his shoulders, and I thought the prettiest one should be perched on his head.

Dottle lit a cigar and puffed out clouds of bluish smoke and said, "I never heard the mating call of the male so clearly sounded on a summer's night." He laughed so hard that he had to get out one of his big handkerchiefs and dab at his eyes with it.

Aunt Sophronia got up from the bench so fast that she brushed against Mr. Bemish, almost knocking him over. He lost his balance and regained it only because he supported himself with one hand on the ground. She must have known that she had very nearly upset him but she went marching toward the house, her back very straight and her head up in the air, and she never once looked back.

Dottle said, "Have I offended her?"

My mother said, "It's late. It's time we went in."

Mr. Bemish must have gone home when we went in the house, but he was back in the yard so early the next morning he might just as well have spent the night. Dottle and I were standing in the kitchen, looking down the back yard. He was drinking coffee out of a mug and I was eating a piece of bread and butter. Our back yard is a pretty sight on a summer morning. It is filled with flowers, and birds are singing, and the air is very cool, and there is a special smell, a summer smell compounded of grass and dew on the grass and flowers, and the suggestion of heat to come later in the day.

We looked out the door and there was Mr. Bemish down on his knees

in front of Aunt Sophronia. She was sitting on the bench and she looked
horrified and she seemed to have been in the act of trying to stop him,
one hand extended in a thrusting-away motion. I thought: His pants legs
will be very damp because there's still dew on the grass, and how did he
get here so early, and did he know that she would be sitting on the bench
almost before sunup?

"Ah, girlie, girlie!" he said, on his knees in our back yard, kneeling
on our thick, soft grass. "Will you marry me?"

"No!"

"Is it," he said, "because I am old?" and his voice went straight up in
pitch just like a scale. "I'm not old. I'm not old. Why, I can still jump
up in the air and click my heels together three times!"

And he did. He got up off his knees and he jumped up, straight up,
and clicked his heels together three times, and landed on the grass, and
there was just a slight thumping sound when he landed.

Aunt Sophronia said, "Mr. Bemish, Mr. Bemish. Don't do that—don't
do that—go away, go home—" And she ran toward the house and he
started after her and then he saw us standing in the door, watching him,
and he stood still. He shouted after her, "I'll put on my best coat and my
best hat and you won't know me—I'll be back—and you won't know
me—"

Dottle glared at him through the screen door and said, "You old fool
—you old fool—"

Mr. Bemish hurried around the side of the house, pretending that he
hadn't heard him.

I did not know when Mr. Bemish would be back, wearing his best coat
and his best hat, but I certainly wanted to see him and, if possible, to
witness his next performance. I decided that whenever Aunt Sophronia
was in the store, I'd be in the store too.

When my father went to eat his dinner at twelve-thirty, Aunt Sophronia
looked after the store. There weren't many people who came in at that
hour; it was the dinner hour and Aunt Sophronia sat in the prescription
room, with the door open, and read the morning newspaper. There was
an old wooden chair, by the window, in the prescription room. It had a
faded painting across the back, a wooden seat and back and arms. It was
a very comfortable chair if you sat up straight, and Aunt Sophronia sat
up very straight. She could look out of the window and see the church
green, see the path that went up Petticoat Lane toward the pine woods,
and she commanded a view of the interior of the store.

I don't think she saw Mr. Bemish when he entered. If she had, she would have gotten out of the chair immediately to wait on him. But she was reading the newspaper, and he came in very quietly. He was wearing a cutaway coat that was too long, and a pair of striped trousers, and he was carrying a silk hat in his hand, a collapsed silk hat. He stopped inside the door and put the hat in shape and then placed it carefully on his head. He looked like a circus clown who is making fun of the ringmaster, mocking him, making his costume look silly.

Mr. Bemish went straight through the store, and stood in front of Aunt Sophronia, and he jumped straight up in the air, like a dancer, and clicked his heels together three times. The bottles on the shelves rattled and the back room was filled with a pinging sound.

"Oh, my goodness," Aunt Sophronia said, frowning. "Oh, my goodness, don't jump like that." And she stood up.

My father came in through the back door and he said, "What's going on in here? What's going on in here?"

Mr. Bemish said, "I was just showing Miss Sophronia that I can still jump up in the air and click my heels together three times before I come back down again."

My father made a noise that sounded like "Boooooh!" but wasn't quite, and Mr. Bemish retreated, talking very fast. "I had asked Miss Sophronia if she would marry me and she said no, and I thought perhaps it was because she thinks I'm too old and not stylish enough and so I got dressed up and I was showing her I could still jump—"

"Get out of here! Get out of here! Get out of here!"

My father's voice kept rising and increasing in volume, and his face looked as though he were about to burst. It seemed to darken and to swell, to get bigger.

Aunt Sophronia said, "Oh, you mustn't talk to him like that—"

My father was moving toward Mr. Bemish, and Mr. Bemish was retreating, retreating, and finally he turned and ran out of the store and ran up Petticoat Lane with his long coattails flapping about his legs.

My father said, "I shouldn't have let him hang around here all these months. I can't leave this store for five minutes that I don't find one of these no-goods hangin' around when I come back. Not one of 'em worth the powder and shot to blow 'em to hell and back. That piano player pawin' the ground and this old white man jumpin' up in the air, and that friend of Johno's, that poet or whatever he is, all he needs are some starched petticoats and a bonnet and he'd make a woman—he's practically one now—and he's tee-heein' around, and if they were all put together in one piece, it still wouldn't be a whole man." My father shook his fist in the air and glared at Aunt Sophronia.

"I guess it's all my fault—" Aunt Sophronia sounded choked-up and funny.

My father said, "No, no, no, I didn't mean that," and patted her arm. "It's all perfectly natural. It's just that we're the only colored people living in this little bit of town and there aren't any fine young colored men around, only this tramp piano player, and every time I look at him I can hear him playing some rags and see a whole line of big-bosomed women done up in sequined dresses standin' over him, moanin' about wantin' somebody to turn their dampers down, and I can see poker games and crap games and—"

My mother came in through the back room. She said, "Samuel, why are you talking about gambling games?"

"I was trying to explain to Sophy how I feel about that piano player."

To my surprise, my mother said, "Has Sophronia asked you how you feel about Mr. Johnson?"

When my father shook his head, she said, "Then I don't think there is any reason for you to say anything about him. I need you in the garden. I want you to move one of my peonies."

I wonder what my mother would say if she knew how my father chased little Mr. Bemish out of his store. I wonder if Mr. Bemish will ever come back.

Mr. Bemish did come back. He came back the following Sunday. We were all in the store, Aunt Sophronia, and Dottle, and Chink and I.

Mr. Bemish sidled in through the door. He looked as though he expected someone to jump out at him and yell, "Go home!" But he came in anyway and he sat down beside me on the bench near the front of the store.

Chink was leaning on the cigar case, talking to Aunt Sophronia, his face very close to hers. I couldn't hear what he was saying, but he seemed to be trying to persuade her to do something, go for a walk, or something, and she was obviously refusing, politely but definitely. Dottle was standing near the back of the store, watching Chink.

Aunt Frank opened the store door, and she stood in the doorway holding the screen door open. She has a cross, sharp way of speaking, very fast, and very unpleasant. She saw me and she said, "Where's Mar-tha?"

I wasn't expecting to see Aunt Frank in the store at that hour and I was so surprised that I didn't answer her.

"What's the mat-ter with you? Cat got your tongue? Didn't you hear what I said? Where's your moth-er?"

"She's over on the other side of the building, in the kitchen. She's having coffee with my father."

She scowled at Chink. "How long's that bearded man been in here talkin' to Sophy?"

Chink turned around and looked toward Aunt Frank. Aunt Sophronia started toward her, moving very fast out from behind the cigar case, saying, "Can I get something for you?"

As Aunt Frank stood there holding the door open, a whole flight of bats came in the store. I say a "flight" because I don't know what else to call a large-sized group of bats. They swooped down and up in a blind, fast flight.

Aunt Frank shrieked, "Ahhh! My hair, watch out for your hair! Ahhhhhh!" and stood up on the bench, and held her black fusty skirts close about her and then pulled them over her head. I decided she had confused mice and bats, that the technique for getting rid of mice was to stand on a chair and clutch one's skirts around one, that is, if you were a lady and pretended to be afraid of mice. I did learn that Aunt Frank was wearing carpet slippers made of dark-gray felt, black cotton stockings, and under the outside layer of skirts there seemed to be a great many layers of black petticoats.

Dottle ran into the back room and held the door tightly shut. There is a glass in the door and he could look out at the rest of us as we dodged the bats. I could see his large white face, and long hair, and I supposed he was as frightened as Aunt Frank that bats would get entangled in his hair, because he squealed, all the rich, buttery quality gone from his voice, just a high-pitched squealing.

Aunt Frank cautiously lowered the outer skirt, fumbled in a pocket, and took out a bottle, not a big bottle, but about the size of an eight-ounce cough-medicine bottle, and she took two or three swigs from it, recorked it, and then re-covered her head.

Chink grabbed a newspaper and slapped at the bats as they circled. "Gotcha. Hi-hi-gotcha—hi-hi-gotcha—hi-hi!" and he folded the newspaper and belted them as they swished past him.

Mr. Bemish stared. I decided that he'd lived with bats and spiders and mice, well, not lived with perhaps, but was so accustomed to them that he could not understand why they should cause all this noise and confusion and fear. He ignored the bats entirely and went to the rescue of his lady love. He clasped Aunt Sophronia to his bosom, covering her head with his hands and arms and he kept murmuring comforting words. "Now, now. I won't let anything hurt you. Nothing can harm you." He took a deep breath and said, quite distinctly, "I love you, my darling. I love you, love you—"

Aunt Sophronia seemed to nestle in his arms, to cuddle closer to him, to lean harder every time a bat swooped past them.

Father came through the back room—he had to wrestle Dottle out of the way before he could get through the door—and he very sensibly held the screen door open, and what with the impetus offered by Chink's folded newspaper, the bats swooped outside.

It was really very exciting while it lasted, what with all the shrieks and the swift movement of the bats. When I began to really look around, the first thing I noticed was that Aunt Sophronia was still huddled in the protective arms of Mr. Bemish. Dottle came out of the back room with his mouth pursed and his cheeks were puffed out a little and I wouldn't have been surprised if he had hissed at Mr. Bemish. He and Chink headed straight towards Mr. Bemish. They are very tall men and Mr. Bemish is short and slender, and as they converged on him, one from the rear and the other from the side, he looked smaller and older than ever.

Aunt Sophronia stepped away from Mr. Bemish. She moved toward Chink. One side of her face was red where it had been pressed hard against the wool of Mr. Bemish's coat.

All of a sudden my father's hand was resting on one of Chink's shoulders. He has large, heavy hands and his hand seemed to have descended suddenly and with great weight. He said, "You'll not start any trouble in my store."

Aunt Frank said, "Bats! Bats!" She indicated that my father was to help her down from the bench. She climbed down awkwardly, holding on to him. "Worse than bats," she said, and she made a wide all-inclusive gesture that took in Chink and Dottle and Mr. Bemish. "Where's Martha?" she demanded. "She still in the kitchen?"

My father nodded. He held the door open for Mr. Bemish, and Mr. Bemish scuttled out. Dottle and Chink went out, too.

I found a dead bat on the floor and sat down on the bench at the front of the store to examine it. It had a very unpleasant smell. But it was such an interesting creature that I ignored the odor. It had rather large, pointed ears that I thought were quite charming. It had very sharp little claws. I could see why the ladies had screamed and covered their heads, because if those claws got entangled in their long hair, someone would have had to cut their hair to get a bat out of it. Aunt Frank's hair isn't long; it is like a sheep's wool, tight-curled and close to the skin or scalp. But I suppose a bat's sharp little claws and peculiar wings snarled up in that might create more of a problem than it would if caught in longer and less tightly curled hair.

The wings of the bat were webbed like the feet of ducks with a thin membranelike tissue that was attached to the body, reaching from the front legs or arms to the back legs and attached to the sides. The body was small in comparison to the wide sweep of those curious wings. I stretched its wings out and they looked like the inside of an opened umbrella, and I couldn't help admiring them. I began to think of all the things I'd heard said about bats, "blind as a bat," and the word "batty" meaning crazy, and I tried to figure out why "batty," probably because a bat's behavior didn't make sense to a human being—its fast, erratic flight would look senseless.

Then Aunt Frank's voice sounded right in my ear, and her horrible breath was in my nose, and she smelled worse than the bat. She said, "You throw that nasty thing away. You throw that nasty thing away."

I thrust the dead bat straight at her black and wrinkled face. "Look out," I yelled. "It'll suck your blood. It's still alive. Look out!"

She jumped away, absolutely furious. "You little vixen," she said, and squealed just like a pig. Then she saw my mother standing in the door of the prescription room. "Mar-tha," she commanded, "you come here and make her throw this nasty thing away. Make her throw it away. She's settin' here playin' with a dead bat."

My mother said, "If you want to look at the bat, take it outside or take it in the back room. You can't keep a dead bat here in the drugstore."

"This can't hurt her. It's dead."

She interrupted me. "Many people are afraid of bats. It doesn't make any difference whether the bats are dead or alive—they are still afraid of them."

I went outside and sat on the front steps and waited. There was a full moon and the light from it made the street and the houses and the church look as though they had been whitewashed. I put the bat beside me on the step. I was going to wait for Aunt Frank, and when she came out of the store and started down the steps, I was going to put the dead stinking bat in one of the big pockets in her skirt—the pocket where she kept her bottle of gin. And when she got home and reached for a drink, I hoped she would discover, encounter, touch with her bony fingers, the corpse of "one of the nocturnal or crepuscular flying mammals constituting the order Chiroptera" as a token of my affection.

I must have waited there on the steps for two hours. My father began putting out the lights in the store. I stayed right there, anticipating the moment when my ancient enemy, Aunt Frank, would come stumbling around the side of the building.

And then—one moment I was sitting on the splintery front steps of the store, and the next moment I was running up Petticoat Lane, going just as fast as I could, because it had suddenly occurred to me that Chink Johnson and Dottle Smith had gone out of the drugstore right behind Mr. Bemish and they hadn't returned.

By the time I reached Mr. Bemish's shop, I was panting. I couldn't catch my breath.

Mr. Bemish's wagon was drawn up close to the side of the shop. The horse was hitched to it. Mr. Bemish was loading the headboard of his beautiful brass bed on the wagon. He was obviously moving—leaving town, at night. He walked in a peculiar fashion as though he were lame. He was panting too, and making hiccuping noises like someone who has been crying a long time, so long that no real sound comes out, just a kind of hiccuping noise due to the contractions of the throat muscles and the heaving of the chest.

As I stood there, he got the headboard on the wagon, and then he struggled with his mattress, and then the springs, and then he brought out his cobbler's bench.

Dottle and Chink stood watching him, just like two guards or two sheriffs. None of us said anything.

I finally sat down on the enormous millstone that served as Mr. Bemish's front step. I sat way off to one side where I wouldn't interfere with his comings and goings.

May-a-ling, his cat, rubbed against me and then came and sat in my lap, with her back to me, facing towards Mr. Bemish.

It didn't take him very long to empty the shop of his belongings. I couldn't help thinking that if we ever moved, it would take us days to pack all the books and the pictures and the china, and all our clothes and furniture. We all collected things. Aunt Sophronia did beautiful embroidery and she collected embroidered fabrics, and mother collected old dishes and old furniture, and my father collected old glass bottles and old mortars, and they all collected books, and then all the rooms had furniture and there were all kinds of cooking pots. No one of us would ever get all of our belongings in one wagon.

Mr. Bemish came out of the shop and walked all around the little building with that peculiar stiff-legged gait. Apparently the only item he'd overlooked was his garden bench. He had trouble getting it in the wagon, and I dumped May-a-ling on the ground and went to help him.

One of Dottle's meaty hands gripped my braid. "He can manage."

I twisted away from him. "He's just a little old man and he's my friend and I'm going to help him."

Chink said, "Leave her alone."

Dottle let go of my hair. I helped put the bench in the wagon, and then went inside the shop with him, and helped him carry out the few items that were left. Each time I went inside the shop with Mr. Bemish I asked him questions. We both whispered.

"Where are you going, Mr. Bemish?"

"Massachusetts."

"Why?"

He didn't answer. His hiccups got worse.

I waited until we'd taken down the green summer curtains and carefully folded them, and put them in the little trunk that held some of his clothes, and put his broom and his dustpan and his tall kitchen cooking stool on the wagon, before I repeated my question. His hiccups had quieted down.

"Why are you leaving, Mr. Bemish?" I whispered.

"They were going to sew me up."

"Sew you up. Did you say—sew you up?"

"Yes."

"Where?" I said, staring at him, thinking: sew up? Sew up what—eyes, nostrils, mouth, ears, rectum? "They were trying to scare you, Mr. Bemish. Nobody would sew up a person, a human being, unless it was a surgeon—after an operation—"

He shook his head. "No," he whispered. "I thought so, too, but—no, they meant it—with my own waxed thread—"

"Did they—"

"Hush! Hush!"

We used this little piece of flowered carpet to wrap his washbowl and pitcher in and then put the whole bulky package it made on the wagon. We went back inside to make sure that we hadn't forgotten anything. The inside of his shop looked very small and shabby and lonely. There wasn't anything left except his stove and he obviously couldn't take that. It was a very big, handsome stove and he kept it quite shiny and clean.

"Can you keep a secret?" he whispered, standing quite close to me. He smelled old and dusty and withered like dried flowers.

I nodded.

He handed me a small velvet bag. "Hide it, girlie," he whispered. "It's some old jewelry that belonged to my mother. Give it to Miss Sophronia at Christmas from me." He patted my arm.

We went outside and he took down the sign with the lady's high-laced shoe painted on it, and put it on the wagon seat. He climbed in the wagon, picked up the reins.

"May-a-ling, May-a-ling," he called. It was the most musical sound I have ever heard used to call a cat. She answered him instantly. She mewed and jumped up on the wagon seat beside him. He clucked to the horse and they were off.

I waited not only until they were out of sight, but until I could no longer hear the creak of the wagon wheels and the clop-clop of the horse's hoofs, and then I turned and ran.

Chink said, "Wait a minute—"

Dottle said, "You don't understand—"

I stopped running just long enough to shout at them, "You both stink. You stink like dead bats. You and your goddamn Miss Muriel—"

Key to the City

●

(1965)

Diane Oliver

"Nora, want to eat your breakfast with me?" Her mother's starched uniform swished as she walked to the door.

"All right, Mama, I'm getting up now." She watched her mother push aside the curtain that separated her bedroom from the hallway. Then she swung both feet to the edge of the bed and stood up. The little girl who slept beside her did not stir as Nora pulled on her blue jeans and tiptoed from the room.

In the kitchen her mother already sat at the table. "Babycake still asleep?" she asked. "That child ought to be completely worn out getting ready for this trip. You'd think we'd been to Chicago and back."

Nora slipped her egg from the skillet to the plate. "At least Mattie isn't so much trouble," she said, "but the two of them sure don't help my packing."

"I wish I could help, but Mrs. Anderson is not going to let me off early."

"She still mad about you leaving?"

Her mother nodded and Nora watched the wrinkles around her mouth deepen into soft brown folds. "Time for me to be leaving." She looked at the battered alarm clock on the center of the table. "Listen, honey, be sure and get the eggs before the girls get up. The chickens deserve a little bit of peace." She picked up her handbag from the kitchen chair and walked out the door.

Nora rinsed her plate in the kitchen sink and, taking the wicker basket from on top the icebox, opened the screen door. Immediately the hens scurried around her, giggling with cackles as they flapped across the front yard. She looked down at the basket in her hand. Here she was gathering eggs like she did every day of her life, and tomorrow the family was leaving for Chicago.

Her daddy had a good part-time job, he said, but he'd gotten so busy he no longer had time to write, not even to send a card for her graduation. She felt strange knowing she would see him in a few hours. Tomorrow morning she and Mattie and Mama and Babycake planned to ride all the way from Still Creek to Chicago without ever leaving the bus except when they all had to go to the bathroom.

Mama probably would have a time with Babycake. Her little sister got sick whenever she rode for a long time, and they couldn't wash her very well in those bus station bathrooms. She knew her daddy would meet them at the downtown Chicago bus station; he would be awfully glad to see them. A lot of people around Still Creek said he'd left them and wasn't going to send for them or even see them again. She had known better. If he said he would send for his family, he would. Besides, when he first married her mama, he promised they'd get away to Chicago. Which was really why Mama took on another job instead of staying home with the kids. With both of them working full time, she figured she could save some money.

At their graduation exercises, the principal had announced the two members of the class who would go on to college. Nora's going to college was the reason they were moving. Her parents said she could go to a branch of the city college practically free and finish up her education. They had planned to move "one of these days" for as long as she could remember.

Nora could repeat their special family formula backwards, frontwards, and even sideways. They had talked about it ever since she was a little girl. Mama and Daddy would get jobs up north, and with the money she herself could earn, she would eventually get through college. Then she would put Mattie through, and Mattie would see that Babycake graduated. And, of course, if any other sisters or brothers came along, they would do the same thing for them.

She waved to Mrs. McAuley, who was hanging out clothes next door. Her wash, like their family's, was conspicuous with the absence of a man's blue work shirts. Nora wondered if Mr. McAuley would ever come home, but the neighborhood's early morning sounds blotted out the memory of him. Behind the chicken coop she could hear the grinding noise of Mr. Johnson's tractor. How funny to think that in a few hours she would no longer hear that familiar sound. Leaving was just a day away, and even thinking about it made her throat feel a little funny.

By the time the eggs were gathered and set up high on top of the icebox,

Mama had long since been off to work. Nora made Mattie and Babycake mayonnaise-and-egg sandwiches for breakfast. After they were through eating, she tried to persuade the two little girls to play house outside. But in an hour they were tired and wanted to help her.

"Go on, Mattie, go back outdoors and play." She tried to keep her impatience from showing.

"But we don't got nothing to play with," Mattie said, determined not to leave. "Margie and Tanker-Belle are all packed up, and you said we won't see them again until we get there."

Mattie's brown eyes began watering as if she were going to cry. Margie and Tanker-Belle were the two dolls of the family. Tanker-Belle had been one of those fancy toaster-cover dolls that some well-meaning aunt on Mama's side had sent as a Christmas gift. Which would have been nice, but they didn't have a toaster.

Mattie had practically confiscated the doll and, for reasons known only to Mattie, had named her Tanker-Belle. She had spent most of her time since Christmas in the Pretend House back of the pecan tree. Tanker-Belle was rather frayed, after having spent several nights in the rain.

Now Nora explained to the little girls that at last the doll was going to have a nice long rest. She had packed Tanker-Belle immediately after breakfast while Mattie was busy with something else. She was now inside the big roasting pan with the dictionary and the kitchen forks. But Mattie insisted that she knew Tanker-Belle was lonesome inside the turkey pan.

"I'll tell you what, Mattie," Nora said as she tried to comfort the sobbing child. "Look on my dresser and get a nickel out of the blue bag. You go find Babycake and you all walk up to Mr. James' store for a double orange Popsicle. Then go play in the Pretend House until lunchtime."

"Can I, Nora! Oh, can I?" Mattie's smile stopped the tears running down her cheeks. She raced out of the little hallway, jumping over boxes, and through the bedroom door for a nickel. In a second she was calling Babycake and the two little girls started up the road.

Five dollars and ninety-five cents' worth of graduation money was left. Nora kept a mental record of her savings since June. Her habit of saving was a reaction, she guessed. Her father had all the good intentions in the world, but whenever they needed money he never had enough. That was one reason why her mother had taken the responsibility of moving the family.

She stooped down and began cramming some books in another cardboard box, in a hurry to move on to something else. By the time the little girls were finished with the Popsicle, it would be time for their naps. Nora tied a string around the box and made a double knot. If she could just have an hour by herself, she could finish the packing.

She had begun scrubbing the kitchen floor when suddenly a noise that sounded like a rock hitting the wire of the chicken coop made her drop the rag and run to the back door.

"Babycake, you and Mattie stop bothering the chickens. We won't get any eggs if you keep on; what's wrong with you all anyway?"

"Babycake wants all the Popsicle, Nora. And you gave it to me, didn't you, Nora?"

By the time Mattie explained about the Popsicle and how Babycake had gotten angry and thrown a rock at the chickens, Babycake was crying. Mattie, upon seeing Babycake's tears, had begun crying herself and Nora stood there, outdone. Here she was faced with two squealing little girls and her with all that work to do.

"I can tell," she said firmly, "that it's time for two naps. Give me the Popsicle and you can eat it after you've had a nap." She marched her sisters through the back door, stopped to deposit the ice cream on the kitchen table, and continued toward the bedroom. While she undressed her sisters, the Popsicle lay forgotten.

In a quarter of an hour Babycake was asleep. Mattie, who was ready to get up again, decided she was not sleepy and began singing to herself. Nora had to stop packing again and tell her to be quiet. She didn't notice the Popsicle until she saw the sticky orange drops on her clean kitchen floor. She wiped off the table and floor and swallowed what was left of the dripping orange Popsicle. There was no getting around it, she'd have to spend another nickel for some more ice cream.

Nora worked all evening, sorting clothes, folding linen, and packing kitchen utensils. Finally, the boxes were ready to go.

In the morning the smell of freshly fried chicken lingered throughout the house. The two fryers Mama had killed last night plus the one Mrs. McAuley brought over would last them the time the trip would take. In the bottom of the lunch basket were three sweet-potato pies and a brown bag full of the Georgia peaches that grew wild in their back yard.

According to the schedule propped on an empty milk bottle on the kitchen table, in a half hour everybody would be ready to pile in the Edwardses' car for the bus station. The Edwardses were going to keep all the house furnishings in their barn until Mama sent for the furniture.

The two big beds already had been dismantled and Mattie's roll-away cot was folded up near the front door. Nora walked from the hall into the living room. The whole house looked so empty, even her father's postcards were missing from the mantel over the fireplace. Suddenly she smiled. All of the furniture was covered with old newspapers their neighbors had saved, and four layers of the *Still Creek Bugle* couldn't possibly revive the sagging sofa cushions.

By seven-thirty Babycake had been freshly washed and ironed for the trip. She was commanded to sit still on the front stoop and announce the Edwardses' arrival. Mattie, who also had been dared to get dirty, kept her company. The two little girls sat on the first step, facing the swing tied to the pine tree. Their sliding feet had trampled the bits of grass growing beneath the rope, and scattered in the yard were a few green weeds the chickens had not pecked away.

Babycake reached over and gave the potted Christmas cactus a good-bye pat. The leaves were shiny because she had poured water over them this morning—Mama insisted the plant be clean when Mrs. Edwards carried the pot home.

All at once there was a honk from the horn, and a long lanky boy, the oldest of the Edwards boys, was running up the steps.

"Pop says are y'all ready yet?" Without giving them a chance to answer he started piling boxes in the trunk of the car. Babycake and Mattie were so scared they would get dirty and get left they did everything Nora told them to do.

"Mattie, pick up the little shoe box . . . Babycake, make sure we got the lunch. No, I'll take care of the lunch, you pick up the hatbox over there." Their little house had never been so cluttered and then so empty. Come to think of it, their neighborhood seldom had seen such excitement.

Everybody in Still Creek was at the bus station to see the Murrays off. There was no need to ask how they'd gotten there. Those few people who had cars drove down and piled in as many neighbors as they could. Uncle Ben, Aunt Mabel's husband, was one of those who had walked the three quarters of a mile to the bus station. Mabel had caught a ride. Anyway, they were all there, a mass of black humanity overflowing the little waiting room marked COLORED.

In one corner of one half of Still Creek Bus Terminal, Mattie sat on an upright box as Aunt Mabel gave her pigtails a quick brushing. When she had tied each end with a bright yellow ribbon, Mabel thumped Mattie on the neck and pushed her off the box toward her mama's voice that attempted to round up the family.

Nora saw Aunt Mabel trying to catch Uncle Ben's eye. Mabel began to speak above the noise in the room.

"Haven't been this many people here since they brought that Jackson boy's body home," she said, "the one who was killed overseas three years ago."

While Uncle Ben and Aunt Mabel discussed the community gatherings at the station during the last five years, Mama was getting ready to buy their tickets. Somebody got up so she could sit down and count out the money for four one-way tickets to Chicago.

Mattie was hanging over her shoulders, wide-eyed. "Mama," she breathed, "are we rich?"

"Hush, child, I'm trying to count." When she had counted out the correct amount of money four times, she tied what was left into a handkerchief and put it in the blue denim purse, which in turn went into her genuine imitation leather cowhide bag. Still counting silently, she made her way to the ticket window. When the man had given her the tickets and counted out the change, Nora felt like giving a glorious hallelujah of relief. At times like this she always felt something wrong was going to happen. She could imagine the fare going up and them without enough money, having to go back home.

With Mama talking to Aunt Mabel, Nora slipped out of the side door for a final look at her hometown. The Georgia landscape was shallow and dull and, to her eyes that had seen no other part of the country, beautiful. Even this early in the morning a thickness had settled over the countryside, covering everything with a film of fine red dust. She fingered the purse inside her pocket. Six dollars she had now—Mrs. Edwards had given her a dime to buy some candy in case she got hungry on the way.

The sound of voices inside the waiting room reached her ears. She could hear Aunt Mabel crying, louder and louder. The voices seemed to reach out and carry her with them. The bus—the bus must have come. Quickly she shut her purse and ran back toward the waiting room.

Sure enough, there was her mother frantically hugging and kissing everybody and thanking them for all the good things they had done for the Murrays. Mattie was pulling Mama's hand and begging her to hurry up before they got left. Seeing Nora, her mother beckoned her to come and get Mattie and Babycake for a final trip to the bathroom.

By the time everybody had been pushed out of the waiting room, the men had most of the luggage stored underneath the bus. Then began the last-minute hugging and kissing and gift giving all over again. Nora felt a dollar bill pressed into her hand. She couldn't help the tears; Uncle Ben really didn't have any money to spare. She bent over and kissed the old man on his cheek.

The bus driver checked his watch and in a dry, matter-of-fact voice announced that anybody who was leaving with him had better hurry up and get on because he was driving in exactly two shakes. Finally the steel door closed. In the rear of the bus, their noses pressed against the windowpanes, the four Murrays waved good-bye to friends and neighbors and to Still Creek, Georgia, "the original home of fine Georgia peaches."

After hours of riding, Nora lost track of the towns they passed. Still Creek seemed so far away and the slight jogging of the bus no longer made her head ache. The whole trip had become a kaleidoscope of sounds and colors. The small towns surrounded with ranch-style houses and green lawns were loose fragments she counted, like turning storybook pages in her mind.

At the next rest stop, Nora decided to stretch her legs in the bus aisle. Mama herself took the little girls inside for a glass of milk and a trip to the bathroom. When the bus started again, she began telling a fairy tale to Mattie, and then suddenly the accident occurred. Little Babycake had stuffed herself with too much sweet-potato custard and she lost all her dinner on the back seat of the bus. They tried to clean up the seat with some old waxed paper, but they couldn't clean and pay attention to Babycake, too.

Babycake started crying. Her stomach hurt and she wanted to go home. Mama tried to hush her, but the more she patted, the more Babycake cried. By the time the sourness had spread throughout the bus, Mama sent Nora up to the bus driver to ask him if he would stop and let Babycake get her stomach settled.

Nora stood up and held on to the seats, cautiously walking up the aisle, toward the back of the bus driver's gray-blue suit. After hours of riding, the jacket still looked freshly pressed, and he didn't even glance up in the mirror as she approached the driver's seat.

"My little sister's sick," she explained. "If she could get some air, my mother said she might feel better." She held on to the pole near the front steps, facing the back of the driver's gray head.

Muttering something unintelligible, he said no. He had lost enough time and would be stopping soon anyway. They would just have to wait like everybody else.

While she was standing in the aisle, the bus picked up speed and turned a sharp curve. Nora felt herself fall against two elderly women, and although the bus was air-conditioned, one was struggling trying to raise the window.

"Niggers," she whispered, her voice grating, colliding with the growl of the motor.

Nora was not certain she had heard the woman speak, but even thinking of the word hurt her ears. Nobody'd ever called her a nigger to her face before. At least never with such anger. She looked into the woman's eyes, seeing the fierce look her father often described as belonging to white people. Fierceness that was hatred. She was conscious of the bus moving, jerking to a stop, and then moving again, but she heard nothing except the woman's words. It was as if the words formed an invisible cloak and only by pushing it away with her thoughts did she keep from being smothered.

She wanted to see her father now—have him take his wife and children from this horrible bus and put them down where they did not have to move ever again. What if . . . no, he would not do that, not after he talked so badly about Mr. McAuley deserting his family six months after they met him in Chicago. The McAuleys stayed in the city not even a year; in December they had come home. Even with the extra money allotted them because of Mr. McAuley's disappearance, they did not have enough money to eat. She dared not even think.

Nora never knew how many rest stops the bus made. Once as she turned toward the window she realized the daylight had changed into darkness. She even forgot to watch for the sign telling them they had crossed the Illinois state line. Mattie wanted to play Cookie Jar, but she could not concentrate on the hand clapping for trying not to remember those words. Nora was almost asleep when the bus turned into an entrance, pulled up to the curb, and stopped.

Because there were so many bundles to carry out, they were the last people getting off the bus. Babycake was the first one to see him. She caught hold of Mama's hand, yelling, "Here we are, here we are," and started to run across the terminal to the man in the black trench coat. Nora had to hold her back. The man Babycake saw was not their father. He was a little too tall, and when he passed the family, he just looked at them strangely.

They stood outside the big glass door with the little packages, waiting and looking through each crowd of people, but no one came.

"You people need help or something?" a woman asked. She walked as if she knew every inch of the ground surrounding the terminal. "If you need a taxi, I'll show you where to stand."

Nora shook her head. "No, thank you, we're waiting for someone." Her eyes dropped to the pavement and for a while she was conscious only of shoes, so many different colors, passing, all walking by them. After fifteen minutes and two "May I help you's," Mama guided them through the revolving door and to a bench in the middle of the station.

"That way he can see us when he comes," she said, sitting down on the bench. Nora again braided Mattie's and Babycake's hair and then there was nothing to do but wait.

Oh, why hadn't he come? He was supposed to be here; they had sent the letter last Friday. She had told him the exact time of their arrival. Twice she'd written it out.

Now Babycake was getting sleepy again. "Where's Daddy?" she asked. "Aren't we there now?"

"Hush up." Her mother motioned for Nora to unlace Babycake's shoes. "Maybe he can't find us," she whispered above the little girls' heads.

An hour passed. Nora stood. "Where you going?" Mattie asked. "Don't you get lost from us, too."

"To check the luggage, it won't take long." Nora began walking down the side of the terminal, near the shiny cigarette machine and past the magazine rack. Everything glittered with a metallic glow, but the fluorescent lighting only emphasized the emptiness within her. She looked up and saw an overhead panel advertising a course in shorthand—gt-gd-jb . . . Then she met Elizabeth Taylor's gaze beneath the sign pointing to the telephone booth.

At once she was aware of what had happened. He was working overtime and had overslept. She had the apartment building's telephone number from one of his first letters. She would call and whoever answered would tell her where to reach him and then he would come get them. With sticky fingers she loosened a dime from her money collection and lifted the receiver. The phone rang once, and a voice answered.

"McConnell's Drugstore—Hello? This is McConnell's Drugstore."

"Please," Nora whispered, "could I speak with Mr. Joseph Murray?"

"Sorry, miss, but no Joe Murray works here."

"Are you sure, don't you know him?"

"No, lady, but if you want to wait I'll check the list of people working in the building."

Then he was back too soon, and he was sorry, no Murray was even listed there.

Nora emerged from the booth and stood at the lockers, wondering if she should look outside, when she felt someone bump into her. She turned quickly, into a woman tugging on a small boy. "Excuse me," the woman murmured, pushing the boy ahead of her.

Abruptly pulling away, Nora ran toward the doors out to the sidewalk into the darkness. She tried to brush the air from her face, but the fingers slightly touching her eyelashes came away damp. She stood outside, her eyes tightly closed, trying not to see them, all three of them huddled on that bench. Then her cheeks were dry.

Nora went back to the station bench and whispered to her mother, who was sitting quietly, Babycake's head nestled in her lap.

"Mama? Oh, Mama, did you know all the time?"

Her mother shook her head and reached for her daughter's hand.

"I couldn't know for sure," she said. "We had to work toward something. Don't you see? We wouldn't have ever gotten out if we didn't work toward something." Her voice was sad and quiet, as if she might slowly start humming Babycake to sleep.

"What are we going to do, Mama? They're bound to make us move out of here sometimes."

"We'll just stay right in this spot," she said, covering Babycake with a coat, "just in case." She turned her face toward the suitcases, and Nora, seeing that her mother might cry, was sorry she had asked.

"Tomorrow we can call the Welfare people. Somebody there can help us find a place to go." Her mother spoke with her eyes fixed on the travel posters on the far side of the room.

That they never before had had to ask for help made no difference to Nora. She felt that they were pieces in a giant jigsaw puzzle, oddly shaped blobs that would never be put together. Here was her mother sitting so quietly, not letting anything upset her. But then that was not so difficult to do, she herself was not conscious of feeling anything. He loved them, he had to. After all, they were his, but sometimes loving became a burden. And if he had met them at the bus station, perhaps they would have become that to him. But they were supposed to be a family, weren't they? She was no longer certain.

Stepping over the suitcases piled near the bench holding Babycake, Nora began sorting bundles. She looked at the clock on the terminal wall; the silvery hands seemed fixed. Strange that it was morning already; outside the sky was still dark.

She'd probably have to babysit for a while, until Mama found a job and a place to leave the little girls during the day. She began fingering the string around the boxes. Today was Saturday and Mattie and Babycake's Sunday dresses would need ironing, but she'd worry about that later. Their hair ribbons did not have to be pressed, if she could ever remember where they were.

Slowly Nora put down the box. Her shoulders slid down the back of the bench. She couldn't press anything. She couldn't even remember where they had packed the iron.

To Da-Duh, in Memoriam

●

(1967)

Paule Marshall

Oh Nana! All of you is not involved in this evil business Death,
Nor all of us in life.
> —Lebert Bethune, "At My Grandmother's Grave"

I did not see her at first, I remember. For not only was it dark inside the crowded disembarkation shed in spite of the daylight flooding in from outside, but standing there waiting for her with my mother and sister I was still somewhat blinded from the sheen of tropical sunlight on the water of the bay which we had just crossed in the landing boat, leaving behind us the ship that had brought us from New York lying in the offing. Besides, being only nine years of age at the time and knowing nothing of islands, I was busy attending to the alien sights and sounds of Barbados, the unfamiliar smells.

I did not see her, but I was alerted to her approach by my mother's hand, which suddenly tightened around mine, and, looking up, I traced her gaze through the gloom in the shed until I finally made out the small, purposeful, painfully erect figure of the old woman headed our way.

Her face was drowned in the shadow of an ugly rolled-brim brown felt hat, but the details of her slight body and of the struggle taking place within it were clear enough—an intense, unrelenting struggle between her back, which was beginning to bend ever so slightly under the weight of her eighty-odd years, and the rest of her, which sought to deny those years and hold that back straight, keep it in line. Moving swiftly toward us (so swiftly it seemed she did not intend stopping when she reached us but would sweep past us out the doorway which opened onto the sea and

199

like Christ walk upon the water!), she was caught between the sunlight at her end of the building and the darkness inside—and for a moment she appeared to contain them both: the light in the long, severe, old-fashioned white dress she wore, which brought the sense of a past that was still alive into our bustling present, and in the snatch of white at her eye; the darkness in her black high-top shoes and in her face, which was visible now that she was closer.

It was as stark and fleshless as a death mask, that face. The maggots might have already done their work, leaving only the framework of bone beneath the ruined skin and deep wells at the temple and jaw. But her eyes were alive, unnervingly so for one so old, with a sharp light that flicked out of the dim clouded depths like a lizard's tongue to snap up all in her view. Those eyes betrayed a child's curiosity about the world, and I wondered, vaguely seeing them, and seeing the way the bodice of her ancient dress had collapsed in on her flat chest (what had happened to her breasts?), whether she might not be some kind of child at the same time that she was a woman, with fourteen children, my mother included, to prove it. Perhaps she was both, both child and woman, darkness and light, past and present, life and death—all the opposites contained and reconciled in her.

"My Da-duh," my mother said formally and stepped forward. The name sounded like thunder fading softly in the distance.

"Child," Da-duh said, and her tone, her quick scrutiny of my mother, the brief embrace in which they appeared to shy from each other rather than touch, wiped out the fifteen years my mother had been away and restored the old relationship. My mother, who was such a formidable figure in my eyes, had suddenly with a word been reduced to my status.

"Yes, God is good," Da-duh said with a nod that was like a tic. "He has spared me to see my child again."

We were led forward then, apologetically, because not only did Da-duh prefer boys but she also liked her grandchildren to be "white," that is, fair-skinned; and we had, I was to discover, a number of cousins, the outside children of white estate managers and the like, who qualified. We, though, were as black as she.

My sister, being the older, was presented first. "This one takes after the father," my mother said and waited to be reproved.

Frowning, Da-duh tilted my sister's face toward the light. But her frown soon gave way to a grudging smile, for my sister, with her large mild eyes and little broad winged nose, with our father's high-cheeked Barbadian cast to her face, was pretty.

"She's goin' be lucky," Da-duh said and patted her once on the cheek. "Any girl child that takes after the father does be lucky."

She turned then to me. But, oddly enough, she did not touch me. Instead, leaning close, she peered hard at me, and then quickly drew back. I thought I saw her hand start up as though to shield her eyes. It was almost as if she saw not only me, a thin truculent child who it was said took after no one but myself, but something in me which for some reason she found disturbing, even threatening. We looked silently at each other for a long time there in the noisy shed, our gaze locked. She was the first to look away.

"But Adry," she said to my mother and her laugh was cracked, thin, apprehensive. "Where did you get this one here with this fierce look?"

"We don't know where she came out of, my Da-duh," my mother said, laughing also. Even I smiled to myself. After all, I had won the encounter. Da-duh had recognized my small strength—and this was all I ever asked of the adults in my life then.

"Come, soul," Da-duh said and took my hand. "You must be one of those New York terrors you hear so much about."

She led us, me at her side and my sister and mother behind, out of the shed into the sunlight that was like a bright driving summer rain and over to a group of people clustered beside a decrepit lorry. They were our relatives, most of them from St. Andrews although Da-duh herself lived in St. Thomas, the women wearing bright print dresses, the colors vivid against their darkness, the men rusty black suits that encased them like straitjackets. Da-duh, holding fast to my hand, became my anchor as they circled round us like a nervous sea, exclaiming, touching us with their callused hands, embracing us shyly. They laughed in awed bursts: "But look, Adry got big-big children!" "And see the nice things they wearing, wristwatch and all!" "I tell you, Adry has done all right for sheself in New York . . ."

Da-duh, ashamed at their wonder, embarrassed for them, admonished them the while. "But oh, Christ," she said, "why you all got to get on like you never saw people from 'Away' before? You would think New York is the only place in the world to hear wunna. That's why I don't like to go anyplace with you St. Andrews people, you know. You all ain't been colonized."

We were in the back of the lorry finally, packed in among the barrels of ham, flour, cornmeal, and rice and the trunks of clothes that my mother had brought as gifts. We made our way slowly through Bridgetown's clogged streets, part of a funereal procession of cars and open-sided buses, bicycles, and donkey carts. The dim little limestone shops and offices along the way marched with us, at the same mournful pace, toward the same grave ceremony—as did the people, the women balancing huge baskets on top their heads as if they were no more than hats they wore to shade them from the sun. Looking over the edge of the lorry I watched as their feet slurred the dust. I listened, and their voices, raw and loud and dissonant in the heat, seemed to be grappling with each other high overhead.

Da-duh sat on a trunk in our midst, a monarch amid her court. She still held my hand, but it was different now. I had suddenly become her anchor, for I felt her fear of the lorry with its asthmatic motor (a fear and distrust, I later learned, she held of all machines) beating like a pulse in her rough palm.

As soon as we left Bridgetown behind, though, she relaxed, and, while the others around us talked, she gazed at the canes standing tall on either side of the winding marl road. "C'dear," she said softly to herself after a time. "The canes this side are pretty enough."

They were too much for me. I thought of them as giant weeds that had overrun the island, leaving scarcely any room for the small tottering houses of sun-bleached pine we passed or the people, dark streaks as our lorry hurtled by. I suddenly feared that we were journeying, unaware that we were, toward some dangerous place where the canes, grown as high and thick as a forest, would close in on us and run us through with their stiletto blades. I longed then for the familiar: for the street in Brooklyn where I lived, for my father who had refused to accompany us ("Blowing out good money on foolishness," he had said of the trip), for a game of tag with my friends under the chestnut tree outside our aging brownstone house.

"Yes, but wait till you see St. Thomas canes," Da-duh was saying to me. "They's canes father, bo." She gave a proud arrogant nod. "Tomorrow, God willing, I goin' take you out in the ground and show them to you."

True to her word Da-duh took me with her the following day out into the ground. It was a fairly large plot adjoining her weathered board and shingle house and consisting of a small orchard, a good-sized canepiece, and behind the canes, where the land sloped abruptly down, a gully. She had purchased it with Panama money sent her by her eldest son, my uncle Joseph, who had died working on the canal. We entered the ground along a trail no wider than her body and as devious and complex as her reasons for showing me her land. Da-duh strode briskly ahead, her slight form filled out this morning by the layers of sacking petticoats she wore under her working dress to protect her against the damp. A fresh white cloth, elaborately arranged around her head, added to her height and lent her a vain, almost roguish air.

Her pace slowed once we reached the orchard, and, glancing back at me occasionally over her shoulder, she pointed out the various trees.

"This here is a breadfruit," she said. "That one yonder is a papaw. Here's a guava. This is a mango. I know you don't have anything like these in New York. Here's a sugar apple." (The fruit looked more like artichokes than apples to me.) "This one bears limes . . ." She went on for some time, intoning the names of the trees as though they were those of her gods. Finally, turning to me, she said, "I know you don't have anything this nice where you come from." Then, as I hesitated: "I said I know you don't have anything this nice where you come from . . ."

"No," I said, and my world did seem suddenly lacking.

Da-duh nodded and passed on. The orchard ended and we were on the narrow cart road that led through the canepiece, the canes clashing like swords above my cowering head. Again she turned and, her thin muscular arms spread wide, her dim gaze embracing the small field of canes, she said—and her voice almost broke under the weight of her pride—"Tell me, have you got anything like these in that place where you were born?"

"No."

"I din' think so. I bet you don't even know that these canes here and the sugar you eat is one and the same thing. That they does throw the canes into some damn machine at the factory and squeeze out all the little life in them to make sugar for you all so in New York to eat. I bet you don't know that."

"I've got two cavities and I'm not allowed to eat a lot of sugar."

But Da-duh didn't hear me. She had turned with an inexplicably angry motion and was making her way rapidly out of the canes and down the slope at the edge of the field which led to the gully below. Following her apprehensively down the incline amid a stand of banana plants whose leaves flapped like elephant's ears in the wind, I found myself in the middle of a small tropical wood—a place dense and damp and gloomy and tremulous with the fitful play of light and shadow, as the leaves high above moved against the sun that was almost hidden from view. It was a violent place, the tangled foliage fighting each other for a chance at the sunlight, the branches of the trees locked in what seemed an immemorial struggle, one both necessary and inevitable. But despite the violence, it was pleasant, almost peaceful in the gully, and beneath the thick undergrowth the earth smelled like spring.

This time Da-duh didn't even bother to ask her usual question, but simply turned and waited for me to speak.

"No," I said, my head bowed. "We don't have anything like this in New York."

"Ah," she cried, her triumph complete. "I din' think so. Why, I've heard that's a place where you can walk till you near drop and never see a tree."

"We've got a chestnut tree in front of our house," I said.

"Does it bear?" She waited. "I ask you, does it bear?"

"Not anymore," I muttered. "It used to, but not anymore."

She gave the nod that was like a nervous twitch. "You see," she said. "Nothing can bear there." Then, secure behind her scorn, she added, "But tell me, what's this snow like that you hear so much about?"

Looking up, I studied her closely, sensing my chance, and then I told her, describing at length and with as much drama as I could summon, not only what snow in the city was like, but what it would be like here, in her perennial summer kingdom.

". . . And you see all these trees you got here," I said. "Well, they'd be bare. No leaves, no fruit, nothing. They'd be covered in snow. You see your canes. They'd be buried under tons of snow. The snow would be higher than your head, higher than your house, and you wouldn't be able to come down into this here gully because it would be snowed under . . ."

She searched my face for the lie, still scornful but intrigued. "What a thing, huh?" she said finally, whispering it softly to herself.

"And when it snows you couldn't dress like you are now," I said. "Oh, no, you'd freeze to death. You'd have to wear a hat and gloves and galoshes and earmuffs so your ears wouldn't freeze and drop off, and a heavy coat. I've got a Shirley Temple coat with fur on the collar. I can dance. You wanna see?"

Before she could answer I began, with a dance called the Truck, which was popular back then in the 1930s. My right forefinger waving, I trucked around the nearby trees and around Da-duh's awed and rigid form. After the Truck I did the Suzy-Q, my lean hips swishing, my sneakers sidling zigzag over the ground. "I can sing," I said and did so, starting with "I'm Gonna Sit Right Down and Write Myself a Letter," then, without pausing, "Tea for Two," and ending with "I Found a Million-Dollar Baby in a Five and Ten Cent Store."

For long moments afterward Da-duh stared at me as if I were a creature from Mars, an emissary from some world she did not know but which intrigued her and whose power she both felt and feared. Yet something about my performance must have pleased her, because bending down she slowly lifted her long skirt and then, one by one, the layers of petticoats until she came to a drawstring purse dangling at the end of a long strip of cloth tied round her waist. Opening the purse she handed me a penny. "Here," she said, half smiling against her will. "Take this to buy yourself a sweet at the shop up the road. There's nothing to be done with you, soul."

From then on, whenever I wasn't taken to visit relatives, I accompanied Da-duh out into the ground, and alone with her amid the canes or down in the gully I told her about New York. It always began with some slighting remark on her part: "I know they don't have anything this nice where you come from," or "Tell me, I hear those foolish people in New York does do such and such . . ." But as I answered, re-creating my towering world of steel and concrete and machines for her, building the city out of words, I would feel her give way. I came to know the signs of her surrender: the total stillness that would come over her little hard dry form, the probing gaze that like a surgeon's knife sought to cut through my skull to get at the images there, to see if I were lying; above all, her fear, a fear nameless and profound, the same one I had felt beating in the palm of her hand that day in the lorry.

Over the weeks I told her about refrigerators, radios, gas stoves, elevators, trolley cars, wringer washing machines, movies, airplanes, the cyclone at Coney Island, subways, toasters, electric lights: "At night, see, all you have to do is flip this little switch on the wall and all the lights in the house go on. Just like that. Like magic. It's like turning on the sun at night."

"But tell me," she said to me once with a faint mocking smile, "do the white people have all these things too or it's only the people looking like us?"

I laughed, "What d'ya mean," I said. "The white people have even better." Then: "I beat up a white girl in my class last term."

"Beating up white people!" Her tone was incredulous.

"How you mean!" I said, using an expression of hers. "She called me a name."

For some reason Da-duh could not quite get over this and repeated in the same hushed, shocked voice, "Beating up white people now! Oh, the Lord, the world's changing up so I can scarce recognize it anymore."

One morning toward the end of our stay, Da-duh led me into a part of the gully that we had never visited before, an area darker and more thickly overgrown than the rest, almost impenetrable. There, in a small clearing amid the dense bush, she stopped before an incredibly tall royal palm which rose cleanly out of the ground and, drawing the eye up with it, soared high above the trees around it into the sky. It appeared to be touching the blue dome of sky, to be flaunting its dark crown of fronds right in the blinding white face of the late morning sun.

Da-duh watched me a long time before she spoke, and then she said very quietly, "All right, now, tell me if you've got anything this tall in that place you're from."

I almost wished, seeing her face, that I could have said no. "Yes," I said. "We've got buildings hundreds of times this tall in New York. There's one called the Empire State Building that's the tallest in the world. My class visited it last year and I went all the way to the top. It's got over a hundred floors. I can't describe how tall it is. Wait a minute. What's the name of that hill I went to visit the other day, where they have the police station?"

"You mean Bissex?"

"Yes, Bissex. Well, the Empire State Building is way taller than that."

"You're lying now!" she shouted, trembling with rage. Her hand lifted to strike me.

"No, I'm not," I said. "It really is; if you don't believe me, I'll send you a picture postcard of it soon as I get back home so you can see for yourself. But it's way taller than Bissex."

All the fight went out of her at that. The hand poised to strike me fell limp to her side, and as she stared at me, seeing not me but the building that was taller than the highest hill she knew, the small stubborn light in her eyes (it was the same amber as the flame in the kerosene lamp she lit at dusk) began to fail. Finally, with a vague gesture that even in the midst of her defeat still tried to dismiss me and my world, she turned and started back through the gully, walking slowly, her steps groping and uncertain, as if she were suddenly no longer sure of the way, while I followed, triumphant yet strangely saddened, behind.

The next morning I found her dressed for our morning walk but stretched out on the Berbice chair in the tiny drawing room where she sometimes napped during the afternoon heat, her face turned to the window beside her. She appeared thinner and suddenly indescribably old.

"My Da-duh," I said.

"Yes, nuh," she said. Her voice was listless and the face she slowly turned my way was, now that I think back on it, like a Benin mask, the features drawn and almost distorted by an ancient abstract sorrow.

"Don't you feel well?" I asked.

"Girl, I don't know."

"My Da-duh, I goin' boil you some bush tea," my aunt, Da-duh's youngest child, who lived with her, called from the shed roof kitchen.

"Who tell you I need bush tea?" she cried, her voice assuming for a moment its old authority. "You can't even rest nowadays without some malicious person looking for you to be dead. Come, girl." She motioned me to a place beside her on the old-fashioned lounge chair. "Give us a tune."

I sang for her until breakfast at eleven, all my brash irreverent Tin Pan Alley songs, and then just before noon we went out into the ground. But it was a short, dispirited walk. Da-duh didn't even notice that the mangoes were beginning to ripen and would have to be picked before the village boys got to them. And when she paused occasionally and looked out across the canes or up at her trees, it wasn't as if she were seeing them but something else. Some huge, monolithic shape had imposed itself, it seemed, between her and the land, obstructing her vision. Returning to the house she slept the entire afternoon on the Berbice chair.

She remained like this until we left, languishing away the mornings on the chair at the window, gazing out at the land as if it were already doomed; then, at noon, taking the brief stroll with me through the ground during which she seldom spoke, and afterward returning home to sleep till almost dusk sometimes.

On the day of our departure she put on the austere, ankle-length white dress, the black shoes, and brown felt hat (her town clothes, she called them), but she did not go with us to town. She saw us off on the road outside her house, and in the midst of my mother's tearful protracted farewell, she leaned down and whispered in my ear, "Girl, you're not to forget now to send me the picture of that building, you hear."

By the time I mailed her the large colored picture postcard of the Empire State Building, she was dead. She died during the famous '37 strike, which began shortly after we left. On the day of her death England sent planes flying low over the island in a show of force—so low, according to my aunt's letter, that the downdraft from them shook the ripened mangoes from the trees in Da-duh's orchard. Frightened, everyone in the village fled into the canes. Except Da-duh. She remained in the house at the window, so my aunt said, watching as the planes came swooping and screaming like monstrous birds down over the village, over her house, rattling her trees and flattening the young canes in her field. It must have seemed to her lying there that they did not intend pulling out of their dive, but, like the hard-back beetles which hurled themselves with suicidal force against the walls of the house at night, those menacing silver shapes would hurl themselves in an ecstasy of self-immolation onto the land, destroying it utterly.

When the planes finally left and the villagers returned, they found her dead on the Berbice chair at the window.

She died and I lived, but always, to this day even, within the shadow of her death. For a brief period after I was grown I went to live alone, like one doing penance, in a loft above a noisy factory in downtown New York and there painted seas of sugarcane and huge swirling Van Gogh suns and palm trees striding like brightly plumed Tutsi warriors across a tropical landscape, while the thunderous tread of the machines downstairs jarred the floor beneath my easel, mocking my efforts.

To Hell with Dying

(1967)

Alice Walker

"To hell with dying," my father would say, *"these children want Mr. Sweet!"*

Mr. Sweet was a diabetic and an alcoholic and a guitar player and lived down the road from us on a neglected cotton farm. My older brothers and sisters got the most benefit from Mr. Sweet, for when they were growing up he had quite a few years ahead of him and so was capable of being called back from the brink of death any number of times—whenever the voice of my father reached him as he lay expiring . . . "To hell with dying, man," my father would say, pushing the wife away from the bedside (in tears, although she knew the death was not necessarily the last one unless Mr. Sweet really wanted it to be), "the children want Mr. Sweet!" And they did want him, for at a signal from Father they would come crowding around the bed and throw themselves on the covers and whoever was the smallest at the time would kiss him all over his wrinkled brown face and begin to tickle him so he would laugh all down in his stomach, and his mustache, which was long and sort of straggly, would shake like Spanish moss and was also that color.

Mr. Sweet had been ambitious as a boy, wanted to be a doctor or lawyer or sailor, only to find that black men fare better if they are not. Since he could be none of those things he turned to fishing as his only earnest career and playing the guitar as his only claim to doing anything extraordinarily well. His son, the only one that he and his wife, Miss Mary, had, was shiftless as the day is long and spent money as if he were trying to see the bottom of the mint, which Mr. Sweet would tell him was the

209

clean brown palm of his hand. Miss Mary loved her "baby," however, and worked hard to get him the "li'l necessaries" of life, which turned out mostly to be women.

Mr. Sweet was a tall, thinnish man with thick kinky hair going dead white. He was dark brown, his eyes were very squinty and sort of bluish, and he chewed Brown Mule tobacco. He was constantly on the verge of being blind drunk, for he brewed his own liquor and was not in the least a stingy sort of man, and was always very melancholy and sad, though frequently when he was "feelin' good" he'd dance around the yard with us, usually keeling over just as my mother came to see what the commotion was.

Toward all of us children he was very kind, and had the grace to be shy with us, which is unusual in grown-ups. He had great respect for my mother, for she never held his drunkenness against him and would let us play with him even when he was about to fall in the fireplace from drink. Although Mr. Sweet would sometimes lose complete or nearly complete control of his head and neck so that he would loll in his chair, his mind remained strangely acute and his speech not too affected. His ability to be drunk and sober at the same time made him an ideal playmate, for he was as weak as we were and we could usually best him in wrestling, all the while keeping a fairly coherent conversation going.

We never felt anything of Mr. Sweet's age when we played with him. We loved his wrinkles and would draw some on our brows to be like him, and his white hair was my special treasure and he knew it and would never come to visit us just after he had had his hair cut off at the barbershop. Once he came to our house for something, probably to see my father about fertilizer for his crops, for although he never paid the slightest attention to his crops he liked to know what things would be best to use on them if he ever did. Anyhow, he had not come with his hair since he had just had it shaved off at the barbershop. He wore a huge straw hat to keep off the sun and also to keep his head away from me. But as soon as I saw him I ran up and demanded that he take me up and kiss me, with his funny beard which smelled so strongly of tobacco. Looking forward to burying my small fingers into his woolly hair, I threw away his hat only to find he had done something to his hair, that it was no longer there! I let out a squall which made my mother think that Mr. Sweet had finally dropped me in the well or something, and from that day I've been wary of men in hats. However, not long after, Mr. Sweet showed up with his hair grown out and just as white and kinky and impenetrable as it ever was.

Mr. Sweet used to call me his princess, and I believed it. He made me feel pretty at five and six, and simply outrageously devastating at the blazing age of eight and a half. When he came to our house with his guitar the whole family would stop whatever they were doing to sit around him and listen to him play. He liked to play "Sweet Georgia Brown," that was what he called me sometimes, and also he liked to play "Caldonia" and all sorts of sweet, sad, wonderful songs which he sometimes made up. It was from one of these songs that I learned that he had had to marry Miss Mary when he had in fact loved somebody else (now living in Chi-ca-go, or De-stroy, Michigan). He was not sure that Joe Lee, her "baby," was also his baby. Sometimes he would cry and that was an indication that he was about to die again. And so we would all get prepared, for we were sure to be called upon.

I was seven the first time I remember actually participating in one of Mr. Sweet's "revivals"—my parents told me I had participated before, I had been the one chosen to kiss him and tickle him long before I knew the rite of Mr. Sweet's rehabilitation. He had come to our house, it was a few years after his wife's death, and he was very sad, and also, typically, very drunk. He sat on the floor next to me and my older brother, the rest of the children were grown-up and lived elsewhere, and began to play his guitar and cry. I held his woolly head in my arms and wished I could have been old enough to have been the woman he loved so much and that I had not been lost years and years ago.

When he was leaving, my mother said to us that we'd better sleep light that night for we'd probably have to go over to Mr. Sweet's before daylight. And we did. For soon after we had gone to bed one of the neighbors knocked on our door and called my father and said that Mr. Sweet was sinking fast and if he wanted to get in a word before the crossover he'd better shake a leg and get over to Mr. Sweet's house. All the neighbors knew to come to our house if something was wrong with Mr. Sweet, but they did not know how we always managed to make him well, or at least stop him from dying, when he was often so near death. As soon as we heard the cry we got up, my brother and I and my mother and father, and put on our clothes. We hurried out of the house and down the road, for we were always afraid that we might someday be too late and Mr. Sweet would get tired of dallying.

When we got to the house, a very poor shack really, we found the front room full of neighbors and relatives and a man met us at the door and said that it was all very sad that old Mr. Sweet Little (for Little was his family name although we mostly ignored it) was about to kick the bucket.

He advised my parents not to take my brother and me into the "death-room," seeing we were so young and all, but we were so much more accustomed to the death-room than he that we ignored him and dashed in without giving his warning a second thought. I was almost in tears, for these deaths upset me fearfully, and the thought of how much depended on me and my brother (who was such a ham most of the time) made me very nervous.

The doctor was bending over the bed and turned back to tell us for at least the tenth time in the history of my family that, alas, old Mr. Sweet Little was dying and that the children had best not see the face of im-placable death (I didn't know what "implacable" was, but whatever it was, Mr. Sweet was not!). My father pushed him rather abruptly out of the way, saying, as he always did and very loudly, for he was saying it to Mr. Sweet, "To hell with dying, man, these children want Mr. Sweet!" which was my cue to throw myself upon the bed and kiss Mr. Sweet all around the whiskers and under the eyes and around the collar of his nightshirt where he smelled so strongly of all sorts of things, mostly liniment.

I was very good at bringing him around, for as soon as I saw that he was struggling to open his eyes I knew he was going to be all right and so could finish my revival sure of success. As soon as his eyes were open he would begin to smile and that way I knew that I had surely won. Once, though, I got a tremendous scare, for he could not open his eyes and later I learned that he had had a stroke and that one side of his face was stiff and hard to get into motion. When he began to smile I could tickle him in earnest for I was sure that nothing would get in the way of his laughter, although once he began to cough so hard that he almost threw me off his stomach, but that was when I was very small, little more than a baby, and my bushy hair had gotten in his nose.

When we were sure he would listen to us we would ask him why he was in bed and when he was coming to see us again and could we play with his guitar, which more than likely would be leaning against the bed. His eyes would get all misty and he would sometimes cry out loud, but we never let it embarrass us for he knew that we loved him and that we sometimes cried too for no reason. My parents would leave the room to just the three of us; Mr. Sweet, by that time, would be propped up in bed with a number of pillows behind his head and with me sitting and lying on his shoulder and along his chest. Even when he had trouble breathing he would not ask me to get down. Looking into my eyes he would shake his white head and run a scratchy old finger all around my hairline, which was rather low down nearly to my eyebrows and for which some people said I looked like a baby monkey.

My brother was very generous in all this, he let me do all the revivaling—he had done it for years before I was born and so was glad to be able to pass it on to someone new. What he would do while I talked to Mr. Sweet was pretend to play the guitar, in fact pretend that he was a young version of Mr. Sweet, and it always made Mr. Sweet glad to think that someone wanted to be like him—of course, we did not know this then, we played the thing by ear, and whatever he seemed to like, we did. We were desperately afraid that he was just going to take off one day and leave us.

It did not occur to us that we were doing anything special; we had not learned that death was final when it did come. We thought nothing of triumphing over it so many times, and in fact became a trifle contemptuous of people who let themselves be carried away. It did not occur to us that if our own father had been dying we could not have stopped it, that Mr. Sweet was the only person over whom we had power.

When Mr. Sweet was in his eighties I was a young lady studying away in a university many miles from home. I saw him whenever I went home, but he was never on the verge of dying that I could tell and I began to feel that my anxiety for his health and psychological well-being was unnecessary. By this time he not only had a moustache but a long flowing snow-white beard which I loved and combed and braided for hours. He was still a very heavy drinker and was like an old Chinese opium-user, very peaceful, fragile, gentle, and the only jarring note about him was his old steel guitar, which he still played in the old sad, sweet, down-home blues way.

On Mr. Sweet's ninetieth birthday I was finishing my doctorate in Massachusetts and had been making arrangements to go home for several weeks' rest. That morning I got a telegram telling me that Mr. Sweet was dying again and could I please drop everything and come home. Of course I could. My dissertation could wait and my teachers would understand when I explained to them when I got back. I ran to the phone, called the airport, and within four hours I was speeding along the dusty road to Mr. Sweet's.

The house was more dilapidated than when I was last there, barely a shack, but it was overgrown with yellow roses which my family had planted many years ago. The air was heavy and sweet and very peaceful. I felt strange walking through the gate and up the old rickety steps. But the strangeness left me as I caught sight of the long white beard I loved so well flowing down the thin body over the familiar quilt coverlet. Mr. Sweet!

His eyes were closed tight and his hands, crossed over his stomach, were thin and delicate, no longer rough and scratchy. I remembered how always before I had run and jumped up on him just anywhere; now I knew he would not be able to support my weight. I looked around at my parents, and was surprised to see that my father and mother also looked old and frail. My father, his own hair very gray, leaned over the quietly sleeping old man, who, incidentally, smelled still of wine and tobacco, and said, as he'd done so many times, "To hell with dying, man! My daughter is home to see Mr. Sweet!" My brother had not been able to come, as he was in the war in Asia. I bent down and gently stroked the closed eyes and gradually they began to open. The closed, wine-stained lips twitched a little, then parted in a warm, slightly embarrassed smile. Mr. Sweet could see me and he recognized me and his eyes looked very spry and twinkly for a moment. I put my head down on the pillow next to his and we just looked at each other for a long time. Then he began to trace my peculiar hairline with a thin, smooth finger. I closed my eyes when his finger halted above my ear (he used to rejoice at the dirt in my ears when I was little); his hand stayed cupped around my cheek. When I opened my eyes, sure I had reached him in time, his were closed.

Even at twenty-four how could I believe that I had failed? that Mr. Sweet was really gone? He had never gone before. But when I looked up at my parents I saw that they were holding back tears. They had loved him dearly. He was like a piece of rare and delicate china which was always being saved from breaking and which finally fell. I looked long at the old face, the wrinkled forehead, the red lips, the hands that still reached out to me. Soon I felt my father pushing something cool into my hands. It was Mr. Sweet's guitar. He had asked them months before to give it to me, he had known that even if I came next time he would not be able to respond in the old way. He did not want me to feel that my trip had been for nothing.

The old guitar! I plucked the strings, hummed "Sweet Georgia Brown." The magic of Mr. Sweet lingered still in the cool steel box. Through the window I could catch the fragrant, delicate scent of tender yellow roses. The man on the high old-fashioned bed with the quilt coverlet and the flowing white beard had been my first love.

Tell Martha Not to Moan

(1968)

Sherley Anne Williams

My mamma a big woman, tall and stout and men like her cause she soft and fluffy looking. When she round them it all smiles and dimples and her mouth be looking like it couldn't never be fixed to say nothing but darling and honey.

They see her now, they sho see something different. I should not even come today. Since I had Larry things ain't been too good between us. But—that's my mamma and I know she gon be there when I need her. And sometime when I come, it okay. But this ain't gon be one a them times. Her eyes looking all ove me and I know it coming. She snort cause she want to say god damn but she don't cuss. "When it due, Martha?"

First I start to say, what. But I know it ain't no use. You can't fool old folks bout something like that, so I tell her.

"Last part of November."

"Who the daddy?"

"Time."

"That man what play piano at the Legion?"

"Yeah."

"What he gon do bout it?"

"Mamma, it ain't too much he can do, now is it? The baby on its way."

She don't say nothing for a long time. She sit looking at her hands. They all wet from where she been washing dishes and they all wrinkled like yo hands be when they been in water too long. She get up and get a dish cloth and dry em, then sit down at the table. "Where he at now?"

"Gone."

215

"Gone? Gone where?" I don't say nothing and she start cussing then. I get kinda scared cause Mamma got to be real mad foe she cuss and I don't know who she cussing—me or Time. Then she start talking to me. "Martha, you just a fool. I told you that man wan't no good first time I seed him. A musician the worst kind of man you can get mixed up with. Look at you. You ain't even eighteen years old yet, Larry just barely two and here you is pregnant again." She go on like that for a while and I don't say nothing. Couldn't no way. By the time I get my mouth fixed to say something, she done raced on so far ahead that what I got to say don't have nothing to do with what she saying right then. Finally she stop and ask, "What you gon do now? You want to come back here?" She ain't never like me living with Orine and when I say no, she ask, "Why not? It be easier for you."

I shake my head again. "If I here, Time won't know where to find me, and Time coming; he be back. He gon to make a place for us, you a see."

"Hump, you just played the fool again, Martha."

"No Mamma, that not it at all; Time want me."

"Is that what he say when he left?"

"No, but . . ."

Well, like the first night we met, he come over to me like he knowed me for a long time and like I been his for awmost that long. Yeah, I think that how it was. Cause I didn' even see him when we come in the Legion that first night.

Me and Orine, we just got our checks that day. We went downtown and Orine bought her some new dresses. But the dress she want to wear that night don't look right so we go racing back to town and change it. Then we had to hurry home and get dressed. It Friday night and the Legion crowded. You got to get there early on the weekend if you want a seat. And Orine don't want just any seat; she want one right up front. "Who gon see you way back there? Nobody. They can't see you, who gon ask you to dance? Nobody. You don't dance, how you gon meet people? You don't meet people, what you doing out?" So we sit up front. Whole lots a people there that night. You can't even see the bandstand cross the dance floor. We sharing the table with some more people and Orine keep jabbing me, telling me to sit cool. And I try cause Orine say it a good thing to be cool.

The set end and people start leaving the dance floor. That when I see Time. He just getting up from the piano. I like him right off cause I like men what look like him. He kind of tall and slim. First time I ever seed a man wear his hair so long and it nappy—he tell me once it an African Bush—but he look good anyway and he know it. He look round all cool. He step down from the bandstand and start walking toward me. He come over to the table and just look. "You," he say, "you my Black queen." And he bow down most to the floor.

Ah shit! I mad cause I think he just trying to run a game. "What you trying to prove, fool?" I ask him.

"Ah man," he say and it like I cut him. That the way he say it. "Ah man. I call this woman my Black queen—tell her she can rule my life and she call me a fool."

"And sides what, nigga," I tell him then, "I ain't black." And I ain't, I don't care what Time say. I just a dark woman.

"What's the matter, you shamed of being Black? Ain't nobody told you Black is pretty?" He talk all loud and people start gathering round. Somebody say, "Yeah, you tell her bout it, soul." I embarrassed and I look over at Orine. But she just grinning, not saying nothing. I guess she waiting to see what I gon do so I stand up.

"Well if I is black, I is a fine black." And I walk over to the bar. I walk just like I don't know they watching my ass, and I hold my head up. Time follow me right on over to the bar and put his arm round my shoulder.

"You want a drink?" I start to say no cause I scared. Man not supposed to make you feel like he make me feel. Not just like doing it—but, oh, like it right for him to be there with me, touching me. So I say yes. "What's your name?" he ask then.

I smile and say, "They call me the player." Orine told a man that once in Berkeley and he didn't know what to say. Orine a smart woman.

"Well they call me Time and I know yo mamma done told you Time ain't nothing to play with." His smile cooler than mine. We don't say nothing for a long while. He just stand there with his arm round my shoulder looking at us in the mirror behind the bar. Finally he say, "Yeah, you gon be my Black queen." And he look down at me and laugh. I don't know what to do, don't know what to say neither, so I just smile.

"You gon tell me your name or not?"

"Martha."

He laugh. "That a good name for you."

"My mamma name me that so I be good. She name all us kids from the Bible," I tell him laughing.

"And is you good?"

I nod yes and no all at the same time and kind of mumble cause I don't know what to say. Mamma really did name all us kids from the Bible. She always saying, "My mamma name me Veronica after the woman in the Bible and I a better woman for it. That why I name all my kids from the Bible. They got something to look up to." But Mamma don't think I'm good, specially since I got Larry. Maybe Time ain't gon think I good neither. So I don't answer, just smile and move on back to the table. I hear him singing soft-like, "Oh Mary, don't you weep, tell yo sister Martha not to moan." And I kind of glad cause most people don't even think bout that when I tell em my name. That make me know he really smart.

We went out for breakfast after the Legion close. Him and me and Orine and German, the drummer. Only places open is on the other side of town and at first Time don't want to go. But we finally swade him.

Time got funny eyes, you can't hardly see into em. You look and you look and you can't tell nothing from em. It make me feel funny when he look at me. I finally get used to it, but that night he just sit there looking and don't say nothing for a long time after we order.

"So you don't like Black?" he finally say.

"Do you?" I ask. I think I just ask him questions, then I don't have to talk so much. But I don't want him to talk bout that right then, so I smile and say, "Let's talk bout you."

"I am not what I am." He smiling and I smile back, but I feel funny cause I think I supposed to know what he mean.

"What kind of game you trying to run?" Orine ask. Then she laugh. "Just cause we from the country don't mean we ain't hip to niggas trying to be big-time. Ain't that right, Martha?"

I don't know what to say, but I know Time don't like that. I think he was going to cuss Orine out, but German put his arm round Orine and he laugh. "He just mean he ain't what he want to be. Don't pay no mind to that cat. He always trying to blow some shit." And he start talking that talk, rapping to Orine.

I look at Time. "That what you mean?"

He all lounged back in the seat, his legs stretched way out under the table. He pour salt in a napkin and mix it up with his finger. "Yeah, that's what I mean. That's all about me. Black is pretty, Martha." He touch my face with one finger. "You let white people make you believe you ugly. I bet you don't even dream."

"I do, too."

"What you dream?"

"Huh?" I don't know what he talking bout. I kind of smile and look at him out the corner of my eye. "I dreams bout a man like you. Why, just last night, I dream—"

He start laughing. "That's all right. That's all right."

The food come then and we all start eating. Time act like he forgot all bout dreams. I never figure out how he think I can just sit there and tell him the dreams I have at night, just like that. It don't seem like what I dream bout at night mean as much as what I think bout during the day.

We leaving when Time trip over this white man's feet. That man's feet all out in the aisle but Time don't never be watching where he going no way. "Excuse me," he say kind of mean.

"Say, watch it, buddy." That white man talk most as nasty as Time. He kind of old and maybe he drunk or an Okie.

"Man, I said excuse me. You the one got your feet in the aisle."

"You," that man say, starting to get up, "you better watch yourself, boy."

And what he want to say that for? Time step back and say real quiet, "No, motherfucker. You the one. You better watch yourself and your daughter, too. See how many babies she gon have by boys like me." That man get all red in the face, but the woman in the booth with him finally start pulling at him, telling him to sit down, shut up. Cause Time set to kill that man.

I touch Time's arm first, then put my arm round his waist. "Ain't no use getting messed behind somebody like that."

Time and that man just looking at each other, not wanting to back down. People was gon start wondering what going on in a few minutes. I tell him, " 'Got something for you, baby,' " and he look down at me and grin. Orine pick it up. We go out that place singing, " 'Good loving, good, good loving, make you feel so clean.' "

"You like to hear me play?" he ask when we in the car.

"This the first time they ever have anybody here that sound that good."

"Yeah," Orine say. "How come you all staying round a little jive-ass town like Ashley?"

"We going to New York pretty soon," Time say kind of snappy.

"Well, shit, baby, you—"

"When you going to New York?" I ask real quick. When Orine in a bad mood, can't nobody say nothing right.

"Couple of months." He lean back and put his arm round me. "They doing so many things with music back there. Up in the City, they doing one maybe two things. In L.A. they doing another one, two things. But, man, in New York, they doing everything. Person couldn't never get stuck in one groove there. So many things going on, you got to be hip, real hip to keep up. You always growing there. Shit, if you 'live and playing, you can't help but grow. Say, man," he reach and tap German on the shoulder, "let's leave right now."

We all crack up. Then I say, "I sorry but I can't go, got to take care of my baby."

He laugh. "Sugar, you got yo baby right here."

"Well, I must got two babies then."

We pull up in front of the partment house then but don't no one move. Finally Time reach over and touch my hair. "You gon be my Black queen?"

I look straight ahead at the night. "Yeah," I say. "Yeah."

We go in and I check first on Larry cause sometimes that girl don't watch him good. When I come in some nights, he be all out the cover and shivering but too sleepy to get back under em. Time come in when I'm pulling the cover up on Orine two kids.

"Which one yours?" he ask.

I go over to Larry bed. "This my baby," I tell him.

"What's his name?"

"Larry."

"Oh, I suppose you name him after his daddy?"

I don't like the way he say that, like I was wrong to name him after his daddy. "Who else I gon name him after?" He don't say nothing and I leave him standing there. I mad now and I go in the bedroom and start pulling off my clothes. I think, that nigga can stand up in the living room all night, for all I care; let Orine talk to German and him, too. But Time come in the bedroom and put his arms round me. He touch my hair and my face and my tittie, and it scare me. I try to pull away but he hold me too close. "Martha," he say, "Black Martha." Then he just stand there holding me, not saying nothing, with his hand covering one side on my face. I stand there trembling but he don't notice. I know a woman not supposed to feel the way I feel bout Time, not right away. But I do.

He tell me things nobody ever say to me before. And I want to tell him that I ain't never liked no man much as I like him. But sometime you tell a man that and he go cause he think you liking him a whole lot gon hang him up.

"You and me," he say after we in bed, "we can make it together real good." He laugh. "I used to think all I needed was that music, but it take a woman to make that music sing, I think. So now stead of the music and me, it be the music and me and you."

"You left out Larry," I tell him. I don't think he want to hear that. But Larry my baby.

"How come you couldn't be free," he say real low. Then, "How you going when I go if you got a baby?"

"When you going?"

He turn his back to me. "Oh, I don't know. You know what the song say, 'When a woman take the blues, / She tuck her head and cry. / But when a man catch the blues, / He grab his shoes and slide.' Next time I get the blues," he laugh a little, "next time the man get too much for me, I leave here and go someplace else. He always chasing me. The god damn white man." He turn over and reach for me. "You feel good. He chasing me and I chasing dreams. You think I'm crazy, huh? But I'm not. I just got so many, many things going on inside me I don't know which one to let out first. They all want out so bad. When I play—I got to be better, Martha. You gon help me?"

"Yes, Time, I help you."

"You see," and he reach over and turn on the light and look down at me. "I'm not what I am. I up tight on the inside but I can't get it to show on the outside. I don't know how to make it come out. You ever hear Coltrane blow? That man is together. He showing on the outside what he got on the inside. When I can do that, then I be somewhere. But I can't go by myself. I need a woman. A Black woman. Them other women steal your soul and don't leave nothing. But a Black woman—" He laugh and pull me close. He want me and that all I care bout.

Mamma come over that next morning and come right on in the bedroom, just like she always do. I kind of shamed for her to see me like that, with a man and all, but she don't say nothing cept scuse me, then turn away. "I come to get Larry."

"He in the other bedroom," I say, starting to get up.

"That's okay; I get him." And she go out and close the door.

I start to get out the bed anyway. Time reach for his cigarettes and light one. "Your mamma don't believe in knocking, do she?"

I start to tell him not to talk so loud cause Mamma a hear him, but that might make him mad. "Well, it ain't usually nobody in here with me for her to walk in on." I standing by the bed buttoning my housecoat and Time reach out and pull my arm, smiling.

"I know you ain't no tramp, Martha. Come on, get back in bed."

I pull my arm way and start out the door. "I got to get Larry's clothes together," I tell him. I do got to get them clothes together cause when Mamma come for Larry like that on Sadday morning, she want to keep him for the rest of the weekend. But—I don't know. It just don't seem right for me to be in the bed with a man and my mamma in the next room.

I think Orine and German still in the other bedroom. But I don't know; Orine don't too much like for her mens to stay all night. She say it make a bad impression on her kids. I glad the door close anyway. If Mamma gon start talking that "why don't you come home" talk the way she usually do, it best for Orine not to hear it.

Orine's two kids still sleep but Mamma got Larry on his bed tickling him and playing with him. He like that. "Boy, you sho happy for it to be so early in the morning," I tell him.

Mamma stop tickling him and he lay there breathing hard for a minute. "Big mamma," he say laughing and pointing at her. I just laugh at him and go get his clothes.

"You gon marry this one?" Every man I been with since I had Larry, she ask that about.

"You think marrying gon save my soul, Mamma?" I sorry right away cause Mamma don't like me to make fun of God. But I swear I gets tired of all that. What I want to marry for anyway? Get somebody like Daddy always coming and going and every time he go leave a baby behind. Or get a man what stay round and beat me all the time and have my kids thinking they big shit just cause they got a daddy what stay with them, like them saddity kids at school. Shit, married or single, they still doing the same thing when they goes to bed.

Mamma don't say nothing else bout it. She ask where he work. I tell her and then take Larry in the bathroom and wash him up.

"The older you get, the more foolish you get, Martha. Them musicians ain't got nothing for a woman. Lots sweet talk and babies, that's all. Welfare don't even want to give you nothing for the one you got now, how you gon—" I sorry but I just stop listening. Mamma run her mouth like a clatterbone on a goose ass sometime. I just go on and give her the baby and get the rest of his things ready.

"So your mamma don't like musicians, huh?" Time say when I get back in the bedroom. "Square-ass people. Everything they don't know about, they hate. Lord deliver me from a square-ass town with square-ass people." He turn over.

"You wasn't calling me square last night."

"I'm not calling you square now, Martha."

I get back in the bed then and he put his arm round me. "But they say what they want to say. Long as they don't mess with me things be okay. But that's impossible. Somebody always got to have their little say about your life. They want to tell you where to go, how to play, what to play, where to play it—shit, even who to fuck and how to fuck em. But when I get to New York—"

"Time, let's don't talk now."

He laugh then. "Martha, you so Black." I don't know what I should say so I don't say nothing, just get closer and we don't talk.

That how it is lots a time with me and him. It seem like all I got is lots little pitchers in my mind and can't tell nobody what they look like. Once I try to tell him bout that, bout the pitchers, and he just laugh. "Least your head ain't empty. Maybe now you got some pictures, you get some thoughts." That make me mad and I start cussing, but he laugh and kiss me and hold me. And that time, when we doing it, it all—all angry and like he want to hurt me. And I think bout that song he sing that first night bout having the blues. But that the only time he mean like that.

Time and German brung the piano a couple days after that. The piano small and all shiny black wood. Time cussed German when German knocked it against the front door getting it in the house. Time want to put it in the bedroom but I want him to be thinking bout me, not some damn piano when he in there. I tell him he put it in the living room or it don't come in the house. Orine don't want it in the house period, say it too damn noisy—that's what she tell me. She don't say nothing to Time. I think she halfway scared of him. He pretty good bout playing it though. He don't never play it when the babies is sleep or at least he don't play loud as he can. But all he thinking bout when he playing is that piano. You talk to him, he don't answer; you touch him, he don't look up. One time I say to him, "Pay me some tention," but he don't even hear. I hit his hand, not hard, just playing. He look at me but he don't stop playing. "Get out of here, Martha." First I start to tell him he can't tell me what to do in my own self's house, but he just looking at me. Looking at me and playing and not saying nothing. I leave.

His friends come over most evenings when he home, not playing. It like Time is the leader. Whatever he say go. They always telling him how good he is. "Out of sight, man, the way you play." "You ought to get out of this little town so somebody can hear you play." Most times, he just smile and don't say nothing, or he just say thanks. But I wonder if he really believe em. I tell him, sometime, that he sound better than lots a them men on records. He give me his little cool smile. But I feel he glad I tell him that.

When his friends come over, we sit round laughing and talking and drinking. Orine like that cause she be playing up to em all and they be telling her what a fine ass she got. They don't tell me nothing like that cause Time be sitting right there, but long as Time telling me, I don't care. It like when we go to the Legion, after Time and German started being with us. We all the time get in free then and get to sit at one a the big front tables. And Orine like that cause it make her think she big time. But she still her same old picky self; all the time telling me to "Sit cool, Martha," and "Be cool, girl." Acting like cool the most important thing in the world. I finally just tell her, "Time like me just the way I am, cool or not." And it true; Time always saying that I be myself and I be fine.

Time and his friends, they talk mostly bout music, music and New York City and white people. Sometime I get so sick a listening to em. Always talking bout how they gon put something over on the white man, gon take something way from him, gon do this, gon do that. Ah shit! I tell em. But they don't pay me no mind.

German say, one night, "Man, this white man come asking if I want to play at his house for—"

"What you tell him, man, 'Put money in my purse?' " Time ask. They all crack up. Me and Orine sit there quiet. Orine all swole up cause Time and them running some kind of game and she don't know what going down.

"Hey, man, yo all member that time up in Frisco when we got fired from that gig and wan't none of our old ladies working?" That Brown, he play bass with em.

"Man," Time say, "all I remember is that I stayed high most of the time. But how'd I stay high if ain't nobody had no bread? Somebody was putting something in somebody's purse." He lean back laughing a little. "Verna's mamma must have been sending her some money till she got a job. Yeah, yeah man, that was it. You remember the first time her mamma sent that money and she gave it all to me to hold?"

"And what she wanna do that for? You went out and gambled half a it away and bought pot with most of the rest." German not laughing much as Time and Brown.

"Man, I was scared to tell her, cause you remember how easy it was for her to get her jaws tight. But she was cool, didn't say nothing. I told her I was going to get food with the rest of the money and asked her what she wanted, and—"

"And she say cigarettes," Brown break in laughing, "and this cat, man, this cat tell her, 'Woman, we ain't wasting this bread on no non-essentials!' " He doubled over laughing. They all laughing. But I don't think it that funny. Any woman can give a man money.

"I thought the babe was gon kill me, her jaws was so tight. But even with her jaws tight, Verna was still cool. She just say, 'Baby, you done fucked up fifty dollars on non-essentials; let me try thirty cents.' "

That really funny to em. They all cracking up but me. Time sit there smiling just a little and shaking his head. Then, he reach out and squeeze my knee and smile at me. And I know it like I say; any woman can give a man money.

German been twitching round in his chair and finally he say, "Yeah, man, this fay dude want me to play at his house for fifty cent." That German always got to hear hisself talk. "I tell him take his fifty cent and shove it up his ass—oh scuse me. I forgot that baby was here—but I told him what to do with it. When I play for honkies, I tell him, I don't play for less than two hundred dollars and he so foolish he gon pay it." They all laugh, but I know German lying. Anybody offer him ten cent, let lone fifty, he gon play.

"It ain't the money, man," Time say. "They just don't know what the fuck going on." I tell him Larry sitting right there. I know he ain't gon pay me no mind, but I feel if German can respect my baby, Time can too. "Man they go out to some little school, learn a few chords, and they think they know it all. Then they come round to the clubs wanting to sit in with you. Then, if you working for a white man, he fire you and hire him. No, man, I can't tie shit from no white man."

"That where you wrong," I tell him. "Somebody you don't like, you supposed to take em for everything they got. Take em and tell em to kiss yo butt."

"That another one of your pictures, I guess," Time say. And they all laugh cause he told em bout that, too, one time when he was mad with me.

"No, no," I say. "Listen, one day I walking downtown and this white man offer me a ride. I say okay and get in the car. He start talking and hinting round and finally he come on out and say it. I give you twenty dollars, he say. I say okay. We in Chinatown by then and at the next stoplight he get out his wallet and give me a twenty-dollar bill. 'That what I like 'bout you colored women,' he say, easing all back in his seat just like he already done got some and waiting to get some more. 'Yeah,' he say, 'you all so easy to get.' I put that money in my purse, open the door and tell him, 'Motherfucker, you ain't got shit here,' and slam the door."

"Watch your mouth," Time say. "Larry sitting here." We all crack up.

"What he do then?" Orine ask.

"What could he do? We in Chinatown and all them colored folks walking round. You know they ain't gon let no white man do nothing to me."

Time tell me after we go to bed that night that he kill me if he ever see me with a white man.

I laugh and kiss him. "What I want with a white man when I got you?" We both laugh and get in the bed. I lay stretched out waiting for him to reach for me. It funny, I think, how colored men don't never want no colored women messing with no white mens but the first chance he get, that colored man gon be right there in that white woman's bed. Yeah, colored men sho give colored womens a hard way to go. But I know if Time got to give a hard way to go, it ain't gon be for no scaggy fay babe, and I kinda smile to myself.

"Martha—"

"Yeah, Time," I say, turning to him.

"How old you—eighteen? What you want to do in life? What you want to be?"

What he mean? "I want to be with you," I tell him.

"No, I mean really. What you want?" Why he want to know I wonder. Everytime he start talking serious-like, I think he must be hearing his sliding song.

"I don't want to have to ask nobody for nothing. I want to be able to take care of my own self." I won't be no weight on you, Time, I want to tell him. I won't be no trouble to you.

"Then what you doing on the Welfare?"

"What else I gon do? Go out and scrub somebody else's toilets like my mamma did so Larry can run wild like I did? No. I stay on Welfare awhile, thank you."

"You see what the white man have done to us, is doing to us?"

"White man my ass," I tell him. "That was my no good daddy. If he'd got out and worked, we woulda been better off."

"How he gon work if the man won't let him?"

"You just let the man turn you out. Yeah, that man got yo mind."

"What you mean?" he ask real quiet. But I don't pay no tention to him.

"You always talking bout music and New York City, New York City and the white man. Why don't you forget all that shit and get a job like other men? I hate that damn piano."

He grab my shoulder real tight. "What you mean, 'got my mind'? What you mean?" And he start shaking me. But I crying and thinking bout he gon leave.

"You laugh cause I say all I got in my mind is pitchers but least they better than some old music. That all you ever think bout, Time."

"What you mean? What you mean?"

Finally I scream. "You ain't going no damn New York City and it ain't the white man what gon keep you. You just using him for a scuse cause you scared. Maybe you can't play." That the only time he ever hit me. And I cry cause I know he gon leave for sho. He hold me and say don't cry, say he sorry, but I can't stop. Orine bamming on the door and Time yelling at her to leave us lone and the babies crying and finally he start to pull away. I say, "Time . . ." He still for a long time, then he say, "Okay. Okay, Martha."

No, it not like he don't want me no more, he—

"Martha. Martha. You ain't been listening to a word I say."

"Mamma." I say it soft cause I don't want to hurt her. "Please leave me lone. You and Orine—and Time, too, sometime—yo all treat me like I don't know nothing. But just cause it don't seem like to you that I know what I'm doing, that don't mean nothing. You can't see into my life."

"I see enough to know you just get into one mess after nother." She shake her head and her voice come kinda slow. "Martha, I named you after that woman in the Bible cause I want you to be like her. Be good in the same way she is. Martha, that woman ain't never stopped believing. She humble and patient and the Lord make a place for her." She lean her hands on the table. Been in them dishes again, hands all wrinkled and shiny wet. "But that was the Bible. You ain't got the time to be patient, to be waiting for Time or no one else to make no place for you. That man ain't no good. I told you—"

Words coming faster and faster. She got the cow by the tail and gon on down shit creek. It don't matter though. She talk and I sit here thinking bout Time. "You feel good . . . You gon be my Black queen? . . . We can make it together . . . You feel good . . ." He be back.

Marigolds

•

(1969)

Eugenia W. Collier

When I think of the hometown of my youth, all that I seem to remember is dust—the brown, crumbly dust of late summer—arid, sterile dust that gets into the eyes and makes them water, gets into the throat and between the toes of bare brown feet. I don't know why I should remember only the dust. Surely there must have been lush green lawns and paved streets under leafy shade trees somewhere in town; but memory is an abstract painting—it does not present things as they are, but rather as they *feel*. And so, when I think of that time and that place, I remember only the dry September of the dirt roads and grassless yards of the shantytown where I lived. And one other thing I remember, another incongruency of memory—a brilliant splash of sunny yellow against the dust—Miss Lottie's marigolds.

Whenever the memory of those marigolds flashes across my mind, a strange nostalgia comes with it and remains long after the picture has faded. I feel again the chaotic emotions of adolescence, illusive as smoke, yet as real as the potted geranium before me now. Joy and rage and wild animal gladness and shame become tangled together in the multicolored skein of fourteen-going-on-fifteen as I recall that devastating moment when I was suddenly more woman than child, years ago in Miss Lottie's yard. I think of those marigolds at the strangest times; I remember them vividly now as I desperately pass away the time waiting for you, who will not come.

I suppose that futile waiting was the sorrowful background music of our impoverished little community when I was young. The Depression that gripped the nation was no new thing to us, for the black workers of rural

Maryland had always been depressed. I don't know what it was that we were waiting for; certainly not for the prosperity that was "just around the corner," for those were white folks' words, which we never believed. Nor did we wait for hard work and thrift to pay off in shining success as the American Dream promised, for we knew better than that, too. Perhaps we waited for a miracle, amorphous in concept but necessary if one was to have the grit to rise before dawn each day and labor in the white man's vineyard until after dark, or to wander about in the September dust offering one's sweat in return for some meager share of bread. But God was chary with miracles in those days, and so we waited—and waited.

We children, of course, were only vaguely aware of the extent of our poverty. Having no radios, few newspapers, and no magazines, we were somewhat unaware of the world outside our community. Nowadays we would be called "culturally deprived" and people would write books and hold conferences about us. In those days everybody we knew was just as hungry and ill clad as we were. Poverty was the cage in which we all were trapped, and our hatred of it was still the vague, undirected restlessness of the zoo-bred flamingo who knows that nature created him to fly free.

As I think of those days I feel most poignantly the tag end of summer, the bright dry times when we began to have a sense of shortening days and the imminence of the cold.

By the time I was fourteen my brother Joey and I were the only children left at our house, the older ones having left home for early marriage or the lure of the city, and the two babies having been sent to relatives who might care for them better than we. Joey was three years younger than I, and a boy, and therefore vastly inferior. Each morning our mother and father trudged wearily down the dirt road and around the bend, she to her domestic job, he to his daily unsuccessful quest for work. After our few chores around the tumbledown shanty, Joey and I were free to run wild in the sun with other children similarly situated.

For the most part, those days are ill defined in my memory, running together and combining like a fresh watercolor painting left out in the rain. I remember squatting in the road drawing a picture in the dust, a picture which Joey gleefully erased with one sweep of his dirty foot. I remember fishing for minnows in a muddy creek and watching madly as they eluded my cupped hands, while Joey laughed uproariously. And I remember, that year, a strange restlessness of body and of spirit, a feeling that something old and familiar was ending, and something unknown and therefore terrifying was beginning.

One day returns to me with special clarity for some reason, perhaps because it was the beginning of the experience that in some inexplicable way marked the end of innocence. I was loafing under the great oak tree in our yard, deep in some reverie which I have now forgotten, except that it involved some secret, secret thoughts of one of the Harris boys across the yard. Joey and a bunch of kids were bored now with the old tire suspended from an oak limb which had kept them entertained for a while.

"Hey, Lizabeth," Joey yelled. He never talked when he could yell. "Hey, Lizabeth, let's go somewhere."

I came reluctantly from my private world. "Where you want to go? What you want to do?"

The truth was that we were becoming tired of the formlessness of our summer days. The idleness whose prospect had seemed so beautiful during the busy days of spring now had degenerated to an almost desperate effort to fill up the empty midday hours.

"Let's go see can we find some locusts on the hill," someone suggested.

Joey was scornful. "Ain't no more locusts there. Y'all got 'em all while they was still green."

The argument that followed was brief and not really worth the effort. Hunting locust trees wasn't fun anymore by now.

"Tell you what," said Joey finally, his eyes sparkling. "Let's us go over to Miss Lottie's."

The idea caught on at once, for annoying Miss Lottie was always fun. I was still child enough to scamper along with the group over rickety fences and through bushes that tore our already raggedy clothes, back to where Miss Lottie lived. I think now that we must have made a tragicomic spectacle, five or six kids of different ages, each of us clad in only one garment—the girls in faded dresses that were too long or too short, the boys in patchy pants, their sweaty brown chests gleaming in the hot sun. A little cloud of dust followed our thin legs and bare feet as we tramped over the barren land.

When Miss Lottie's house came into view we stopped, ostensibly to plan our strategy, but actually to reinforce our courage. Miss Lottie's house was the most ramshackle of all our ramshackle homes. The sun and rain had long since faded its rickety frame siding from white to a sullen gray. The boards themselves seemed to remain upright, not from being nailed together, but rather from leaning together like a house that a child might have constructed from cards. A brisk wind might have blown it down, and the fact that it was still standing implied a kind of enchantment that was stronger than the elements. There it stood, and as far as I know is standing yet—a gray rotting thing with no porch, no shutters, no steps, set on a cramped lot with no grass, not even any weeds—a monument to decay.

In front of the house in a squeaky rocking chair sat Miss Lottie's son, John Burke, completing the impression of decay. John Burke was what was known as "queer-headed." Black and ageless, he sat, rocking day in and day out in a mindless stupor, lulled by the monotonous squeak-squawk of the chair. A battered hat atop his shaggy head shaded him from the sun. Usually John Burke was totally unaware of everything outside his quiet dream world. But if you disturbed him, if you intruded upon his fantasies, he would become enraged, strike out at you, and curse at you in some strange enchanted language which only he could understand. We children made a game of thinking of ways to disturb John Burke and then to elude his violent retribution.

But our real fun and our real fear lay in Miss Lottie herself. Miss Lottie seemed to be at least a hundred years old. Her big frame still held traces of the tall, powerful woman she must have been in youth, although it was now bent and drawn. Her smooth skin was a dark reddish-brown, and her face had Indian-like features and the stern stoicism that one associates with Indian faces. Miss Lottie didn't like intruders either, especially children. She never left her yard, and nobody ever visited her. We never knew how she managed those necessities which depend on human interaction—how she ate, for example, or even whether she ate. When we were tiny children, we thought Miss Lottie was a witch and we made up tales, which we half believed ourselves, about her exploits. We were far too sophisticated now, of course, to believe the witch nonsense. But old fears have a way of clinging like cobwebs, and so when we sighted the tumbledown shack, we had to stop to reinforce our nerves.

"Look, there she is," I whispered, forgetting that Miss Lottie could not possibly have heard me from that distance. "She's fooling with them crazy flowers."

"Yeh, look at 'er."

Miss Lottie's marigolds were perhaps the strangest part of the picture. Certainly they did not fit in with the crumbling decay of the rest of her yard. Beyond the dusty brown yard, in front of the sorry gray house, rose suddenly and shockingly a dazzling strip of bright blossoms, clumped together in enormous mounds, warm and passionate and sun-golden. The old black witch-woman worked on them all summer, every summer, down on her creaky knees, weeding and cultivating and arranging, while the house crumbled and John Burke rocked. For some perverse reason, we children hated those marigolds. They interfered with the perfect ugliness of the place; they were too beautiful; they said too much that we could not understand; they did not make sense. There was something in the vigor with which the old woman destroyed the weeds that intimidated us. It should have been a comical sight—the old woman with the man's hat on her cropped white head, leaning over the bright mounds, her big backside in the air—but it wasn't comical, it was something we could not name. We had to annoy her by whizzing a pebble into her flowers or by yelling a dirty word, then dancing away from her rage, reveling in our youth and mocking her age. Actually, I think it was the flowers we wanted to destroy, but nobody had the nerve to try it, not even Joey, who was usually fool enough to try anything.

"Y'all git some stones," commanded Joey now, and was met with instant giggling obedience as everyone except me began to gather pebbles from the dusty ground. "Come on, Lizabeth."

I just stood there peering through the bushes, torn between wanting to join the fun and feeling that it was all a bit silly.

"You scared, Lizabeth?"

I cursed and spat on the ground—my favorite gesture of phony bravado. "Y'all children get the stones, I'll show you how to use 'em."

I said before that we children were not consciously aware of how thick were the bars of our cage. I wonder now, though, whether we were not more aware of it than I thought. Perhaps we had some dim notion of what we were, and how little chance we had of being anything else. Otherwise, why would we have been so preoccupied with destruction? Anyway, the pebbles were collected quickly, and everybody looked at me to begin the fun.

"Come on, y'all."

We crept to the edge of the bushes that bordered the narrow road in front of Miss Lottie's place. She was working placidly, kneeling over the flowers, her dark hand plunged into the golden mound. Suddenly—zing—an expertly aimed stone cut the head off one of the blossoms.

"Who out there?" Miss Lottie's backside came down and her head came up as her sharp eyes searched the bushes. "You better git!"

We had crouched down out of sight in the bushes, where we stifled the giggles that insisted on coming. Miss Lottie gazed warily across the road for a moment, then cautiously returned to her weeding. Zing—Joey sent a pebble into the blooms, and another marigold was beheaded.

Miss Lottie was enraged now. She began struggling to her feet, leaning on a rickety cane and shouting, "Y'all git! Go on home!" Then the rest of the kids let loose with their pebbles, storming the flowers and laughing wildly and senselessly at Miss Lottie's impotent rage. She shook her stick at us and started shakily toward the road, crying, "Git 'long! John Burke! John Burke, come help!"

Then I lost my head entirely, mad with the power of inciting such rage, and ran out of the bushes in the storm of pebbles, straight toward Miss Lottie, chanting madly, "Old witch, fell in a ditch, picked up a penny and thought she was rich!" The children screamed with delight, dropped their pebbles, and joined the crazy dance, swarming around Miss Lottie like bees and chanting, "Old lady witch!" while she screamed curses at us. The madness lasted only a moment, for John Burke, startled at last, lurched out of his chair, and we dashed for the bushes just as Miss Lottie's cane went whizzing at my head.

I did not join the merriment when the kids gathered again under the oak in our bare yard. Suddenly I was ashamed, and I did not like being ashamed. The child in me sulked and said it was all in fun, but the woman in me flinched at the thought of the malicious attack that I had led. The mood lasted all afternoon. When we ate the beans and rice that was supper that night, I did not notice my father's silence, for he was always silent these days, nor did I notice my mother's absence, for she always worked until well into evening. Joey and I had a particularly bitter argument after supper; his exuberance got on my nerves. Finally I stretched out on the pallet in the room we shared and fell into a fitful doze.

When I awoke, somewhere in the middle of the night, my mother had returned, and I vaguely listened to the conversation that was audible through the thin walls that separated our rooms. At first I heard no words, only voices. My mother's voice was like a cool, dark room in summer— peaceful, soothing, quiet. I loved to listen to it; it made things seem all right somehow. But my father's voice cut through hers, shattering the peace.

"Twenty-two years, Maybelle, twenty-two years," he was saying, "and I got nothing for you, nothing, nothing."

"It's all right, honey, you'll get something. Everybody out of work now, you know that."

"It ain't right. Ain't no man ought to eat his woman's food year in and year out, and see his children running wild. Ain't nothing right about that."

"Honey, you took good care of us when you had it. Ain't nobody got nothing nowadays."

"I ain't talking about nobody else, I'm talking about *me*. God knows I try." My mother said something I could not hear, and my father cried out louder, "What must a man do, tell me that?"

"Look, we ain't starving. I git paid every week, and Mrs. Ellis is real nice about giving me things. She gonna let me have Mr. Ellis's old coat for you this winter—"

"Damn Mr. Ellis's coat! And damn his money! You think I want white folks' leavings? Damn, Maybelle"—and suddenly he sobbed, loudly and painfully, and cried helplessly and hopelessly in the dark night. I had never heard a man cry before. I did not know men ever cried. I covered my ears with my hands but could not cut off the sound of my father's harsh, painful, despairing sobs. My father was a strong man who could whisk a child upon his shoulders and go singing through the house. My father whittled toys for us and laughed so loud that the great oak seemed to laugh with him, and taught us how to fish and hunt rabbits. How could it be that my father was crying? But the sobs went on, unstifled, finally quieting until I could hear my mother's voice, deep and rich, humming softly as she used to hum for a frightened child.

The world had lost its boundary lines. My mother, who was small and soft, was now the strength of the family; my father, who was the rock on which the family had been built, was sobbing like the tiniest child. Everything was suddenly out of tune, like a broken accordion. Where did I fit into this crazy picture? I do not now remember my thoughts, only a feeling of great bewilderment and fear.

Long after the sobbing and the humming had stopped, I lay on the pallet, still as stone, with my hands over my ears, wishing that I too could cry and be comforted. The night was silent now except for the sound of the crickets and of Joey's soft breathing. But the room was too crowded with fear to allow me to sleep, and finally, feeling the terrible aloneness of 4 a.m., I decided to awaken Joey.

"Ouch! What's the matter with you? What you want?" he demanded disagreeably when I had pinched and slapped him awake.

"Come on, wake up."

"What for? Go 'way."

I was lost for a reasonable reply. I could not say, "I'm scared and I don't want to be alone," so I merely said, "I'm going out. If you want to come, come on."

The promise of adventure awoke him. "Going out now? Where to, Lizabeth? What you going to do?"

I was pulling my dress over my head. Until now I had not thought of going out. "Just come on," I replied tersely.

I was out the window and halfway down the road before Joey caught up with me.

"Wait, Lizabeth, where you going?"

I was running as if the Furies were after me, as perhaps they were—

running silently and furiously until I came to where I had half known I was headed: to Miss Lottie's yard.

The half-dawn light was more eerie than complete darkness, and in it the old house was like the ruin that my world had become—foul and crumbling, a grotesque caricature. It looked haunted, but I was not afraid, because I was haunted, too.

"Lizabeth, you lost your mind?" panted Joey.

I had indeed lost my mind, for all the smoldering emotions of that summer swelled in me and burst—the great need for my mother, who was never there; the hopelessness of our poverty and degradation; the bewilderment of being neither child nor woman and yet both at once; the fear unleashed by my father's tears. And these feelings combined in one great impulse toward destruction.

"Lizabeth!"

I leaped furiously into the mounds of marigolds and pulled madly, trampling and pulling and destroying the perfect yellow blooms. The fresh smell of early morning and of dew-soaked marigolds spurred me on as I went tearing and mangling and sobbing while Joey tugged my dress or my waist crying, "Lizabeth, stop, please stop!"

And then I was sitting in the ruined little garden among the uprooted and ruined flowers, crying and crying, and it was too late to undo what I had done. Joey was sitting beside me, silent and frightened, not knowing what to say. Then: "Lizabeth, look."

I opened my swollen eyes and saw in front of me a pair of large callused feet; my gaze lifted to the swollen legs, the age-distorted body clad in a tight cotton nightdress, and then the shadowed Indian face surrounded by stubby white hair. There was no rage in the face now, now that the garden was destroyed and there was nothing any longer to be protected.

"M-miss Lottie!" I scrambled to my feet and just stood there and stared at her, and that was the moment when childhood faded and womanhood began. That violent, crazy act was the last act of childhood. For as I gazed at the immobile face with the sad, weary eyes, I gazed upon a kind of reality which is hidden to childhood. The witch was no longer a witch but only a broken old woman who had dared to create beauty in the midst of ugliness and sterility. She had been born in squalor and lived in it all her life. Now at the end of that life she had nothing except a falling-down hut, a wrecked body, and John Burke, the mindless son of her passion. Whatever verve there was left in her, whatever was of love and beauty and joy that had not been squeezed out by life had been there in the marigolds she had so tenderly cared for.

Of course, I could not express the thing that I knew about Miss Lottie as I stood there awkward and ashamed. The years have put words to the things I knew in that moment, and as I look back upon it, I know that that moment marked the end of innocence. People think of the loss of innocence as meaning the loss of virginity, but this is far from true. Innocence involves an unseeing acceptance of things at face value, an ignorance of the area below the surface. In that humiliating moment I looked beyond myself and into the depths of another person. This was the beginning of compassion, and one cannot have both compassion and innocence.

The years have taken me worlds away from that time and that place, from the dust and squalor of our lives and from the bright thing that I destroyed in a blind childish striking out at God-knows-what. Miss Lottie died long ago and many years have passed since I last saw her hut, completely barren at last, for despite my wild contrition she never planted marigolds again. Yet there are times when the image of those passionate yellow mounds returns with a painful poignancy. For one does not have to be ignorant and poor to find that this life is barren as the dusty yards of our town. And I, too, have planted marigolds.

After Saturday Night
Comes Sunday

(1971)

Sonia Sanchez

It had all started at the bank. She wuzn't sure, but she thot it had. At that crowded bank where she had gone to clear up the mistaken notion that she wuz $300.00 overdrawn in her checking account.

Sandy had moved into that undersized/low expectation of niggahs/being able to save anything bank/meanly. She wuz tired of people charging her fo they own mistakes. She had seen it wid her own eyes, five checks: four fo $50 the other one fo $100 made out to an Anthony Smith. It wuz Winston's signature. Her stomach jumped as she added and re-added the figures. Finally she dropped the pen and looked up at the business/suited/ man sitten across from her wid crossed legs and eyes. And as she called him faggot in her mind, watermelon tears gathered round her big eyes and she just sat.

Someone had come for her at the bank. A friend of Winston's helped her to his car. It wuz the wite/dude who followed Winston constantly wid his eyes. Begging eyes she had once called 'em, half in jest, half seriously. They wuz begging now, along wid his mouth, begging Sandy to talk. But she cudn't. The words had gone away, gotten lost, drowned by the warm/ april/rain dropping in on her as she watched the car move down the long/ unbending/street. It was her first spring in Indianapolis. She wondered if it wud be beautiful.

He wuz holding her. Crying in her ear. Loud cries, almost louder than the noise already turning in her head. Yeh. He sed between the cries that he had messed up the money. He had . . . he had . . . oh babee. *C'mon, Sandy, and talk. Talk to me. Help me, babee. Help me to tell you what I got to tell you for both our sakes.* He stretched her out on the green/

237

oversized/couch that sat out from the wall like some displaced trailer waiting to be parked.

I'm hooked, he sed. I'm hooked again on stuff. It's not like befo though when I wuz 17 and just beginning. This time it's different. I mean it has to do now wid me and all my friends who are still on junk. You see I got out of the joint and looked around and saw those brothers who are my friends all still on the stuff and I cried inside.. I cried long tears for some beautiful dudes who didn't know how the man had 'em by they balls. Baby, I felt so sorry for them and they wuz so turned around that one day over to Tony's crib I got high wid 'em. That's all, babee. I know I shouldn't have done that. You and the kids and all. But they wuz dudes I wuz in the joint wid. My brothers who wuz still unaware. I can git clean, babee. I mean, I don't have a long jones. I ain't been on it too long. I can kick now. Tomorrow. You just say it. Give me the word/sign that you understand, forgive me for being one big asshole and I'll start kicking tomorrow. For you, babee. I know I been laying some heavy stuff on you. Spending money we ain't even got—I'll git a job, too, next week—staying out all the time. Hitting you fo telling me the truth 'bout myself. My actions. Babee, it's you I love in spite of my crazy actions. It's you I love. Don't nobody else mean to me what you do. It's just that I been acting crazy but I know I can't keep on keepin' on this way and keep you and the children. Give me a whole lot of slack during this time and I can kick it, babee. I love you. You so good to me. The meanest thing that done ever happened to me. You the best thing that ever happened to me in all of my 38 years and I'll take better care of you. Say something, Sandy. Say you understand it all. Say you forgive me. At least that, babee.

He raised her head from the couch and kissed her. It was a short cooling kiss. Not warm. Not long. A binding kiss. She opened her eyes and looked at him, and the bare room that somehow now complemented their lives, and she started to cry again. And as he grabbed her and rocked her, she spoke fo the first time since she had told that wite/collar/man in the bank that the bank was wrong.

The-the-the-the bab-bab-bab-ies. Ar-ar-ar-are th-th-th-they o-o-okay? Oh my god. I'm stuttering. Stuttering, she thot. Just like when I wuz little.

Stop talking. Stop talking, girl. Write what you have to say. Just like you used to when you wuz little and you got tired of people staring at you while you pushed words out of an unaccommodating mouth. Yeh. That was it, she thot. Stop talking and write what you have to say. Nod yo/ head to all of this madness. But rest yo/head and use yo/hands till you git it all straight again.

She pointed to her bag and he handed it to her. She took out a pen and notebook and wrote that she wuz tired, that her head hurt and wuz spinning, and that she wanted to sleep fo a while. She turned and held his face full of little sores where he had picked fo ingrown hairs the nite befo. She kissed them and let her tongue move over his lips, wetting them. He smiled at her and sed he wud git her a coupla sleeping pills. He wud also pick up some dollies fo himself cuz Saturday was kicking time fo him. As he went out the door he turned and sed, *Lady, you some lady. I'm a lucky M.F. to have found you.* She watched him from the window and the sun hit the gold of his dashiki and made it bleed yellow raindrops.

She must have dozed. She knew it wuz late. It was dark outside. The room was dark also and she wondered if he had come in and gone upstairs where the children were napping. What a long nap the boys were taking. They wud be up all nite tonite if they didn't wake up soon. Maybe she shud wake them up, but she decided against it. Her body wuz still tired and she heard footsteps on the porch.

His voice was light and cracked a little as he explained his delay. He wuz high. She knew it. He sounded like he sounded on the phone when he called her late in the nite from some loud place and complimented her fo understanding his late hours. She hadn't understood them, she just hated to be a complaining bitch. He had no sleeping pills, but he had gotten her something as good. A morphine tablet. She watched his face as he explained that she cud swallow it or pop it into the skin. He sed it worked better if you stuck it in yo/arm. As he took the tablet out of the cellophane paper of his cigarettes, she closed her eyes and, fo a moment, she thot she heard someone crying outside the house. She opened her eyes.

His body hung loose as he knelt by the couch. He took from his pocket a manila envelope. It had little spots of blood on it and, as he undid the rubber bands, she saw two needles, a black top wid two pieces of dirty, wite cotton balls in it. She knew this wuz what he used to git high wid.

•

I-I-I-I don-don-don-don't wa-wa-want none o-o-o-of that stuff, ma-a-a-a-a-n. Ain't th-th-th-that do-do-do-dope, too? I-I-I-I just just just just wa-wa-wa-nnnt-ted to sleep. I'm o-o-o-kay now. She picked up her notebook and pen and started to write again.

I slept while you wuz gone, man. I drifted on off as I looked for you to walk up the steps. I don't want that stuff. Give me a cold beer though, if there's any in the house. I'll drink that. But no stuff man, she wrote. I'm yo/woman. You shudn't be giving me any of that stuff. Throw the pill away. We don't need it. You don't need it any mo. You gon kick and we gon move on. Keep on being baddDDD togetha. I'll help you, man, cuz I know you want to kick. Flush it down the toilet! You'll start kicking tomorrow and I'll get a babysitter and take us fo a long drive in the country and we'll move on the grass and make it move wid us, cuz we'll be full of living/alive/thots and we'll stop and make love in the middle of nowhere, and the grass will stop its wintry/brown/chants and become green as our Black bodies sing. Heave. Love each other. Throw that stuff away, man, cuz we got more important/beautiful/things to do.

As he read the note his eyes looked at hers in a half/clear/way and he got up and walked slowly to the john. She heard the toilet flushing and she heard the refrigerator door open and close. He brought two cold beers and, as she opened hers, she sat up to watch him rock back and forth in the rocking chair. And his eyes became small and sad as he sed, half-jokingly, *Hope I don't regret throwing that stuff in the toilet,* and he leaned back and smiled sadly as he drank his beer. She turned the beer can up to her lips and let the cold evening foam wet her mouth and drown the gathering stutters of her mind.

The sound of cries from the second floor made her move. As she climbed the stairs she waved to him. But his eyes were still closed. He wuz somewhere else, not in this house she thot. He wuz somewhere else, floating among past dreams she had never seen or heard him talk about. As she climbed the stairs, the boys' screams grew louder. *Wow. Them boys got some strong lungs,* she thot. And smiled.

It wuz 11:30 and she had just put the boys in their cribs. She heard them sucking on their bottles, working hard at nourishing themselves.

She knew the youngest twin wud finish his bottle first and cry out fo more milk befo he slept. She laughed out loud. He sho cud grease.

He wuz in the bathroom. She knocked on the door, but he sed for her not to come in. She stood outside the door, not moving, and knocked again. *Go and turn on the TV*, he said, *I'll be out in a few minutes.*

It wuz 30 minutes later when he came out. His walk wuz much faster than befo and his voice wuz high, higher than the fear moving over her body. She ran to him, threw her body against him and held on. She kissed him hard and moved her body 'gainst him til he stopped and paid attention to her movements. They fell to the floor. She felt his weight on her as she moved and kissed him. She wuz feeling good and she cudn't understand why he stopped. In the midst of pulling off her dress he stopped and took out a cigarette and lit it while she undressed to her bra and panties. She felt naked all of a sudden and sat down and drew her legs up against her chest and closed her eyes. She reached for a cigarette and lit it.

He stretched out next to her. She felt very ashamed, as if she had made him do something wrong. She wuz glad that she cudn't talk cuz that way she didn't have to explain. He ran his hand up and down her legs and touched her soft wet places.

It's just, babee, that this stuff kills any desire for THAT! I mean, I want you and all that but I can't quite git it up to perform. He lit another cigarette and sat up. *Babee, you sho know how to pick 'em. I mean, wuz you born under an unlucky star or sumthin'? First, you had a nigguh who preferred a rich/wite/woman to you and Blackness. Now you have a junkie who can't even satisfy you when you need satisfying.* And his laugh wuz harsh as he sed again, *You sho know how to pick 'em, lady.* She didn't know what else to do so she smiled a nervous smile that made her feel, remember times when she wuz little and she had stuttered thru a sentence and the listener had acknowledged her accomplishment wid a smile and all she cud do was smile back.

He turned and held her and sed, *Stay up wid me tonite, babee. I got all these memories creeping in on me. Bad ones. They's the things that make kicking hard, you know. You begin remembering all the mean things you've done to yo/family/friends who dig you. I'm remembering now all the heavee things I done laid on you in such a short time. You hardly had a chance to catch yo/breath when I'd think of sum new game to lay on you. Help me, Sandy. Listen to my talk. Hold my hand when I git too*

*sad. Laugh at my fears that keep poppin' out on me like some childhood
disease. Be my vaccine, babee. I need you. Don't ever leave me, babee,
cuz I'll never have a love like you again. I'll never have another woman
again if you leave me.* He picked up her hands and rubbed them in his
palms as he talked, and she listened until he finally slept and morning
crept in through the shades and covered them.

He threw away his works when he woke up. He came over to where
she wuz feeding the boys and kissed her and walked out to the backyard
and threw the manila envelope into the middle can. He came back inside,
smiled and took a dollie wid a glass of water, and fell on the couch.

Sandy put the boys in their strollers in the backyard where she cud
watch them as she cleaned the kitchen. She saw Snow, their big/wite/
dog, come round the corner of the house to sit in front of them. They
babbled words to him but he sat still guarding them from the backyard/
evils of the world.

She moved fast in the house, had a second cup of coffee, called their
babysitter and finished straightening up the house. She put on a short
dress which showed her legs, and she felt good about her black/hairy legs.
She laughed as she remembered that the young brothers on her block
used to call her a big/legged/momma as she walked in her young ways.

They never made the country. Their car refused to start and Winston
wuz too sick to push it to the filling station for a jump. So they walked
to the park. He pushed her in the swing and she pumped herself higher
and higher and higher till he told her to stop. She let the swing come
slowly to a stop and she jumped out and hit him on the behind and ran.
She heard him gaining on her and she tried to dodge him but they fell
laughing and holding each other. She looked at him and her eyes sed, *I
wish you cud make love to me, man.* As she laughed and pushed him
away she thot, *but just you wait til you all right, Winston, I'll give you
a workout you'll never forget,* and they got up and walked till he felt badly
and went home.

He stayed upstairs while she cooked. When she went upstairs to check
on him, he was curled up, wrapped tight as a child in his mother's womb.
She wiped his head and body full of sweat and kissed him and thought
how beautiful he wuz and how proud she wuz of him. She massaged his
back and went away. He called fo her as she wuz feeding the children
and asked for the wine. He needed somethin' else to relieve this saturday/
nite/pain that was creeping up on him. He looked bad, she thot, and
raced down the stairs and brought him the sherry. He thanked her as she
went out the door and she curtsied, smiled and sed, *Any ol time, man.*
She noticed she hadn't stuttered and felt good.

By the time she got back upstairs he was moaning and turning back and forth on the bed. He had drunk half the wine in the bottle, now he wuz getting up to bring it all up. When she came back up to the room he sed he was cold, so she got another blanket for him. He wuz still cold, so she took off her clothes and got under the covers wid him and rubbed her body against him. She wuz scared. She started to sing a Billie Holiday song. Yeh. God bless the child that's got his own. She cried in between the lyrics as she felt his big frame trembling and heaving. *Oh god,* she thot, *am I doing the right thing?* He soon quieted down and got up to go to the toilet. She closed her eyes as she waited fo him. She closed her eyes and felt the warmth of the covers creeping over her. She remembered calling his name as she drifted off to sleep. She remembered how quiet everything finally wuz.

One of the babies woke her up. She went into the room, picked up his bottle and got him more milk. It wuz while she wuz handing him the milk that she heard the silence. She ran to their bedroom and turned on the light. The bed wuz empty. She ran down the stairs and turned on the lights. He was gone. She saw her purse on the couch. Her wallet wuz empty. Nothing was left. She opened the door and went out on the porch, and she remembered the lights were on and that she wuz naked. But she stood fo a moment looking out at the flat/Indianapolis/street and she stood and let the late/nite/air touch her body and she turned and went inside.

My Man Bovanne

(1972)

Toni Cade Bambara

Blind people got a hummin jones if you notice. Which is understandable
completely once you been around one and notice what no eyes will force
you into to see people, and you get past the first time, which seems to
come out of nowhere, and it's like you in church again with fat-chest
ladies and old gents gruntin a hum low in the throat to whatever the
preacher be saying. Shakey Bee bottom lip all swole up with Sweet Peach
and me explainin how come the sweet-potato bread was a dollar-quarter
this time stead of dollar regular and he say uh hunh he understand, then
he break into this *thizzin* kind of hum which is quiet, but fiercesome just
the same, if you ain't ready for it. Which I wasn't. But I got used to it
and the onliest time I had to say somethin bout it was when he was playin
checkers on the stoop one time and he commenst to hummin quite
churchy seem to me. So I says, "Look here, Shakey Bee, I can't beat you
and Jesus too." He stop.

So that's how come I asked My Man Bovanne to dance. He ain't my
man mind you, just a nice ole gent from the block that we all know cause
he fixes things and the kids like him. Or used to fore Black Power got
hold their minds and mess em around till they can't be civil to ole folks.
So we at this benefit for my niece's cousin, who's runnin for somethin
with this Black party somethin or other behind her. And I press up close
to dance with Bovanne who blind and I'm hummin and he hummin,
chest to chest like talkin. Not jammin my breasts into the man. Wasn't
bout tits. Was bout vibrations. And he dug it and asked me what color
dress I had on and how my hair was fixed and how I was doin without a
man, not nosy but nice-like, and who was at this affair and was the canapés

dainty-stingy or healthy enough to get hold of proper. Comfy and cheery
is what I'm tryin to get across. Touch talkin like the heel of the hand on
the tambourine or on a drum.

But right away Joe Lee come up on us and frown for dancin so close
to the man. My own son, who knows what kind of warm I am about;
and don't grown men call me long distance and in the middle of the night
for a little Mama comfort? But he frown. Which ain't right since Bovanne
can't see and defend himself. Just a nice old man who fixes toasters and
busted irons and bicycles and things and changes the lock on my door
when my men friends get messy. Nice man. Which is not why they
invited him. Grass roots you see. Me and Sister Taylor and the woman
who does heads at Mamies and the man from the barbershop, we all there
on account of we grass roots. And I ain't never been souther than Brooklyn
Battery and no more country than the window box on my fire escape.
And just yesterday my kids tellin me to take them countrified rags off my
head and be cool. And now can't get Black enough to suit em. So everybody passin sayin My Man Bovanne. Big deal, keep steppin and don't
even stop a minute to get the man a drink or one of them cute sandwiches
or tell him what's goin on. And him standin there with a smile ready case
someone do speak he want to be ready. So that's how come I pull him
on the dance floor and we dance squeezin past the tables and chairs and
all them coats and people standin round up in each other face talkin bout
this and that but got no use for this blind man who mostly fixed skates
and skooters for all these folks when they was just kids. So I'm pressed
up close and we touch talkin with the hum. And here come my daughter
cuttin her eye at me like she do when she tell me about my "apolitical"
self like I got hoof and mouf disease and there ain't no hope at all. And
I don't pay her no mind and just look up in Bovanne shadow face and
tell him his stomach like a drum and he laugh. Laugh real loud. And
here come my youngest, Task, with a tap on my elbow like he the third-
grade monitor and I'm cuttin up on the line to assembly.

"I was just talkin on the drums," I explained when they hauled me
into the kitchen. I figured drums was my best defense. They can get ready
for drums what with all this heritage business. And Bovanne stomach just
like that drum Task give me when he come back from Africa. You just
touch it and it hum thizzm, thizzm. So I stuck to the drum story. "Just
drummin, that's all."

"Mama, what are you talkin about?"

"She had too much to drink," say Elo to Task cause she don't hardly
say nuthin to me direct no more since that ugly argument about my wigs.

"Look here, Mama," say Task, the gentle one. "We just tryin to pull your coat. You were makin a spectacle of yourself out there dancing like that."

"Dancin like what?"

Task run a hand over his left ear like his father for the world and his father before that.

"Like a bitch in heat," say Elo.

"Well uhh, I was goin to say like one of them sex-starved ladies gettin on in years and not too discriminating. Know what I mean?"

I don't answer cause I'll cry. Terrible thing when your own children talk to you like that. Pullin me out the party and hustlin me into some stranger's kitchen in the back of a bar just like the damn police. And ain't like I'm old old. I can still wear me some sleeveless dresses without the meat hangin off my arm. And I keep up with some thangs through my kids. Who ain't kids no more. To hear them tell it. So I don't say nuthin.

"Dancin with that tom," say Elo to Joe Lee, who leanin on the folks' freezer. "His feet can smell a cracker a mile away and go into their shuffle number posthaste. And them eyes. He could be a little considerate and put on some shades. Who wants to look into them blown-out fuses that—"

"Is this what they call the generation gap?" I say.

"Generation gap," spits Elo, like I suggested castor oil and fricassee possum in the milk shakes or somethin. "That's a white concept for a white phenomenon. There's no generation gap among Black people. We are a col—"

"Yeh, well never mind," says Joe Lee. "The point is, Mama . . . well, it's pride. You embarrass yourself and us, too, dancin like that."

"I wasn't shame." Then nobody say nuthin. Them standin there in they pretty clothes with drinks in they hands and gangin up on me, and me in the third-degree chair and nary a olive to my name. Felt just like the police got hold to me.

"First of all," Task say, holdin up his hand and tickin off the offenses, "the dress. Now that dress is too short, Mama, and too low-cut for a woman your age. And Tamu's going to make a speech tonight to kick off the campaign and will be introducin you and expecting you to organize the council of elders—"

"Me? Didn nobody ask me nuthin. You mean Nisi? She change her name?"

"Well, Norton was supposed to tell you about it. Nisi wants to introduce

you and then encourage the older folks to form a Council of the Elders
to act as an advisory—"

"And you going to be standing there with your boobs out and that wig
on your head and that hem up to your ass. And people'll say, 'Ain't that
the horny bitch that was grindin with the blind dude?' "

"Elo, be cool a minute," say Task, gettin to the next finger. "And then
there's the drinkin. Mama, you know you can't drink cause next thing
you know you be laughin loud and carryin on," and he grab another
finger for the loudness. "And then there's the dancin. You been tattooed
on the man for four records straight and slow draggin even on the fast
number. How you think that look for a woman your age?"

"What's my age?"

"What?"

"I'm axin you all a simple question. You keep talkin bout what's proper
for a woman my age. How old am I anyhow?" And Joe Lee slams his
eyes shut and squinches up his face to figure. And Task run a hand over
his ear and stare into his glass like the ice cubes goin calculate for him.
And Elo just starin at the top of my head like she goin rip the wig off
any minute now.

"Is your hair braided up under that thing? If so, why don't you take it
off? You always did so a neat cornroll."

"Uh huh," cause I'm thinkin how she couldn't undo her hair fast
enough talking bout cornroll so countrified. None of which was the subject. "How old, I say?"

"Sixtee-one or—"

"You a damn lie, Joe Lee Peoples."

"And that's another thing," say Task on the fingers.

"You know what you all can kiss," I say, gettin up and brushin the
wrinkles out my lap.

"Oh, Mama," Elo say, puttin a hand on my shoulder like she hasn't
done since she left home and the hand landin light and not sure it supposed
to be there. Which hurt me to my heart. Cause this was the child in our
happiness fore Mr. Peoples die. And I carried that child strapped to my
chest till she was nearly two. We was close is what I'm trying to tell you.
Cause it was more me in the child than the others. And even after Task
it was the girl-child I covered in the night and wept over for no reason
at all less it was she was a chub-chub like me and not very pretty, but a
warm child. And how did things get to this, that she can't put a sure hand
on me and say Mama we love you and care about you and you entitled
to enjoy yourself cause you a good woman?

"And then there's Reverend Trent," say Task, glancin from left to right like they hatchin a plot and just now lettin me in on it. "You were suppose to be talking with him tonight, Mama, about giving us his basement for campaign headquarters and—"

"Didn nobody tell me nuthin. If grass roots mean you kept in the dark I can't use it. I really can't. And Reven Trent a fool anyway the way he tore into the widow man up there on Edgecomb cause he wouldn't take in three of them foster children and the woman not even comfy in the ground yet and the man's mind messed up and—"

"Look here," say Task. "What we need is a family conference so we can get all this stuff cleared up and laid out on the table. In the meantime I think we better get back into the other room and tend to business. And in the meantime, Mama, see if you can't get to Reverend Trent and—"

"You want me to belly rub with the Reven, that it?"

"Oh damn," Elo say and go through the swingin door.

"We'll talk about all this at dinner. How's tomorrow night, Joe Lee?" While Joe Lee being self-important I'm wonderin who's doin the cookin and how come nobody ax me if I'm free and do I get a corsage and things like that. Then Joe nod that it's O.K. and he go through the swingin door and just a little hubbub come through from the other room. Then Task smile his smile, lookin just like his daddy and he leave. And it just me in this stranger's kitchen, which was a mess I wouldn't never let my kitchen look like. Poison you just to look at the pots. Then the door swing the other way and it's My Man Bovanne standin there sayin Miss Hazel but lookin at the deep fry and then at the steam table, and most surprised when I come up on him from the other direction and take him on out of there. Pass the folks pushin up towards the stage where Nisi and some other people settin and ready to talk, and folks gettin to the last of the sandwiches and the booze fore they settle down in one spot and listen serious. And I'm thinkin bout tellin Bovanne what a lovely long dress Nisi got on and the earrings and her hair piled up in a cone and the people bout to hear how we all gettin screwed and gotta form our own party and everybody there listenin and lookin. But instead I just haul the man on out of there, and Joe Lee and his wife look at me like I'm terrible, but they ain't said boo to the man yet. Cause he blind and old and don't nobody there need him since they grown up and don't need they skates fixed no more.

"Where we goin, Miss Hazel?" Him knowin all the time.

"First we gonna buy you some dark sunglasses. Then you comin with me to the supermarket so I can pick up tomorrow's dinner, which is goin to be a grand thing proper and you invited. Then we goin to my house."

"That be fine. I surely would like to rest my feet." Bein cute, but you got to let men play out they little show, blind or not. So he chat on bout how tired he is and how he appreciate me takin him in hand this way. And I'm thinkin I'll have him change the lock on my door first thing. Then I'll give the man a nice warm bath with jasmine leaves in the water and a little Epsom salt on the sponge to do his back. And then a good rubdown with rose water and olive oil. Then a cup of lemon tea with a taste in it. And a little talcum, some of that fancy stuff Nisi mother sent over last Christmas. And then a massage, a good face massage round the forehead which is the worryin part. Cause you gots to take care of the older folks. And let them know they still needed to run the mimeo machine and keep the spark plugs clean and fix the mailboxes for folks who might help us get the breakfast program goin, and the school for the little kids and the campaign and all. Cause old folks is the nation. That what Nisi was sayin and I mean to do my part.

"I imagine you are a very pretty woman, Miss Hazel."

"I surely am," I say just like the hussy my daughter always say I was.

Jevata

•

(1977)

Gayl Jones

I didn't see Jevata when she ran Freddy away from her house, but Miss
Johnny Cake said she had a hot poker after him, and would have killed
him too, if he hadn't been faster than she was. Nobody didn't know what
made her do it. I didn't know either then, and I'm over there more than
anybody else is. Now I'm probably the onliest one who know what did
happen—me and her boy David. Miss Johnny Cake don't even know,
and it seem like she keep busier than anybody else on Green Street. People
say what make Miss Johnny so busy is the Urban Renewal come and
made her move out of that house she was living in for about forty years,
and all she got to do now is sit out there on the porch and be busy. Once
she told me she felt dislocated, and I told Jevata what she said, and Jevata
said she act dislocated.

Miss Johnny Cake ain't the onliest one talking about Jevata neither.
All up and down Green Street they talking. They started talking when
Jevata went up to Lexington and brought Freddy back with her, and they
ain't quit. They used to talk when I'd come down from Davis town to
visit her. Then I guess they got used to me. I called myself courting her
then. We been friends every since we went over to Simmons Street School
together, and we stayed friends. I guess all the courting was on my side
though, cause she never would have me. I still come to see about her
though. I was coming to see about her all during the time that Freddy
was living with her.

"I don't see what in the world that good-lookin boy see in her," Miss
Johnny Cake would say. "If I was him and eighteen, I wouldn't be courting
the mama, I be courting the daughter. He ain't right, is he, Mr. Floyd?"

I wouldn't say anything, just stand with my right foot up on the porch while she sat rocking. She was about seventy, with her gray hair in two plaits.

"I don't see what they got in common," Miss Johnny said.

"Same thing any man and woman got in common," I said.

"Aw, Mr. Floyd, you so nasty."

Before Freddy came, Jevata used to have something to say to people, but after he came she wouldn't say nothing to nobody. She used to say I was the only one that she could trust, because the others always talked about her too much. "Always got something to say about you. Caint even go pee without them having something to say about you." She would go on by and wouldn't say nothing to nobody. People said she got stuck up with that young boy living with her. "Woman sixty-five going with a boy eighteen," some of the women would say. "You seen her going up the street, didn't you? Head all up in the air, that boy trailin behind her. Don't even look right. I be ashamed for anybody to see me trying to go with a boy like that. Look like her tiddies fallen since he came, don't it? But you know she always have been like 'at though, always looking after boys. I stopped Maurice from going down there to play. But you know if he was like anybody else he least be trying to get some from the daughter too."

Now womens can get evil about something like that. Wasn't so much that Jevata was going with Freddy, as she wouldn't say nothing to them while she was doing it. Now if she'd gone over there and said something to them, and let them all in her business and everything, they would felt all right then, and they wouldn't a got evil with her. "Rest of us got man trouble, Miss Jevata must got boy trouble," they'd laugh.

Now the boy's eighteen, but Jevata ain't sixty-five though, she's fifty, cause I ain't but two years older than her myself. I used to try to go with her way back when we was going to Simmons Street School together, but she wouldn't have me then, and she won't have me now. She married some nigger from Paris, Kentucky, one come out to Dixieland dance hall that time Dizzy Gillespie or Cab Calloway come out there. Name was Joe Guy. He stayed with her long enough to give her three children. Then he was gone. I was trying to go with her after he left, but she still wouldn't have me. She mighta eventually had me if he hadn't got to her, but after he got to her, seem like she wouldn't look at no mens. Onliest reason she'd look at me was because we'd been friends for so long. But first time I tried to get next to her right after he left, she said, "Shit, Floyd, me and you friends, always have been and always will be." I asked her to marry me, but she looked at me real evil. I thought she was going to tell me I could just quit coming to see her, but she didn't. After that she just wouldn't let me say nothing else about it, so I just come over there every chance I get. She got three childrens. Cynthy the oldest. She sixteen. Then she got a boy fourteen, name David, and a little boy five, name Pete. Sometime she call him Pete Junebug, sometime Little Pete.

Don't nobody know where in Lexington she went and got Freddy. Some people say she went down to the reform school they got down there and got him. It ain't that he's bad or nothing, it's just that they think some-thing's wrong with him. I didn't know where she got him myself, because it was her business and I figured she tell me when she wanted to, and if she didn't wont to, she wouldn't.

Miss Johnny Cake lives over across the street from Jevata, and every time I pass by there, she got to call me over. Sometimes I don't even like to pass by there, but I got to. She thinks I'm going to say something about Jevata and Freddy, but I don't. I just listen to what she's got to say. After she's said her piece, sometimes she'll look at me and say, "Clarify things to me, Mr. Floyd." I figure she picked that up from Reverend Jackson, cause he's always saying, "The Lord clarified this to me, the Lord clarified that to me." I ain't clarified nothing to her yet.

"He's kinda funny, ain't he?" she said one day. That was when Freddy and Jevata was still together. It seemed like Miss Johnny Cake just be sitting out there waiting for me to come up the street, because she would never fail to call me over. Sitting up there, old seventy-year-old woman, couldn't even keep her legs together. One a the men on the street told me she been in a accident, and something happened to that muscle in her thighs, that's supposed to help you keep your legs together. I believed him till he started laughing, and then I didn't know whether to believe him or not.

"That boy just don't act right, do he? He ain't right, is he, Mr. Floyd? Something wrong with him, ain't it?" She waited, but not as if she expected an answer. I guess she'd got used to me not answering. "You reckon he's funny? Naw, cause he wouldn't be with her if he was funny, would he? I guess she do something for him. She must got something he wont. God knows I don't see it. Mr. Floyd, you just stand up there and don't say nothing. Cat got your tongue, and Freddy got hers." She looked at me grinning. I blew smoke between my teeth. "If you wonted to, I bet you could tell me everything that go on in that house."

I said I couldn't.

"Well, I know she sixty-five, cause she used to live down 'ere on Poke

Street when I did. She might look like she forty-five, and tell everybody she forty-five, but she ain't. Now, if that boy was *right*, he be trying to go with Cynthy anyway. That's what a *right* boy would do. But he ain't right. He don't even *look* right, do he, Mr. Floyd?"

I told her he didn't look no different from anybody else to me.

Miss Johnny grinned at me. "You just don't wont to say nothin' against her, do you? Ain't no reason for you to take up for him, though, cause he done cut you out, ain't he?"

I said I was going across the street. She said she didn't see why I want to take up for him, cut me out the way he did.

One day when I came down the street, Freddy was standing out in the yard, his shirt sleeves rolled up, standing up against the post, looking across the street at Miss Johnny, looking evil. I didn't think Miss Johnny would bother me this time. I waved to her and kept walking. She said, "Mr. Floyd, ain't you go'n stop and have a few words with me? You got cute, too?" I went over to her porch before I got a chance to say anything to Freddy. He was watching us, though. Green Street wasn't a wide street, and if she talked even a little bit as loud as she'd been talking, he would have heard.

"Nigger out there," she said, almost at a whisper. "Keep staring at me. Look at him."

She kept patting her knees. I didn't turn around to look at him. I was thinking, "He see those bloomers you got on."

"Look at him," she said, still low.

"Nice day, ain't it?" I said, loud.

"Fine day," she said, loud, too, then whispered, "I wish he go in the house. I don't even like to look at him."

I said nothing. I lit a cigarette. She started rocking back and forth in her rocker, and closed her eyes, like she was in church. Or like I do when I'm in church.

"You have you a good walk?" she asked, her eyes still closed.

I said, "Okay."

We were talking moderate now.

"You a fool you know that? Walk all the way out here from Davis town, just to see that woman. She got what she need, over there."

I hoped he hadn't heard, but I knew he had. I wondered if I was in his place, if I would have come over and said something to her.

"You know you a fool, don't you?" she asked again, still looking like she was in church.

I didn't answer.

"You know you a fool, Mr. Floyd," she said. She rocked a while more, then she opened her eyes.

"But I reckon you say you been a fool a long time, ain't no use quit now."

I turned a little to the side so I could see out of the corner of my eye. He was still standing there. I couldn't tell if he was watching or not. I felt awkward about crossing the street now. I gave Miss Johnny a hard look before I crossed. She only smiled at me.

"Mr. Floyd," Freddy said. He always called me Mr. Floyd. He was still looking across the street at Miss Johnny. I stood with my back to her. He asked me to walk back around the yard with him. I did. I stood with my back against the house, smoking a cigarette.

"I caint stand that old woman," he said. "You see how she was setting, didn't you? Legs all open. I never could stand womens sit up with their legs all open. 'Specially old women."

I said they told me she couldn't help it.

"I had a aunt use to do that," he said. "She can help it. She just onry. Ain't nothin wrong with that muscle. She just think somebody wont to see her ass. Like my aunt. Used to think I wonted to see her ass, all the time."

I said nothing. Then I asked, "How's Jevata . . . and the children?"

"They awright. Java and Junebug in the house. Other two at school."

I finished my cigarette and was starting in the house.

"Think somebody wont to see her ass," Freddy said. He stayed out in the yard.

Jevata was in the kitchen ironing. She took in ironing for some white woman lived out on Stanley Street.

"How you, Floyd?" she asked.

"Not complaining," I said. I sat down at the kitchen table. She looked past me out in the back yard where Freddy must have still been standing.

"What Miss Busy have to say about me today?" she asked, looking back at me.

"Nothin'."

"You can tell me," she said. "I won't get hurt."

"Miss Johnny wasn't doing nothing but out there talking bout the weather," I said.

"Weather over here?" she asked.

I smiled.

She looked back out in the yard. I thought Freddy was still standing out there, but when I turned around in my seat to look, he wasn't. He must have gone back around to the front of the house.

"How you been?" she asked me as if she hadn't asked before, or didn't remember asking.

She wasn't looking at me, but I nodded.

"I never did think I be doing this," she said. "You 'member that time I told you Joe and me went down to Yazoo, Mississippi, and this ole, white woman come up to me and asked me did I iron, and I said, 'Naw, I don't iron.' I wasn't gonna iron for *her*, anyway."

I said nothing. I had already offered to help Jevata out with money, but she wouldn't let me. I worked with horses, and had enough left over to help. Now, I was thinking, she had *four* kids to take care of.

"He found a job yet?" I asked.

She looked at me, irritated. She was sweating from the heat. "I told him he could take his time. He ain't been here long. He need time to get adjusted."

I was wondering how much adjusting did he need. It was over half a year ago since she went and got him.

"You don't think Freddy's evil, do you?" she asked.

I looked at her. I didn't know why she asked that. I said, "Naw, I don't think he's evil." She went back to ironing. I just sat there in the kitchen, watching her. After a while Freddy came in through the back door. He didn't say anything. He passed by, and I saw him put his hand on her waist. She smiled but didn't turn around to look at him. He went on into the front of the house. I sat there about fifteen or twenty minutes longer, and then I got up and said I was going.

"Glad you stopped by," Jevata said.

I said I'd probably be back by sometime next week, then I went out the back way.

Miss Johnny not only caught me when I was coming to see Jevata, but she caught me when I was leaving.

"I never did think that bastard go in the house," she said. "Sometime I wish the Urban Renewal come and move me away from here. They dislocate me once, they might as well do it again."

I was thinking she probably heard Reverend Jackson say, "When the devil dislocate you, the Lord relocate you."

"How's Miss Jevata doing?" she asked.

"She's awright," I said.

"Awright as you can be with a nigger like that on your hands. If it was me, I be ashamed for anybody see me in the street with him. If he wont to go with somebody, he ought to go with Cynthy. I didn't tell you what I seen them doing last night?"

"What?" I asked frowning.

"I seen 'em standing in the door. Standing right up in the door kissing. Thought nobody couldn't see 'em with the light off. But you know how you can see in people's houses. Tha's the only time I seen 'em though. But still if they gonna do something like that, they ought to go back in there where caint nobody see 'em, and do it. Cause 'at ain't right. Double sin as old as she is. And they sinned again, cause you spose to go in your closet and do stuff like that."

I said nothing.

"You know I'm right, Mr. Floyd."

I still said nothing.

"Naw, you prob'ly don't know if I'm right or not," she said.

I looked away from her, over across the street at Jevata's house.

"Tiddies all sinking in," she said. "I don't see what he see in her. Look like she ain't got no tiddies no more. I don't see what he see in her. You think I'm crazy, don't you? I just don't like to see no old womens trying to go with young boys like that. I guess y'all ripe at that age, though, ain't you?"

I said I couldn't remember back that far.

"Floyd, you just a nigger. You just mad cause you been trying to go with her yourself. I bet you thought y'all *was* going together, didn't you? Everybody else thought so too, but not me. I didn't."

I turned around to look at her. She kept watching me.

"Ain't no use you saying nothing neither, cause I know you wasn't. I can tell when a man getting it and when he ain't."

I started to tell her I could tell when a woman wonts it and can't have it, but I just told her I'd be seeing her.

"You got a long walk back to Davis town, ain't you, Mr. Floyd?"

The next time I was down to Jevata's only the girl was at home. I asked her where her mama was. She said she and Freddy took Junebug downtown to get him some shoes. She told me Jevata had been mad all morning.

"Mad about what?" I asked.

"Mad cause Miss Johnny told Freddy to go up to the store for her."

"To get what?"

"A bottle of Pepsi Cola."

"Did he go?"

"Naw, he sent Davey." Then she said, "I don't know what makes that woman so meddlesome, anyway."

We were in the living room. I hadn't set down when I heard Jevata wasn't there. She was still standing, her arms folded like she was cold. She was frowning.

"What is it?" I asked.

"I guess I do know why she so meddlesome, why they all so meddlesome," she said.

I waited for her to go on.

"They talking about them, ain't they, Mr. Floyd? People all up and down the street talking, ain't they?" She didn't ask the question as if she expected an answer. She was still looking at me, frowning. She was a big girl for sixteen. She could've passed for eighteen. And she acted older than she was. She acted about twenty.

"Sometimes I'm ashamed to go to school. Kids on this street been telling everybody up at school. But you know I wouldn't tell Mama. I don't wont to hurt her. I wouldn't do anything to hurt her."

I was thinking Jevata probably already knew, or guessed that people who didn't even know her might be talking about her.

I didn't say anything.

"They saying nasty things," she said.

I still didn't say anything. She kept looking at me. I put my hand on her shoulder. She was the reason I understood how Jevata could feel about Freddy, those times I felt attracted to Cynthy, wanting to touch those big breasts. I took my hand away.

"Just keep trying not to hurt her," I said.

She was looking down at the floor. I kept watching her breasts. They were bigger than her mama's. I was thinking of Mose Mason, who they put out of church for messing with that little girl him and his wife adopted. The deacons came to the house and he said, "I ain't doing nothing but feeling around on her tiddies. I ain't doing nothin' y'all wouldn't do." They was mad, too. "They ack like they ain't never wont to feel on nobody," Moses told me when we was sitting over in Tiger's Inn. "Shit, I bet they do more feeling Saturday night than it take me a whole damn week to do. And then they come sit up under the pulpit on Sunday morning and play like they hands ain't never touched nothin' but the Holy Bible. Saying 'amen' louder than anybody. Shit, don't make me no difference, though, whether I'm with 'em or not cause the Baptist is sneaky, anyway. Sneak around and do they dirt."

"I can hear them," Cynthy said quietly. "I can hear her telling him to hold her. 'Hold me, Freddy,' she say. I can hear her telling him he's better to her than my daddy was."

I couldn't think of anything to tell her. I wanted to touch her again, but didn't dare.

When Jevata came in, she said, "Cynthy tell you what that bitch did?" I nodded.

"I know what she wonts, bitch," she said. "I know just what she wonts with him."

She asked me if I wanted something to eat. I said, Naw, I'd better be going. I'd been just waiting around to see her.

"Why did she try to kill 'im, Mr. Floyd?" Miss Johnny asked. It was a couple of weeks after Jevata had gone after Freddy with the poker.

"I don't know," I said. I had my right foot up on the porch and was leaning on my knee, smoking.

"Got after Cynthy, didn't he? I bet that's what he did."

"He didn't bother Cynthy," I said, angry. But I didn't know whether he did or not.

"I bet tha's what he did. I bet she went somewhere and come back and found them in that house." She started laughing.

"I don't know what happened," I said.

"Seem like she tell you, if she tell anybody," Miss Johnny said.

I threw my cigarette down on the ground, and mashed it out.

"I wish she let me come over there and get some dandelions like I used to, so I can make me some wine out of 'em," she said.

"If Freddy was over there, you could tell him to get you some," I said.

"I wouldn't tell 'at nigger to do nothing for me," she said. She was angry. I looked at her for a moment, and then I walked out of the yard.

When I got to Jevata's, she was sitting in the front room with her housecoat on, the same dirty yellow one Cynthy said she was wearing the day she threatened to kill Freddy. Cynthy said she hadn't been out of the house since she chased Freddy out. I asked her if she was all right.

"Ain't complaining, am I?" she said. She said she had some Old Crow back there in the kitchen if I wanted some. I said, "Naw, thank you." She hadn't been drinking any herself, which surprised me. She didn't drink much anyway, but I thought maybe with Freddy gone, she might.

"Shit, Floyd, why you looking at me like that?" she asked.

"I didn't know I was looking at you any way," I said.

"Well, you was."

I said nothing.

"I seen Miss Bitch call you over there. What she wont this time?"

"She wonts to know why," I said.

"I ain't told *you* why."

"And you won't, will you?"

She looked away from me, then she said, "You know it always have took me a long time, Floyd."

She didn't say anything else, and I tried not to look at her the way I had been looking. She sat on the edge of the couch with her hands together, like she was nervous, or praying. Her shoulders were pulled together in a way that made her look like she didn't have any breasts.

Cynthy came in the front room, and asked me how I was.

"Awright."

"Mama, supper's ready," she said.

"Stay for supper, won't you, Floyd?" Jevata asked me.

"Yeah."

"Cynthy, where's Freddy?" Jevata asked suddenly.

Cynthy looked at me quickly, then back at Jevata.

"He's not here, Mama," Cynthy said.

"Floyd, you ain't seen Freddy, have you?" Jevata asked me.

I just looked at her. I couldn't even have replied as calmly as Cynthy had managed to. I just kept looking at her. Jevata laughed suddenly, a quick, nervous laugh, then said, "Naw, y'all, I don't mean Freddy, I mean where's Little Pete, y'all. I don't mean Freddy I feel like a fool now."

I said nothing.

"He's down the road playing with Ralph," Cynthy said.

"Well, tell him to come on up here and get his supper."

"What about David, Mama?"

"You take his plate in there to him. I don't wont to see him."

"Yes, m'am."

I looked at Cynthy, puzzled, then I said I would take it. Jevata looked at me, but said nothing.

David was lying on the bed. I set his plate down on the chair by the bed. He didn't say anything.

"You know something about this, don't you?" I asked.

He still said nothing.

"I b'lieve you know what happened."

"Go way and leave me alone!" David said. "You ain't my daddy."

I stood looking at him for a moment. He still lay on his belly. He had half turned around when he was hollering, but he hadn't looked at me. I finally left the room. When I came back in the kitchen, Little Pete was sitting at the table and Cynthy was putting the food on the table.

"Where's Jevata?" I asked.

Cynthy said nothing.

"I just ask her when Freddy was coming back and then she start acting all funny. I didn't do nothin', Mr. Floyd."

"I know you didn't," I said.

Cynthy looked at me and sat my plate down on the table. I sat down with them. Jevata didn't come back.

"Don't you think you better take your mama a plate," I said to Cynthy.

"She said she didn't wont nothin'," she said.

I stood up.

"She looked like she didn't wont nothin', Mr. Floyd," Cynthy said.

I sat back down.

I knew there was one place I could find out where Freddy was. I took the bus to Lexington, then went over to the barbershop over in Charlotte Court, right off Georgetown Street.

"Any y'all know Freddy Coleman?" I asked.

They didn't answer. Then, one man sitting up in the chair, getting his hair trimmed around the sides, cause he didn't have any in the top, said, "What you got to do with him?"

"Nothin'," I said. "I just wont to know where he is."

"I used to know. He used to keep the yard down here at Kentucky Village."

Some of the other men started laughing. Kentucky Village was a school for delinquent boys. I asked what was funny.

"Close to them KV boys, wasn't he?" one of the men said.

The man in the chair started laughing. "He never did do nothing. Just used to stand up there with the rake. Womens be passing by looking. Didn't do 'em no good." He asked me why I wanted him.

"I'm just looking for him," I said.

They looked at each other, like people who got a secret. They were trying not to laugh again.

"You can try that liquor store up the street. They tell me his baby hang out over there."

The rest of the men started laughing. I left them and went up to the liquor store. Somebody told me Freddy was living in an apartment up over some restaurant off Second Street.

I found the place and went upstairs and knocked on the door. He wasn't glad to see me.

"How you find me?" he asked.

I came in before he asked me to. I stayed standing.

"What do you wont?" he asked. "Finding out where I am for *her*?"

"Naw, for myself," I said.

I looked around. The living room was small. Only a couch and a couple of chairs, and a low coffee table. On the coffee table was a hat with feathers on it. It was a woman's hat. We were both standing. I didn't sit down without him asking me to. He wasn't saying anything and I wasn't. I was thinking he *was* a good-looking man, almost *too* good-looking. The onliest other man I knew was *that* good-looking was Mr. Pindar, a fake preacher that used to go around stealing people's money. He used to get drunks off the street and have them go before the congregation and play like he had changed their life. And people would believe it, too. He was so good-looking the women would believe it, and preached so good the men would believe it.

Freddy kept standing there looking at me. I kept looking at him.

"Where's my ostrich hat?" It was a man's voice, but somehow it didn't sound like a man.

Freddy looked embarrassed, he was frowning. He hollered he didn't know where it was.

"You seen my ostrich hat, honey?" the man asked again. He came in, like he was swaying, saw me and stopped cold. He said, "How do," snatched the hat from the table and went back in the other room.

Freddy wasn't looking at me. I said I'd better be going.

"He's crazy," Freddy said quickly. "He live down at Eastern State, and he's crazy."

Eastern State was the mental hospital.

"He got a room down at Eastern State," Freddy said. "They let him out every day so he can get hisself drunk. That's all he do is get hisself drunk."

I said nothing. The man had come back in the room, and was standing near the door, pouting, his lower lip stuck out. Freddy hadn't turned to see him.

I started to go. Freddy reached out to put his hand on my arm, but didn't. He looked like he didn't want me to go.

"I was going to ask you to come back to her," I said, my eyes hard now. I ignored the man standing there, pouting. "I was going to tell you she needs you."

Freddy looked like he wanted to cry. "You know she kill me if I go back there," he said.

"Why?" I asked.

He said nothing.

I went toward the door again and he came with me. He still hadn't turned around to see the man. I asked him why again. Then I wanted another why. I asked him why did he go with her in the first place.

He said nothing for a long time, then he reached out to touch my arm again. I don't know if he would have stopped again this time, but I stood away from him.

"She was going to the carnival. You know, the one they have back behind Douglas Park every year, the one back there. She was passing through Douglas Park and seen me sitting up there all by myself. She ask me if I wont to go to the carnival. I don't know why she did. Maybe she thought I was lonesome, but I wasn't. I was sitting up there all by myself. She took me with her, you know. They had this man in this tent who was swallowing swords and knives, you know like they do. She wanted to take me there, so I went. We was standing up there watching this man, up close to him. We was standing up close to each other too, and then all a sudden Miss Jevata kind of turned her head to me, you know, and said kind of quiet-like, 'You know, Miss Jevata could teach you how to swallow lightning,' she said. That was all she said. She didn't say nothing else and she didn't say that no more. I don't even know if anybody else heard her. But I think that's why I went back with her. That was the reason I went with her."

I said nothing. When I closed the door, I heard something hit the wall.

"Freddy did something to David, didn't he," I asked her.

"Naw, it wasn't David," Jevata said. She was sitting with her hands together.

I frowned, watching her.

"Petie come and told me Freddy tried to throw him down the toilet. I didn't believe him."

"If he tried he would've," I said. "What did him and David do?"

She kept looking at me. I was waiting.

"I seen him go in the toilet," she said finally. "Him and David went back in the toilet together. He didn't even have his pants zipped up when he come back to the house."

I was over by her when she burst out crying. When she stopped, she asked me if I could do something for her. I told her all she had to do was ask. When she told me she still loved Freddy, that she wanted me to get him back for her, I walked out the door.

I thought I wouldn't see her again. When the farm I worked for wanted me to go up to New Hampshire for a year to help train some horses, I went. I told myself when I did come back, I was through going out there, but I didn't keep my promise to myself.

When I got there, Miss Johnny wasn't sitting out on her porch, but Jevata was sitting out on hers—with a baby, sitting between her breasts. She was tickling the baby and laughing. When she looked up at me, she was still laughing.

"Floyd, Freddy back," she said. "Freddy come back."

I didn't know what to say to her. I asked if Cynthy was at home. She said yes. I went in the house. Cynthy was standing in the living room. She must have seen me coming.

"Freddy back?" I asked.

She put her hands to her mouth, and drew me toward the kitchen.

"Naw, she mean the baby," she said. "She named the baby Freddy."

"Is it his?" I asked.

She hesitated, frowning, then she said, "Yes." She got farther into the kitchen and I went with her.

"She didn't wont to have him at first. At first she tried to get rid of him."

I kept looking at her. She was a grown woman now. I remembered when I first started coming there, right after her daddy left. Every time I'd come, she'd get the broom and start sweeping around my feet, like she was trying to sweep me out of the house. Now she looked at me, still frowning, but I could tell she was glad to see me. She said she knew I'd been sending them the money, but Jevata thought Freddy had.

I said nothing. I stood there for a moment, then I said I'd better be going.

"You will come back to see us?" she asked quickly, apprehensively. "We've missed you."

I looked at her. I started to move toward her, then I realized that she meant I might be able to help Jevata.

"Yes, I'll be back," I said.

She smiled. I went out the door.

"You little duck, you little duck, Freddy, you little duck," Jevata said, tickling the baby, who was laughing. A pretty child.

"You be back to see us, won't you, Floyd?" she asked when I started down the porch.

"Yes," I said, without turning around to look at her.

Sister Detroit

•

(1978)

Colleen McElroy

When Buel Gatewood bought his Gran Turismo Hawk, folks around
Troost Avenue and Prospect Boulevard hadn't learned how to talk about
Vietnam yet. After all, Bubba Wentworth had just returned from Korea,
and the V.A. had helped him get a job at Swift Packing House. Grace
Moton was just recovering from having to bury her brother, who'd been
shot in a border skirmish at the Berlin Wall. "Ain't much of a wall if it
can't stop bullets." Grace had wept. And Andre Clayton had taken his
sissy self off to some white school in the East just to test all that Supreme
Court business about integration.

But Buel Gatewood had plunked down a goodly portion of several
paychecks in full certainty that with his deluxe edition $3,400 Hawk, he
would own the best wheels on the block for some time to come. There
was one thing for certain about that notion: he was going to have the
biggest car payments on the block for at least five years.

Still, there was no doubt that Buel's Hawk was tough enough. It was
all grille and heavy chrome borders, black like a gangster's car, but road-
ready for a sporty-otee like Buel. "Any car got the name of Hawk is bound
to be good," Buel had said. "That's the name of that wind that blows off
the lake in Chicago. Hawk! That wind says: Look out, I'm the Hawk and
I'm coming to get you. Now I got me a Hawk, so look out!"

In that car Buel could outgun DeJohn Washington's '54 Coupe de Ville,
and outshine the Merc Meteor his brother, Calvin, owned. And, despite
its retractable hardtop, he simply dismissed the Ford V-8 Roger Payton

264

had bought on the grounds that only somebody working in a gas station could afford a gas guzzler. "I don't go around talking 'bout other folks' mistakes," he'd said, but according to Buel, almost everything about Roger and the others was a mistake. Unlike Calvin, Buel had a high school diploma and didn't have to tend bar at Rooster's Tavern. And he didn't have to haul cow shit at Swift Packing, like DeJohn, or nickel-and-dime in a gas station alongside Roger. He had a good-paying job with Arbor Industrial Services, and, once he bought his Hawk, he'd settled into outrunning the competition. That competition completely surrounded Buel and his Turismo Hawk.

That year the Detroit exhibition of cars featured Freedom, bumper to bumper on a disc-shaped turntable. It amazed the public to see all that shiny metal swirling past them. That crowd should have come to Buel's neighborhood, where cars dazzled owners and passersby alike. The traffic moving down Brush Creek Boulevard, Blue Parkway, or The Paseo alone would have been enough to put Detroit on the map, but with the added interstate traffic between Kansas and Missouri, between the city and the suburbs, between the haves and have-nots, the need to have bigger and better wheels kept folks buying cars: Mustangs, Barracudas, Cougars, Mercs, Caddies, or Falcons, speed-ohs or rattletraps, FOB factory or custom-cut to the owner's specs.

Cars were a part of the neighborhood, the status symbol of having arrived into your own, with wheels. Cars were the black man's stock portfolio, his rolling real estate, his assets realized. What roads the city didn't provide by way of streets, it made convenient with expressways that cut through the length of the town, leaving a trail of cheap motels, used-car lots, and strip joints at one end, and Swift Packing House and the bridge to the Kansas side at the other end. Any of the roads from the center of town allowed easy access to a state highway, but the convenience was counted only by those who needed to flee the city or cross the state line.

Real estate developers in the select sections of the inner city that were being upgraded for white residents called those expressways "The River of Lights." Folks around Buel's neighborhood called them "The Track," and tried turning their backs on the whole business unless they were unlucky enough to have a reason to skip town.

Sometimes Buel and his friends had vague dreams of eating up roadway in a hot machine of their choice, but Andre had been the only one to find a fast exit east, and when he'd left the city, he'd just vanished as far as Buel and the rest of the Technical High School class of '62 were concerned. Andre might have vanished, but Brush Creek, Swope Parkway, and Pershing Road were always there. And when cars from the neighborhood around Troost and Prospect passed each other on the road, their owners would honk their horns in recognition.

If someone had taken a photo of Buel, DeJohn, Roger, and Calvin back in 1964, they could have spotted the contentment on those four faces. In those days everything they set out to do seemed easy, especially when they stayed within the boundaries of the world they knew, places they could reach on one tank of gas. They couldn't imagine, did not bother to imagine, anything pushing them farther than that point. That would come later. For now, it was enough to wait for Sunday afternoon, when Buel or one of the others would say, "Let's show Nab some tail feathers and floorboard these hogs."

On a good day, when the heat and humidity were in agreement, when there was no snow blowing off the Kansas plains or winds whipping north toward Chicago, the men took to the roads, their cars spit-clean from the fish-eye taillights and split-wing trim to the sleek roofs and grillwork. Their only worry was the occasional cop on the Nab ready to grab them as they sped past a billboard or crossed the state line at rocket speed. When Miss Swift raised her skirts over the Intercity Viaduct and they smelled the rancid odors of dirty meat, they knew they were heading west. And when the messages on billboard after billboard along Highway 40 were shattered by blinking neon-like black lights on a disco floor, they were heading east.

But for the women, those cars were the excuses that helped their men stay as fickle as the tornadoes that occasionally passed through the heart of town, the winds that sometimes danced through living rooms and took everything a family had managed to scrape out of a pinch-penny job, and sometimes turned corners down the centers of streets as if they were following traffic patterns. For the women those cars were merely another way to haul them from the house to a day job—"the hook between Miss Ann and the killing floor," as Autherine Franklin would say—because, for the women, the cars were to be looked at and paid for, but never driven.

Anna Ruth Gatewood remembered the family gossip about her Aunt Charzell, who had driven a Packard to Oklahoma City in 1927 all by herself. "The only way she did it was she dressed like a man and she was so light she could pass for some old honkie anyway." But Anna Ruth's family had fallen on hard times, and there were no Packards available for the women when the men could barely hang on to a job long enough to support one car.

Even when some old fool, like Dennis Frasier, went on pension and bought a new car, keeping the old car for a runabout and the new one for churchgoing, women weren't likely to take the wheel. All of them had excuses for not being able to drive: Luann Frasier claimed she was too old, Nona Payton said her babies made her too nervous, and Autherine Franklin told everyone she was too tired to do anything after spending all day scrubbing Miss Ann's floors out in the suburbs.

When Buel bought his Hawk GT, Anna Ruth told everyone that Buel had never said "boo" to her about buying a car, and if he had, she would have taken driving lessons before he'd signed the papers.

"He just showed up with it," she said. "Drove up to the house, big as cuff, and walked up the path like he'd just hopped off the Prospect bus and come home from work, as usual."

According to Anna Ruth, Buel had sat down on the sofa, picked up the paper, and folded it back to the sports page the way he always did. But about a quarter of an hour after he'd been in the house, Anna Ruth came to the window to see what the commotion on the street was all about.

What she saw was a jet-black Studebaker Hawk surrounded by half the neighbors on College Street.

At first Anna Ruth didn't connect the car with Buel. All she saw was the top of the car, a bright swatch of black metal, a glob of shiny color that looked like the smear of tar road crews poured in the ruts along Brush Creek Boulevard every spring. At first she couldn't even determine what kind of car it was.

"Looked like some kind of funeral car," she said later. "First word that come into my head when I seen that car was *death*. If I was gonna buy a car and spend all that money, I'd have bought me a pink one, something bright and pretty like them cotton candy cones they sell over at Swope Park in the summer. But that thing looked like somebody had been laid out and the undertaker had come calling."

"Girl, if he was my husband," Autherine Franklin said, "I'd make him give me the keys to that car. That's why I don't have no intention of marrying that no-good DeJohn Washington. Can't never depend on men for nothing."

Anna Ruth almost told Autherine that men were all she'd ever depended on, but she held her tongue. Everybody knew Autherine was fast and loose, and that was why she and DeJohn didn't get married. But if anyone said anything to Autherine about it, she'd be ready to go upside their heads, and since Autherine was her best friend, next to Nona Payton, Anna Ruth had better sense than to pick a fight over nothing.

"I was thinking about going over to the YWCA," Nona said. "Tell me they got driving lessons over there for anybody to take."

"Girl, Roger ain't gonna let you spend no money learning how to drive," Autherine and Anna Ruth said at the same time.

Then they both leaned back and laughed at the sharpness of their perceptions. It was comforting to see some part of the world clearly, and the three of them had been friends for so long they clearly saw each other's worlds, even if they could not see their own.

What was happening to change their own worlds did not make itself known until Buel had owned his car for nearly a year. But in that time, he and Anna Ruth more or less settled into a routine, an edgy kind of quarreling mixed with hard loving that told the world they were still newlyweds. Each morning Anna Ruth still took the Prospect bus to the Plaza and her stockroom job in Ladies' Apparel. And each morning Buel drove his Hawk one block north of Arbor Industrials, where he parked and walked the rest of the way for fear one of his bosses might see the car and think he was trying to be a big shot.

"I ain't got the patience to be teaching you to drive," Buel told Anna Ruth. "Ain't no reason for a woman to be driving. Women too nervous. Besides, you got me to do your driving for you." He laughed and stroked her ass to make her forget the idea of his car.

No matter how many times they argued the logic of her learning to drive, or how many times Anna Ruth offered to help with the weekly Simoniz, the only time she sat in that Studebaker was on Sundays. And even then she only got a ride to church. Getting home was her problem, because Sundays Buel and his buddies went to Rooster's to listen to whatever game was being broadcast on the radio. Anna Ruth knew the seasons by sports more than she did by weather: football in the fall, basketball in late winter, track in the spring, and baseball all summer. In a pinch the guys even listened to golf or tennis, anything to keep their standing arrangement of Rooster's after church, then onto the Interstate or Highway 40 and one of the bag-and-bottle clubs until late Sunday night. Except for an occasional family gathering at one of their parents' houses, little had interfered with the boys' routine in the two years since they'd left high school.

None of Anna Ruth's complaints could keep Buel away from Rooster's after church.

Buel said, "Anna Ruth, you ought to feel good when I drive up to the church and help you out of this baby right there in front of the preacher."

"I'd feel a lot better if I was driving this baby by my lonesome," she said.

And Nona said, "Ain't that just like a man? Thinking that just 'cause he can drive you to church, you got to feel happy 'bout him driving off and leaving you alone at night."

"How you think they kept all them slaves in line?" Autherine asked. "Told them God meant for them to be slaves, that's how. Fed them a whole bunch of crap about God and church. That's why I don't like going to nobody's church. When I really want to talk to God, I just get down on my knees and commence to speaking."

"Honey, when you get down on your knees, you talking to Ajax and Spic and Span," Nona laughed.

"Nona Pettigrew Payton, we been friends since the second grade," Autherine snapped, "but if you don't watch your mouth, I'm gone make you one dead friend."

"Just hush," Anna Ruth said. "You know you don't mean that. Now just hush, both of you. I swear, seems I spent half my life listening to you two snapping at each other."

Autherine was ready to take the argument one step further, but Nona paid attention to what Anna Ruth had said.

"Aw, girl, come on," Nona said to Autherine. "You know I didn't mean nothing. Let's walk over to Bishop's and get a fish sandwich we can turn red with some Louisiana hot sauce."

"Ohh, now you talking," Autherine shouted, and linked arms with both Anna Ruth and Nona.

Still dressed in their Sunday best, they left church and headed toward Bishop's.

At one point their path took them down a two-block stretch of Brush Creek Boulevard. The trees lining the four-lane street rustled with the wind, and debris, caught in the backwash, swirled down the creek bed that separated the traffic patterns into two lanes on either side of a concrete abutment. The creek itself was concrete, paved over years ago by the Pendergast political machine, which owned the local concrete plant. Now it resembled a spillway for a dam site, except it was flat, like the rest of the landscape, with sections of sewer pipe cut in half and laid open along a winding mile stretch through the middle of the city. And it was either full or empty. In dry seasons a trickle of water oozed through the mud that crept up in the middle where the concrete sections didn't quite meet. But the creek offered the neighborhood sudden flash floods during the wet seasons. In those times crossing the boulevard could be perilous, and more than one person had suddenly been faced with the prospect of drowning while the rest of the city stayed high and dry.

Still, the creek had its advantages, meager as they may have been. It separated the rush of traffic up and down the busy boulevard, and the trees stirred the wind so that gas fumes did not linger the way they did along Blue Parkway, The Paseo, and other thoroughfares. And in the winter, when the snows froze into ice, neighborhood kids used the creek as a playground, while the hot summer air left the trees heavy with fragrance, and wildflowers bloomed in the cracks edging the creek.

It was rough walking those two blocks, but Anna Ruth and her friends knew what kind of jaunty flash they made, laughing and high-stepping their way to Bishop's. Some days they walked to a chorus of car horns honking their owners' approval at the sight of three foxy ladies. Autherine had more interest in pointing out who was behind the wheel of a passing Bonneville, or a two-toned Barracuda, or a fishtailed Plymouth. Anna Ruth was busy counting the number of women maneuvering their old man's Oldsmobile or Falcon or Fleetwing. Only Nona was interested in how much money had been wasted engineering the Brush Creek project.

But Nona had always been the curious one of the group. As a child, she'd been more interested in playing Monopoly than pick-up-sticks or jacks. And in high school she'd taken a course in drafting along with her Executive Secretary program. Even now she was enrolled in night school in an effort to upgrade her job with the most successful black dentist in the city from receptionist to bookkeeper. Nona liked to read better than she liked to dance, and Nona had a library card that she used at least once a month. So Nona had been labeled the brains of the group.

"You so stuck up, you got no business over here in Tech," Autherine had told her one spring day after typing class. "You ought to be at Richmond where you could be wearing them football sweaters and going to the prom."

But Richmond wouldn't take Roger Payton, and more than anything else in the world, Nona Pettigrew wanted to be with Roger Payton. It was probably Nona who had put the idea of marriage into Anna Ruth Simpson's head. Anna Ruth had liked Buel well enough, but she hadn't thought much beyond her next date with him. Nona had plans for Roger Payton, and when she consulted Autherine and Anna Ruth on the best way to make Roger aware of those plans, the fever of marriage struck Anna Ruth as well. The three of them had giggled and plotted, and three months after Roger and Buel graduated, there had been a double wedding, with Autherine and DeJohn acting as witnesses for both couples.

Once they were married, Anna Ruth had settled into not thinking past any given day again, but Nona simply worked around Roger's Midwestern ideas of what a wife should be and enrolled in night school. By the summer of 1964 she was working her way to convincing herself that she needed a driver's education course as well as those bookkeeping courses she took while Roger was on duty nights at the gas station, and by spring she would have enrolled if the country hadn't been faced with Johnson's Tonkin Gulf Resolution.

Suddenly the United States was fighting in Vietnam and Roger Payton was one of the first men in the neighborhood to be drafted. Within six months all of them were in uniform, and in the six-square-mile area between Prospect and Troost, families were learning to pronounce the names of places that even President Johnson had trouble wrapping around his tongue: Phan Rang, Chu Yang Sin, Quang Ngai, Dong Hoi.

Like everyone else, the women had been totally unprepared for the impact of Vietnam, but of them all, Autherine seemed hardest hit by the news of her man called to war. She saw it as a plot against black folks, and even after she helped DeJohn pack his clothes and sell his car, she preached against his participation in some white man's war games.

"Going to church and going to war is all black folks is allowed," she shouted. "We ought to form our own state. Let them white folks fight it out amongst themselves."

And as she wept and ranted, refusing to go to church anymore, refusing to go to movies or even press her hair in her protest against white injustice, Anna Ruth and Nona saw the revolutionary she would become within the next three years. But by the beginning of 1965, Nona and Anna Ruth became more troubled over the decrease in letters they received from their husbands.

Now walking along Brush Creek was a problem, no matter what the season. They ignored the cars that honked at them and tried to imagine what kind of scenery the men could see in that place called Vietnam, a small speck on the map that Nona had helped them locate one day in the library. Now each of them found ways to occupy their time, especially the nights, and Nona, free to take any classes she wished without hiding them from Roger, finally enrolled in a driver's ed course.

"I aim to tell him," she said to Autherine. "I aim to tell Roger all about that driving course next time I hear from him, but I don't want to be throwing him no surprises until I'm sure he got the other letters I sent him. I ain't heard from him since last September, and here it is January."

"I got a letter from Buel in November. Said he was being transferred to Roger and DeJohn's company. But I ain't heard from him since."

"DeJohn don't write much, but I should've been hearing from him 'bout now. Last thing I heard, they was moving them farther north."

"Well, if I know the boys, they got themselves some hootch and up there painting the town," Anna Ruth laughed.

The others laughed with her, but no one believed what she'd said. The news was filled with stories of war casualties; B. L. Jefferson's boy had been killed on a destroyer in the South China Sea, and the Andersons, over on Bales Street, had lost a son and two nephews. And everyone was beginning to have news of another name added to the list of those missing in action. In June the names Roger Payton, Buel Ray Gatewood, and Calvin Gatewood were added to that list. And in June DeJohn's mother told Autherine she'd received a letter from the War Department telling her that DeJohn had been fatally wounded.

"Those cocksuckers can't even say *dead*," she screamed. "Just some shit about casualties and missing. Like we gonna turn a corner and find them standing there grinning. This is *some* shit. I want you to know, this is *some* shit."

"I just can't believe Roger's dead," Nona said. "Roger wouldn't just go off and die on me."

"Honey, Roger didn't die on *you*," Autherine snarled. "He died on Uncle Sam. He died fighting for some white man. He died same as DeJohn and Buel and Calvin."

"I don't believe Buel is dead," Anna Ruth said in a flat voice. "I just don't believe it."

"And Roger can't be dead," Nona wept. "Look. He didn't even sell his car." She pointed to the Ford parked at the curb in front of her house. "He left the car right there. I mean, you can't see him going off and leaving that car."

"I don't see nothing but that car," Autherine said. "I don't see nothing but that car out there rotting in the rain. Ain't nobody in it. Roger ain't in his car, and Buel ain't in his. They might as well have sold them. Might as well have done what DeJohn did and sold that shit. And if you got any sense, that's what you'll do."

"I'm not gonna sell that car until Roger comes home and tells me in person to sell it."

"Then that car's gonna be sitting there till hell freezes over," Autherine snapped.

But Nona finished her driving course, and on Sundays, when Autherine didn't have a Black Panthers meeting, Nona would take her for a ride, the two of them zipping along Blue Parkway, The Paseo, the Interstate

Viaduct, and Highway 40 in Roger Payton's Ford Skyliner. Loneliness for Nona became those Sunday rides where she tried to duplicate the outings Roger had taken, Buel and the others trailing him. Only Nona had Autherine spouting Black Nationalist doctrines in the passenger's seat beside her. Anna Ruth refused to come with them.

Anna Ruth said her Sundays were too busy. She had to make sure Buel's Hawk received its weekly Simoniz, she told them. And she had to attend meetings at the church where she helped the auxiliary track down government addresses so the ladies could write to the War Department and ask them to send their men home.

On Sundays Nona and Autherine drove by Anna Ruth's house on College Street, but every Sunday Anna Ruth was too busy to join them. Through that whole summer Anna Ruth seemed too busy to have any time for them at all. By fall, Nona and Autherine noticed how Anna Ruth didn't wait for the weekend to Simoniz Buel's car. Often they would see her washing the whitewalls, polishing the chrome, or waxing that car on Wednesdays or Fridays or Saturdays, only to do the whole job again on Sundays. And more and more, Anna Ruth retreated into a kind of unquiet muteness that was more like a scream than a silence.

And in early December, four months after the Watts riots, when the winds blowing off the prairie seemed loaded with little crystals of ice, and the bare limbs of trees along Brush Creek Boulevard crackled in the thin air, Anna Ruth snapped and took the wheel of Buel Ray Gatewood's Gran Turismo Hawk.

It seemed so natural, sliding into the driver's seat. For months she'd brushed the upholstery and floor with a clothes brush to keep the dust from eating the fabric. For months she'd polished the steering wheel, the wraparound windshield and dash. And from time to time, on orders from Buel, she'd started the engine and let the car idle. But on that day she'd slipped it into drive, popped the brakes, and eased away from the curb.

She was on Brush Creek before Nab spotted her. At three o'clock, when the cop pulled her over, she'd put the car in neutral and waited patiently.

It surprised her a bit that she didn't feel frightened. It wasn't as if she knew what she was going to say, but she had felt that heart-pounding rush she remembered feeling the day she'd worked Buel around to asking her to marry him, or the first time, a few days later, when she'd slept with him. In her rearview mirror she watched the cop lock his cycle in park, and waited until he tapped on the glass before she cranked down the window.

"It's my husband's car. He's in the army in Nam," she told him when he asked for her driver's license. "He's missing in action so I'm taking care of his car till he gets back."

The cop never blinked an eye. "I'm gonna have to take your keys," he said. "Why don't you just park this heap close to the curb and let me have your keys."

"This ain't no heap," Anna Ruth snapped. "It's a Gran Turismo Hawk, and it belongs to my husband. He's in Nam. Missing in action . . ."

"We got two hundred thousand boys in Vietnam, and not a one of them took his car. You got no driver's permit for this thing, so you park it. This car is impounded."

The cop walked to the rear of the car to take down the license number, and Anna Ruth leaned over to start the engine. She gunned it, giving the 255 horsepower full rein.

"Easy there, girl," the cop said. "Don't get fancy on me. Just slide on into that curb."

Anna Ruth slipped it out of neutral into drive, then while she was still inhaling, into reverse. The engine responded as if it had been starving for attention. In one fluid, sudden movement Anna Ruth took out the cop's motorcycle, and if that Nab hadn't stepped back, she'd have nailed him, too. Then she slammed it into gear and raced down Brush Creek. She was four blocks away before the cop stopped slapping his hat against his knee and yelling, "Goddammit! Goddammit!"

Passersby gawked, and some, heading toward Bishop's or Maxine's Bar-b-que, called to friends to see the sight. "Nab got creamed!" they shouted, and the news spread up and down the street like brushfire. Unfortunately, Anna Ruth had left the cop's radio intact.

But that was not her concern at the moment. When the cop finally realized he could call for help, Anna Ruth was careening off parked cars along the boulevard. Her foot seemed frozen on the accelerator, and when she entered The Paseo, she skidded into a spin at the icy intersection, circling twice before she headed north, leaving five crippled cars stuck in the middle of the street behind her. The police call reached patrol cars at 3:18 p.m. By 3:20 she was spotted on The Paseo, and two cars gave chase.

Somewhere along that thoroughfare, Anna Ruth came into her own, and the occasional clatter of metal when she sideswiped a parked car or grazed a driver too slow to move out of her path no longer made her gasp. When she saw Nab behind her, she left The Paseo at Plymouth and returned to it later off Linwood. The snowplows had been working in her favor. In fact, the weather was in her favor. It was a gloomy day, but cold and clear, so cold that no one was out that Sunday unless they had to be. So cold that slush hadn't formed on the roadway and the ashes left by the plow crews were still on top of the ice. Despite the damage she'd caused, for the most part, the path ahead of her was clear. But behind her there was a stream of police cars.

She had decided to head for the Interstate Viaduct and the Kansas side, but Nab began to descend in all directions, and she had to crisscross her own path across The Paseo and back. Once, when she was parallel to The Paseo on Troost, she saw two cop cars coming toward her. The units behind her knew they had her cornered, but Anna Ruth jerked the wheel and in one wild open circle of a swing, headed in the opposite direction, weaving between and around the cars that had been trailing her. Three cars ran into each other to avoid a head-on with Anna Ruth's Hawk.

As the cop driving the second car pulled himself from the wreck, he looked at Anna Ruth's retreating taillights and shook his head in begrudging admiration. "Goddamn, that bitch can drive," he said.

But whatever luck Anna Ruth had found in encountering very little traffic on newly plowed streets was about to run out. By all accounts, the police had brought in twelve units by the time she reached the last lap of her odyssey. By all accounts, Anna Ruth had traveled the length of The Paseo from Brush Creek to the Viaduct intersection and back by the time Nab had cut off her escape route. And just as she reentered the neighborhood, just before a line of squad cars flanked the street and forced her onto the lawn of the Technical High School, she'd left behind her a trail of more than twenty damaged cars.

But in those last two miles Anna Ruth had gathered a cheering section. Folks in the area between Troost and Prospect lined the street, yelling directions that would place her out of Nab's path. And sometimes folks blocked Nab's path by shoving junk cars that had been abandoned in the neighborhood in front of the cops. Young boys threw rocks, practicing for the riots that were soon to come to the city. And old men, rising from their Sunday afternoon slumber, marked the day as a turning point.

Nona caught up with Autherine just as Anna Ruth swerved off Brush Creek onto Euclid. Autherine had been helping make posters for a Panthers meeting in the basement of the school, and when Nona banged on the door and called to her, she was just warming up to an argument with a fellow Panther about the causes of revolution. The news of Anna Ruth's rebellion erased her need to convince the man.

The two women were running down the front stairs of the school when Anna Ruth turned onto the block. At the opposite end the police had parked several paddy wagons. Behind her, a phalanx of patrol cars, sirens blasting and lights flashing, raced toward her.

Perhaps she would have made it if Old Man Frasier had not been backing out of his driveway at that moment. Frasier had heard all the noise, and his neighbor, Charleston Davis, told him some crazy woman was tearing up Brush Creek. That was a sight the old man felt determined not to miss. He could not have known Anna Ruth had detoured off Brush Creek and was aiming for a new route north along Blue Parkway. He eased the big Pontiac out of his driveway and directly into Anna Ruth's path.

Even from the stairs, Nona and Autherine could see Anna Ruth didn't have much of a choice between Old Man Frasier or the school's snow-impacted lawn.

"Damn! I 'bout made Kansas, Nona," Anna Ruth whispered after the police had pulled her out of the wrecked Studebaker. "Halfway there and driving by myself."

Nona shushed her and, cradling her head, rocked her until the ambulance attendants got the stretcher ready.

"Buel's gonna be mad at me," Anna Ruth said. "Buel's gonna come home and find out I wrecked his car, and he's gonna have my ass."

"Don't worry about it, baby," Nona told her. "By the time Buel gets here, we gonna have everything fixed."

Autherine watched the cops trying to handcuff Anna Ruth even as the medics were placing her on the stretcher. "This is some shit!" Autherine shouted. "Some shit!"

Folks who lived around Troost and Prospect could do nothing but agree with her.

comin to terms

(1 9 7 9)

Ntozake Shange

they hadnt slept together for months/ the nite she pulled the two thinnest blankets from on top of him & gathered one pillow under her arm to march to the extra room/ now 'her' room/ had been jammed with minor but telling incidents/ at dinner she had asked him to make sure the asparagus didnt burn so he kept adding water & they, of course/ waterlogged/ a friend of hers stopped over & he got jealous of her having so many friends/ so he sulked cuz no one came to visit him/ then she gotta call that she made the second round of interviews for the venceremos brigade/ he said he didnt see why that waz so important/ & with that she went to bed/ moments later this very masculine leg threw itself over her thighs/ she moved over/ then a long muscled arm wrapped round her chest/ she sat up/ he waz smiling/ the smile that said 'i wanna do it now.'

mandy's shoulders dropped/ her mouth wanted to pout or frown/ her fist waz lodged between her legs as a barrier or an alternative/ a cooing brown hand settled on her backside/ 'listen, mandy, i just wanna little'/ mandy looked down on the other side of the bed/ maybe the floor cd talk to him/ the hand roamed her back & bosom/ she started to make faces & blink a lot/ ezra waznt talkin anymore/ a wet mouth waz sittin on mandy's neck/ & teeth beginnin to nibble the curly hairs near her ears/ she started to shake her head/ & covered her mouth with her hand sayin/ 'i waz dreamin bout cuba & you wanna fuck'/ 'no, mandy, i dont wanna fuck/ i wanna make love to . . . love to you'/ & the hand became quite aggressive with mandy's titties/ 'i'm dreamin abt goin to cuba/ which isnt important/ i'm hungry cuz you ruined dinner/ i'm lonely cuz you embarrassed my friend: & you wanna fuck'/ 'i dont wanna fuck/ i told you

277

that i wanna make love'/ 'well you got it/ you hear/ you got it to yr self/
cuz i'm goin to dream abt goin to cuba'/ & with that she climbed offa
the hand pummelin her ass/ & pulled the two thinnest blankets & one
pillow to the extra room.

the extra room waz really mandy's anyway/ that's where she read & cro-
cheted & thot/ she cd watch the neighbors' children & hear miz nancy
singin gospel/ & hear miz nancy give her sometimey lover who owned
the steepin tavern/ a piece of her mind/ so the extra room/ felt full/ not
as she had feared/ empty & knowin absence. in a corner under the window/
mandy settled every nite after the cuba dreams/ & watched the streetlights
play thru the lace curtains to the wall/ she slept soundly the first few nites/
ezra didnt mention that she didnt sleep with him/ & they ate the breakfast
she fixed & he went off to the studio/ while she went off to school he
came home to find his dinner on the table & mandy in her room/ doing
something that pleased her. mandy was very polite & gracious/ asked how
his day waz/ did anything exciting happen/ but she never asked him to
do anything for her/ like lift things or watch the stove/ or listen to her
dreams/ she also never went in the room where they usedta sleep together/
tho she cleaned everywhere else as thoroughly as one of her mother's
great-aunts cleaned the old house on rose tree lane in charleston/ but she
never did any of this while ezra waz in the house/ if ezra waz home/ you
cd be sure mandy waz out/ or in her room.

one nite just fore it's time to get up & the sky is lightening up for sunrise/
mandy felt a chill & these wet things on her neck/ she started slapping
the air/ & without openin her eyes/ cuz she cd/ feel now what waz goin
on/ ezra pushed his hard dick up on her thigh/ his breath covered her
face/ he waz movin her covers off/ mandy kept slappin him & he kept
bumpin up & down on her legs & her ass/ 'what are you doin ezra'/ he
just kept movin. mandy screamed/ 'ezra what in hell are you doin.' &
pushed him off her. he fell on the floor/ cuz mandy's little bed waz right
on the floor/ & she slept usually near the edge of her mattress/ ezra stood
& his dick waz aimed at mandy's face/ at her right eye/ she looked away/
& ezra/ jumped up & down/ in the air this time/ 'what are you talkin
abt what am i doin/ i'm doin what we always do/ i'm gettin ready to fuck/
awright so you were mad/ but this cant go on forever/ i'm goin crazy/ i
cant live in a house with you & not fu . . . / not make love. i mean.'

mandy still lookin at the pulsing penis/ jumpin around as ezra jumped around/ mandy sighed 'ezra let's not let this get ugly/ please, just go to sleep/ in yr bed & we'll talk abt this tomorrow.' 'what do you mean tomorrow i'm goin crazy' . . . / mandy looked into ezra's scrotum/ & spoke softly 'you'll haveta be crazy then' & turned over to go back to sleep. ezra waz still for a moment/ then he pulled the covers off mandy & jerked her around some/ talkin bout 'we live together & we're gonna fuck now'/ mandy treated him as cruelly as she wd any stranger/ kicked & bit & slugged & finally ran to the kitchen/ leavin ezra holdin her torn nitegown in his hands.

'how cd you want me/ if i dont want you/ i dont want you niggah/ i dont want you' & she worked herself into a sobbin frigidaire-beatin frenzy . . . ezra looked thru the doorway mumblin. 'i didnt wanna upset you, mandy. but you gotta understand. i'm a man & i just cant stay here like this with you . . . not bein able to touch you or feel you'/ mandy screamed back 'or fuck me/ go on, say it niggah/ fuck.' ezra threw her gown on the floor & stamped off to his bed. we dont know what he did in there.

mandy put her gown in the sink & scrubbed & scrubbed til she cd get his hands off her. she changed the sheets & took a long bath & a douche. she went back to bed & didnt go to school all day she lay in her bed. thinkin of what ezra had done. i cd tell him to leave/ she thot/ but that's half the rent/ i cd leave/ but i like it here/ i cd getta dog to guard me at nite/ but ezra wd make friends with it/ i cd let him fuck me & not move/ that wd make him mad & i like to fuck ezra/ he's good/ but that's not the point/ that's not the point/ & she came up with the idea that if they were really friends like they always said/ they shd be able to enjoy each other without fucking without having to sleep in the same room/ mandy had grown to cherish waking up a solitary figure in her world/ she liked the quiet of her own noises in the night & the sound of her own voice soothin herself/ she liked to wake up in the middle of the nite & turn the lights on & read or write letters/ she even liked the grain advisory show on tv at 5:30 in the mornin/ she hadda lotta secret nurturin she had created for herself/ that ezra & his heavy gait/ ezra & his snorin/ ezra & his goin-crazy hard-on wd/ do violence to . . . so she suggested to ezra that they continue to live together as friends/ & see other people if they wanted to have a more sexual relationship than the one she waz offering . . . ezra laughed. he thot she waz a little off/ til she shouted 'you cant imagine me without a wet pussy/ you cant imagine me without yr goddamned dick stickin up in yr pants/ well yr gonna learn/ i dont start comin to life cuz you feel like fuckin/ yr gonna learn i'm alive/ ya hear' . . . ezra waz usually a gentle sorta man/ but he slapped mandy this time & walked off . . . he came home two days later covered with hickeys & quite satisfied with himself. mandy fixed his dinner/ nothin special/ & left the door of her room open so he cd see her givin herself pleasure/ from then on/ ezra always asked if he cd come visit her/ waz she in need of some company/ did she want a lil lovin/ or wd she like to come visit him in his room/ there are no more assumptions in the house.

Requiem for Willie Lee

•

(1979)

Frenchy Hodges

I teach, you know, and it was summer, one of the few times we get to
be like children again. Summers we pack up and go somewhere that only
rich folk year-round can afford. And if we can only afford a day and a
night, we take what we can get and do not count the loss. For twenty-
four hours we groove fine on the dollar we have to spend, and in my
purse with the credit cards was exactly eighteen dollars: a ten, a five, and
three ones.

El Habre is a rustic resort area halfway between Los An and Sanfran.
Not a swanky place, but fronting two miles of the most beautiful oceanic
view, the junglic-beach is splattered with endless numbers of summer-
camp type cabins whitewashed and dingy gray measuring about nine by
nine and most of them claiming five sleeping places. Crowded with beds,
they can only be used for sleeping. Such is El Habre.

But El Habre has one thing more. El Habre has one of the most popular
clubhouses in the world and people who have no intention of ever seeing
the cabins—some never even knowing they exist—come to enjoy the
fun, the food, and the fine show of stars. So, one lazy summer afternoon
near the end of my vacation, Gaile (my hostess) and I and her little girl
Donaile set out in my trusty old Mercedes for remote El Habre.

Now we, like many people, didn't know of the need for reservations
and we experienced a foreboding of the wait to come when we saw the
acres and acres of cars in the Temporary Guests' parking lot. We parked
and were ushered by red-coated attendants through a multi-turnstile entrance to a waiting room as we cracked private jokes about the three of
us and the only occasional dark faces in evidence among the sea of white.

The waiting room was a comfortable no-nonsense place with white straight-backed chairs placed everywhere. There were perhaps a hundred people or more. Only three others were black, an older couple looking for all the world like contented grandparents, which in fact they were, as we learned from the restless little boy of about four who was with them. To my right were two hippie couples making jokes and telling stories about places they'd been and things they'd done. Most of the people were encouraging them to keep up this light show by laughing animatedly at every joke and story punch line. I was sorta enjoying them myself, exchanging ain't-they-sick glances with Gaile as we kept a wary eye on Donaile across the room playing with the little grandboy.

Somewhere in the middle of all this, the door burst open and in came Willie Lee, tall, lean, reed-slender, country-sun-and-rain-black, and out of place. In his right hand was a little girl's. With his left he closed the door. He then thrust this hand to some hidden place in the bosom of his black denim jacket and stood for a moment deliberately surveying the room. Though he had a pleasant, mischievous schoolboy face, he seemed to be about twenty-two or three. Right away I knew him. Well, not *him*, but from some wellspring of intuition I knew into him and sensed some sinister intent enter that room in the winsome grin and bold arresting gaze that played around the room.

Silence played musical chairs around the group and the hippies were *it*, ending a story that was just begun. All eyes were on the man and the child at the door.

He swaggered Saturday-night-hip-style to a seat across the room from Gaile and me, sat, and the little girl leaned between his knees looking smug and in-the-know about something she knew and we did not. Willie Lee his name was, he said, but somewhere later I heard the child call him Bubba.

Oh, Willie Lee, where did you come from and why are you here where you don't belong with that do-rag on your head, and those well-worn used-to-be-bright-tan riding boots on your feet, and that faded blue sweatshirt and those well-worn familiar-looking faded dungarees? Willie Lee, why did you come here and I know it's a gun or a knife in your jacket where your left hand is and you ain't gonna spoil my last-of-summer holiday!

"What do you think?" *sotto voce*, I said to Gaile.

"Methinks the deprived has arrived," *sotto voce*, her reply.

From the time he entered, he took over.

"Don't let me stop nothing, gray boys," he said to the storytellers. "We just come to have some fun. Yeah! Spread around the goodwill!" He threw back his head and laughed.

That was when I noticed fully the little girl. She was watching him, laughing to him like she knew what was to come and was deliciously waiting, watching him for the sign. She seemed to be about nine. He stuck out his hand and carefully looked at his watch.

"Yeah!" he said, stretching out his legs from some imaginary lounge chair. "Whatcha say, Miss Schoolteacher?" He laughed, looking boldly amused at me.

Years of teaching and I knew him. Smart, a sharp mind, very intelligent and perceptive but reached by so many forces before me, yet coming sometimes and wanting something others had not given, others who didn't know how, some not knowing he needed, grown in the street and weaned on corners, in alleys, and knowing only a wild creative energy seeking something all humans need. I knew him, looked in his eyes and perceived the soul lost and wandering inside.

"I say forget it, Willie Lee. That's what I say."

A momentary look of recognition crossed his face and when he realized what we both knew, he laughed a laugh of surprise that even here some remnant of his failed past jumped out to remind him of the child he'd been, yet appreciating too, I think, that here it was he in charge, not I.

Gaile had tensed as I spoke. "Come here a minute, Baby," she called to Donaile, but the child was already on her way to her mother, and quickly positioned herself between her legs. She stood facing this newly arrived pair and stared at them. The little girl, Willie's sister he said, made a face at the smaller child who then hid her face in her mother's lap. Still, I looked at Willie Lee. Then I looked away, regretting having acknowledged his person only to have that acknowledgment flung laughingly back in my face, and I resolved to have no more to say to him but to try and figure out what his plan was and how to escape it unharmed.

Again, he must have read my mind.

"Folks," he said, "my sister and I just come to have a little fun. She's had a little dry run of what to expect, and it's coming her birthday and I told her, 'Donna,' I say, 'I'ma let you have a little piece of the action up at El Habre.' She'll be seven next week, you know, and well, it's good to learn things while you young." He laughed again.

Then turned to a flushed-looking man sitting on his left.

"Hey, Pops, how's business on Wall Street?" That laugh again.

The poor man looked for help around the room and, finding none in the carefully averted eyes, finally perceived Willie Lee waiting soberly for his answer.

"Nnnnn-not in the ssss-stock market," he said, to which Willie Lee guffawed.

I found myself looking intently at that laughing face, trying to figure out what to do and how to do it. I reviewed the entrance from the parking lot. We'd come through a turnstile such as large amusement parks have and we'd been ushered to this side room to wait for reservations. Now where were those uniformed ushers who'd directed us here? One had come and called out a party of five about forty minutes ago. I decided to give up my waiting position and be content to read about this fiasco in tomorrow's paper.

So deciding, I stood up resolutely, took Donaile's hand and said to Gaile, "Let's go," and started for the door. The whole room stumbled from its trance to begin the same pilgrimage.

Coldly, "Stop where you are, *everybody*!" he said, arresting us, and we turned to look at him standing and calmly holding a gun.

Defeated, I dropped the child's hand and stood there watching the others return to their original seats.

You will not hurt me, Willie Lee. I stood still, looking at him.

"Slim, you and the sister can go if you want to," he said, looking levelly at me. Dreamlike I saw a little lost boy sitting in my class, wanting something—love maybe—but too lost, misguided, and misbegotten and too far along on a course impossible to change and too late if we but knew how.

"Thank you," I said, and Gaile and I went out the door, each of us holding one of Donaile's hands.

Something was wrong at the turnstiles, and the sky had turned cloudy and dark. Instead of the neatly dressed ushers we'd seen coming in, there were two do-rags-under-dingy-brim-hatted fellows wearing old blue denims and black denim jackets calmly smoking in the graying day.

When they saw us, I felt the quick tension as cigarettes were halted in midair.

"Where y'all going, Sistuhs?" the short pudgy one said.

"We got tired of waitin' and *he* said we could go," I answered, standing still and looking at them intently.

They looked at each other a moment.

Then, "I think y'all better wait a while longer," the tall droopy-eyed one said.

Some sixth sense told me we'd be safer inside, and then I saw the bulge of the gun at the pudgy one's side sticking from the waist of his pants.

"You're probably right," I said, and with studied casualness, we turned and went back to the room we'd just left.

Things had started to happen inside. Willie Lee was brandishing the little black and sinister gun as he methodically went to each person collecting any valuables people were wearing and money from pockets and bags.

"Get your money out, Slim," he said to me as we came back inside.

Distinctly, I remember returning to my seat, locating my billfold, extracting eight dollars—the five and three ones, thinking I'd not give any more than I *had* to and holding the three ones in my hand and stashing the five in my skirt pocket.

He was snatching watches from wrists and rings from fingers and making people empty their pockets and purses to him and putting these things in a dingy little laundry bag with a drawstring. People seemed dazed in their cooperation while the little girl, Donna, carted booty from all over the room in wild and joyful glee. The room was hot and deathly quiet. Then her hand was in my skirt pocket and she was gone to him and his bag with my three singles and the five.

Gaile was just sitting there and Donaile was leaning quietly between her legs. And I was thinking. Where is everybody? What have they done to them? We'd heard nothing before *he* came. Then I heard something. I heard the sirens and my mouth dropped open. Oh, no! Don't come now. I sat wishing they had not come just then with Willie's job unfinished and the child in the throes of her wild pre-birthday glee!

Then he was standing in front of me.

"I'm sorry, Slim, but you see how it is!" he said with amused resolution.

He grabbed the not-on-Wall-Street man, pushed him roughly toward the door.

"Okay, everybody out," he said.

Things got confusing then. Outside we vaguely heard shouts and what I guess was gunfire, and not the holiday fireworks it sounded like. We all went rushing to the door. The door got jammed, then was not. More shots were heard and screams and cries. Outside, amid rushing legs, a turnstile smoker lay groaning and bleeding on the ground. The child Donna ran screaming to where he groaned and lay. Holding tight to Donaile's hand, Gaile and I ran toward the turnstile amid wild and crowded confusion. Then someone was holding me.

"Let me go!"

"Bitch, come with me!" a mean voice said. "You too, Bitch, and bring the kid!" This to Gaile.

We were shoved and pushed into the rear seat of a Scaporelli's Flower Delivery station wagon. Crowded next to us were the two hippie girls clinging to each other and crying. The back doors were slammed, and

Willie Lee hustled the pleading Wall Street man in the front seat, jumping in behind him. And Droopy-Eye of the turnstile jumped in the driver's seat, and started the car. Donaile was crying and clinging to Gaile. The course we took was bizarre and rash because people were running everywhere. And still more people were running from the gilded entrance of the El Habre Clubhouse to scatter confusedly along the course we sped. Too many people scattered along this fenced-in service drive where running people and a racing car should never be. He tried to dodge them at first, blowing his horn, but they would not hear and heed, so soon he was knocking them down, murdering his way toward a desperate freedom. The blond hippie girl began to heave and throw up on her friend. I closed my eyes, begging the nightmare end. And then I smelled the flowers. Looking back, I saw them silently sitting there.

I looked at the back of Willie Lee's head, where he, hunched forward, gun in hand, tensely peered ahead.

"Willie Lee, it just won't work." I kept my eyes on the back of his head.

"Shut up, Bitch," Droopy-Eye said.

Willie Lee looked back to me.

"Man, that's Miss Schoolteacher. She knows *everything*," he exaggerated. "Slim, it'll work 'cause *you* part of our exit ticket now, since Ol' Sam here brought y'all in."

"Willie Lee, give it up," I said.

"Man, let's dump the dizzy bitch! I was just grabbing anybody," he excused himself. Then as an afterthought, "I never did like schoolteachers no way."

Then up ahead they saw the gate.

"Hey, Sam, crash that gate. No time to stop," Willie said, peering behind.

"Man, ain't no cops gonna run down no people. You got time to open that gate!" This from a man who'd run people down.

Willie Lee peered again through the flowers at the road behind.

"Willie Lee, the road will end when you reach the gate. It's a dirt road then where you have to go slow, unless," I added, "you're ready to die and meet your maker."

"Damn, this bitch think she know everything!" Droopy-Eye said while Willie Lee just looked at me.

Donaile was crying still. Gaile was, too. Wall Street was now quietly sitting there, just sitting and staring straight ahead. The hippie girls were crying.

I turned around and looked behind. The running people had receded in the distance, framed in stage-like perspective by the big El Habre Clubhouse where we'd been going to enjoy an afternoon show. And tomorrow my vacation would end, if my life didn't end today.

Droopy-Eye stopped the car and Willie Lee got out and opened the gate. Now began dust and sand as the station wagon plowed too fast down the gravelly, dusty road. Down before us, we could see the ocean's white-capped waves. And between us and the ocean was the circular courtyard flanked by four or five small buildings and one other building larger than the rest.

"The road will end at those buildings," I said. "What you gonna do then, Willie Lee?"

"I'ma chunk yo' ass in the ocean, Bitch, if you don't shut up."

I kept looking levelly at Willie Lee. He kept hunched forward, looking down the slowly ending road. We reached the courtyard entrance, a latticed, ivy-covered archway, and Droopy drove the station wagon through.

"Oh, shit, the road *do* end!" Droopy moaned as he stopped the car.

When the motor was cut, we heard the ocean's waves, and back in the distance, the people running and screaming behind. Why are they coming this way, I wondered, remembering the time we kids ran home to our burning house. They must be cabin dwellers, I thought.

"What now, Willie Lee?" I said.

Willie and Droopy jumped out of the car.

"Okay, everybody out!" Willie directed.

When Wall Street, the last, had finally climbed out, Willie shouted, "Okay, Slim, y'all take off. Sam, you take Wall Street, and the two girls come with me." And they began to hustle the three toward the bigger building with the cafeteria sign.

Thank you, Willie Lee, for letting me free. Gaile and Donaile ran toward the woods where the cabins were and where beyond was the busy sea. As I ran behind them, I looked back to see Sam and Willie crashing in the cafeteria door, dragging and pushing the man and the girls inside, just as a Wonder Bread truck began to enter the courtyard from behind. It was filled with guns-ready police. I screamed to Gaile to wait for me.

When we'd reached the bottom of the hill, we heard shouting and gunfire. We ran on, cutting right to a service path that led through the green woods lush with undergrowth. About every fifty feet on either side of the path were the cabins, whitewashed, dank, and gray. Running and running, stopping some to breathe and rest and to try and soothe the terrified child. *You shouldn't have come here, Willie Lee, bringing your sister to see you fail.* Soon we heard others coming, loud and excited in the tragedy of this day.

Why couldn't you stop, Willie Lee, when it started going wrong and kept on going that way? You're not a fool, because I know you from each year you've been in my classes, and when I've tried to teach you, reach you, touch you, love you, you've snarled, "Take your hands off me," and I've kept myself to myself and tried my best to forget every one of you and this afternoon at El Habre was part of my plan to get as far away from you as I can and here you are set on tearing up my turf. Will I never get away from you?

Once while I stopped resting, some people passed.

"They killed the one with the droopy eyes," they said, "but the other was only wounded and got away."

"He's coming this way, they say."

Then another: "I got my gun in the cabin. When I git it, I'ma help hunt'im and I hope I get to blow'im away."

"They say he's looking for his girlfriend, a teacher or somebody that got away."

Willie Lee, why are you looking for me? Why don't you give yourself up and die? Will I never get away from you?

"Gaile, I've got to go find him," I said. "You take Donaile and try to get away."

I didn't stay for her protest but started walking resolutely back over the path we'd come. The day was dark and the woods were dark and the clouds were dark in the sky. I met and passed people who looked curiously at me. He is looking for me, I thought, and maybe they wondered, thought they knew. I had visions of him knocking people down, shooting anyone trying to stop him, keep him from having his way. Still, why *was* he looking for me? And then I knew. For the same reason I was now looking for him. He was my student who'd failed and I was the teacher who'd failed him. Not for hostage, not for harm, but to die! To die near me who knew him. Well, not *him*, but knew into him just the same. He, who's going to die. Is dying. And now he knows. And I'm the only person who knows him and can love the little boy hurting inside.

His jacket was gone and so was his do-rag and blood was caked in his straightened unkempt hair. His eyes unseeing, he peered ahead and stumbled dying past me.

"Willie Lee," I called his name.

He stopped and in slow motion, semi-crouched, gun half-raised, he turned, peering at me through time. In the green-gray light, I opened wide my arms and silently bade him come. He dropped his gun and came paining into my arms.

It was another world then. People continued to run by, bumping us as they did. Glancing about, I saw a cabin nearby.

"Let's go in here," I said.

"Yeah, this what I want," he said. "Someplace to stop."

I looked inside and saw the cabin was bare except for the beds. I climbed through the door and helped him in, leading him to the one double bed. Two singles above and one single below on the side.

"What is this place?" he asked in wonder as our eyes grew accustomed to the darker inside. Drab even in this darkened day.

"This is one of the resort cabins," I said. "Part of El Habre too."

"What do they *do* here?" he asked.

"Sun and swim and sleep," I said. "Hear the ocean on the beach below?"

"And for this, shit, people *pay*?" He gestured around the room in unbelieving wonder.

"Yes," I said, "for this, *Shit*"—I looked to him and was held by his waiting eyes—"people pay. For the sun and the earth and the good growing things and the moon, and the dawn and the dew, people take their hard-earned bread and come here and stay and pay. *They pay!*"

Until then, I had been calm. *Steady, Teach, or you'll lose again.* I softer added, "*We* pay. We all pay."

He was quiet then and dropped his head. He looked at his hands and then at his feet. Then he looked at me.

Soberly, "Well, I spoiled it for them today, didn't I? I spoiled it today real bad," he chuckled, "didn't I?" Then he threw back his head and laughed and laughed.

And I threw back my head and just laughed and laughed hugging him.

"Yes, you did!" I said. "Yes, you really did!"

Perhaps our laughter called the people. And there they were outside the cabin windows peering and laughing in. I went to the windows then and gently pulled the shades and as best I could, I comforted the dying man, making a requiem for him, for myself, and for all the world's people who only know life through death.

Damon and Vandalia

•

(1985)

Rita Dove

DAMON

They came out of the darkness past the bamboo patch so like a fistful of
spears, and as they threaded a path between Clark's battered yellow Volkswagen and my blue Peugeot, I saw she was carrying a plastic bag filled
with some sort of grain—rice, perhaps. Clark rose to meet them; wind
swooped from the incline and blew the kerosene lamp out. I stood up, a
reflex I didn't know I had—old-world charm surging in this colonial,
barrel chest—and stumbled over the ice bucket. Drunker than I realized.
Bourbon and Texan heat go devilishly well together, a gentle pair passing
practically unnoticed, leaving one languid and curious.

But all this unexpected activity. I stumbled, fell to one knee; in the
warm, vegetal dark I stayed, palms pressed tight around the sweating
aluminum bucket until they ached from the cold. What seemed to take
centuries: a male drawl, then her voice, upbeat, saying *birdseed*; Clark's
laugh *I must give both of you a hug come here*. Then I was on my feet
again and walking towards them, unsummoned, hands dripping and a
chest spiked with gasps. It was a scene to be repeated in endless
variations—she await, earth's bounty in her arms; I bowed, my hands
cupping all I had to offer—gifts that changed their form even as I held
them out to her, stones melting to tears.

VANDALIA

That evening of high wind and heat, I was finely tuned to every sound,
every movement, merry and skittish as a schoolgirl without knowing why.
My mood pleased Michael, and he smoothed his neat Afro and tried on

290

his new smile, the one that went so well with his professor's pipe. The bamboo stood guard, a pale green organ in shadows.

We drank a lot. Somewhere around midnight, Clark ran out of ice and the trays lay forgotten on the back steps, condensation spreading in an ever darkening stain. The creek sang its ghost song, calling for a sign from the sky. Lukewarm whiskey, now, in tall glasses. The wind gushed, diving into the chimney of the lamp. We took turns lighting the wick; my fingers shook as I slid the wooden match from its box. Damon began to chatter in Japanese—I thought he was talking gibberish, until Clark said he had spent his childhood in Japan—and then I found him pretentious. Without saying so. And each matchstick a long-stemmed, unopened rose.

DAMON

Protons and electrons—barometers of the human body, scientifically proven aphrodisiacs and depressants: the heavy, dragged-out feeling before a summer storm—and afterwards, the air discharging and you with it, purpling ions, all is electricity. More and more often she came from the city, escaping the proton-laden skyscrapers and traffic, her hair crinkling from sweat, her brown skin as glossy, each day a bit darker, as the bark of a cherry tree. By the time she reached our place the negatively-spiced air of the countryside had taken effect, and she showed no sign of exhaustion or tension. It was as if she were high. She told me that she was frightened of cacti—the flat peppery lobes, the tufted spikes—and that she found the drive through the mesquite wasteland strangely exciting, like the exhilaration of a soldier after surviving a battle.

VANDALIA

Michael, his pipe and his southern inferiority complex. Talk right, learn to play tennis, never lose control. Make something of yourself. There's a way to "go about" everything.

We were to meet after his faculty meeting and I had chosen the bar. I should have known The Diamond Cowboy could only be what it was, booths of black leather and men in tight jeans dancing with each other, their tooled boots shuffling across the dark red floor. I ordered a Carta Blanca and sat down to wait. Then Clark came up. He danced expertly, Mr. Cool, just like a black dude. He was cruising and I was waiting for Michael; we bolstered each other, ignoring the others so as to appear more desirable.

Then Michael had come, and I could tell Clark liked him and that Michael was jealous. I didn't explain, not at first. Clark bought a round;

Michael began to loosen. *You'll have to come visit me*—Clark laughed, his arms around both of us—*in my love nest in the country. And meet my boyfriend, naturally.*

DAMON

I was born in Japan of a father who loved all that wasn't England and a mother doomed to follow him, but determined to take England with her wherever she went. We travelled throughout the Far East in service of the Company. It was a childhood of seas and pine woods and mountains, of inscrutable manners before all adults and spankings when I slipped out to play with the Japanese children. Those children bullied me mercilessly. I was Gulliver among the Lilliputians; they expected danger in my robust British frame and so they struck before I could or would, or so they thought. (But I was tame—oh, I was tame and stupid with my rosy cheeks.) I loved them so, those children, and I wanted to be like them—small and dirty and full of abandon and laughing as they pinched and kicked me. In the English school, haven for diplomats' sons, I excelled in running and in debate; alone, in bed, watched by the chill pine, I spoke Japanese like a sailor, cursing fiercely into the crisp pillow.

VANDALIA

Our neighborhood was a garden of smells—the rank smoke of the rubber factories, the grapey breeze that passed for spring, the witch-water bitterness of collard greens—all these thick scents mingled and clung to the skin in silent collusion.

And in the endless alternating shifts in the tire factory, six to two to ten to six, I was born—a change of pace, a breath of fresh air in the lives of my parents. And in the accepted custom of lower-class black families, they chose for their daughter a name that would stand out, a name suited for the special fate awaiting this child, their contribution to history, and so they named me Vandalia. Vandalia the vivacious, the valiant, the vibrant. A lightness and a treachery, like the beguiling flames of a snowstorm. Softly: Vandalia.

Until fourth-grade geography, when a classmate went up to the map to point out Chicago and instead cried out *Look, here's Vandalia!*, and everyone wondered, and the teacher took me up to the map so I could see for myself. Later, in the public library, I looked it up in the encyclopedia: A city in south central Illinois, seventy-five miles southwest of Springfield, on the Kaskaskia River. Dairy and grain region. Founded 1809, enjoying the position as state capital 1819–39, now the seat of

Fayette county. Industry: cereal production and the manufacture of transformers, shoe heels, clothing and telephone booths. Population: 5,160 (1960 census).

I thought you knew, the teacher said, and what I felt was shame. My parents and their neighbors had never ventured beyond the once-thriving canal town of their youth—one had only to look at my name to see. And I had thought I was unique, a fine joke. At least 5,160 people knew how ignorant we were.

DAMON

When I was old enough I was sent—as a punishment, it seemed at the time—"home." Education in Eton. The neat quadrangles, the livid lawns boxed in by stone, grey and raw. At last to be dwarfed, to look up to Something. The autumn evenings, the deep and aching blue through the dormitory windows, booze and philosophy in small spaces, the sharp animal scent of wool and male bodies warming the room, their sweat as stimulating, as exciting as a strong black tea. My roommate moaned in his sleep; I dared not rise and comfort him.

Later I fled across the Atlantic to central Canada and its furred creatures, lakes to fish and woods to fell, enough wilderness to get lost in—for three years, when it spit me out and over the border to North Dakota, where I thought I'd die until I learned to turn my fear to good use and began to run—to train until the heart-muscle swoll to meet the fear, beating to the *tropp* of track shoes on cinder, *endure, endure*. Marathon runner. Time to think of nothing but the body's thunder.

I ran my way to the university; I knew I couldn't escape it all along. Track scholarship—and again the slap on the ass and the innocent guffaw, the slick knotted thighs and the gang showers and the hair in the eyes, stinging, and the smell of strong black tea, that cool lightning at the base of my spine. I trained. I ran until my chest threatened to burst; but when I finally collapsed into knees and elbows on the grass next to the high-jump pit, he was waiting, smiling, with his boy's face and his long slim legs.

VANDALIA

My job—the job that buys my freedom from the industrial midwest, from factory smoke and acrid stink of simmering greens—is to type film scripts into a computer. Green letters, squarish stencils poured through with light, appear on the darkened screen. When the screen's full, I read it for mistakes, type them over—and the computer inserts the corrections, the lines readjusting automatically to accommodate the addition. I type the entire script on an ever-rolling scroll of light impressions, and when it is finished I print it out—the laser printer spitting out a page every few seconds, perfectly typed pages of eight-and-a-half-by-eleven bond with the appropriate margins and numerated and italics where indicated, the whole shebang.

A job unrelieved by physical contact or mental strain, a job of our time. I devise ways of coping; I pretend I am a sculptor, gaze into a block of blackish green marble until my gaze meets resistance, and so defining contour. I type in obscenities, I invent dialogues between the barber and his philandering wife and erase them the moment before Print Out. Though increasingly I have to admit that I feel nothing while I am typing; it is no more probing the stone as it is writing in air.

DAMON

I change jobs like drinking water—and wherever I go, what the tap brings forth tastes different—smooth with fluorine, salty from the pump, sweet as the brook running through pine woods (or is it the brook that runs through childhood, the rush that comes when one is unfamiliar with the world, a not-yet-tiredness), the metal-sour smack of reservoir fluids pulled from pits on the outskirts of town and strained from one steel tank to another, the liquid flowing clearer and more anonymous with every filter . . . And as I grow accustomed to the new flavor of a drink I regard as delicious, yes, vital, something fades, life balks. So I break camp; I shed skins.

The jobs I've had: waiter, lumberjack, student, gardener. Whenever I needed money I did free-lance translations—instruction booklets for Japanese imports, from cassette recorders to automobiles through to the inevitable cameras.

But since Clark, I've languished under a curious lassitude, content to let whatever happens happen, the demands of the moment sluicing over me like a sexual flush. When Clark got hired as a curator at the University of Texas, I followed him to Austin. I followed him to the garden house in the country and took the hammer he held out; I planted the herb garden *parsley sage rosemary and thyme.* I accepted the duties assigned me, cook and mechanic and romantic foreigner.

VANDALIA

Clark knew. And said nothing, silently accepting the gifts I brought, shamefaced tribute. It was a habit I had learned from Michael's friends, liberal white intellectuals who went to Europe each summer and brought back quaint rules of etiquette: they could never accept a dinner invitation without showing up with a box of chocolates under their arm or flower heads bobbing, distressed, over a horn of blazing tissue paper.

My gifts were unusual—a reflection, says Michael, of my trusting personality. Now I outdid myself. Seed for the bird feeder. An olive retriever, metal jaws on a long stem. A wicker jar for crickets. Crayons, forty-eight in a yellow flip-top box.

Damon did nothing, all day. Hung around. Whenever I came, my latest ornament carefully presented for Clark's carefully registered delight, he was lounging on the back terrace. Walked in casually, hands balled in the deep pockets of his khaki pants, shirtsleeves rolled loosely below the elbows and the collar open, revealing a reddened vee of skin and the first crisp curls of chest hair. How strange that a man who tanned so easily should burn right there. And he never took his shirt off.

Clark knew, without asking, what I wanted, running around the kitchen in his ill-fitting jogging shorts, chopping limes, sloshing tonic over a tower of ice cubes. A half hour, no more. Else Michael would worry something had happened to me on the road.

And every time he appeared in the back door, fists in pocket, I knew he had been waiting.

DAMON

Clark is gone. He came back from the supermarket with a bag full of fruit, among them limes, a netted sackful. Said he couldn't stand it anymore, took a sharp knife and slit the throat of the net so the limes spilled all over. I scrambled for the rolling limes and Clark stood there, watching as I gathered them to my lap, a palette of fragrant green. Then he turned. *Get it over with*, he said, walking out.

VANDALIA

A *cold fish*, my mother frowned, following the flattened pear of a white woman's buttocks down the street. *Couldn't warm up an ice cube, much less a man.*

It was the morning after Labor Day and we went downtown to shop for last-minute school supplies—and maybe a dress for me, if any decent ones were on sale. I was ten and she thought I didn't understand. I didn't—but I remembered until I was old enough.

She said it in self-defense, unaware she was rubbing a little brighter the myth. I think she was even proud, who knows . . . this woman who wanted so much to learn that she taught herself French with the help of a tattered primer found at a rummage sale, calling out the names as she laid the groceries on the table: *oeufs, jambon, pommes de terre, poulet.* No word for turnip greens. No word for chitterlings, for sweet potato pie. A woman with so much and nowhere to give it but her house and family, what she'd been taught was enough. And I her daughter, cold.

DAMON

The third day. Again Clark did not come home after work; for two days he hadn't returned before ten or even midnight. No words had passed between us; we were both exhausted. The knife lay next to the bowl of limes, exactly where I had placed it.

All day the sky had weighed on the earth like a large sweating hand. And suddenly, without warning, water loosened over the house—a wonder that flattened the weeds and released a cool, metallic perfume. The roar was deafening. From sheer nervousness I ran outdoors, peeling off my shirt and throwing it into the herb garden. Bare-chested I was monstrous, a Caliban; I held back my face for the rain to pelt eyelids and cheeks, throat and forehead. I was a harpooned whale; I wanted to be drummed blind.

VANDALIA

The cloudburst overcame me as I turned into the driveway; I switched off the engine but kept the ignition on, watching the windshield wipers plough a dry space that was promptly inundated again. All a matter of timing—if I blinked, counterpoint, to the blades' click, the windshield was always clear. I sat for five minutes or so, blinking. On the seat beside me stood a birdcage constructed entirely from toothpicks, each sliver individually stained and varnished. There was a ladder inside the cage, leaning against one side, and a tiny wooden swing. The swing moved in time with the wipers . . .

The yellow Volkswagen was nowhere to be seen but the Peugeot was there, blue hood well into the bamboo patch. Had they gone away for the weekend? I could walk up to the door and check. Or I could drive back. In this rain.

DAMON

All I remember is that I took the birdcage from her and set it on the table. I was dripping, shivering; I asked her if I could get her something, a towel or a drink. Then, of course, it was over too quickly—she moved slightly·

and I overran her; I nearly swallowed those gasping lips in my efforts to find the contours inside the skin. She drew back instinctively, her mouth and chin slick and glistening from my kiss, and I apologized; *forgive me* I said again and again, as I licked from her neck and ears the salt and bitter of sweat and cologne. For an instant I thought of those cold and wet Japanese winters spent whispering into the crook of a pillow; I had never been more terrified.

VANDALIA

The thundering around us and the silence between. He stood in the door to the terrace, bare-chested, the red vee of collar skin an arrow pointing down, down, and his khakis soaked and wrinkled, clinging to his legs. It was as if I were there and not there at the same time; I watched and felt myself being watched, I closed my eyes to disappear.

When we had finished, he placed his palm between my legs, cupping and defining, his face as wondering as a child's, amazed that that's all there was—no magic, no straining muscular desire.

It is possible we have never met. It is possible that this is fiction and, though we are always moving towards each other, the scene will fade at the last moment. There are times when I have not left the car, when the birdcage of sticks does not swing, buffeted by the rain, when I have not entered the house with Clark gone and the limes waiting on the counter, exhaling their insidious perfume.

DAMON

When I am with Clark there is consolation—the same bones beneath the same skin, how they float around, or rest quiet, or tense.

Now I know I am not modest though I pretend to be. Now I know I did not follow Clark to Texas but led him there; we ran away together but I pointed out the way; I chose the spiked and prickling desert as our retreat, I pressed for a house in the countryside, I glimpsed the wild bamboo, luxuriant, beside the creek and said *This is mine*.

I could not make a move until Clark spilled the limes over the kitchen counter, but then I moved. Now Vandalia is the one who waits—and when it doesn't happen, the thing she was waiting for (but I'm not sure even she knows what it is), she begins to grow vague, her eyes looking only at the surface of the world, not the world itself, not me, and I've lost her, again.

What I think about when we make love: the blip fading on the screen. What I feel: Vandalia flattening, spreading into a map, the map of my longing. Her skin is taut as a mask and mine is loose over its bones like an elephant's. The small of my back curves into her until there is nothing left. And I am small, small when she touches me.

VANDALIA

It is summer; I have done something wrong. *Wait till your father gets home* my mother says, and sends me to my room. Instead, I wait for her to disappear down the basement to check on the laundry—then I slip through the door and down the front walk. Quiet. Asphalt softening in the sun, undulating like black greased waves. A tar smell.

Across the street is a vacant lot with a maple tree in it, the flat starred leaves casting an irregular circle of shade. I go to this tree and climb it; I swear never to come down again.

For a while nothing happens. The broad leaves are cool on my arms and legs. The tar smell mixes with the non-smell of air. What does it mean, to do something wrong? I am alive but I am never where I think I am—for instance, I am not in this tree, I am far away. The six o'clock whistle blows and Father's Buick comes trundling down the street; now things will happen.

The screen door slams; *Vandalia* they call. I will not come down I am not here. Where I am the streets are swept and flowers line the windows. There is a Sears & Roebuck where I am, and a soda fountain and in the center of town a grassy square with a white bandstand right in the middle, and around the bandstand green benches but no one is ever sitting on them. I walk down the glittering sidewalk and everybody knows my name. *Vandalia*, they say, again and again.

The World of Rosie Polk

(1987)

Ann Allen Shockley

I

The hot afternoon sun, inflating the summer sky of 1952, made a sheath of flat, scorching heat rise and fall against her with the jerking movements of the truck. Rosie had been riding all day and night with the others crammed against her, the smell of unwashed bodies and acrid breaths piercing her nostrils like a privy. She knew it was worse for the ones in the middle, cramped in by more heat and odors. Because she had been among the first to join Big Ernest's crew back in Virginia, she had a choice place at the side of the truck, where nothing was in front of her except the wooden railing that fenced them in like cattle. Between the makeshift bars, she could see the asphalt of Highway 13, lanced on each side with sprawling farmland. The fields were ripe for picking now. The migrant season was in full bloom.

She twisted her head to look through the rear window of the truck to see how Big Ernest was doing, driving all that distance by himself. He was bent hard over the wheel of the ancient Chevy, as if his clinched position would certainly keep the truck moving. The black derby hat, which he always wore, was cocked low over his eyes, and the usual unlit cigar was clamped wetly in his wide mouth. She often wondered why he just didn't chew tobacco instead of a lifeless tube. Someone once told her that he kept a gun in the truck to keep anybody dissatisfied from jumping off. As far as she knew, nobody ever tried to jump off, and nobody messed with Big Ernest.

Rosie pulled her large straw hat lower over her face to shield the lined

299

brownness of it against the sun. She was only thirty-four, but her stiff, crinkled hair was graying rapidly, and the jaws of a previously handsome, strong face now had sunken hollows from the absence of teeth removed long ago and never replaced. She had once been tall and straight as an oak tree. Now, from the stoop work of picking, lifting, and dragging in the fields, her shoulders were rounded, but not so much as those of some of the women on the truck. Lord, she thought, trying to exercise her stiff muscles in the limited body space, what the fields that birth beans, tomatoes, peas, and corn can do to a person. Somehow, she had still managed to hold on, due to the strength in her back, if nothing else. She had to, for this was her life: the few weeks in the year when she earned her living bent to pick the food from the land.

"God, it's hot!" a female voice complained, startling her, reminding her that these humans beside her did speak.

"Sho' is," Rosie agreed, looking down at Maybelline sprawled heavily on a stool much too small for her obese size. On account of being unable to stoop any longer in the fields, Maybelline went along to cook the food, wash clothes, and mind children too young to become field weeds arched like sickles in the images of their parents. Everybody liked jovial, yellow Maybelline. They liked her booming laughter rising straight and honest from her guts, her raucous manner with the men, and knowledgeableness with the women. Maybelline could stop fights, wipe away tears, and bring the sunshine of the Lord into the private pits of hell. Since they wanted Maybelline to ride in comfort, they found her a stool from a trash heap to sit on, while they slumped upon the piles of blankets, crates, and cardboard suitcases that housed their possessions, or stood until they could stand no more—the children, women, and men.

"I hope it don't rain. I didn't make but twelve dollars last week pickin' them strawberries on old man Grimes's farm. He's too stingy to pay more'n ten cents a quart. And him sellin' 'em for more. After I paid for food and the rent, wasn't nothin' hardly left for Charlie and me," Rosie said, fretting.

"Un-huh, I know. It's mighty hard," Maybelline replied, pulling a red polka-dot handkerchief out of her dress pocket to wipe her face. She had begun to sweat a lot, even when it wasn't hot. The heat just went through her in the winter as well as summer, causing water to form drops the size of peas on her face. The unhealthy sweat went along with the pains in her legs and back.

Rosie turned around to see where Charlie was. Charlie looked a lot like her with his flat features, but not about his too old, vacant, staring eyes. He was piled atop the brown army blanket bulging with their belongings. His chest was bare, and the oversized, worn-out jeans he had on were drawn with a cord under his protruding navel. The whorls of tight hair covering his oblong-shaped head were tangled and needed combing.

When Charlie saw his mother looking at him, he shouted across to her, "Mama, I'm thirsty. I want some sweetin' water!"

Rosie looked away. She had bought him pop at the last stop, an endless distance in her memory somewhere down the road. Twenty cents for a grape soda. Big Ernest wrote it down in that dirty notebook he kept in his hip pocket. The notebook was always showing, always reminding them about owing him. Big Ernest was a sonofabitch. But what could *she* do? With the money he cheated out of them, he could at least buy a good truck that had a top on it to haul them around. It was by the grace of God they hadn't run into any rain on this trip. All Big Ernest wanted to do was gyp them and sip on his cheap red wine. When the wine got to telling on him, he would get mean and nasty and cuss them all out just to be cussing. Call them a bunch of ignorant niggers. Sometimes, it was a wonder one of those strapping young men didn't draw back and knock the shit out of him. But they needed Big Ernest like he needed them. He needed workers, and they a crew boss to carry them where the work was and to take care of them like children. They couldn't do it alone.

Numbness entombed her feet and legs. Lord, she was tired of riding. Big Ernest turned off the highway, and now they were traveling back roads. This meant they must be nearing Ridgeville, where the snap beans were and the factory that wanted them for canning.

Charlie shouted again to her, "Mama—I'm thirsty!"

Worrisome just like his daddy, Floyd, she thought. Although she was never sure if it was Floyd or Pete that time. She giggled, remembering. Both were sure hot after her. In those days, she was really something. She had more hair and young tender meat on her bones. She hadn't started having all them children yet. The first time had been Mary when she was fifteen. Mighty young to be having a baby, but there has to be *some* love in a person's life, especially when there is nothing else. Her family had strayed apart long before. She had had a hard time with Mary. Wasn't no midwife in that camp, or woman who knew much about trouble in childbirth. She had lain alone in fear and pain and blood until, in desperation, someone went into town for a doctor, who refused to come because he didn't wait on nigger patients, least of all, nigger migrant workers. A week later, Mary died.

Afterward, having the others wasn't too bad, since she had already been torn open. The second was Lula, born in Florida; Lonnie, in Georgia; and, last, Charlie, in Maryland, during tomato-picking time. She didn't know where Lula was. Lula had gone off with a boy three years ago. Poor Lonnie was dead—killed in Fruitland, Maryland, over sixty cents in a crap game. His death put a real hurting on her, for Lonnie worked right beside her and gave her money. The law didn't even want to go into the camp and get the man who did it. Just niggers killing niggers. And, too, some were just scared to go into a camp nicknamed Bloodsville, for there people were as used to killing as breathing.

The loud blaring of a car's horn passing them untangled the coil of her thoughts. A long, sleek blue car went by them recklessly. She could see the staring eyes in the white children's faces leaning far out of the windows to gape back at all the niggers jammed in the back of the noisy old truck. She watched the car until it was no more. The truck rumbled on down the narrow road into the stark hot desert of the day.

II

By twilight time, the truck ended its journey on the land of John Tilghman. The work crew, twenty-five of them, tried to straighten up and put life into their stiff muscles. They dropped slowly off the truck, the feel of the hard, firm ground almost coming as a shock. Arms reached up to help women with sleeping children.

"Thank God, we're here at last!" Maybelline breathed the sigh of relief for them all.

The camp was five miles outside of town on a barely used dirt road. To Rosie, the place was similar to the others; only it didn't appear to be as bad as the one they had just left. The decrepit rows of unpainted shanty houses, with jagged metal roofs and sagging boards for steps, were propped up on concrete blocks. Some still had windows and doors intact. A pump for water was at the end of the houses which faced each other across a dusty path, strewn with the debris of cans, bottles, and crates left over from whoever was there last. The outdoor toilet sat in the distance behind the houses, and back of it was a graveyard of rusted washtubs, wheelbarrows, and flabby tires.

As if attempting to hide the living quarters from the front, where the highway bordered the farm, acres and acres of planted corn, snap beans, and tomatoes stretched beneath the sky. This broad expanse of land had been amassed by John Tilghman's family through generations in Sussex County. The Tilghman family lived in town and made its money off crops grown and harvested by migrants and shipped in Tilghman trucks to wholesalers in Philadelphia and Wilmington. John Tilghman rarely came near the camp. This he left to his longtime friend and field boss, who took care of the things Tilghman had no stomach for. To the field workers, John Tilghman was merely a name.

Rosie looked around at the place like all the many others she had seen and lived and worked on. "My Lord," she murmured to herself, "don't nothin' ever change for me?"

"Com'on, you people. Let's git a move on!" Big Ernest shouted, stumbling out of the truck, eyes bloodshot. His old khaki army shirt was soaking wet in the back, the shirttail hanging out over baggy green cotton pants. It was rumored he had been a corporal in the army once. Steadying himself, he straightened up before them, planting his short, squat legs apart, hands on hips, eyeing them beneath the brim of the derby hat. This stance had given him the name Big Ernest.

"Now git yourselves one of them places to stay in. Tomorrow, we start real early in the fields. Done wasted 'nough time on the road."

"Hey—Big Ernest. I'm in a real bad way for some smokes—" a man called out to him.

"Fuck them cigarettes now and let's git this shit off'n this truck!" Big Ernest snapped back, pointing a finger at the vehicle still loaded with possessions.

A white Buick came careening down the side road, kicking up dust and coming to a squealing stop beside the truck. A middle-aged white man with thinning blond hair looked out of the car at them.

"There's Mista Todd," Big Ernest muttered low, teeth biting hard on the soggy cigar.

The man gave a long, beckoning sound on his horn, and Big Ernest moved away from them, bracing himself to walk evenly over to the car. The group quietly watched the men talking, the white man's lips moving the most, while Big Ernest kept nodding his head up and down. Out of deference or because it was hot, Big Ernest had taken his hat off and Rosie could see his smooth, nut-brown head.

Charlie tugged at her dress. "Mama, I'm thirsty!"

The white man in the Buick turned his attention back to the crew again, scrutinizing the workers with speculative, hard work eyes. Then he gunned the powerful motor to turn around in the dust and drive hurriedly out of the yard.

"All right, you niggers, listen to me—" Big Ernest began, slapping his hat on again while walking back to them. "That was Mista Todd—the field boss. He says that he don't want no one leaving here until these fields are picked clean and all the money owed him for rent and such is paid off. I'm goin' into town to the store for you and git your eatin's or anythin' else you want. If you ain't got the money, I'll put it down in the book. Tomorrow, we start *work*. Mista Todd said you better do a good job, for he's thinkin' mighty hard *and* long 'bout gittin' some Puerto Ricans to come in and do the work. Y'all don't want *that* to happen, do you, or your black asses'll be out of work!"

Why's he always talkin' 'bout our black asses and his'n is just as black too? Rosie pondered to herself. She felt Charlie's movements clinging to her skirt, as though he too understood Big Ernest's threat.

Then, out of the openness, a man's deep voice shouted out: "Aw, Ernest, cut out that talk 'bout Puerto Ricans. That ain't nothin' but to make these people work harder and cheaper."

A startled hush fell over the group as the man who had spoken up to Big Ernest approached them, seemingly from nowhere out of the dwindling, dusky twilight.

Before Rosie realized it, the words came out over the tiredness and anger submerged within her, bred from the long trip and the insensitiveness of Big Ernest. "Mista, you sure done spoke the God's awful truth!"

The stranger's gaze fell hard upon her for a moment, and then back again to focus on Big Ernest. "You know I'm right, Ernest, so cut that tryin' to scare these people."

"Now you just wait a minute there, Jackson," Big Ernest snapped back, reaching into his shirt pocket for a new cigar. "Nobody asked *you* to git into this. You just mind *your* business and I'll take care of *mine*—these people here. Now y'all haul ass and git that stuff off'n my truck!"

As the crew scattered at the lash of the order, Rosie squinted to see Jackson better—the man who had come out of the dark holes of the shacks to challenge Big Ernest. He loomed tall and black and ugly as sin before her. The more she stared at the strongly built stranger with the jagged knife scar making a split from the corner of his right eye down to his upper lip, she knew this was a man to be feared and respected. His ears stuck out like jutting cliffs, and, unlike all the other men here, he had a beard covering most of his lower face. It was hard for her to tell how old Jackson was; for him and the rest, time had made a quick swath in their lives, like the Grim Reaper hurrying death through decay.

"Jackson"—Big Ernest was still standing there looking at him too—

"don't you start no trouble with me," he warned, chewing hard on the unlit cigar. "You just be glad I'm lettin' you work with this crew."

"You ain't got nothin' to do with me, Ernest, and you know it!" the man, Jackson, said evenly, grit edging the words.

"Hey, we got things to do." Maybelline's voice interrupted, coming loud from the tangled knot of weary people pausing to listen. "Can't git nothin' done standin' 'round like this."

"Yeah, g'wan, *git*," Big Ernest echoed, relieved to regain his authority.

Charlie tugged on her again. "Mama, I'm thirsty!"

"Thirsty myself, son. Let's go see what kind of water that pump's givin' up."

"Don't want no pump water. Want sweetin' water!" Charlie bellowed.

At that moment, Jackson's eyes settled upon them, dark, piercing, amused as he looked at her and the boy. She felt the others moving around and against her as they carried their blankets, suitcases, crates, and brown paper bags stuffed with all they owned to the vacant houses. For some reason, she found herself rooted there, until Jackson's gigantic frame came over to her. He walked slowly, with a slight limp in his left leg. The cast-off khaki army trousers he wore, like Big Ernest did sometimes, fit snugly to his well-muscled thighs. There was power in him, and for a sensitive moment while watching him approach her, she felt a sensuous response she hadn't known in a long time warmly stroke her body, settling in the V-angle of her legs. She rebuked herself. She was too old to be feeling like that again. *That* feeling had died with Charlie's coming—eight years ago. Hadn't it?

"You sure got spunk, lady," he said, softly, standing in front of her. "Out of all these people, you got spunk! I like people like that." Then, looking down at Charlie, he grinned. "Boy's thirsty. I got some nice cold water in my place and a piece of ice to go in it."

"I don't want no *water*!" Charlie persisted, sensing an ally in this man who was taking time to talk to him. "I want sweetin' water."

"We'll git that some other time," Jackson promised. "Right now, I'll give you what's on hand. Water!"

"I got to git my stuff off'n the truck," Rosie said.

"I'll git it for you," Jackson offered. "And I'm goin' to show you a right nice place hidden by a clump of trees past the rest. Got a cookstove and two beds."

"*Two* beds?" Rosie sighed. "Me and Charlie just been sleepin' together the best way we can."

"Which one is your'n?" Jackson asked, following her back to the truck.

"The big brown blanket over there." She pointed.

He climbed on the truck and reached for her bundle, lifting the weight of it with ease. "Com'on 'fore somebody else finds that place."

The one-room house was in better condition than the others, with simulated brick siding and the two windows unbroken. The beds were iron with old straw mattresses. A kerosene stove sat in a corner by a sink that did not have running water. The center of the room was occupied with a rickety, scarred brown table surrounded by three mismatched chairs.

"Used to be a crew leader's place long time ago," he explained, watching her show pleasure at the surroundings. "I'm in back of you a little piece." He stopped, frowning. "What's your name?"

"Rosie," she said quietly. "Rosie Polk."

"All right, Rosie Polk. While you gittin' things together, I'll take the boy and give him his water."

"His name's Charlie."

"Let's go, Charlie. You can bring your mama some water back, too."

She watched them leave—the big man with her son. Then she turned to untie the knot of the blanket and unpack to stay in what was home, at least for now.

III

Early morning of the next day, Rosie, with Charlie beside her, began the long stretching hours in the fields picking snap beans. The heat was oppressive, bearing down on figures going through the puppetlike down and up movements of picking the beans and putting them into hampers, then dragging them along the parallel rows to the checker.

Rosie, like the other women, wore a wide-brimmed straw hat on top of a handkerchief covering her head and ears, and pants, beneath the shapeless dress, to protect her legs from the insects. Dresses distinguished the women from the men stooped in the fields. There was little talking between the workers harvesting the crops. Too much of an exchange of words would impede the progress of filling the hampers, whose numbers meant pay.

Rosie stopped for a moment to straighten up, taking the tail end of her dress to fan her face. At the far end of the row, she could distinguish Jackson with his belt of tickets. He was the checker and examined the hampers to see if there were any bad beans picked; he gave the workers a ticket for each full hamper. This was a good job and showed that Jackson was favored by the white field boss. Rosie smiled, thankful that the checker was Jackson. She knew some who were meaner than hell, dumping full loads on the ground just because one or two bad beans or tomatoes were in them. Jackson saw her looking at him and waved. She waved back, blinking in the glare of the sun. The friendly gesture in the open fields brightened her spirits.

"Wonder where *he* come from?" She had forgotten Leroy was picking on the other side of her. He had paused to rest too, taking off his tattered shirt to wipe the sweat off his face and chest. Leroy had been with the crew all the way too. He was a burnt-orange color and looked as if he had some Indian mixed up in him.

"Don't know, since he was already here. Big Ernest sure don't like him!" she replied, chuckling.

"Maybe he knows somethin' 'bout Big Ernest *we* don't know," Leroy scoffed, putting the sweat-dampened shirt back on.

"Maybe." Rosie grunted, stooping again to the beans.

Leroy looked down at her form like an overdressed scarecrow. "Which place you stayin' in, Rosie?"

She straightened up again to see his face grinning at her meaningfully. "Not your'n," she flared back.

Leroy threw back his head, laughing loudly. "Just thought you might like some comp'ny some night."

"All right, you people over there. Stop all that yakkin' and git to work!" They saw Mister Todd shouting at them menacingly. "Can't git no beans picked like that."

"Damn white sonofabitch," Leroy muttered, under his breath.

"Stoopin' and pickin'," Rosie said, shaking her head. " 'Fore I die, I'd sure like to know how it feels to do somethin' else in this life."

"Well, you ain't ever goin' to know," Leroy said, spitting into the dirt. " 'Cause that's all you can do."

IV

Until Saturday of the next week, which was payday, nine days off, Rosie and Charlie ate baloney stew and drank grape sodas. Going home in the evening past Maybelline's house, she could smell the big pot of greens and fatback cooking for those who bought meals from her. Charlie would eat his food quickly, sopping up the stew juice with day-old bread, then curl up on the bed and go to sleep, tired from the fields.

One evening after she had cleaned up the plates and lit the kerosene lamp, a knock sounded on the door, and she heard someone calling her name.

"Rosie?" It was Jackson standing outside in the darkness. "Just thought I'd come by and see how you and the boy are doin'."

"Charlie's gone to sleep. Ain't easy workin' in the fields for a little boy."

"Ain't no kind of life for a boy *or* woman," Jackson added, entering the dim, smoky shadows of the room.

"Man much neither," Rosie went on sadly. "I've seen some ole men just fall right over and die in the field. That's the only way you can leave it—free."

Jackson sat down in one of the chairs by the table. A clothesline was strung across the room with her clothes and Charlie's hanging on it. The washing gave the room a wet-damp smell. Some of the grimy dirt and insecticide used for spraying the crops still stubbornly stained the pant legs. All the washboard scrubbings in the world wouldn't get them out.

Rosie sat down at the table with him. His clean white T-shirt and blue pants made her aware that she hadn't washed or changed her field clothes. When all you did was live to work from morning to night, you didn't think about nothin' else—not even yourself.

Jackson took out a pack of cigarettes and offered her one. She shook her head. She had given up smoking a long time ago. Somehow, the smoke didn't mix with the dust and spray and heat from the sun bursting her lungs. She watched him drag deeply on the cigarette, like he enjoyed it so much. She tried to remember the last time she sat with a man like this—talking and watching him smoke, the cigarette starkly white between his black fingers.

"Where you from, Jackson?" she asked, thinking that he must be from someplace afar that made good, strong black men.

"Georgia. But I live 'round here now. Came to these parts two years ago following the crops. Got tired of movin', movin', and movin', so I just stayed. Man gits tired." He flicked the cigarette ashes in the empty soda bottle left on the table. "Mista Todd let me stay on to do odd jobs 'round here. Said I was dependable and a good worker. You know how white folks like to have a special nigger." He winked at her. "Anyways, he's got some cows and chickens down the road a piece, and planting time, I runs the tractor here."

She watched him out of the corner of her eye, not wanting to look directly at him. For some reason, she felt shy around him. He sat leaned back in the chair with his legs spread wide. Furtively, she glanced at the crotch of his pants. Warmth stole over her like a heated spring. He grinned, as if knowing her thoughts.

"You live by yourself?" Quickly, her hand covered her mouth, ashamed of the question that had slipped out. It was the same as asking if he had a woman.

Now he laughed, and she saw his teeth, even and bright. She ran her tongue unconsciously around the inside of her mouth where her back jaws were ragged with teeth and spaces in between. She wanted to laugh back, respond to him, but dared not.

"Yeah, I live by myself. Can cook right good too. You and the boy come over for supper Sat'day. I'll show you."

Surprise transfigured her face into almost childishness. No one had ever cooked for her except her mother; then after she got old enough, she took over the chores.

"*Cook* for us!" This time, she forgot the missing teeth and laughed aloud at the thought. A *man* cooking for her and Charlie!

"Sure. You two com'on over and see. I'll show you. I learnt to cook when I was ten. My mama died when we was little. My daddy tried to keep all five of us younguns together—somehow. He worked in the factory and fields and put *us* to work. Made us go to school too," he said proudly, putting out the cigarette butt in the bottle. "Up to the fifth grade. Then he got hisself a woman who just moved right in and took over. By then, I knew it was time for me to leave. Started gittin' crowded after *she* started havin' babies."

She listened quietly, amazed that he had gone to the fifth grade. She had hardly made it to the third. She glanced over at Charlie, still sleeping soundly, curled into a ball. Poor Charlie. He was like her, never staying in a place long enough to finish anything.

"Well, Rosie, I'm goin' so's you can git to sleep. It's been a long day," he said, getting up.

"All our days are long," she murmured wearily.

"Don't forgit—Sat'day," he called back, closing the door softly to keep from awakening the boy.

No, she wouldn't forget. Thinking about it would help her to get through the rest of the days that were alike in their unvaried sameness.

V

The following day was clouded with threats of rain. They worked harder, faster, feverishly to fill as many baskets as they could before the rain started. Rain meant no work, no work meant no pay, and no pay was being indebted for living.

By noon, the dreaded rain came in a furious torrent, as if the devil were in the sky mocking them. It rained all day and night, and continued on into the next morning. Boredom set in and, with it, frustration. To occupy time, the women washed clothes that refused to dry in the dampness that crept into the shanties from cracks and holes in the floors and walls. The children became restless, cooped up in the cramped quarters where there was nothing else to do but take care of the younger ones, while impatient parents took it out on them by screaming epithets. The men spent the time gambling with promises until payday and sending Big Ernest back and forth into town for wine bought on credit.

Rosie used up her time trying to scrub away the encrusted dirt left over by those before her. The thought of Saturday night helped to brighten the gloom of the rain. She had just put a bucket under the spot where the roof was leaking when the door swung open and Leroy entered without knocking. He came in dripping wet, dressed in an old black rubbery raincoat, smelling of wine and grinning like a fool.

"Hey, Rosie." He smirked, hanging his coat on a nail by the door. "Thought maybe you'd be lonesome on a day like this." Swaying, he slumped down in the chair where Jackson had sat before.

"No time to git lonesome." She frowned at him. "Got things to do."

"Oh, hell. Forgit them things to do. Here," he invited, pulling a pint bottle of wine out of his pocket, "have a li'l taste. Make you feel like a new woman."

She moved to pull the blanket closer around Charlie, asleep on the bed. "Naw, Leroy."

He swigged noisily from the bottle, wiping his mouth with the back of his hand. "What's the best thing to do on a day like this with the rain fallin' and ever'thin'?"

Ignoring him, Rosie sat down to darn Charlie's underwear. That was the best way to get rid of Leroy, she decided, pretend like he wasn't there.

Brushing aside her disdainful silence, he went on garrulously. "*Lovin'*.

That's the best thing to do when it's rainin'. Takes away all your worries—makes the sun shine again."

She heard his chair scrape the floor as he moved closer to reach over and squeeze her breast. "That's exactly what you need!"

"Git your hands off'n me, Leroy!" She slapped angrily at him.

"Aw, now, Rosie," he began, voice low, wheedling. "I ain't never seen a woman yet who wasn't interested in a little lovin' now and then. And *I'm* the one who can give it like the doctor ordered. Your man, Leroy. Right here!"

"G'on home, Leroy, and leave me alone," she said, getting up to go back to the box of clothes where others needing patching were.

In one quick motion, he sprang out of the chair, grabbing her from behind. She felt the push of his hard body against her and smelled his sour cigarette smell. She tried to twist out of his grasp as he began kissing the back of her neck and side of her cheek. His breath came faster as he half pulled and pushed her to the bed. Here, he threw her down, falling on top of her, while his hand ran paths under her dress and up her legs, touching her body.

"Com'on, Rosie," he pleaded, "you know you want it."

She stiffened against him, tightening her legs together, reaching beneath the mattress for what would stop him. "You better let go of me, Leroy, 'fore I stick this knife clean up your behind!"

He let go of her, rolling over to the side of the bed and getting up. "Since when'd *you* git so touchy?" he sneered. "I heard that, one time, all somebody had to do was tap you on the shoulder and your dress'd fly up!"

"Git out of here, Leroy."

Charlie awakened, stared at them sleepily, then closed his eyes again. He had seen his mother and men before.

"Okay, I'm goin'. But you ought to be glad I'm even in-ter-ested. Ugly as *your* black ass is!"

The words tore through her more ravishing than pain. "Look who's got the nerve to call somebody ugly!" she flung back weakly at the sound of his leaving.

She stayed on the bed with her eyes tightly closed, refusing to open them until she was certain he was gone. Outside, the rain thrashed ominously against the thin walls of the house. The sound of fate.

VI

It rained for three days. When the sun finally came out, they went back into the muddy fields, feet sinking into the soft ground. By the time Saturday came, Rosie owed for the rent and the food bought on credit. In the pay line, she heard a woman grumbling, "Always owin', owin', owin'. After owin', ain't nothin' left. One of these days, I ain't goin' to owe nothin' 'cept to the Lord."

Later that evening, she bathed Charlie in the big round tub that she washed clothes in. Then she dressed him in a clean pair of pants patched at the knees and a faded yellow shirt. She combed and brushed his hair, applying Vaseline to make the tight curls softer. Afterward, she got herself ready, putting on the one good dress she had, a cotton print with a wide skirt, and tied her hair up in a bandanna. Holding Charlie by the hand, she walked self-consciously over to Jackson's.

On the way, she saw Maybelline sitting on her stoop. "Jackson tolt me y'all were comin' over to dinner. Just be sure eatin's all!" She guffawed, slapping her heavy thigh.

"Maybelline, you got a nasty mind!" Rosie laughed back good-naturedly, hurrying Charlie along.

Jackson's house was different. It had electricity and two rooms. The front room had a stove with an old brown icebox beside it, a sink, and sagging upholstered chairs with grease-stained backs. The table was set and covered with a red plastic cloth that almost matched the curtains at the windows. One large light bulb hung on a wire down over the table. The second room was small, with a pine bed and a chest of drawers with the bottom drawer missing. A curtain separated the rooms.

"Supper's all ready," he announced proudly, gesturing toward the stove.

"I'm hungry!" Charlie said, running over to bounce up and down on a chair. He hadn't seen a chair with springs before.

"He's always hungry," Rosie said, apologetically.

"Growin' boys got appetites. I cooked some black-eyed peas, rice, and ham hocks."

"Hum-m-m. Sure smells good."

"Y'all sit down and help yourselves. You goin' to git brownskin service."

"Uh-huh! Ain't nothin' I like better'n brownskin service!" Rosie breathed, sitting down.

When dinner was over, they talked and Jackson played piggyback with Charlie. When the evening sky deepened, she began to feel a twinge of regret, hating to go back to her place, which wasn't as bright and cheerful as this.

"Like my cookin'?" he asked, smiling.

"Real good." She smiled back, forgetting the hole of her mouth.

"You need to smile more, Rosie," he said gently.

"Takes happenin's to make a person smile."

"I know we got it rough. It's our luck. But we might as well try to git a little pleasure out of life while we can. We only come this way once."

From afar, they could hear children playing. A woman cursed and a man laughed. The sound of a bottle being flung out of a window splintered the evening like cracked ice.

"Let's go into town," Jackson said abruptly.

"Into *town?*" she repeated, the idea completely foreign to her. She looked down at what she wore: the long, shapeless dress bought at a rummage sale, where clothes still held the odor of their owners, and shoes run over from wear.

"Sure. We goin' to take a ride. Look at the sky and see other folks. Right, boy?"

Charlie jumped up eagerly, happy with the thought of leaving this place. All he did was work. He went nowhere and saw nothing but the same old people all the time.

"Big Ernest don't let us go into town," Rosie said hesitantly.

Jackson stood up, his full length stretching almost to the ceiling. "Rosie, Big Ernest don't rule *me*. I knew him *when*. Back there in the army in Alabama when all we did to fight the war was clean up the mess hall and polish white officers' boots. You see this scar on my face?" he asked, running a finger down the length of the crooked line. "That's when Big Ernest thought he could try to boss me but found out diff'rent. He thought being a corporal made him Jesus. Treated us like dirt. I showed him one night off base that he wasn't no black God 'cause of a coupla stripes. Only he ain't got no scars to show for it—'ceptin' when he sees me and 'members. He had a knife and I just had my fists." Jackson took Charlie's hand. "Okay, boy, let's all go for that ride."

Jackson had an ancient, rusty blue Plymouth without a right fender. Somehow, through nursing and amateur tampering, he kept it running. The back seat was torn out and only the springs remained.

"Ain't much," he said modestly, "but I bought it for almost nothin' from Mista Todd. He's got a junkyard down the road. It'll git us into town." He laughed, opening the door for them.

When they got into town, Main Street was busy with people shopping or milling around talking. There was a five-and-dime store, Acme, drug-store, clothing shop, bank, bowling alley, and liquor store with a noisy barroom in the rear.

Jackson, Rosie, and Charlie made a strange trio, walking slowly down the street. Charlie was wide-eyed and speechless, gaping at the lighted windows and storewares. The people on the street stared at them in anger and repugnance, giving them plenty of space to pass. They were out-siders—migrant workers—drifting flotsam on Tilghman's place. These people were known to be ignorant and mean with it. The townspeople wished that they didn't have to be there, but they were needed. Even the town's blacks moved over as they passed, branding them as dumb nigger field hands. Two or three of the townsmen recognized Jackson, and their gaze softened. They *knew* him.

Jackson bought Charlie his first ice-cream cone, which he ate very slowly, savoring the strange chocolate flavor. They passed George Kleen's Clothing Shop, and Rosie stopped to peer in at the dresses displayed on white mannequins.

"My, ain't they pretty? That green one's sure nice. If I can pick 'nough next week and it don't rain no more—" She said nothing else, knowing she wouldn't ever pick enough.

They walked on into and against the fading, long summer night. Cars honked horns, neighbors shouted to each other, children ran boisterously ahead of parents down the street. Rosie didn't know when she had felt this good before—like a person. When they got back to the camp, she slept well and without dreams.

VII

Sunday morning, she was awakened by a knock on her door. "Rosie, got somethin' for you and the boy."

"Just a minute," she called, quickly pulling on the old work pants and shirt over her gown.

Upon hearing the knock, Charlie sprang out of the bed. "Mama, it's Jackson!"

Jackson came in carrying two packages under his arms. Charlie ran over to him, grabbing his legs. "What'cha got?" he asked excitedly.

"This one's for you. And the big one's your mama's."

"What'd you go and buy somethin' for us for?" Rosie questioned, confusion and surprise clouding her face.

"Person who works all the time ought to have somethin' for them-selves—*sometimes*." Jackson looked away from what he saw in her eyes.

Shakily she opened the box and took out the green dress nestled between tissue paper. "Jackson—you went and bought the dress in the window!"

"Yeah. Went back last night just 'fore the store closed. Got Charlie some new pants and a ball. Can't 'spect a boy to grow up without havin' a ball once in his life. Can you?"

Charlie tore open his package, exposing the pants and the bright red ball. Rosie watched him happily bouncing the ball up and down. The last toy he had was a miniature fire truck with one wheel off given to him for Christmas by a church group.

"Jackson, you spent all your money on *us*," Rosie chastised him softly.

"Not quite all. And what if I did? I'm makin' somebody happy."

Rosie held the dress up before her, smiling, forgetting her almost empty mouth.

"We goin' into town in style next Sat'day night. So don't forgit to wear that dress!"

The next Saturday, they dressed up in their new clothes and went once again into town with Jackson. This time, Rosie didn't mind the stares and whispers.

Later, in the darkness of his room, he enfolded her in his arms and made slow love to her. She discovered the tenderness of him, the massive power of his giving and taking. She felt wanted again and needed, and shuddered at the flow of warmth within her. She had had many men before, but because Jackson was the most gentle of them all, she now knew what it meant to really have a man. Patiently, he helped her to climb with him and reach the summit of passion. Afterward, she slept in the protection of his mountainous frame.

Working in the fields wasn't as bad now for her. She had Jackson to fill her day thoughts and be with her at nights. She lived the days as they came, treasuring each, for she knew they soon would have to move to follow the crops. Leaving men and having them leave her had been woven into the pattern of her existence.

Finally, when the fields were picked clean, Big Ernest told them to get ready to move out. They were going on up Route 13 north to Pennsylvania. Big Ernest had contracted work on another farm.

In the early grayness of Sunday's dawn, she awakened Charlie. "We got to leave here now. Work's all done."

Charlie turned over sleepily, rubbing his eyes. "Why we gotta go, Mama? Always goin'. Why can't we stay here with Jackson?"

" *'Cause we got to go!*" she cried out angrily, not wanting to be reminded. "Git your things and put 'em in the blanket."

Outside, she could hear the movements of people preparing to leave: the talk, grumbling, cries of still-sleepy children. Big Ernest's shouts rose high above the other sounds. "Hustle it up. Crops gotta be picked. Git the lead outa your asses!"

Rosie knotted the blanket with their things and dragged it out the door. She was abandoning the house occupied by her and those before her and the ones who would come after her. It was now just another place in the backwash of her life.

The morning sky was sullen with clouds. She didn't want rain. Not while riding in that truck. Someone threw her bundle on the truck for her. Silently Charlie climbed up and took his place on the blanket, which he protected and which protected him. His life was now molded into acceptance. She found a place beside him near the rail.

Maybelline, planted precariously on her stool, looked at her quietly. "Kind of looks like rain, don't it, Rosie?"

Rosie nodded. She didn't want to talk now. She looked at the line of shanties and strained to see Jackson's place where she was leaving a piece of her behind. She looked down to see Charlie looking at it too.

"Everybody in!" Big Ernest called, climbing into the cabin of the truck, derby low over his eyes, cigar stationed in his mouth. The truck's motor started and stopped.

"Oh, Lordy, don't tell me the thing ain't goin' to move?" Someone giggled.

The motor coughed, sputtered, and finally turned over. Rosie stared out of her mind's eye into nothing.

"Ever' place we go, we leave a little sumpin' behind, honey," Maybelline said gently. "And we takes a little sumpin' with us."

Suddenly the truck jerked to a stop, toppling some of the standing bodies against each other. They saw Big Ernest getting out of the truck cursing. "Goddam crazy nigger! You want to git killed? Standin' there in the middle of the road like a dumb-assed fool!"

"There he is, honey." Maybelline chuckled, raising herself up laboriously to look over the side of the truck. "Standin' there big as a giant."

Rosie peered over the railing to see Jackson looming tall, naked to the waist, barefooted in the road, looking like he had just gotten out of bed.

"Rosie! Com'on down from there!"

"G'wan," Maybelline urged, laughing. "Can't you hear that man yellin' his fool head off for you?"

She felt immobile among the bodies around her, remembering other men in the past who had called her name, men with whom it always turned out to be the same. Why should she? Nothing was ever any different in this gray world of hers.

"Nigger," Big Ernest snarled at Jackson, "you keepin' my crew from gittin' on the road. Time counts in this biz'ness."

Jackson's eyes darted back at Big Ernest, then returned to the truck as swiftly as a fly could light and leave. "Rosie!"

Her words were not intended to be spoken aloud, but somehow they slipped out. "Ain't no use. Goin' to be just like with the rest of 'em."

"You don't know that, honey," Maybelline soothed, squeezing her hand. "Things *do* change sometimes for some of us—for the best."

"Mama." Charlie tugged pleadingly at her skirt. "Jackson wants you."

She moved slowly at first, feeling all eyes upon her. Then faster over the crates, boxes, and people, with Charlie trying to drag their blanket that she had forgotten. She jumped off the truck straight into the vise of his arms, the blanket landing at her feet.

"Just where in hell you think *you* goin'?" Big Ernest confronted her, hands on his hips. "Git back up there in that truck."

"Ain't gittin' back up there," Rosie shot back, anger rising within her. There he was giving orders, always giving orders. "Sick of trucks," she went on, letting her longtime pent-up frustrations cascade out at him. "All my life, I been doin' nothin' but gittin' on and off trucks. Ridin' and gittin' no place."

A flicker of surprise crossed Big Ernest's face. None of the crew had ever talked back to him like that before. Not even a man. Incensed, he threw her a mean look. "You my worker. 'Sides, you owe me money," he added triumphantly.

"Money?" Jackson repeated, stepping between them. "How much?"

"A hundred dollars."

Rosie frowned in bewilderment. How could crackers, baloney, sweetin' water for Charlie, beans, and kerosene for cooking come to that much? Especially when she had been repaying him.

"I don't believe you," Jackson said coldly.

"Oh? Well, look. See, it's right here in the book." Big Ernest extracted a greasy notepad from his pocket. "I 'member 'cause she's been owin' since we started out."

Jackson's face hardened, the scar quivering like something alive. "I knows all 'bout how you keeps them books, Big Ernest," he said warningly. "You keeps 'em so's you can have the people owin' all the time."

"Now you wait a minute, Jackson." Big Ernest edged forward menacingly. "You callin' me a cheat?"

Rosie watched Big Ernest's hands. He could be mighty quick with a knife or gun. She moved nearer to Jackson. Big Ernest had better not try anything.

"I'm goin' to give you fifty dollars," Jackson stated firmly, reaching into his wallet. "And that's all. Now git and leave us be."

The people in the truck watched in silence, straining to hear, to see, to know. Someone snickered, and a man coughed mockingly.

Big Ernest stared hard and long at Jackson, whose eyes locked unwaveringly with his. Finally he muttered low, "Damn crazy nigger." Spitting in the dust, he wheeled around to go back to the truck.

" 'Bye, Rosie!" Maybelline shouted over the roar of the motor. " 'Member what I tolt you!"

"One less body on this old heap takin' up space!" a voice called back teasingly.

"You didn't think I was goin' to let you go, did you?" Jackson grinned, holding her close. "You goin' to stay here with me. Be my wife."

Wife! Not woman. She felt a wave of giddiness. None in the past had offered her that. Tears streamed down her cheeks. Ashamed and happy, she smiled as the thought overtook her. "Why, I don't even know your whole name." Those who worked in the fields didn't bother with more than one name—Joe, Pete, Lucy. Wasn't no need. "A wife ought to know that."

"You goin' to be Mrs. Joe Louis Jackson."

"Hum-m-m, I likes that." Suddenly she laughed. "My, my, somebody sure knew what to name *you!*"

"Suits you fine too." He smiled, taking her hand and Charlie's. "Com'on, let's go home."

Hoodoo

●

(1988)

Connie Porter

In the closet under the stairs at 79-B All-Bright Court the albino girl lies and dreams. She dreams there is a door at the end of the sloping closet, a small door. Through the door there comes a black boy. He is small when he comes through the door, but once in the closet he is big and sits with his knees to his chest. The boy has come to bring the albino girl color. He has come with a small tin of watercolors.

He opens the tin and paints her soft, fat white body. The boy paints with short, quick strokes that feel like the licking of a cat's tongue. He mixes the colors and paints her black. He uses them all up to make her black.

The girl is allowed outside then. She can be seen. The wind blows on her and the sun shines. Its light does not hurt her eyes. She is loved. Her mother and father love her. The boy loves her, and she and the boy dance. There is something in the dance that summons rain. It falls like a punishment and washes the color away. The rain makes her ugly again, and she runs back inside. She hides in the closet, and the boy follows her. He tells her he will bring color again. He will go home for crayons.

"They won't wash away," he says.

And the boy makes himself small again and goes back through the small door. But before the black boy can come back, the colorless girl awakens.

She awakens to find the door at the end of the closet has disappeared, and she has been sleeping. She has been hiding and dreaming in the closet because she is not loved. Her parents hate her. This child is a punishment. She is a spell worked up by her grandmother.

•

"She working a spell," Zena's mother said when Zena told her of Greene's kindness.

"She never even talked to you before. Why should she start now?" her mother asked.

"Because I'm having Karo baby. It's her grandchild," Zena said.

"I'm not so sure that's not a spell, too."

"Oh, Mama," Zena said.

"Don't you 'Oh, Mama' me. You was too young to remember when Greene first come up here. That was the same summer them bats came."

It was back in 1964 that Greene and her six children came up from Florida. They just showed up at the All-Bright Court in a dusty yellow pickup. No one knew them, and not a week after they moved in, the bats came.

Out of twilight they appeared as shadows, first a few, then hundreds. But under the pale light of the new moon they became bats. An ashy boy led a group of boys on a hunt. With baseball bats and sticks they managed to kill a few bats they chased off from the main group. No one had ever seen anything like it before, and when one of the women mentioned it to Greene, she said, "I want to get my hands on one of them bats. I could use one of them bats."

And that was all it had taken. The next morning, "What she want with a bat?" was the question being asked by the women from one end of All-Bright Court to the other.

"And where them bats come from out of nowhere?"

"You reckon she called them?"

"And *what* she was going to do with a bat?"

"What you think! She into hoodoo."

"If they come back tonight, you tell your son to leave them bats alone, hear? He don't need to be catching no bats for her."

"And hey, girl, you see her teeth? They all gold. Looking in her mouth make you feel like you falling in a pit."

All of Greene's teeth were covered in gold, and none of the women knew how she could afford them. Despite the fact she wore a silver band, no husband had come north with her. But Greene had no trouble attracting men.

"Country nigger" is what the women said of Greene. Of the men they said, "Only a country nigger would think her mouth look good."

This did not stop some of their husbands from passing in and out of her back door. They came to explore the riches of her mouth. They left knowing the secrets beneath her tongue. These men left behind four more children, and Greene tied asafetida bags around their necks.

All her children wore the bags, including the ones who had come up from Florida. The bags and strings turned black and greasy and smelled of garlic, but Greene's children never seemed to get sick.

No one could ever remember them getting chicken pox, measles, whooping cough, mumps, not even a cold. Most children stayed away from them because the bags gave off such an odor, but Zena did not.

She came near Karo. She danced with him. She held his hand for pop-the-whip. It was Zena who convinced Karo to take the stinking, dirty bag from his neck back in 1966.

"It's stupid," Zena said. "It don't really protect you from germs. That's country. You know the school nurse say y'all don't get sick 'cause don't nobody come in breathing distance of y'all. Why don't you just take it off?" Zena asked.

And this and Zena's smile was all that it took for Karo to break the string and throw the bag away.

He told his mother the string had broken and he had lost the bag in a field. Greene said nothing. Karo was almost twelve, anyway. He didn't need it anymore. But when he went to sleep, Greene sat on the edge of his bed and raised the lids of his eyes to find Zena dancing in the back of them.

Greene never disliked Zena. She was never nasty to her, but she was not nice either. Sometimes Zena would be there in Greene's house, just like air, just like she had always been there. And Greene never spoke to her. How could you speak to air?

Greene had ten children and other women's husbands to look after. She had no time to take notice of Zena. She was tired much of the time. But a look of tiredness in her eyes was not that. It was the evil eye. Greene caused the sewers to back up more often. She caused the winters to be harsher, and the rivers to rise higher in spring. She could cause ringworms and mange to appear on children's scalps. She could even make husbands cleave not unto their wives, but come to her seeking treasure. Greene was accused of being a country nigger who had not left her ways behind. Her accusers knew because they were country niggers, too.

They were all from the South, and most were from the country. They claimed Birmingham, Fayetteville, Jacksonville, Jackson, New Orleans. But they were from Plain Dealing, Zenith, Goshen, Acme, Gopher. They came from specks on the map. They knew the country and its ways well.

They had seen spells cast, fields dry up, floods come, moles cast into women's wombs. And then there were the bats.

The bats had come with Greene's arrival. They had only come that one night, and they had never come back. That could not be ignored.

Zena's mother could not keep her away from Karo, so she warned her about Greene.

"You stay from out her house, you hear?" her mother said. "And don't be eating nothing she cook. I mean nothing. Ain't no telling what she might cook up in it."

Zena and Karo married in 1972. She was pregnant, and though Karo was only eighteen, Greene signed for him to marry. He went off and joined the Navy.

And it was in Zena's fifth month that she became sick. Her stomach was upset for a week and her urine turned dark. There was a milkiness, a whiteness that passed across her irises. It passed across slowly, like a thin cloud against a windless night sky. After two days of sickness Zena admitted to her mother she had eaten at Greene's. She had some potato salad and collards.

"She working a spell. I'm telling you, she working something on the baby. She done something to mark the baby," Zena's mother said.

"That's crazy, Mama. That's just a bunch of country talk."

But Zena never felt right after her dinner at Greene's. She was always tired, and there was an uneasiness inside her, a cold whiteness that moved from Zena's eyes and into her womb. The baby seemed to pick it up. It made the baby still.

The doctor at the clinic said there was nothing wrong, but the birth of the baby proved the doctor wrong.

She was a fat white baby with white hair and pink lips. All of the color had been washed from her.

Karo had been out to sea when the baby was born, and when he came home and saw her, he did not want to even touch her. He refused to hold her. The child was ugly, and Zena kept her hidden in the house. Both of their families shunned the child, but Greene had come over to see her once.

She came to bring an asafetida bag for the child. She tied it around the baby's neck and told Zena, "I knows what these people be saying about me, but it ain't true. I ain't no conjure woman. But how can you tell people that? People believes what they want to." That was the most Greene had ever said to her, and before she left Zena's house, she repeated, "People believes what they want to."

Zena took the bag from the baby's neck and threw it away, and she kept the baby hidden.

The paperboy has managed to see this all-white child, though. He has seen her far off in the darkness of the afternoon house, her milky blue eyes staring at him. She has never come to the door, but only sat and stared as he opened the door and placed the paper on the floor.

After her nap today, after the colorless girl awakens to find the door at the end of the closet has disappeared, she goes and sits in the cool darkness of the living room. And when she hears the paperboy coming up the stairs of the porch, she comes to the door.

He opens the screen door and stares at the child. He stares at her white skin, her woolly white hair, her full pink lips. He smiles at her and hands her the paper.

Though he has not come from the closet, she thinks he is the black boy from her dream. Her milky blue eyes move rapidly as she tries to focus on the boy. But the brightness of the afternoon sun takes her vision away, and the boy becomes a shadow.

"Do you have the crayons?"

The boy is confused, and before he can answer, the girl's mother is there. She is floating above her, just like air. And she strikes the child. She knocks the child to the floor. The sheets of paper spill over her, and the door slams.

"I told you to stay away from the door. No one want to see you. Don't nobody come here to see you," her mother says.

It seems as though talking to this child hurts, as if with each word she is spitting sand.

The boy sees the girl get up, and her mother's hand printed pink across her face. Before he leaves the porch, he sees the girl run from the door and disappear into the closet under the stairs.

Willie Bea and Jaybird

———————————————————•———————————————————

(1991)

Tina McElroy Ansa

When Willie Bea first saw Jaybird in The Place, she couldn't help herself. She wanted him so bad she sucked in her bottom lip, cracked with the cold, then she ran her tongue so slowly over her top lip that she could taste the red Maybelline lipstick she had put on hours before. He looked like something that would be good to eat, like peach cobbler or a hot piece of buttered cornbread.

She had just entered the bar clutching her black purse under her arm and smiling to try to make herself look attractive among the six o'clock crowd of drinkers and dancers and socializers, every one of them glad to be done with work for the day. He was there at the end of the bar in his golden Schlitz uniform sharing a quart of Miller High Life beer with a buddy. Willie Bea noticed right away how he leaned his long frame clear across the bar, bent at the waist, his elbows resting easily on the Formica counter. There didn't seem to be a tense bone in his lean, efficient body.

He look like he could go anywhere in the world, Willie Bea thought as she followed her big-butt friend Patricia as she weaved her way to a nearby table already jammed with four of her friends, two men, two women. "If somebody put him in a white jacket and a flower in his buttonhole, he could pass for an actor in a Technicolor movie."

As the jukebox started up again, playing a driving Sam and Dave number, he looked around the bar, picked up his glass of beer, and headed toward her table with his chin held high over the other patrons. When he smoothly pulled up a chair to her table and straddled it backwards, Willie Bea crossed her stick legs and pinched her friend Pat's thigh under the table to give her some Sen-Sen for her breath.

"Hey, Little Mama, you got time for a tired working man?"

She had to remember to wipe the uncomfortable moisture from the corners of her mouth with her fingertips before she could respond to him.

She still felt that way, four years after they had started going together, when she looked at him.

Nothing gave her more pleasure than to be asked her marital status with Jaybird around.

"Willie Bea, girl, where you been keeping yourself?" some big-mouthed woman would shout at her over the din of the jukebox at The Place. "I ain't seen you in a month of Sundays. You still living with your aunt, ain't you?" This last expectantly with pity.

Willie Bea would roll her shoulders and dip her ears from side to side a couple of times in feigned modesty.

"Naw, girl, I *been* moved out of my aunt's," Willie Bea would answer. "I'm married now. I live with my . . . *husband*."

The old horse's big mouth would fall open, then close, then open as if she were having trouble chewing this information.

"Husband? Married??!!"

"Uh-huh. That's my husband over there by the jukebox. Naw, not him. My Jay is the tall light-skinned one, the one with the head full of curly hair."

Willie Bea never even bothered to look at her inquisitor when she pointed out Jay. She could hear the effect the weight of the revelation had had on the woman. And Willie Bea only glanced smugly at the old cow as she raced around the bar nearly knocking over a chair to ask her friends and companions why no one told her that skinny little shiny-faced Willie Bea had a man.

"I thought she was sitting there mighty sassy-looking."

Even Willie Bea would have admitted it. Most days, she did feel sassy, and it was Jaybird who made her so. He burst into the bathroom while she was in the bathtub and pretended to take pictures of her with an imaginary camera. He teased her about flirting with Mr. Maurice, who owned the store on the corner near their boardinghouse, when the merchant sliced her baloney especially thin, the way she liked it.

Now, she really thought she was cute, with her little square monkey face and eager-to-please grin, a cheap jet-black Prince Valiant wig set on the top of her head like a wool cap with her short hair plaited underneath and a pair of black eyeglasses so thick that her eyes looked as if they were in fish bowls.

Jaybird had done that to her. He even called her "fine," an appellation

that actually brought tears to her eyes, made huge and outlandish by the
Coke-bottle-thick glasses.

"Fine." It was the one thing in life Willie Bea longed to be. She had
no shape to speak of. She was just five feet tall and weighed about ninety
pounds. But she did her best to throw that thing even though she had
very little to throw.

"If I had me a big old butt like you, Pat," she would say to her friend,
"ya'll couldn't stand me."

The pitiful little knot of an ass that she had was her sorrow, especially
after noticing from Jaybird's gaze that he appreciated a full ass. His favorite
seemed to be the big heart-shaped ones that started real low and hung
and swayed like a bustle when the woman walked. Many mornings, Jay
lay in bed watching Bea move around the room getting dressed and
thought, Her behind ain't no bigger than my fist. But he didn't dare say
anything, even as a joke. He knew it would break her heart.

But since she knew she didn't have a big ass, she did what she had
done since she was a child when someone told her what she was lacking:
She pretended she did and acted as if her ass was the prize one in town.
The one men in juke joints talked about.

Wherever she went—to the market, to work cleaning houses, to The
Place, downtown to shop—she dressed as if she had that ass to show off.

She wore tight little straight skirts that she made herself on her landlady's
sewing machine. Skirts of cotton or wool or taffeta no wider than twelve
inches across. Not that wide, really, because she wanted the skirt to "cup,"
if possible, under the pones of her behind and to wrinkle across her crotch
in front. Using less than a yard of material and a Simplicity quickie pattern
she had bought years before and worked away to tatters, she took no more
than an hour to produce one of her miniature skirts.

On Sundays, when the house was empty of other boarders or quiet
from their sleep, Willie Bea used her landlady's sewing machine that she
kept in the parlor. The steady growl of the old foot-pedal-run Singer
disturbed no one. In fact, on those Sundays she and Jaybird went out and
she did no sewing, the other tenants of the large white wooden house felt
an unidentified longing and found themselves on the verge of complaining
about the silence.

Willie Bea looked on the ancient sewing machine, kept in mint condition by the genial landlady who always wore plaid housedresses and her
thin crimpy red hair in six skinny braids, as a blessing. She didn't mind
that the machine was a foot-propelled model rather than an electric one.
It never occurred to her to expect anything as extravagant as that. For

her, the old machine was a step up from the tedious hand-sewing that she had learned and relied on as a child. With the waistbands neatly attached and the short zippers eased into place by machine, her skirts had a finished look that would have taken her all night to accomplish by hand.

Many times, she felt herself rocking gently to the rhythm she set with her bare feet on the cold iron treadle to ease a crick in her stiff back before she realized that she had been at the job nonstop all afternoon. Just using the machine made her happy, made her think of men watching her at the bus stops in her new tight skirt and later, maybe, these same men letting some sly comment drop in front of Jaybird about her shore looking good.

She imagined Jaybird jumping in the men's faces, half angry, half proud, to let them know that was his *wife* they were talking about. Just thinking of Jaybird saying "my wife" made her almost as happy as her being able to say "my husband."

She loved to go over in her head how it had come to pass, their marriage. They had been living together in one room of the boardinghouse at the top of Pleasant Hill for nearly three years, with him seeming to take for granted that they would be together for eternity and with her hardly daring to believe that he really wanted her, afraid to ask him why he picked her to love.

As with most of his decisions, movements, he surprised her.

One evening in August, he walked into their room and said, "Let's get married." As if the idea had just come to him, his and original. She responded in kind.

"Married? Married, Jay?" she said, pretending to roll the idea around in her head awhile. Then, "Okay, if you want."

It was her heart's desire, the play-pretty of her dreams, being this man's wife.

She bought stiff white lace from Newberry's department store to make a loose cropped sleeveless overblouse and a yard of white polished cotton and sewed a tight straight skirt for the ceremony at the courthouse.

When they returned to their room for the honeymoon, Willie Bea thought as she watched him take off his wedding suit that no other man could be so handsome, so charming, so full of self-assured cockiness . . . and still love her.

He was tall and slender in that way that made her know that he would be lean all his life, never going sway-backed and to fat around his middle like a pregnant woman. He was lithe and strong from lifting cases and kegs of Schlitz beer all day long, graceful from leaping on and off the running board of the moving delivery truck as it made its rounds of bars and stores.

Once when he had not seen her, Willie Bea had spied him hanging fearlessly off the back of the beer truck like a prince, face directly into the wind, his eyes blinking back the wind tears, a vacant look on his face. His head full of curly hair quivering in the wind. The setting sunlight gleamed off the chrome and steel of the truck, giving a golden-orange color to the aura that Willie Bea felt surrounded him all the time.

Overcome by the sight, Willie Bea had had to turn away into an empty doorway to silently weep over the beauty of her Jaybird.

Jaybird even made love the way she knew this man would—sweet and demanding. When her friend Pat complained about her own man's harsh, unfeeling fucking, Willie Bea joined in and talked about men like dogs. But first, in her own mind, she placed Jaybird outside the dog pack.

"Girl, just thank your lucky stars that you ain't hooked up with a man like Henry," Pat told her. "Although God knows they all alike. You may as well put 'em all in a croker sack and pick one out. They all the same. One just as good as the other. Just take your pick."

"Uh-huh, girl, you know you telling the truth," Willie Bea would answer.

"Why, that old dog of mine will just wake any time of the night and go to grabbing me and sticking his hand up my nightdress. He don't say nothing, just grunt. He just goes and do his business. I could be anything, a sack of flour, that chair you sitting on."

"What you be doing?" Willie Bea asked in her soft singsong voice, even though she already knew because Pat always complained about the same thing. But she asked because she and Pat had grown up together, she had been Pat's friend longer than anyone outside of her family. And Willie Bea knew what a friend was for.

"Shoot, sometimes I just lay there like I *am* a sack of flour. I thought that would make him see I wasn't getting nothing out of his humping. Then I saw it didn't make no difference to him whether I was having a good time or not. So, now, sometimes I push him off me just before he come. That makes him real mad. Or I tell him I got my period.

"Some nights, we just lay there jostling each other like little children jostling over a ball. I won't turn over or open up my legs and he won't stop tugging on me."

"Girl, both of ya'll crazy. That way, don't neither of you get a piece. That's too hard," Willie Bea said sincerely.

"Shoot, girl, some nights we tussle all night." Pat gave a hot dry laugh.

"Henry thinks too much of hisself to fight me for it, really hit me upside my head or yell and scream, 'cause with those little paper-sheer walls, everybody next door would know our business. So while we fighting, it's real quiet except for some grunts and the bed squeaking."

Then, she laughed again.

"I guess that's all you'd be hearing anyway."

Willie Bea tried to laugh in acknowledgment. Once Pat told her, "Shoot, girl, I've gotten to liking the scuffling we do in bed better than I ever liked the screwing."

That made Willie Bea feel cold all over.

"It's like it make it more important," Pat continued. "Something worth fighting for. Some nights when he just reach for me like that, it's like he calling me out my name. And I turn over ready to fight.

"I would get somebody else, but they all the same, you may as well pick one from the sack as another. But look at you, Bea. You just agreeing to be nice. You don't believe that, do you?"

"I didn't say nothing," Willie Bea would rush to say. "I believe what you say about you and Henry. I believe you."

"That ain't what I mean and you know it. I'm talking about mens period."

"I know what you saying about men."

"Yeah, but you don't think they all alike, do you?" Pat asked.

Willie Bea would start dipping her head from side to side and grinning her sheepish closed-mouth grin.

"Go on and admit it, girl," Pat would prod.

After a moment, Willie Bea would admit it. "I don't know why he love me so good."

Then, Pat would sigh and urge her friend to tell her how sweet Jay was to her . . . in bed, at the table, after work. Especially in bed.

Willie Bea balked at first, each time the subject came up. But she always gave in, too. She was just dying to talk about Jaybird.

Most women she knew held the same beliefs that Pat did about men. They sure as hell didn't want to hear about her and the bliss her man brought her. She had found they may want to hear about "you can't do with him and can't do without him" or how bad he treat you and you still can't let him go. All of that. But don't be coming around them with those thick windowpane eyes of hers all bright and enlarged with stories of happiness and fulfillment. Those stories cut her other girlfriends and their lives to the quick.

But her friend Pat, big-butt Pat, urged Bea to share her stories with her. Sometimes, these reminiscences made Pat smile and glow as if she were there in Willie Bea's place. But sometimes they left her morose.

Willie Bea, noticing this at first, began leaving out details that she thought made Pat's love pale in comparison. But Pat, alert to nuances in the tales, caught on and insisted that Willie Bea never leave stuff out again if she was going to tell it.

And Willie Bea, eager to tell it all, felt as if she were pleasing her friend as much as herself. So she continued telling stories of love and dipping her ear down toward her shoulder in a gay little shy gesture.

"When Jaybird and me doing it, he has this little grufflike voice he uses when he talks to me."

"Talk to you? What ya'll be doing, screwing or talking?" Pat would interrupt, but not seriously.

"He says things like, 'Is that all? That ain't all. I want it all. Uh-huh.' "

At first, Willie Bea was embarrassed disclosing these secrets of her and Jaybird's passionate and tender lovemaking. But Pat seemed so enthralled by her stories that Willie Bea finally stopped fighting it and gave herself over to the joy of recounting how Jaybird loved her.

Pat never told Willie Bea that many of the women at The Place talked under their breaths when Jaybird and Willie Bea came in together.

"He may sleep in the same bed with her, but I heard he put an ironing board between 'em first," some said.

"He can't really want that little old black gal. He just like her worshiping the ground he walk on," another would add.

Pat knew Willie Bea would have tried to kill whoever said such things. But even Pat found it hard to believe sometimes that her little friend had attracted Jaybird.

Mornings, Pat watched Willie Bea step off the city bus they both took to their jobs, her too-pale dime-store stockings shining in the early light, her narrow shoulders rotating like bicycle pedals in the direction opposite the one she sent her snake hips inside her straight skirt, and thought how changed her friend was by the love of Jaybird. Now, that walk is something new, Pat thought, as the bus pulled away from the curb.

Willie Bea, who lived two blocks above Pat, got on the bus first, then alit first when she got near the white woman's house she cleaned five days a week. Pat stayed on until the bus reached downtown near the box factory where she worked. They rode to and from work together nearly every day.

So, one evening when Pat wasn't on the bus when she got on returning home, Willie Bea began to worry about her. All that one of Pat's co-workers on the bus said when Willie Bea asked was, "She left work early."

I wonder if she's sick, Willie Bea thought.

She was still thinking about her friend when the bus began making its climb up Pleasant Hill. I better stop and see 'bout her, Willie Bea thought.

She was still standing with her hand near the signal wire when the bus slowed to a stop in front of the cinder-block duplex where Pat lived, and Willie Bea saw the gold of a Schlitz beer uniform slip back inside the dusty screen door of her friend's house.

The bus driver paused a good while with the bus door open waiting for Willie Bea to leave. Then he finally hollered toward the back of the bus, "You getting off or not?"

Willie Bea turned around to the driver's back and tried to smile as she took her regular seat again. When she reached her boardinghouse, she was anxious to see Jaybird and ask him who the new man was working on the beer truck. But he wasn't home.

She sat up alone on the bed in the boardinghouse room long after it grew dark.

Willie Bea didn't know how long she had been asleep when she heard the rusty doorknob turn and felt a sliver of light from the hall fall across her face. Jaybird almost never stayed out late without her or telling her beforehand.

"You okay, Jay?" she asked sleepily.

He only grunted and rubbed her back softly. "Go back to sleep, Bea," he said. "I'm coming to bed now."

Willie Bea lay waiting for Jaybird to say something more, to say where he had been, to say he saw her friend Pat that day. But he said nothing.

And when he did finally slip into bed, it felt as if an ironing board was between them.

Song of Roland

●

(1993)

Jamaica Kincaid

His mouth was like an island in the sea that was his face; I am sure he had ears and nose and eyes and all the rest, but I could see only his mouth, which I knew could do all the things that a mouth usually does, such as eat food, purse in approval or disapproval, smile, twist in thought; inside were his teeth and behind them was his tongue. Why did I see him that way, how did I come to see him that way? It was a mystery to me that he had been alive all along and that I had not known of his existence and I was perfectly fine—I went to sleep at night and I could wake up in the morning and greet the day with indifference if it suited me, I could comb my hair and scratch myself and I was still perfectly fine—and he was alive, sometimes living in a house next to mine, some-times living in a house far away, and his existence was ordinary and perfect and parallel to mine, but I did not know of it, even though sometimes he was close enough to me for me to notice that he smelt of cargo he had been unloading; he was a stevedore.

His mouth really did look like an island, lying in a twig-brown sea, stretching out from east to west, widest near the center, with tiny, sharp creases, its color a shade lighter than that of the twig-brown sea in which it lay, the place where the two lips met disappearing into the pinkest of pinks, and even though I must have held his mouth in mine a thousand times, it was always new to me. He must have smiled at me, though I don't really know, but I don't like to think that I would love someone who hadn't first smiled at me. It had been raining, a heavy downpour, and I took shelter under the gallery of a dry-goods store along with some other people. The rain was an inconvenience, for it was not necessary;

there had already been too much of it, and it was no longer only outside, overflowing in the gutters, but inside also, roofs were leaking and then falling in. I was standing under the gallery and had sunk deep within myself, enjoying completely the despair I felt at being myself. I was wearing a dress; I had combed my hair that morning; I had washed myself that morning. I was looking at nothing in particular when I saw his mouth. He was speaking to someone else, but he was looking at me. The someone else he was speaking to was a woman. His mouth then was not like an island at rest in a sea but like a small patch of ground viewed from high above and set in motion by a force not readily seen.

When he saw me looking at him, he opened his mouth wider, and that must have been the smile. I saw then that he had a large gap between his two front teeth, which probably meant that he could not be trusted, but I did not care. My dress was damp, my shoes were wet, my hair was wet, my skin was cold, all around me were people standing in small amounts of water and mud, shivering, but I started to perspire from an effort I wasn't aware I was making; I started to perspire because I felt hot, and I started to perspire because I felt happy. I wore my hair then in two plaits and the ends of them rested just below my collarbone; all the moisture in my hair collected and ran down my two plaits, as if they were two gutters, and the water seeped through my dress just below the collarbone and continued to run down my chest, only stopping at the place where the tips of my breasts met the fabric, revealing, plain as a new print, my nipples. He was looking at me and talking to someone else, and his mouth grew wide and narrow, small and large, and I wanted him to notice me, but there was so much noise: all the people standing in the gallery, sheltering themselves from the strong rain, had something they wanted to say, something not about the weather (that was by now beyond comment) but about their lives, their disappointments most likely, for joy is so short-lived there isn't enough time to dwell on its occurrence. The noise, which started as a hum, grew to a loud din, and the loud din had an unpleasant taste of metal and vinegar, but I knew his mouth could take it away if only I could get to it; so I called out my own name, and I knew he heard me immediately, but he wouldn't stop speaking to the woman he was talking to, so I had to call out my name again and again until he stopped, and by that time my name was like a chain around him, as the sight of his mouth was like a chain around me. And when our eyes met, we laughed, because we were happy, but it was frightening, for that gaze asked everything: who would betray whom, who would be captive, who would be captor, who would give and who would take, what would I do. And when our eyes met and we laughed at the same time, I said, "I love you, I love you," and he said, "I know." He did not say it out of vanity, he did not say it out of conceit, he only said it because it was true.

His name was Roland. He was not a hero, he did not even have a country; he was from an island, a small island that was between a sea and an ocean, and a small island is not a country. And he did not have a history; he was a small event in somebody else's history, but he was a man. I could see him better than he could see himself, and that was because he was who he was and I was myself but also because I was taller than he was. He was unpolished, but he carried himself as if he were precious. His hands were large and thick, and for no reason that I could see he would spread them out in front of him and they looked as if they were the missing parts from a powerful piece of machinery; his legs were straight from hip to knee and then from the knee they bent at an angle as if he had been at sea too long or had never learnt to walk properly to begin with. The hair on his legs was tightly curled as if the hairs were pieces of thread rolled between the thumb and the forefinger in preparation for sewing, and so was the hair on his arms, the hair in his underarms, and the hair on his chest; the hair in those places was black and grew sparsely; the hair on his head and the hair between his legs was black and tightly curled also, but it grew in such abundance that it was impossible for me to move my hands through it. Sitting, standing, walking, or lying down, he carried himself as if he were something precious, but not out of vanity, for it was true, he was something precious; yet when he was lying on top of me he looked down at me as if I were the only woman in the world, the only woman he had ever looked at in that way—but that was not true, a man only does that when it is not true. When he first lay on top of me I was so ashamed of how much pleasure I felt that I bit my bottom lip hard—but I did not bleed, not from biting my lip, not then. His skin was smooth and warm in places I had not kissed him; in the places I had kissed him his skin was cold and coarse, and the pores were open and raised.

Did the world become a beautiful place? The rainy season eventually went away, the sunny season came, and it was too hot; the riverbed grew dry, the mouth of the river became shallow, the heat eventually became as wearying as the rain, and I would have wished it away if I had not become occupied with this other sensation, a sensation I had no single word for. I could feel myself full of happiness, but it was a kind of happiness I had never experienced before, and my happiness would spill out of me and run all the way down a long, long road and then the road would come to an end and I would feel empty and sad, for what could come after this? How would it end?

Not everything has an end, even though the beginning changes. The first time we were in a bed together we were lying on a thin board that was covered with old cloth, and this small detail, evidence of our poverty—people in our position, a stevedore and a doctor's servant, could not afford a proper mattress—was a major contribution to my satisfaction, for it allowed me to brace myself and match him breath for breath. But how can it be that a man who can carry large sacks filled with sugar or bales of cotton on his back from dawn to dusk exhausts himself within five minutes inside a woman? I did not then and I do not now know the answer to that. He kissed me. He fell asleep. I bathed my face then between his legs; he smelt of curry and onions, for those were the things he had been unloading all day; other times when I bathed my face between his legs—for I did it often, I liked doing it—he would smell of sugar, or flour, or the large, cheap bolts of cotton from which he would steal a few yards to give me to make a dress.

What is the everyday? What is the ordinary? One day, as I was walking toward the government dispensary to collect some supplies—one of my duties as a servant to a man who was in love with me beyond anything he could help and so had long since stopped trying, a man I ignored except when I wanted him to please me—I met Roland's wife, face to face, for the first time. She stood in front of me like a sentry—stern, dignified, guarding the noble idea, if not noble ideal, that was her husband. She did not block the sun, it was shining on my right; on my left was a large black cloud; it was raining way in the distance; there was no rainbow on the horizon. We stood on the narrow strip of concrete that was the sidewalk. One section of a wooden fence that was supposed to shield a yard from passersby on the street bulged out and was broken, and a few tugs from any careless party would end its usefulness; in that yard a primrose bush bloomed unnaturally, its leaves too large, its flowers showy, and weeds were everywhere, they had prospered in all the wet. We were not alone. A man walked past us with a cutlass in his knapsack and a mistreated dog two steps behind him; a woman walked by with a large basket of food on her head; some children were walking home from school, and they were not walking together; a man was leaning out a window, spitting, he used snuff. I was wearing a pair of modestly high heels, red, not a color to wear to work in the middle of the day, but that was just the way I had been feeling, red with a passion, like that hibiscus that was growing under the window of the man who kept spitting from the snuff. And Roland's wife called me a whore, a slut, a pig, a snake, a viper, a rat, a lowlife, a parasite, and an evil woman. I could see that her mouth formed a familiar hug around these words—poor thing, she had been used to saying them. I was not surprised. I could not have loved Roland the way I did if he had not loved other women. And I was not surprised; I had noticed immediately the space between his teeth. I was not surprised that she knew about me; a man cannot keep a secret, a man always wants all the women he knows to know each other.

I believe I said this: "I love Roland; when he is with me I want him to love me; when he is not with me I think of him loving me. I do not love you. I love Roland." This is what I wanted to say, and this is what I believe I said. She slapped me across the face; her hand was wide and thick like an oar; she, too, was used to doing hard work. Her hand met the side of my face: my jawbone, the skin below my eye and under my chin, a small portion of my nose, the lobe of my ear. I was then a young woman in my early twenties, my skin was supple, smooth, the pores invisible to the naked eye. It was completely without bitterness that I thought as I looked at her face, a face I had so little interest in that it would tire me to describe it, Why is the state of marriage so desirable that all women are afraid to be caught outside it? And why does this woman, who has never seen me before, to whom I have never made any promise, to whom I owe nothing, hate me so much? She expected me to return her blow but, instead, I said, again completely without bitterness, "I consider it beneath me to fight over a man."

I was wearing a dress of light-blue Irish linen. I could not afford to buy such material, because it came from a real country, not a false country like mine; a shipment of this material in blue, in pink, in lime green, and in beige had come from Ireland, I suppose, and Roland had given me yards of each shade from the bolts. I was wearing my blue Irish-linen dress that day, and it was demure enough—a pleated skirt that ended quite beneath my knees, a belt at my waist, sleeves that buttoned at my wrists, a high neckline that covered my collarbone—but underneath my dress I wore absolutely nothing, no undergarments of any kind, only my stockings, given to me by Roland and taken from yet another shipment of dry goods, each one held up by two pieces of elastic that I had sewn together to make a garter. My declaration of what I considered beneath me must have enraged Roland's wife, for she grabbed my blue dress at the collar and gave it a huge tug; it rent in two from my neck to my waist. My breasts lay softly on my chest, like two small pieces of unrisen dough, unmoved by the anger of this woman; not so by the touch of her husband's mouth, for he would remove my dress, by first patiently undoing all the buttons and then pulling down the bodice, and then he would take one breast in his mouth, and it would grow to a size much bigger than his mouth could hold, and he would let it go and turn to the other one; the saliva evaporating from the skin on that breast was an altogether different sensation from the sensation of my other breast in his mouth, and I would divide myself in two, for I could not decide which sensation I wanted to take dominance over the other. For an hour he would kiss me in this way and then exhaust himself on top of me in five minutes. I loved him so. In the dark I couldn't see him clearly, only an outline, a solid shadow; when I saw him in the daytime he was fully dressed. His wife, as she rent my dress, a dress made of material she knew very well, for she had a dress made of the same material, told me his history: it was not a long one, it was not a sad one, no one had died in it, no land had been laid waste, no birthright had been stolen; she had a list, and it was full of names, but they were not the names of countries.

What was the color of her wedding day? When she first saw him was she overwhelmed with desire? The impulse to possess is alive in every heart, and some people choose vast plains, some people choose high mountains, some people choose wide seas, and some people choose husbands; I chose to possess myself. I resembled a tree, a tall tree with long, strong branches; I looked delicate, but any man I held in my arms knew that I was strong; my hair was long and thick and deeply waved naturally, and I wore it braided and pinned up, because when I wore it loosely around my shoulders it caused excitement in other people—some of them men, some of them women, some of them it pleased, some of them it did not. The way I walked depended on who I thought would see me and what effect I wanted my walk to have on them. My face was beautiful, I found it so.

And yet I was standing before a woman who found herself unable to keep her life's booty in its protective sack, a woman whose voice no longer came from her throat but from deep within her stomach, a woman whose hatred was misplaced. I looked down at our feet, hers and mine, and I expected to see my short life flash before me; instead, I saw that her feet were without shoes. She did have a pair of shoes, though, which I had seen: they were white, they were plain, a round toe and flat laces, they took shoe polish well, she wore them only on Sundays and to church. I had many pairs of shoes, in colors meant to attract attention and dazzle the eye; they were uncomfortable, I wore them every day, I never went to church at all.

My strong arms reached around to caress Roland, who was lying on my back naked; I was naked also. I knew his wife's name, but I did not say it; he knew his wife's name, too, but he did not say it. I did not know the long list of names that were not countries that his wife had committed to memory. He himself did not know the long list of names; he had not committed this list to memory. This was not from deceit, and it was not from carelessness. He was someone so used to a large fortune that he took it for granted; he did not have a bankbook, he did not have a ledger, he had a fortune—but still he had not lost interest in acquiring more. Feeling my womb contract, I crossed the room, still naked; small drops of blood spilt from inside me, evidence of my refusal to accept his silent offering. And Roland looked at me, his face expressing confusion. Why did I not bear his children? He could feel the times that I was fertile, and yet each month blood flowed away from me, and each month I expressed confidence at its imminent arrival and departure, and always I was overjoyed at the accuracy of my prediction. When I saw him like that, on his face a look that was a mixture—confusion, dumbfoundedness, defeat—I felt much sorrow for him, for his life was reduced to a list of names that were not countries, and to the number of times he brought the monthly flow of blood to a halt; his life was reduced to women, some of them beautiful, wearing dresses made from yards of cloth he had surreptitiously removed from the bowels of the ships where he worked as a stevedore.

At that time I loved him beyond words; I loved him when he was standing in front of me and I loved him when he was out of my sight. I was still a young woman. No small impressions, the size of a child's forefinger, had yet appeared on the soft parts of my body; my legs were long and hard, as if they had been made to take me a long distance; my arms were long and strong, as if prepared for carrying heavy loads; I was not beautiful, but if I could have been in love with myself I would have been. I was in love with Roland. He was a man. But who was he really? He did not sail the seas, he did not cross the oceans, he only worked in the bottom of vessels that had done so; no mountains were named for him, no valleys, no nothing. But still he was a man, and he wanted something beyond ordinary satisfaction—beyond one wife, one love, and one room with walls made of mud and roof of cane leaves, beyond the small plot of land where the same trees bear the same fruit year following year—for it would all end only in death, for though no history yet written had embraced him, though he could not identify the small uprisings within himself, though he would deny the small uprisings within himself, a strange calm would sometimes come over him, a cold stillness, and since he could find no words for it, he was momentarily blinded with shame.

One night Roland and I were sitting on the steps of the jetty, our backs facing the small world we were from, the world of sharp, dangerous curves in the road, of steep mountains of recent volcanic formations covered in a green so humble no one had ever longed for them, of three hundred and sixty-five small streams that would never meet up to form a majestic roar, of clouds that were nothing but large vessels holding endless days of water, of people who had never been regarded as people at all; we looked into the night, its blackness did not come as a surprise, a moon full of dead white light travelled across the surface of a glittering black sky; I was wearing a dress made from another piece of cloth he had given me, another piece of cloth taken from the bowels of a ship without permission, and there was a false pocket in the skirt, a pocket that did not have a bottom, and Roland placed his hand inside the pocket, reaching all the way down to touch inside of me; I looked at his face, his mouth I could see and it stretched across his face like an island and like an island, too, it held secrets and was dangerous and could swallow things whole that were much larger than itself; I looked out toward the horizon, which I could not see but knew was there all the same, and this was also true of the end of my love for Roland.

Notes

1. Anna Julia Cooper, *A Voice from the South* (New York: Oxford University Press, 1988), p. 121.
2. There are currently three anthologies of short stories by African-American women available: Elizabeth Ammons, ed., *Short Fiction by Black Women, 1900–1920* (New York: Oxford University Press, 1991); Marcy Knopf, ed., *The Sleeper Wakes, Harlem Renaissance Stories by Women* (New Brunswick, N.J.: Rutgers University Press, 1993); and Asha Kanwar, ed., *The Unforgetting Heart: An Anthology of Short Stories by African American Women* (1859–1993) (San Francisco: Aunt Lute Books, 1993). While these books are all well done, the first two look at stories from a given time period, and the third discusses the work of black women writers in relation to the plight of the untouchable women in India.
3. This method of critical analysis attempts to look at these stories on the basis of what a community of readers contemporaneous with the author would have been able to understand. See Alex Preminger et al., *The New Princeton Encyclopedia of Poetry and Poetics* (Princeton, N.J.: Princeton University Press, 1993), p. 254. See also Claudia Tate, *Domestic Allegories of Political Desire* (New York: Oxford University Press, 1992), p. 232, which describes the "first readers" of post-Reconstruction black women novelists (who published between 1877 and 1915) as a "very small number of academically trained professionals, for example ministers, doctors and teachers, as well as tradesmen and tradeswomen such as caterers, seamstresses, tailors, hairdressers, stenographers, typists and cobblers," who made up the black middle and working class of that period. In later historical periods, the black male and female readership becomes increasingly more educated, with female college graduates from black schools finally outnumbering men in the 1940s.
4. Ammons, *Short Fiction by Black Women*, p. 12.
5. T. O. Beachcroft, *The Modest Art* (London: Oxford University Press, 1968), p. 11.
6. Ibid., p. 15.
7. Edgar Allan Poe, "Review of Twice Told Tales," in Nathaniel Hawthorne, *The Complete Short Stories* (New York: Doubleday, 1959), p. 9.
8. Thomas A. Gullason, "The Short Story: An Underrated Art," in *Short Story Theories*, ed. Charles E. May (Ohio: Ohio University Press, 1976), p. 29.

9. Nadine Gordimer, "The Flash of Fireflies," in May, *Short Story Theories*, p. 180.
10. Interview with George Kent in Roseann P. Bell, Bettye J. Parker, and Beverly Guy-Sheftall, eds., *Sturdy Black Bridges: Visions of Black Women in Literature* (New York: Anchor-Doubleday, 1979), p. 218.
11. The story is a murder mystery involving two brothers, Stephen and Jesse Boorn, who are convicted and sentenced to hang for the murder of Russell Colvin, a fellow Manchester, Vermont, townsman. Colvin had disappeared seven years before the arrest and conviction of the brothers. The Boorns' conviction is based on false testimony: Jesse's confession to the authorities that he saw Stephen murder Colvin; and Colvin's son's testimony that he saw Stephen knock his father down. There is no explanation why the men lied. When Colvin is found living in New Jersey, he is brought back to Manchester, and legal proceedings are begun to absolve and free the brothers.
12. We believe that "A True Story of Slave Life" is not fiction for the following reasons: First, Brown entitled it "A True Story . . ." Second, the account reads as a narrative or an anecdote, that is, without the drama of a story. Third, the persons named in the event existed and lived in Philadelphia in 1852, when the account was published. Mr. Purvis, who first took in Elizabeth Carter, is Robert Purvis, who was married to Harriet Forten, one of three black Forten sisters who were well-known abolitionists. (Harriet's sister Sarah was a good friend of Angelina Grimké.) The late James Forten, referred to in the narrative as the father-in-law, died in 1842 and may have been the son of James Forten, Sr., also black and a wealthy Philadelphia sailmaker and abolitionist. See *Black Women in America*, vol. I, ed. Darlene Clark Hine (Brooklyn, N.Y.: Carlson Publishing, 1993), pp. 443, 444, 505.
13. Frances Smith Foster, ed., *A Brighter Coming Day: A Francis Ellen Watkins Reader* (New York: The Feminist Press, 1990), p. 28. For information on the nineteenth-century woman's rationale for social and political service, see also Mary Helen Washington, ed., *Invented Lives: Narratives of Black Women 1860–1960* (New York: Anchor-Doubleday, 1987), p. 77.
14. Hortense J. Spillers, introduction to *Clarence and Corinne; or God's Way*, by Mrs. A[melia]. E. Johnson, 1890; reprint (New York: Oxford University Press, 1988), p. xxvii.
15. Ammons, *Short Fiction by Black Women*, p. 3. For details of black periodicals in the United States before the founding of *The Crisis* in 1910, see Penelope L. Bullock, *The Afro-American Periodical Press 1838–1909* (Baton Rouge: Louisiana State University Press, 1981).
16. Norman A. Graebner, *A History of the United States*, vol. II (New York: McGraw-Hill, 1970), p. 547.
17. Tate, *Domestic Allegories of Political Desire*, p. 62.
18. Herbert G. Gutman, *The Black Family in Slavery and Freedom, 1750–1925* (New York: Pantheon, 1976), pp. 270, 275. Gutman points out that "most slaves were not denied the right to marry but most slave marriages were unaccompanied by civil ritual. That did not mean that slave marriages lacked

ritual. Substitute marriage rituals developed among the slaves. In all cultures, marriage, which signalizes the social acceptance of rights and duties concerning such matters as sexual access, co-residence, and economic obligation, is accompanied by public ceremony or ritual."

19. Tate, *Domestic Allegories of Political Desire*, p. 109.
20. Ibid., p. 181.
21. Also see Ammons, *Short Fiction by Black Women*, p. 16.
22. Frantz Fanon, *The Wretched of the Earth* (New York: Grove Press, 1963), p. 39. Fanon identified the desire of the oppressed to take the place of the oppressor with the observation: "What native has not dreamed of taking the master's place?"
23. The introduction to *The Works of Alice Dunbar-Nelson*, vol. 2, ed. Elizabeth Ammons (New York: Oxford University Press, 1988), p. xxxvi.
24. Tate, *Domestic Allegories of Political Desire*, p. 210.
25. Henry Louis Gates, Jr., in *The Signifying Monkey* (New York: Oxford University Press, 1988), p. 54, states: "Scholars have for some time commented on the peculiar use of the word *signifyin(g)* in black discourse. Though sharing some connotations with the standard English-language word, *signifyin(g)* has rather unique definitions in black discourse . . . [I]t is useful to look briefly at one suggested by Roger D. Abrahams:

> Signifying . . . can mean any of a number of things . . . It certainly refers to the trickster's ability to talk with great innuendo, to carp, cajole, needle, and lie. It can mean . . . the propensity to talk around a subject, never quite coming to the point . . . making fun of a person or situation . . . speaking with the hands and eyes, and in this respect encompasses a whole complex of expressions and gestures. Thus it is signifying to stir up a fight between neighbors by telling stories; it is signifying to make fun of a policeman by parodying his motions behind his back; it is signifying to ask for a piece of cake by saying, "my brother needs a piece a cake."

> Petry's signification takes the form of improvisation. So fundamental to the very idea of jazz, improvisation is "nothing more" than repetition and revision. Gates states, "In this sort of revision . . . where meaning is fixed, it is the realignment of the signifier that is the signal trait of expressive genius. The more mundane the fixed text ("April in Paris," by Charlie Parker, "My Favorite Things," by John Coltrane), the more dramatic is the Signifyin(g) revision" (p. 63).

26. Somerset Maugham, *A Writer's Notebook* (New York: Doubleday, 1949), p. 151.
27. Bell, Parker, and Guy-Sheftall, *Sturdy Black Bridges*, pp. viii, 23, 24.
28. Washington, *Invented Lives*, introduction, p. xx. There are also two other excellent anthologies edited by Mary Helen Washington containing short stories and excerpts from novels and/or other materials: *Black-Eyed Susans: Classic Stories by and About Black Women* (Garden City, N.Y.: Anchor-

Doubleday, 1975); and *Midnight Birds: Stories of Contemporary Black Women Writers* (Garden City, N.Y.: Anchor-Doubleday, 1980).

29. William Faulkner, *Light in August* (New York: Random House, 1972), p. 111.

30. Gates, *The Signifying Monkey*, p. 5.

31. Barbara Christian, in *Black Feminist Criticism* (New York: Pergamon, 1985), p. 3, points out that the conjure woman image is so strong that "in New Orleans, the center of Catholicism in the South, Marie Laveau, the great voodoo mambo [was] . . . one of its most powerful citizens for half a century."

Biographies

TINA MCELROY ANSA, 1949–
Born in Macon, Georgia, Tina McElroy Ansa graduated from Spelman College in 1971. She has worked as a journalist for the *Atlanta Constitution* and the *Charlotte Observer* (North Carolina) and has taught writing and journalism at Clark College (Atlanta) and other colleges. In 1990 she was a writer-in-residence at her alma mater. In addition to working as a free-lance journalist and book reviewer, Ansa writes short stories and essays and has published two novels, *Baby of the Family* (1989), the story of a girl born with a caul, and *Ugly Ways* (1993), the account of three sisters who return home to bury their mother. *Ugly Ways* was number 1 on several black bookseller lists, including the African-American Best Sellers List/Blackboard List. Ansa is an avid gardener and an amateur naturalist. She lives with her husband, a filmmaker, on St. Simons Island, Georgia, and in 1989 directed its grass-roots festival, which seeks to preserve the heritage of the original slave inhabitants.

TONI CADE BAMBARA, 1939–
Named Toni Cade at her birth in New York City, the author adopted the name Bambara in 1970 when she discovered it as part of a signature on a sketchbook she found in her great-grandmother's trunk. Bambara published her first short story, "Sweet Town," in 1959, the same year she received her B.A. from Queens College in New York City. While enrolled as a graduate student of modern American fiction at the City College of New York, she worked as a social worker, published another short story, "Mississippi Ham Rider" (1961), and studied at the Commedia del' Arte in Milan, Italy. She received an M.A. in 1965. For the next four years, Bambara taught at City College, published stories in various magazines, and participated in the black nationalist and women's liberation movements, which were gathering momentum during the 1960s and early 1970s. However, realizing that neither addressed the concerns of African-American women, she edited *The Black Woman: An Anthology* (1970), in which a range of black women write on issues relevant to their lives. The volume is the first of its kind in the United States, and its year of publication is now generally recognized as marking the beginning of the twentieth-century renaissance of black women's literature. Bambara followed this with another anthology, *Tales and Stories for Black Folks* (1971), which was designed to teach young people the value of telling

stories. She is also the author of two short-story collections, *Gorilla, My Love* (1972) and *The Sea Birds Are Still Alive* (1977). Her novel *The Salt Eaters* (1980) won the American Book Award. An activist for women's rights, Bambara met with the Federation of Cuban Women in Cuba in 1973 and was a guest of the Vietnamese Women's Union in Vietnam in 1975. She has taught at Rutgers and was a writer-in-residence at Spelman College. She presently resides in Philadelphia with her daughter.

MARITA BONNER, 1899–1971

One of four children, Marita Bonner was born and raised in Brookline, Massachusetts. She earned a B.A. in English and Comparative Literature from Radcliffe College in 1922. For the following eight years she taught high school in Washington, D.C., where she became friends with Georgia Douglas Johnson, Langston Hughes, Countee Cullen, Alain Locke, Jessie Fauset, and Jean Toomer, among other writers who would make their mark during the Harlem Renaissance. As a member of the "S" Salon, a group of writers who met weekly at Johnson's home, Bonner was encouraged to write. In 1925, she won the *Crisis* essay award for "On Being Young—a Woman—and Colored," which dealt with the constraints America placed on black women. In 1927, she won that journal's short story award for "Drab Rambles," which contains two vignettes showing the inhuman treatment of blacks. The same year she won the *Crisis* best play award for "The Purple Flower," which calls for a bloody revolution to protest racism. Bonner married a Brown University graduate in 1930 (in her prize-winning essay she emphasized that black women should seek husbands they can look up to without looking down on themselves) and moved to Chicago. She bore three children and, although she continued to teach, wrote little after 1940. Bonner died in a fire in her Chicago apartment.

EUGENIA COLLIER, 1928–

Eugenia Collier was born and raised in Baltimore. She received a B.A. in English from Howard University in 1948, an M.A. in American Literature from Columbia University in 1950, and a Ph.D. in American Civilization from the University of Maryland in 1976. "Marigolds" (1969), which won the Gwendolyn Brooks Award in Fiction, was Collier's first published short story. *Breeder and Other Stories* (1991) is a collection of her short fiction, and *Spread My Wings* (1992) is a historical novel about a young woman who was held in slavery long after the Civil War ended. Collier has also published poetry and a number of critical essays on African-American literature. A college teacher since 1955, Collier is presently chairperson of the Department of English and Language Arts at Morgan State University in Baltimore. She has "tried to see as much of the black world as possible," taking trips to, among other places, West Africa, Brazil, Suriname, Guyana, and Saudi Arabia. A divorced woman with three sons and six grandchildren, she reads from her works at community organizations, colleges, and universities.

RITA DOVE, 1952–
Born in Akron, Ohio, Rita Dove graduated summa cum laude from Miami University, in Oxford, Ohio, attended the University of Tübingen in Germany as a Fulbright Fellow, and earned an M.A. from the University of Iowa. She is the author of a collection of short stories, *Fifth Sunday* (1985); a novel, *Through the Ivory Gate* (1992); a one-act play, "The Siberian Village" (1991); and numerous volumes of poetry, including the Pulitzer Prize–winning *Thomas and Beulah* (1985), which explores the significance of black migration from the South through the experience of her grandparents. Dove's literary essays have appeared in *The New York Times Book Review* and other publications. She has won numerous academic and literary honors, including a Guggenheim Fellowship and two honorary doctorates; is on the editorial boards of several literary journals, including *Callaloo*; and in 1993 was named Poet Laureate of the United States. She is Commonwealth Professor of English at the University of Virginia, plays the cello and viola with a university music consort, and sings soprano with a university opera workshop. She resides in Virginia with her husband and daughter.

ALICE DUNBAR-NELSON, 1875–1935
Born in New Orleans to a middle-class family, Alice Moore Dunbar-Nelson graduated from Straight College (now Dillard University) in 1892 and went on to study at Cornell, Columbia, the Pennsylvania School of Industrial Art, and the University of Pennsylvania. Of mixed ancestry—white, black, and American Indian—she had reddish-blond baby curls and a fair complexion, which enabled her to pass for white when she was intent on experiencing the high culture (operas, bathing spas, art museums) of a Jim Crow society. Nonetheless, in the essay "Brass Ankles Speaks," she recalls her "miserable" childhood, when other schoolchildren taunted her because she was a "light nigger, with straight hair!" Dunbar-Nelson published two collections during her lifetime: *Violets and Other Tales* (1895), a potpourri of "promising juvenilia"—fiction, poetry, and essays; and *The Goodness of St. Rocque* (1898), a collection of short stories about Creole life that helped create a black story tradition for a reading public conditioned to expect only plantation and minstrel stereotypes. Earning a living as a teacher, a secretary, and a columnist, Dunbar-Nelson also fought for the rights of black people and was the first African-American woman elected to the Delaware Republican State Committee. She married three times, initially to the poet Paul Laurence Dunbar.

JESSIE REDMON FAUSET, 1882–1961
The youngest of seven children born to an African Methodist Episcopal minister and his wife in a middle-class family in Camden, New Jersey, Jessie Redmon Fauset studied classical languages at Cornell University, graduating Phi Beta Kappa in 1905. She earned an M.A. at the University of Pennsylvania, studied at the Sorbonne, attended the second Pan-African Congress in Paris in 1921, and visited Africa in 1924. She taught high school for most of her life, but always sought greater use of her talents. In 1919, W. E. B. Du Bois chose her to be the

literary editor of *The Crisis*, where she was considered a "midwife," helping to cultivate the talents of young Harlem Renaissance writers such as Claude McKay, Jean Toomer, Countee Cullen, George Schuyler, Arna Bontemps, and Langston Hughes. She also edited a monthly *Crisis* magazine for children. Fauset wrote four novels in nine years: *There Is Confusion* (1924), *Plum Bun* (1929), *Chinaberry Tree* (1931), and *Comedy, American Style* (1933). They examine attitudes within the black community toward miscegenation, class pretensions, and extramarital and interracial relationships. A new analysis of her fiction indicates that she was especially concerned with the impact of race on women and the limitations placed on black women by their own communities. She married in 1929.

ANGELINA WELD GRIMKÉ, 1880–1958
The daughter of former mulatto slave Archibald Grimké (whose father was his owner), who married a wealthy Northern white woman, Angelina Weld Grimké was born in Boston and raised by her father. Her mother was believed to have been institutionalized. Grimké was a privileged child; her father was a nationally known lawyer and the executive director of the National Association for the Advancement of Colored People (NAACP). Educated at exclusive private schools, she graduated in 1902 from Boston Normal School for Gymnastics (now Wellesley College). She taught English in Washington, D.C., high schools until her retirement, and in 1926 moved to New York City, where she died in 1958. A drama, *Rachel*, is her only book published before the *Selected Works of Angelina Weld Grimké* (edited by Carolivia Herron), but Grimké published poetry, short stories, and nonfiction (reviews and biographical sketches) in *Opportunity* and other monthly publications. Most of her fiction dealt with racism, specifically, lynching. *Rachel* is about a young woman who is driven mad when she fears that the fate of her father, who was lynched in the South, could befall any children she might bear. Grimké was a lesbian, but, in order to please her father, she never lived with another woman.

FRANCES ELLEN WATKINS HARPER, 1825–1911
Frances Ellen Watkins Harper was born free in the slave state of Maryland, possibly fathered by a white man. It is believed that her mother died when she was three. Raised by an aunt and educated until thirteen at an academy for "Negro youth" that was founded by her uncle, a prominent minister and abolitionist, Harper studied the Bible, Greek, Latin, and elocution. After she left school, Harper worked as a domestic. At twenty she published her first volume of poetry, and by the time she was thirty, her name was included in most compendiums of prominent black Americans. She left the South in 1850 and later found that she could not return, since Maryland had passed a law that forbade free blacks from entering the state upon penalty of enslavement. She taught school and lectured for the antislavery movement, working closely with Frederick Douglass and Ida B. Wells. She was also a founding member of the National Council of Negro Women. In 1860, she married; four years later, her husband died, leaving her with a daughter and three stepchildren. The best-known and best-loved black

poet before Paul Laurence Dunbar (1872–1906), Harper was concerned with abolition, religion, and women's rights. Her extant prose includes essays, speeches, letters, short stories, and a novel, *Iola Leroy, or Shadows Uplifted* (1892), which portrays a mulatto who refuses to pass into white society and chooses instead to devote her life to racial uplift.

FRENCHY JOLINE HODGES, 1940–
Born in Dublin, Georgia, Frenchy Hodges earned a B.S. in English at Fort Valley State College in 1964. In 1973 she was awarded a fellowship at Atlanta University, where she received an M.A. in Afro-American studies, concentrating on literature. Hodges has taught school in Quitman, Georgia, and Detroit, Michigan. Also an actress, she played starring roles in "God's Trombones," "A Hand Is on the Gate," "Baptism," and "Who's Got His Own" at Concept East Theater in Detroit; and also in Larry Blame's "Little Old Ladies" at the Detroit Repertory Theater. Hodges is also a poet. Her belief that "life is a legend happening in an eternal minute, and art is the sapping of substance from reality cased in illusion, helping man continue through this eternal minute" is reflected in her work. Hodges lives in Detroit.

ZORA NEALE HURSTON, 1901–1960
The fifth child born to a minister and his wife living in the all-black town of Eatonville, Florida, Zora Neale Hurston was thirteen when her mother died; she finished high school in Baltimore and enrolled in Howard University. After two years in Washington, she moved to New York; a scholarship eventually enabled her to enter Barnard College, where she received a B.A. in English in 1928. She wrote four novels, two books of folklore, an autobiography, and short stories. Best known are the folktale collection *Mules and Men* (1935) and the novel *Their Eyes Were Watching God* (1937). Skillfully woven into her novels, which are set within an all-black or mostly black background, is her belief that color- and race-identity are independent of character. Hurston also produced a Broadway concert and wrote movies for Paramount Studios. In 1934 she was awarded a fellowship to study anthropology and folklore; and in 1936 and 1937 she garnered two Guggenheim Fellowships to study the practice of magic in the West Indies. A controversial figure during the Harlem Renaissance, she contested the notion that the black race needed defending, an idea which originated, she believed, from the same racist ideology that said black people were inferior. She died forgotten and penniless in a Florida welfare home.

GAYL JONES, 1940–
Born in Lexington, Kentucky, Gayl Jones grew up listening to stories her mother wrote, and still considers herself a storyteller as opposed to a fiction writer. She received a B.A. from Connecticut College and an M.A. (1973) and a D.A. (1979) from Brown University. Her two novels, *Corregidora* (1976) and *Eva's Man* (1979), reflect the strong voice of the storyteller and Jones's interest in the blues, while exploring the complex and painful way some black men have treated black women.

She was profoundly disappointed when these two works brought scathing criticism from some black male critics, who read her fictional inventions as reflections of her personal estimation of black men. Among her other published works are a collection of short stories, *White Rat* (1977); four plays; two volumes of poetry, *Song for Anninho* (1981) and *Xarque and Other Poems* (1985); and *Liberating Voice* (1991), a scholarly work on the oral tradition in the literature of African-American writers. From 1975 to 1981, Jones taught at the University of Michigan.

JAMAICA KINCAID, 1949–
Born Elaine Potter Richardson to Annie Richards in St. Johns, Antigua, the author was brought up believing that her mother's husband, a carpenter, was her father; she did not know her biological father until later in life. When Kincaid was nine years old, her mother gave birth to the first of three sons. At sixteen, Kincaid emigrated to the United States, where she became a citizen. Since 1974, her work has appeared almost exclusively in *The New Yorker*, where she became a staff writer in 1976. *At the Bottom of the River* (1983) is a collection of her short stories and other short pieces. Her two novels, *Annie John* (1985) and *Lucy* (1990), deal almost entirely with intense relationships between women. She has also published *A Small Place* (1988), a political analysis of Antigua that is highly critical of the European and American exploitation of the island. Married and the mother of two children, she resides in the Northeast.

NELLA LARSEN, 1893–1964
Born in Chicago of a West Indian father and a Danish mother, Nella Larsen was two years old when her father died. Her mother remarried a white man, with whom she had a second daughter. Nella attended private school with her half sister, studied science at Fisk University, and later attended the University of Copenhagen. In 1915 she received a nursing degree from Lincoln Hospital in New York City and became assistant superintendent of nurses at Tuskegee Institute in Alabama. In 1919, Larsen married a physicist (they were divorced in 1933) and became a librarian at a public library in Harlem. As a socialite wife she met a cadre of black authors—including James Weldon Johnson, Jessie Fauset, Jean Toomer, and Langston Hughes—who encouraged her to write. Larsen published the novels *Quicksand* (1928) and *Passing* (1929) and several short stories, and was the first African-American woman to win a Guggenheim Fellowship for creative writing. She captured in impressive detail the mannerisms, values, concerns, and emotional conflicts of the black nouveau riche during the Harlem Renaissance. But plagiarism charges, never substantiated, ended her career. She spent her later life as a supervising nurse in New York City. She died in obscurity.

PAULE MARSHALL, 1929–
Born Valenza Pauline Burke in Brooklyn, New York, to emigrant parents from Barbados, Paule Marshall graduated cum laude and Phi Beta Kappa from Brooklyn College in 1954. Her fiction writing began when she started composing vignettes at the end of her workday as a researcher and staff writer for a New York magazine.

Her short stories are collected in *Soul Clap Hands and Sing* (1961) and *Reena and Other Stories* (1984). Marshall has written four novels, the most recent of which is *Daughters* (1991). Her works deal with, among other subjects, black life in this country and in the Caribbean. Marshall has won numerous awards, including a Guggenheim Fellowship (1960) and the prestigious John D. and Catherine T. MacArthur Fellowship (1992). She is presently a professor of English and creative writing at Virginia Commonwealth University. Divorced and remarried, she is the mother of a grown son.

COLLEEN MCELROY, 1935–
Born an "army brat" in St. Louis, Missouri, Colleen McElroy attended the University of Maryland, and earned a doctorate from the University of Washington, where she is now a professor of English. The author of two collections of short stories, *Jesus and Fat Tuesday and Other Short Stories* (1987) and *Driving Under the Cardboard Pines* (1990), six books of poetry, and a textbook on speech and language development, McElroy has received fellowships from the National Endowment for the Arts and the Fulbright Foundation, and has won a poetry award from the *Cincinnati Poetry Review*, and fiction awards from *Callaloo* and *Prairie Schooner*. She has lectured at numerous colleges and universities and traveled abroad extensively. Her work has been translated into Italian, Russian, German, Serbo-Croatian, and Malagasy. She resides in the Pacific Northwest.

DIANE OLIVER, 1934–1966
Born in Charlotte, North Carolina, Diane Oliver attended the University of North Carolina at Greensboro and was a student at the Writer's Workshop of the University of Iowa. Her short stories appeared in several anthologies, including *Prize Short Stories of 1967: The O. Henry Awards*. Oliver also served as a guest editor at *Mademoiselle* and won honorable mention in one of the magazine's fiction competitions. She died in an automobile accident a few days before she was to receive her master's degree.

ANN PETRY, 1911–
The daughter of Peter C. Lane, one of the first black pharmacists registered in Connecticut, and Bertha James, a businesswoman, Ann Petry was born and raised in Old Saybrook, Connecticut. She studied pharmacology at the University of Connecticut and later worked in her family's drugstore alongside an aunt, who was the first black woman pharmacist in the state. After Petry's marriage in 1928 she moved to New York, where she worked for several social services agencies and was a reporter for a Harlem newspaper. Her first novel, *The Street* (1946), about the life of a single black woman in Harlem in the 1940s, won a Houghton Mifflin Literary Fellowship and became a best-seller, which sold 1.5 million copies. Petry is the author of two other novels, *Country Place* (1947) and *The Narrows* (1953); four children's books; and a collection of short stories, *Miss Muriel and Other Stories* (1989). She has received several honorary doctorates. She and

her husband reside in Old Saybrook, a short distance from the James Pharmacy, which still bears her aunt's name. They have a grown daughter.

CONNIE PORTER
The second youngest of eight siblings, Connie Porter grew up in Buffalo, New York, graduated from the State University of New York at Buffalo in 1981, and earned an M.F.A. in fine arts from Louisiana State University. A scholar and a fellow at the Bread Loaf Writer's Conference, she has taught at, among other schools, Emerson College and the University of Southern Illinois at Carbondale. Her first novel, *All-Bright Court* (1991), was named to the American Library Association's Notable Book List and to *The New York Times* Notable Books of the Year. "Hoodoo," published in 1988, is a chapter from the novel. Porter has also published three children's books about a child named Addy living in slavery in the mid-1800s.

SONIA SANCHEZ, 1934–
Born in Birmingham, Alabama, and raised in New York City, Sonia Sanchez graduated from Hunter College in 1955. A leading activist during the civil rights movement in the 1960s, she is the author of twelve books, including numerous volumes of poetry and a collection of stories for young readers, and the editor of *We Be Word Sorcerers: 25 Stories by Black Americans* (1973), an anthology of short stories by black Americans. Sanchez is the recipient of several major awards, including the P.E.N. Writing Award in 1969, the National Institute of Arts and Letters Grant in 1970, a National Endowment for the Arts fellowship, and an American Book Award for her book of poetry *Homegirls and Handgrenades* (1984). She has also published several "poemplays," including *Uh Huh, But How Do It Free Us?*, whose theme has become a metaphor for her work. She uses black speech to illuminate the deplorable conditions endured by African Americans. The recipient of an honorary doctorate from Wilberforce University and a professor at Temple University, where she holds the Laura Carnell Chair in English, Sanchez has lectured at more than five hundred universities and colleges in the United States and abroad. She lives with her three children in Philadelphia.

NTOZAKE SHANGE, 1948–
Ntozake Shange was born Paulette Williams, the first of four children to Paul and Eloise Williams, a surgeon and a psychiatric social worker, in Trenton, New Jersey. She was exposed to music, dance, and literature as a young child, and also had the opportunity to meet many celebrities, including W.E.B. Du Bois, Dizzy Gillespie, Charlie Parker, Josephine Baker, Chuck Berry, and Miles Davis, who were friends of her parents. Shange earned a B.A. with honors in American Studies from Barnard College in 1970 and an M.A. from the University of Southern California in 1973. An early marriage ended in divorce, and, plagued with a deep sense of alienation and rage, she made several suicide attempts. In 1975, after teaching college, she moved to New York, where her play *for colored girls who have considered suicide, when the rainbow is enuf*—which recalls ex-

periences of women who have been rejected, verbally and physically abused, and discredited—won several awards, including an Obie. It was the first play by a black woman to appear on Broadway after Lorraine Hansberry's *A Raisin in the Sun*. Shange has published short stories, novels, and poetry, as well as plays. Her most recent work, *Love Space Demands* (1991), is a collection of poems. Her major themes are the abuse of women and children and their survival in the face of loneliness, rejection, and rape. Shange assumed her African name in 1971. Ntozake means "she who comes with her own things"; Shange means "who walks like a lion." Heralded as a feminist author, as much concerned with the plight of black men as with that of women, she is the recipient of several honors and awards, including a Guggenheim Fellowship in 1981. She resides in Philadelphia with her twelve-year-old daughter.

ANN ALLEN SHOCKLEY, 1927–
Born in Louisville, Kentucky, Ann Allen Shockley graduated from Fisk University and earned an M.S. in library science from Case Western Reserve University. She has worked as a librarian at various colleges and universities and is presently associate librarian for special collections and university archivist at Fisk University. In the late 1940s and early 1950s she wrote newspaper columns on black issues for white-owned newspapers in Maryland and Delaware. She is the author of more than thirty short stories and two novels. In her collection of stories, *The Black and White of It* (1980), she explores lesbian relationships within the constraints of a racist and heterosexual society. *Loving Her* (1974) was the first novel by a black woman to feature a black lesbian as its central character. *Say Jesus and Come to Me* (1982) satirically confronts homophobia in the black church. Shockley has also edited a book-length bibliography and several scholarly reference works. She has won numerous awards and grants and has lectured widely. She has two grown children.

MARY ELIZABETH VROMAN, 1923–1967
Born in Buffalo, New York, and raised in the West Indies, Mary Elizabeth Vroman attended Alabama State College. "See How They Run" was published in the *Ladies' Home Journal* and made into the movie *Bright Road* in 1953. Vroman published the novel *Esther* in 1963 and the young adult novel *Harlem Summer* in 1968. In 1965 she published *Shaped to Its Purpose: Delta Sigma Theta, the First Fifty Years*, the history of a black sorority. Vroman was the first black woman to become a member of the Screen Writers' Guild. In 1952, she received a Christopher Award for inspirational magazine writing. She died from complications following surgery in 1967.

ALICE WALKER, 1944–
One of America's most prolific writers, Alice Walker was the last of eight children born to sharecroppers in Eatonton, Georgia. She attended Spelman College in Atlanta, and, to distance herself from the South, transferred to Sarah Lawrence College in Bronxville, New York, where she graduated in 1965. While in college,

she had an abortion and, in her senior year, traveled to Africa. Both experiences were later incorporated in her writings. Returning to the South to work on voter registration, she married a white civil rights lawyer in 1967. She subsequently held several teaching and writer-in-residence positions and won numerous awards. Her books span twenty-two years and include two collections of short stories, *In Love and Trouble* (1973) and *You Can't Keep a Good Woman Down* (1981); five volumes of poetry; two essay collections; a biography of Langston Hughes; and five novels, including *The Color Purple* (1982). Winner of a Pulitzer Prize and an American Book Award, *The Color Purple* depicts the dehumanization of women. While Walker's work embodies a host of themes, a central one is that when a woman goes in search of her mother's gardens she will ultimately find her own. Walker has a grown daughter, and currently resides on a ranch outside San Francisco, California, where she continues to write.

DOROTHY WEST, 1912–

The only child of a free woman and an ex-slave, Dorothy West grew up in Boston and attended Boston University and the Columbia School of Journalism. When she was eighteen, her short story "The Typewriter" won an *Opportunity* magazine literary prize. In 1927 she had a small part in *Porgy*, and traveled to London with the original stage company. During the 1930s, she visited Russia with Langston Hughes to make a film, which was never completed. She later became editor of *Challenge*, a literary magazine that listed among its contributors Claude McKay, Zora Neale Hurston, and Countee Cullen. In 1937 West founded *New Challenge*, with Richard Wright as associate editor. However, only one issue was ever published. She later joined the Federal Writers' Project of the Work Projects Administration, which employed artists during the Depression to research archival projects on American history. West published several short stories, numerous articles, and one novel, *The Living Is Easy* (1948), which satirized affluent black Bostonians who allowed class differences to separate them from the concerns of working-class black communities. Dorothy West currently lives in Martha's Vineyard, Massachusetts, where she continues to write short stories as well as a column for the *Martha's Vineyard Gazette*.

FANNIE BARRIER WILLIAMS, 1855–1944

Born in Brockport, New York, Fannie Barrier Williams grew up with a brother and a sister in a sheltered and affluent environment, graduating from the State Normal School at Brockport. Her father, a barber and a coal merchant, owned his home and was an active leader in the predominantly white community. Williams did not experience racism until she went South after the Civil War to teach freed slaves. She quickly left for a teaching post in Washington, D.C., where she met a young law student from Georgia who was an 1881 graduate of the University of Michigan and a former Alabama schoolteacher. When he completed his law degree in 1887, they were married and moved to Chicago. He was one of eleven assistant attorneys in northern Illinois and later became a Chicago district attorney. Williams gained notoriety at the 1893 Chicago World's

Fair, where she addressed the National Association of Representative Women on the need for fair employment for black women. In 1894 she was the first black woman admitted (following a fourteen-month debate) to an exclusive white women's club. She championed Booker T. Washington's ideas about industrial education and the need for white philanthropy, and served on the boards of various black charitable organizations. Williams was the Chicago reporter for the *Women's Era*, a monthly newspaper that disseminated news about black women's organizations. "After Many Days: A Christmas Story" may be her only published work of fiction.

SHERLEY ANNE WILLIAMS, 1944–
Sherley Anne Williams, the youngest of three sisters, was born and raised in a low-income housing project in Bakersfield, California. After her mother's death when Sherley was sixteen, she occasionally picked cotton, cut grapes, and worked as a stock clerk to help the sister who cared for her make ends meet. She earned a B.A. in history at a California State University college in 1966, spent one year in graduate school at Howard University, and received an M.A. from Brown University in 1972. She also taught in the Black Studies Department at Brown. Her first published short story, "Tell Martha Not to Moan" (1968), has appeared in several anthologies. Williams has also published literary criticism, including *Give Birth to Brightness: A Thematic Study in Neo-Black Literature,* which analyzes the work of James Baldwin and Ernest Gaines. Her first book of poetry, *The Peacock Poems* (1975), was nominated for a National Book Award in 1976. This work and a second collection, *Some One Sweet Angel Chile* (1982), deal with her early life, when her family "followed the crops" and she felt part of the "dispossessed." She has also published a novel, *Dessa Rose,* an illuminating neo-slave narrative that focuses on a black woman who leads an insurrection. Williams, a single mother of one son, is a professor of literature at the University of California, San Diego.